Cressida McLaughlin

The
Canal Boat
Café

...ssy was born in South East London surrounded by books
...with a cat named after Lawrence of Arabia. She studied
...lish at the University of East Anglia and now lives in
...wich with her husband, David. When she isn't writing,
...sy spends her spare time reading, returning to London or
...oring the beautiful Norfolk coastline. She is also the author
... _Christmas Tail_, originally a four-part e-serialization, set
...e fictional world of Primrose Terrace.

...you'd like to find out more about Cressy, visit her on
...er and on Facebook. She'd love to hear from you!

...ressidaMcLaughlinAuthor
...CressMcLaughlin

Also by Cressida McLaughlin

Primrose Terrace series

Wellies and Westies
Sunshine and Spaniels
Raincoats and Retrievers
Tinsel and Terriers

A Christmas Tail – The Complete Primrose Terrace Story

Cressida McLaughlin

The Canal Boat Café

HARPER

Harper
An imprint of HarperCollins*Publishers* Ltd
The News Building
1 London Bridge Street
London SE1 9GF

www.harpercollins.co.uk

This paperback original 2016
1

First published in Great Britain as four separate ebooks in 2016 by HarperCollins*Publishers*

First published as one edition in 2016 by HarperCollins*Publishers*

A catalogue record for this book
is available from the British Library

ISBN: 978-0-00-813603-1

Set in Birka by Palimpsest Book Production Ltd, Falkirk, Stirlingshire

Printed and bound in Great Britain by
Clays Ltd, St Ives plc

For David, for everything.

Acknowledgements

I have loved every minute of writing this book, and I have had lots of help and encouragement along the way.

A HUGE thank you to Kate Bradley, who is a wonderful person and editor, who steers me in the right direction, has faith in me and never fails to make me smile. I am so lucky that I get to work with her. The same goes for the whole HarperCollins team, who make everything fun, exciting and – from my point of view, though possibly not always theirs – easy. Special thanks to Charlotte Brabbin, who is extremely patient and generally brilliant. And to Katie Moss, Kim Young, Martha Ashby and Ann Bissell. To Alice Stevenson and Alexandra Allden, for putting my words in such a desirable package, with truly stunning covers.

To the copy-editors and proofreaders who have worked on my book at various stages, either for the parts or the whole novel: Rhian McKay, Kati Nicholl, Anne O'Brien and

Linda Joyce. I so appreciate everything they have done to knock my words into shape.

Thank you to the brilliant and unstoppable Hannah Ferguson. She's a dream agent, and I still feel amazed to be working with her.

To Kirsty Greenwood and Alex Brown, who are gurus of the book world, have supported and helped me more than I can say, and have become awesome friends. I don't know what I would do without you.

I am endlessly inspired – and encouraged – by some wonderful authors. I have to mention Katie Marsh, Isabelle Broom, Vicky Walters, Lisa Dickenson, Lucy Robinson, Holly Martin, Cesca Major, Katey Lovell and Elly Griffiths, but the list could go on and on.

To anyone who has read my books, tweeted or messaged me about them, you are the people who make all the hard work so worthwhile. For years I dreamed about readers contacting me to say how much they'd loved, or been moved by, my writing, and now it ACTUALLY happens. Thank you for reading, and for taking the time to get in touch.

I've only ever taken holiday trips on canal boats, and have never had to deal with the daily complications of living on one, so I turned to books for accuracy. *The Liveaboard Guide: Living Afloat on the Inland Waterways* by Tony Jones, and *How to Live on a Canal Boat: An Alternative Lifestyle* by Vaughan Tucker were particularly helpful. Any errors are down to my failure to understand how it works.

Thank you to Anne, for her friendship and her boat knowledge, and for the publication day bellinis. To Katy C for being generally awesome, and for suggesting character names for future books – one day she might pick one that I'll feel comfortable using, but it's unlikely to be Willimon. To Judy,

Lisa and Sandra – I don't get to see them often enough, but their love and support is super evident even from afar. To Kate G, for putting things into perspective and always making me laugh.

To my mum and dad, for taking me to Sevenoaks Wildlife Reserve when I was little, for helping to inspire my love of nature, and for the unforgettable kingfisher moment. Without their support, and their endless capacity for listening and advice, I wouldn't be doing this. To Lucy, for being my Big Sis.

To David, the most wonderful and patient husband, who has supported me unquestionably from the very beginning; watching the whole of Netflix while I've hidden myself away to write, bringing me coffee and cooking me delicious meals, and never once complaining. He makes this possible, and I am eternally grateful for his love and generosity. I know that part of him would quite like to live on a boat, and having immersed myself in the lifestyle to write *The Canal Boat Café*, I am pretty tempted, but there's one problem I can never get past – where would we put all our books?

Chapter 1

As Summer Freeman turned into the square of concrete that proudly advertised itself as Willowbeck's car park, her hands gripped the steering wheel, her fingers red from the cold.

It looked the same.

It had the same faded lines marking the spaces, the same notice above the pay-and-display machine reminding her that parking was free between November and March, the same wooden signpost with arrows pointing to 'The Black Swan', 'The River Great Ouse', 'The Towpath'. A thin sliver of frost topped the arrows, giving them a Christmassy flourish even though it was mid-February.

There was no arrow pointing to 'The Canal Boat Café', something Madeleine, Summer's mother, had always grumbled about. *Why should the pub get a sign, when we're as much a public eating establishment as they are?* It had been the same argument, over and over, her mum only half-joking. Madeleine had thrived on the competition between her and the pub's owners, Dennis and Jenny Greenway, at least until their relationship had changed irreversibly.

Summer parked in the farthest corner, next to the butcher's van, as if she wanted to hide her presence from anyone who might be passing. She had thought about Willowbeck a lot in the last eight months, its beauty and buzz coming to her in pictures as vivid as photographs, but she had never got as far as the question of returning. It was a forty-minute drive from Cambridge, where she lived, and in the opposite direction to the studio where she worked as a sign writer. But the journey north that morning, past the imposing outline of Ely Cathedral, was one that she could do in her sleep, even though it had been so long since she'd last taken the route. Her mum had owned the café and now it was hers, but she had abandoned it like a broken toy, the memories, the thought of taking her mum's place, too painful to consider.

She stepped out of the car, her breath misting, and wrapped her red wool coat tightly around her, folding her arms across her chest. She locked the old Polo and walked slowly across the car park, her steps echoing in the February morning quiet. She wished that she'd brought Latte with her. The young Bichon Frise always lifted Summer's spirits, but she didn't know exactly what she was going to face and she hadn't wanted to risk her little dog being in the way, or not knowing what to do with her.

Summer stood on the road, facing the river.

To her right was the small row of shops. She could see only the backs of them now, but she knew they were the butcher's, owned by Adam and his son Charlie, the newsagent's that sold more Willowbeck postcards than it did newspapers, and a gift shop. Summer loved the soft pastels, the cosiness of the shelves of candles, cushions, and door signs with slogans about dogs and life on the river. She had a sign on the wall of her tiny Cambridge flat that her mum had bought her. It read: *I'd rather be on my boat*. Over the last eight months, Summer hadn't agreed with the sentiment, but now her hand had been forced.

To her left stood the Black Swan. It was a big cream building, the paintwork around the doors and windows black and glossy, the gentle slope of grass that led towards the river dotted with picnic tables. In front of her were Willowbeck's moorings, big enough for six narrowboats moored bow to stern along the towpath. Four of the moorings were residential, and one of those was her mother's.

Summer took a deep breath and walked forward, her view of the river widening as she got closer to the water. Today it was dark and smooth as glass, the trees that shaded the opposite towpath bare of their usual leaves. She smiled as a couple strolled past her, an eager Jack Russell terrier sniffing at the ground. All the permanent moorings were taken. Valerie's purple narrowboat, *Moonshine*, was furthest left, in front of the pub, and next to hers was *The Canal Boat Café*. The lights were ablaze, but the serving hatch was closed, no blackboard outside offering fresh coffee and cakes. Summer swallowed, knowing that the chill she was feeling wasn't just to do with the weather, and delayed stepping aboard for a few more moments.

On the right was Norman Friend's boat, *Celeste*. The old man was nowhere to be seen, hibernating from the cold below decks. The mooring between *Celeste* and *The Canal Boat Café*, which had been waiting for a new occupant the last time Summer had been to Willowbeck, was now taken up with a beautiful narrowboat coloured red, gold and black, *The Sandpiper* written in a flourishing font on the side. Summer could appreciate the quality of the artistry, and had often dreamed – in happier times – that one day her designs would decorate the boats that slid serenely up and down the river. But recently, all thoughts of the river, and of the boats, had been tainted by her grief and she'd shut herself up in her studio, taking on any commission that would keep her mind away from the creeping thoughts of the day her mum had died.

'Summer? Summer, is that you?' The voice was high and breathy and snapped Summer out of her daydream. Valerie Brogan popped her head out of the doors at the bow of *The Canal Boat Café,* then stepped on to the deck. Her red hair was like a blazing fire licking over her shoulders, her cheeks flushed, her long purple dress the colour of her own boat. 'Summer, thank God you're here.' She held her arms wide, and Summer walked forward, hovering just out of reach. 'Come aboard, come aboard. You can't rescue me from there.'

Summer gave Valerie what she hoped was a warm smile, and walked across the plank that connected the towpath to the boat. Valerie wrapped her arms around her, smothering her in the scent of coffee, and an underlying sweetness of jasmine incense. 'You have no idea how much I've missed you. How long has it been? Eight months?'

Summer tried to nod, her head pressed against Valerie's shoulder. *Seven months and twenty-six days,* thought Summer. 'Yes,' she said, 'about that.'

'Come inside then. Come and—' Valerie looked directly at Summer, sighed, and then gestured behind her. 'It's not the best it's ever looked. I'll say that now.'

Summer followed Valerie through the doors, and gasped. The café took up the front half of the boat, and was big enough for six two-seater tables. At the back was the counter that served as the throne of Madeleine's mini-empire. She had sold cakes and scones and coffee, either to those inside, or from the hatch that looked out on to the towpath, treating every customer like a dear friend, the blackboard behind her advertising daily specials. The chairs and tables were painted royal blue with red accents, matching the exterior paintwork of the boat, and even the outdoor furniture, stored on the boat in winter, fitted the colour scheme.

At least, that was the image that Summer had held on to: everything running smoothly, Madeleine so proud of her beautiful café. But now, as she stood in the doorway, icy air whispering around the tops of her boots, that shred of reassurance was torn away.

The café was empty of customers, which was a good thing considering the state of it. The tables were in disarray, chairs askew as if people had left in a hurry, and some of the blue paintwork had been scratched, revealing the wood underneath. A bag's worth of coffee beans was scattered across the floor, collecting in the corners with dust and, Summer noticed, a couple of sizeable spiders. The windows were smeared on the inside as well as out, and some of the bunting had been pulled down. The counter looked like it was dealing with the aftermath of a squirrel raid, crumbs and plates and mess everywhere, and the smell of burnt coffee caught in her throat. Valerie shrugged her shoulders, her expression contrite, but Summer knew this was her own fault.

'It's not too bad,' she said tentatively, running her finger along the top of one table. It caught on a splinter.

'It's worse,' Valerie said. 'I've been trying, Summer, I really have. But even during the winter, customers are always popping in. It's not always full, but there's a steady stream and there's never a minute to recover, and then by the end of the day I'm so shattered.'

'It's not your fault,' Summer whispered. 'What's happened here?' She approached the stricken coffee machine.

'It's stopped working. It just belches steam and spray and makes whirring noises, and then, when I was trying to fix it this morning, I knocked the beans over. And what with Jenny,' she looked away, 'really pushing the cakes in the Black Swan, I'm not sure that this place, Maddy's place . . .' Her words drifted off and she glanced at the counter, where a few Jammie Dodgers sat under a glass dome with a sign saying '*Ten pence each*'. 'Maddy's not happy with me, I know it.'

Summer turned to Valerie, her hands clenching into fists. 'What?'

'Her presence is strong. She can see me failing.' Valerie crouched and picked up some coffee beans, shoving them into the pocket of her dress. 'She forgives me, of course, but even so.'

'Valerie,' Summer said, trying to keep her voice even, 'please let's focus on getting things back on track. I'm sure it won't take long.' She pushed a chair flush against a table, hoping it would make things look instantly brighter. It didn't.

'Summer,' Valerie said, giving her a warm smile, 'it is so good to see you. I don't know why I didn't call you sooner.'

'It's good to see you too,' Summer said weakly. They both knew that Valerie had phoned Summer before this, but Summer had chosen to ignore her calls, unable to see herself back in the place where her mother – and she – had been so happy. 'And I'm sorry,' she added. 'I'm so sorry, Valerie. You shouldn't have had to look after this place, you've got your own life to lead.'

'But I was Maddy's best friend. I'm next door. I wouldn't have been able to forgive myself if I hadn't at least tried to keep the café going. And I've fitted my readings in around it. But I do fear my efforts have made things worse than if it hadn't been open at all. And the coffee machine was the last straw. If we can't sell steaming cups of coffee on a February morning, then we've got no hope.'

'So that's what I'll look at first.' Summer shrugged off her coat and hung it over a chair, rolled up the sleeves of her grey jumper and pulled her wavy, strawberry-blonde hair into a messy ponytail with the hairband that lived constantly on her wrist. The stainless steel was hot to the touch, the coffee grinder at the side empty, and when she opened up the bowels of the machine, steam hit her in the face. She turned away, grasping for a cloth, and found a tea towel that looked as if it hadn't been washed in weeks. She wiped her face on her jumper.

Valerie hovered beyond the counter, her long silver earrings dangling. 'So how've you been, Summer? I've missed you. Willowbeck's missed you.'

Summer busied herself with the coffee machine, scooping out chunks of sodden coffee grounds that had been left to pile up, causing the machine to jam. 'Not too bad, thanks. Work's busy and we've had a few more people join the cooperative, so the studio's always got a good atmosphere. Christmas was . . . a bit hard,' she added, her voice dropping.

'Oh my love,' Valerie said, 'how could it not be, without Maddy there? Are your father and brother keeping well?'

'They're fine,' Summer said. 'Ben's still up in Edinburgh, but he came to Dad's for Christmas. It was strange, though.' She hadn't had a full family Christmas since her parents had divorced, nearly eight years before, but the traditional occasions at her dad's had always been balanced by the time spent with her mum. More often than not they'd celebrated in the Black Swan, but sometimes they'd taken the boat further up the river and discovered other pubs, her mother quickly becoming the centre of attention, happy to talk to everyone, always smiling, and Summer getting swept up in it, finding her own confidence in Madeleine's presence. Without that, Christmas had felt hollow, her mother's absence overwhelming.

'It felt strange here, too,' Valerie said. 'Willowbeck seemed much quieter.'

Summer closed her eyes. 'Of course,' she said. 'Of course it was.'

She leant against the counter, dumping handfuls of coffee sludge into the dirty tea towel, and looked at Valerie. Her mum's best friend had always matched Madeleine for vibrancy, both of them appearing much younger than early fifties, Valerie's boat *Moonshine* hosting psychic readings, fortune-telling, astrology charts. A treasure-trove of magic and mysticism that Summer could never quite get her head around.

Somehow, she'd allowed herself to forget that Valerie was almost as close to her mother as she was. Valerie had lived alongside her for years, had lost her too, and instead of running away like Summer had, she'd tried to carry on where Madeleine no longer could.

It was no wonder that the café had gone downhill, but how much worse would it have been if Valerie had left Summer to deal with it? It would be completely closed, never mind a few scratches and an unappealing selection of cakes.

Summer heard footsteps along the towpath, a couple chatting as they passed the moorings. She sighed and moved the coffee grains around with her fingers. 'I'm sorry, Valerie,' she said again.

'Oh hush,' Valerie said. 'You're here now.'

Summer winced, knowing her apology was inadequate and Valerie was being too forgiving. 'I think I've fixed the coffee machine.'

'You have?' Valerie's eyes widened.

'It was blocked up. I'll give it a good clean and then we can look at some of the other bits.'

'I'll get the dustpan and brush.'

'Have we got any cakes?' Alongside the Jammie Dodgers was a tray of what looked like flapjack, but was thin enough to be peanut brittle.

Valerie caught Summer's eye. 'I'm not much of a baker.'

'No,' Summer said. 'Neither am I. That was always Mum's thing. So . . .' She glanced around her, waiting for a flash of inspiration. She could get some ingredients, fill the café with the smell of baking and entice people in. But what could they do immediately? Even if the seating area needed more work, they had the hatch, which at the moment was closed to the world. Ely and the nearest supermarket was only a ten-minute drive away, she'd be back in no time. 'Is the butcher's still open at weekends?'

'Saturday and Sunday mornings,' Valerie said. 'Another few hours before they close.'

'Great. Give me five minutes.' She washed her hands in the sink, put the sodden tea towel and coffee grounds in a carrier bag and tied it up, and then put her coat on and stepped outside.

The air was biting, sharp and cold compared to the belching coffee machine she'd had her head inside, and the water looked bottomless. She shuddered and stepped on to the towpath, glancing inside *The Sandpiper* as she passed it, but was met only with darkness. Next was *Celeste*. It cheered her to think of Norman still in there, even if he was the least sociable person in Willowbeck. He spent most of his time on his deck, fishing, and grumbling when other boats disturbed the calm of the water. For someone who lived on the river, he was particularly intolerant of other boat owners.

She couldn't believe how quickly everything slipped back into place in her mind: Valerie and her readings, Norman, the butcher's. The beautiful river, where she'd watched the orange and blue flash of kingfishers, the robin that perched on the tiller or the roof, the cacophony of ducks and geese and swans. It was quiet this morning, the colour of the narrowboats bright against the muted silvery-grey of frosty Willowbeck, but somehow that made it more of a blank canvas for all Summer's memories.

Except that they all included her mum, laughing or winking at someone, her blonde hair pulled scruffily back, gingham apron on; taking a batch of cherry scones out of the oven; leaning out of the hatch to talk to a passing family, then turning to Summer and telling her a story about when she and Blaze were only knee-high. However many times Summer's older brother had reminded Mum that he'd legally changed his name to Ben, Madeleine had insisted on referring to him as Blaze, his given name. Summer knew she had got off lightly, but she loved being named after her mum's favourite season.

Summer found she'd stopped on the towpath, and was tracing the lettering on Norman's boat with her finger, following the curved lines of *Celeste*. There was a loud banging from inside and Summer jumped back as the doors on to the bow deck opened and Norman, looking exactly the same as the last time she'd seen him, navy flat cap, torn green cable-knit jumper and patchy grey beard, appeared and pointed at her.

'Norman,' Summer said, breaking into a smile. 'It's really good to see you. It's been a long time, but you look just the same.'

He nodded once. 'T'off my boat.'

'What?' She frowned.

'Y'll take the paint off.' He jutted his chin in her direction, and Summer dropped her hand. Of course. He would know that Valerie had been struggling at the café, even if he hadn't spoken to anyone. Summer realized that she had a lot to make up for, and not just with Valerie.

'Sorry, I – I'm sorry, Norman.'

'Hhm,' he grunted. 'Wha' fer?'

Summer looked at him. 'For not being here.'

'Why? S'all the same t'me.'

'OK,' Summer said, clearing her throat. 'Well, I'm going to do bacon rolls from the café this morning. Would you like one?'

'Hhmmm,' Norman said, his eyes, shadowed by grey bushy brows, watching her the whole time.

'Right then,' Summer said brightly. 'Have a good day.' She gave him a quick wave and hurried towards the butcher's.

The welcome she got was cheerier, even if it wasn't much warmer inside the shop than out. The sawdust on the floor, she was sure, was unnecessary, but Adam had always kept his business as traditional as possible.

'Are my eyes deceiving me?' Adam said, looking up from where he was scribbling something in a book. 'I thought you'd given up this place.'

'I'm back,' Summer said, 'for today at least. How are you? How's Charlie?'

'He's out back,' Adam said. 'Turning into a good apprentice. It's the same as ever; we're still busy, still doing lots of deliveries. What can I do for you?'

13

Summer looked at the items under the glass. 'I'd like some of your bacon please, smoked. Quite a bit, actually.'

Adam raised his eyebrows. He had thinning mid-brown hair, a cheerful face, and a red and white striped apron over his white coat. 'You're back in the café, then?'

Summer shifted from one foot to the other. 'I'm helping Valerie out. I thought, as it's so cold, bacon sandwiches might go down well. I'm glad you're busy,' she added. 'It seems so quiet here today. I've hardly seen anyone. Is it like this all the time now?'

'It's still early, girl,' Adam said. 'But I've seen that it's struggling a bit, your café.' He weighed out the rashers, his face fixed in concentration.

Summer's words disappeared. She wanted to tell him it wasn't hers, that she had never asked for it, that the last thing she had wanted was to be in charge, because that meant her mum wasn't there to run it any more.

'Of course,' Adam continued, when she failed to fill the space, 'winter months it's going to be quieter, isn't it? It'll soon pick up. And Valerie's a trooper, isn't she?'

'Yes, she's been amazing for even trying to keep it going.' She bit her lip, realizing how mean that sounded. Adam handed over the bacon and she got her purse out, paid and thanked him, then hurried outside, wondering if it was possible to get it wrong with everyone in Willowbeck before lunchtime. Of course, she thought, looking up at the Black Swan, she'd do that with Jenny and Dennis just by being here.

When she got back to the café Valerie had moved the chairs and tables to the edges of the space, and was polishing the floor, all trace of coffee beans and spiders gone. The smell of pine-scented cleaner filled the air. 'I thought I'd give it a going-over,' she said.

'It looks better already. I've got bacon, but we need rolls – do you have any?'

'Oh no,' Valerie admitted. 'I could barely come up with any cakes, let alone think of doing sandwich fillings. The newsagent's sells white bread.'

Summer chewed her lip. 'I think rolls would be better. Will you be all right if I disappear for half an hour, get a few bits from Ely? I could get some cakes up and running too.'

Valerie nodded and smiled. 'I knew you'd fix it all,' she said.

'I'm not,' Summer protested. 'Anyone would struggle running the café entirely on their own. I'm helping you get back on your feet, that's all.'

'It's not *my* feet that should be here. I'm doing this for Maddy and for you, Summer, but I have my own job to be getting on with. The money I get for my readings is even more important now.' She gestured around her, and Summer felt her cheeks redden, realizing that Valerie would have had to buy supplies as well as everything else. 'I was never cut out for this,' Valerie continued. 'Maddy left the café to you, and you loved it, didn't you? Being here with her.'

'Of course I did. But I have my job, my flat – and I've got a dog now. I never lived here, because—'

'Because it was Maddy's. But, Summer,' Valerie put her mop down, 'she's not here. The living space is empty, the café's failing. It's turning into a ghost ship . . .'

Summer gave Valerie a sharp look, but she carried on unperturbed.

'And I know that Maddy wants you here, carrying it on for her. You've shown, already, that you were meant to be here.'

'I've cleaned out the coffee machine and bought some

15

bacon,' Summer said, exasperation creeping into her voice. 'That's all. This place is still a mess, we've got hardly anything to sell, and there aren't any customers. I can cook all the bacon I want, but if there's nobody to eat it then what's the point? I know you've given up a lot to keep it running, but I can't just come back, Valerie. It isn't that simple.'

'So sell it,' Valerie said, her hazel eyes meeting Summer's. 'Get rid of the boat. Be done with it.'

Summer froze.

'I'm serious. If you don't want to be here, then sell it and do something else with your mum's money. There's no point in it limping along like this.'

Summer shook her head.

'I'm not trying to be cruel, Summer, but really, you have to do something.'

'I have to go to the supermarket,' Summer said, backing towards the door.

'Well,' Valerie said, sploshing the mop into the bucket and then sweeping it in a wide, soapy puddle over the floor, 'that's a start.'

By the time she returned from Ely with carrier bags full of cake ingredients and crusty white and wholemeal rolls, the hatch at the side of the boat was open and Valerie was leaning out, handing blue cardboard coffee cups to a young couple togged up in woolly hats and gloves. Summer hurried aboard, her eyes widening at the transformation.

The floor was clean, the tables and chairs back in place and crumb-free, waiting for repairs and decoration. The counter was gleaming, the Jammie Dodgers nowhere to be seen, and the smell coming from the coffee machine made Summer yearn for a spiced latte.

'Wow.'

'They were our first customers,' Valerie said. 'Appeared as soon as I opened the hatch. I've cleaned up a bit, but the offerings are pretty paltry.'

'Hopefully this will help,' Summer said, holding up her bags. 'Let's get the bacon on; I can sort out the rolls and then mix up some brownies.'

'Ooh,' Valerie said, her voice taking on a dreamy tone, 'you and your brownies. Maddy always said they were the best thing she sold.'

'Hardly,' Summer said, but she felt a smile tug at her lips – until she saw the state of the kitchen.

'I haven't had a chance to come back here yet,' Valerie said.

'That's OK,' Summer murmured. She glanced at the door that led to the cabin, her mum's living quarters compressed because of the café taking up half the length of the boat. She'd watched countless films on the sofa, curled up alongside her mum, the boat undulating softly.

Summer never got over how snug her mum's living space was, but her mouth dried out at the thought of stepping in there now. How could it have any warmth to it when Madeleine was gone? She thought of Valerie's words, about how her mum's presence was strong, and imagined her sitting on the sofa staring at the blank television screen, her pale face devoid of emotion.

She shook her head angrily – she was not about to indulge Valerie's ghostly beliefs – dropped her bags on the floor and stared at the scatter of plates, spoons and mixing bowls covering every surface and filling the sink.

'Tell me what I can do,' Valerie said from the doorway.

'Can you keep serving coffee?' Summer asked. 'I need to make this place gleam and then I can start cooking.'

'You're sure you don't want me to do that?'

'I'm sure,' Summer said. 'You've cleaned the café, Valerie, now it's my turn to get my hands dirty.' She ran hot water and began piling things into the sink.

It wouldn't take long to get the kitchen back to its former, polished glory, but Summer knew that wouldn't be enough to rescue the café, to return it to the sparkling, welcoming place that Maddy had put her heart into. And after getting over the initial hurdle of returning to Willowbeck and *The Canal Boat Café*, Summer wasn't sure that she had the will to stick it out.

By eleven o'clock, they were serving their first bacon sand-wiches through the hatch on to the towpath. The inside of the café still needed some work – the scratches needed to be fixed, the windows polished and the whole place given a thorough, deep clean – not to mention the personal touches, like flowers on the tables, that Maddy had always taken so much time over. But at least they were open, they were serving, and a batch of brownies was in the oven.

Sweat was running down Summer's back, and her face was flushed, her wavy hair turning to frizz in the heat from the oven. She had put all her energy into cleaning and then baking, feeling that she could do more behind the scenes than out at the front, talking to customers. Besides, she hadn't been at Willowbeck for months; the regulars would be more familiar with Valerie – if there were any regulars left.

'Summer, do you think we should put the blackboard out now?'

Summer wiped her hands on a tea towel and, checking the oven timer, followed Valerie into the café. It looked brighter, despite the smeared windows limiting the amount of sun that was coming in. The counter was clean, the cake domes were waiting for fresh brownies, and a glass full of snowdrops that Summer had picked on her walk back from the car sat next to the till. Before she'd had a chance to respond, Valerie hugged her, squeezing tightly, her earring grazing Summer's cheek.

'Blackboard,' Summer managed.

'Look what you've done,' Valerie said. 'Look what a difference you make.'

'*We've* done this,' Summer said, gently wriggling out of Valerie's grasp, 'and it's not there yet. Besides, anyone could have helped – it's the difference between one pair of hands and two. That's all.'

Valerie shook her head. 'Stop being so humble. You were meant to run this café.'

Summer swallowed. 'No I wasn't,' she said quietly. 'Mum was. This should still be Mum's.'

Valerie seemed to deflate, the light leaving her eyes, and Summer felt instantly guilty. But she couldn't, help it. Her mum had been robbed of her life far too soon, and when she was living it to the full, too. Summer hadn't been able to reconcile herself with what had happened, or the fact that she was partly to blame.

'I'll do the blackboard,' she said, grabbing the A-frame from where it was leaning against the counter, and the coloured chalks. Her feet echoed on the wooden floor and the boat swayed slightly as she walked through the café and out on to the deck, and then across to the towpath. She set the A-frame near the open hatch and crouched, pressing her bare knees into the ground, the leather of her boots cracking.

She thought for a moment, and then, in blue chalk, wrote: *Keep out the cold with a fresh bacon roll.* The writing was bold and swirly. Whenever Summer had worked on the boat with her mum, Madeleine had got her to do this part.

Summer was a sign writer by trade, and it came naturally to her, the lettering looking professional, evenly spaced and not misshapen. *Add a coffee or tea,* she added underneath in red chalk, *for an extra 50p.* She'd just started on her final line when she felt a presence behind her. 'What's this?' the familiar voice said, and Summer pressed too hard and snapped the chalk. She crouched, and then pushed herself to standing, brushing dirt off her knees before turning to face Jenny.

'What does it look like?' Summer said, pulling herself up to her full, five-foot-four height, trying to minimize the feeling of being talked down to.

'Like you haven't got a cat in hell's chance of selling anything,' Jenny said. 'People won't be endeared to you because of a few childish rhymes.' She was dressed in black, her auburn hair pulled back, her fringe framing her pinched face. Summer thought she must be in her mid-forties, but she looked older than Madeleine had, which was probably another reason – on top of all the others – that Jenny had taken against her.

'But maybe they'll see that we're welcoming. Anyway,' Summer said, 'Valerie's been doing it all on her own, and now I'm back to help. What makes you think we can't be successful?'

'Because things have changed, Summer. Hasn't Valerie told you?'

Summer glanced at the boat. 'Told me what?'

'We sell professional cakes now, and we're open from ten. You should see the kitchen, the utilities we've got. Why not

21

come over and sample some of the red velvet cake I made yesterday? It's as light as a feather, and still moist.'

Summer folded her arms. 'I can't imagine you mean that.'

'Of course I do,' Jenny said, giving her such a wide smile that Summer thought for a second that all might be forgiven. 'That'll prove to you that your pathetic attempt at a café is finished.'

Summer felt a surge of defiance that shocked her. 'You're wrong.'

'Sometimes the truth hurts, Summer. I should know that better than anyone. It's admirable of you to come down here and try to rescue it, but you have to face up to the fact that you're at the helm of a sinking ship.'

'But we're a café,' Summer said. 'It says it there, on the side, in beautiful writing.' She pointed to the boat. 'You're a pub. I bet hardly anyone knows that you sell cakes as well, and just because you've got a new blender and some fancy recipe books doesn't mean they're any better than ours.'

Jenny's expression hardened into anger. 'You haven't got a hope,' she hissed, 'not any more. The sooner you come to terms with that, the better.'

'Why do you get to make the rules?' Summer asked. 'Why can't we both do our own thing and not get in each other's way?'

'You know why.'

'But I haven't done anything wrong,' Summer said, trying and failing to end the argument. 'You can't attack me just because of what happened months ago. Why do we need to have this battle? If I'm going to be coming back here—' Summer stopped, the words on her lips before she'd had time to consider them.

'Are you?' Jenny shot back.

22

She stared at the pub owner, at her conservative outfit of black trousers and a black shirt, professional but devoid of personality, at the challenge in her face, and realized she didn't have the answer.

'Maybe,' she managed, but she knew her indecision was all that Jenny needed.

Jenny gave her a triumphant smile, and then spun on her heels. 'Count your losses, Summer. Go back to your life, and leave this place in the past.'

Summer watched her climb the path that cut through the grassy slope, up to the front of the pub. 'Crap,' she murmured. She turned back to the blackboard and saw Valerie peering at her out of the hatch, a worried look on her face.

Seeing Jenny had been as bad as Summer had feared it would be, but it had also lit a flame inside her. For the first time that day she felt some of the passion for *The Canal Boat Café* that she knew her mum had had. What Jenny had said was untrue, and even if Summer wasn't ready to come back to Willowbeck more permanently, she couldn't let her win.

'So Jenny's really upped the ante with the baking,' she said as she took her own batch of brownies out of the oven, the heat hitting her, quickly followed by the rich smell of melting chocolate and butter.

Valerie nodded. 'They don't just do the standard pub food any more. Dennis refurbished their kitchen last year, not long after . . . after the summer.'

Summer frowned. 'Really?'

'I suppose there was a space to fill,' Valerie said quietly.

'No,' Summer replied, 'that can't be why. I mean, perhaps for Jenny, but I can't imagine Dennis ever taking that attitude.'

Valerie caught Summer's eye. 'I'm not sure he would have had a choice.'

Summer exhaled loudly, put the brownies on the cooling rack, and turned back to her scone mixture, wiggling her fingers before diving in. It was her favourite part, rubbing the butter and flour together, and today she was going to treat the dough as a culinary stress ball.

'So you've not had much cheeriness from the pub these last few months, then?'

'Dennis smiles at me, when she's not around.'

'Damned by association?'

'I don't think Jenny has a good day unless she can have an argument with someone.'

'And then force them to eat a cake,' Summer added. 'That must get confusing for people.'

Valerie tittered, the sound small and unconvincing. Summer had noticed that much of the older woman's confidence was gone, and she deferred to Summer for everything. She turned away from her mixture, gestured for Valerie to move into the café and followed her out with the brownies. They weren't nearly cool enough, but sticky, melting brownies were better than no brownies, and the February wind coming through the hatch would soon cool them down.

She put them on the plate, leaving the glass dome off, and made two coffees. She gave one to Valerie and sat at one of the tables, Valerie sitting opposite her.

'It must have been lonely here, since Mum died.' It hurt Summer to say the words, but over the last few hours she'd realized that if she couldn't even say it, then she couldn't do anything about the boat's predicament with any kind of conviction.

'I have my readings,' Valerie said into her coffee. 'And I've been serving customers, however ineffectively. Mr Dawson from the village gets a latte on his way to work, strolling along the towpath in his suit, and passing boat owners are always friendly, commenting on the colour of *Moonshine*.'

'Dark lavender's a beautiful colour,' Summer admitted. 'And unusual for a narrowboat. But even so, with the pub being so hostile – do you ever go in there?'

'Sometimes, when I want a hot meal and I haven't got the energy to cook. I have no grudge with them, and as I said, Dennis is always amicable, and the other staff are pleasant enough.'

'But Norman's a bit reclusive, so I guess down here . . .' She looked out of the window as a couple of mallards swam past, the drake's green feathers glinting in the sun. 'Who's in *The Sandpiper*? That wasn't here before.'

'Oh, that's Mason,' Valerie said looking up, her face brightening. 'He's very nice.'

'Who is he?'

'He's some nature buff, goes around hunting for birds and geese.'

Summer wrinkled her nose. 'Like a twitcher?'

'It's his job – he writes and takes photos for magazines. He's got a strong aura, good and kind.'

'Right,' Summer said. 'Sounds like he's companionable then.'

'Oh he is – a bright spark.'

There was a knocking at the hatch and Summer jumped up, ready to serve a customer, and then realized the customer was a beautiful silver tabby. The cat jumped elegantly down into the café and Summer scooped him up so that his face was pressed against her cheek, his purring loud in her ear.

'Harvey,' she said, 'oh, I've missed you.' She grinned and

25

returned to the table, the cat content in her arms. 'How are they?'

'Good,' Valerie said. 'Harvey's going through a phase of trying to catch moths, which is never a good idea on a boat. And after what happened to his brother, too.'

'No!' Summer said, and then directed her attention to the cat. 'That's a very silly thing to do, isn't it, Harvey?' Harvey closed his eyes in contentment. 'How's Mike?'

Mike was Harvey's brother. A smaller cat, he had fallen into the river as a kitten and been rescued by Valerie jumping alarmingly in after him, a frantic Ophelia with her red hair streaming out behind her.

'He's fine,' Valerie said. 'Though he's never recovered his adventurous spark after that incident.' She reached out and stroked Harvey's silky fur. 'He does sometimes surprise my clients, snoozing on the sofa until halfway through a reading, when he'll pop his head up and meow, or jump on to their laps. It's not entirely professional, but I can't bear to move him. His world is my boat, and I'm not going to limit him further. And Harvey's adventurous enough for both of them. He's not averse to trying out other people's boats if a window or door has been left open.'

'God, I wonder if he's got on to Norman's boat. If only you could talk,' Summer said, rubbing the fur between Harvey's eyes.

'His latest thing is antagonizing Mason's dog,' Valerie said, sighing.

'What kind of dog has he got?' Summer asked, feeling a pang of longing at the thought of Latte, alone in her flat.

Valerie waved her hand. 'Smallish, scruffy. A bit of a terror if you ask me, though I wouldn't say it to Mason's face. I've caught Harvey screeching at him, tail puffed out, more than

26

once, but the dog always comes back for more – as if he enjoys it.'

Summer couldn't help but laugh. 'Sounds like a pretty straightforward relationship to me.'

Valerie gave her a curious look. 'Do you know what, Summer Freeman? That's the first time I've heard you laugh since you've been back here.'

Summer opened her mouth, but her lack of response was forgotten as there was a gentle rat-a-tat at the serving hatch, this time from a human visitor rather than a feline one.

'Hello? Any chance of a cuppa? My hands are freezing.' A face appeared and Valerie rushed to greet the customer, an older gentleman with a shock of white hair and a brown jacket zipped up to the neck, and Summer slipped back to the kitchen to carry on with her scones. As she rubbed the mixture between her fingers, she realized how much she'd shut herself off, and how unfair that had been to Valerie. At least she didn't seem too lonely, was able to go in the pub and had a new, friendly neighbour, even if he did sound a little on the geeky side.

Summer put the scones in the oven and looked at her watch. It was two o'clock and, realistically, the café would only be open until four. She glanced again at the doorway into the living space and shuddered. She didn't want to admit to being spooked out – it was just a couple of empty rooms – but she had to be away from the boat before it got dark. She chided herself, wished again that she had Latte's uncomplicated companionship, and started clearing up.

She remembered that she had mentioned her bacon rolls to Norman and decided that if he wasn't prepared to come to them – and she hadn't really expected him to – then she would take one to him. She'd surprised herself by how much she'd enjoyed seeing Valerie again, as well as getting back into baking, and part of her knew that this couldn't be a one-off, not if she wanted the café to survive. Maybe she could come back every other weekend. Regardless, she wanted Jenny and the people of Willowbeck to know *The Canal Boat Café* was back in business, and getting Norman onside seemed like a good place to start.

She fried some more bacon, sliced open a crusty roll and finished it with a dollop of ketchup.

'Do you know what coffee Norman likes? I can't remember.'

Valerie smiled. 'He thinks coffee is a new-fangled invention. He only ever drinks tea.'

Summer's eyes widened. 'Oh, that's right! I wonder what would happen if I took him a spiced gingerbread latte with whipped cream and cinnamon sprinkles?'

'He'd throw it in the river.'

'I'll take him a tea, then.'

She banged on the door at the bow deck, concerned that the bacon roll would be cold by the time he got it. She couldn't hear anything, so she knocked again. Eventually, she heard a whumph, and a couple of bangs, and then the door opened an inch.

'What?' Norman asked.

'I brought you a bacon roll and a tea. It's a welcome back gift, and I thought it'd warm you up a bit.'

'I've not be'n anywhere. Always be'n here.'

'No, I meant me.' Summer frowned. 'So I suppose it's not "welcome back", but "nice to see you".'

'Y'said that earlier.'

'I'm saying it again. It *is* nice to see you. How have things been?'

'Did y'say that's bacon?' Norman eyed the roll, wrapped in a couple of napkins, warily.

Summer nodded. 'From the butcher, so it's really good.'

Norman's gaze angled up, scrutinizing Summer. 'All right,' he said.

'What?'

'All right, I'll take it.' He held his hands out, and Summer put the cardboard cup and the bacon roll into them.

'Enjoy,' she said brightly, despite the fact he had made her feel like he was doing her a favour.

His head moved in what could almost be a nod of thanks, then he went inside and shut the door.

Summer sighed and hugged her arms around her. The sun was starting to descend and it was getting colder. She was surprised that, as far as she could see, the river remained unfrozen. She jumped down from the deck of *Celeste* and walked slowly past *The Sandpiper*.

There was a light on inside now and Summer resisted the urge to press her face against the window. Mason, the nature journalist. She couldn't imagine the stories he wrote ever got really dramatic – herons decimating local koi carp colonies in residential ponds, the arrival of a rare wading bird from Africa – but living on a boat would get him closer to nature, and if she was honest, she'd love to see some of the photos.

She was almost back at the boat when there was a commotion from inside, raised voices – Valerie's and one other – and a dog barking. She picked up her pace and had almost reached the deck when a stocky, scruffy terrier raced past her, with what looked like a large chunk of bacon in its mouth.

'Is that *our*—' she started, as a man shot through the door and almost collided with her, grabbing her by the arms just in time.

'Sorry! That's my dog, he's just stolen Valerie's bacon and I need to . . .' but his words faded as the dog, clearly deciding against its escape, trotted back and stood in front of him, the bacon sticking out of its mouth. The man loosened his grip on Summer and crouched down, appraising his dog as if unsure what the next step was. The dog's dark eyes were bright with mischief, its tail wagging constantly, defiant in front of its owner. The man sighed and then, to Summer's surprise, lifted up the camera that was hanging round his neck, trained it on his dog, and took a photo.

Summer stared at them, her mouth open.

'Drop it, Archie,' he said. 'Now.' Archie didn't let go of the bacon. 'Archie,' the man said, a warning in his voice. He held his hand out. Archie moved further away.

'Archie,' he repeated, more forcefully this time. The terrier hesitated, looked up at Summer and then dropped the chunk of bacon, complete with dog drool, into his owner's hand.

The man stared at it for a moment, murmured something to his dog that Summer couldn't quite hear and then stood.

'I'm sorry for running into you,' he said.

Summer shook her head, trying to ignore the ruined bacon he was holding. 'No, it's—'

'Oh, Summer,' Valerie said, hurrying out to join them on the deck. 'You've met Mason, then? I'm sorry it's not an ideal introduction.'

Mason gave her a sharp look, and Summer gawped. '*This* is Mason?'

'Why are you surprised?' Mason asked. 'What've you heard about me? I'm so sorry about Archie. I had no idea

30

you were . . .' His words trailed off, and he looked at her, his eyes narrowing. Summer couldn't help but do the same.

His eyes were dark and, as Valerie had indicated, seemed kind despite the situation. They were framed by dark brows and his face, in turn, was framed by a halo of near-black curls, unruly and teased-out. Summer wondered how soft they were, and resisted the urge to reach out and tug a few strands. He wore a washed-out denim jacket over a white T-shirt and dark jeans, a green wool scarf his only concession to the cold. The camera round his neck was chrome and black, modern, but styled like a vintage Leica. It looked expensive.

'So you're Summer,' he said eventually, echoing her words.

'You've heard about me too,' Summer said, her mouth drying out. She knew Valerie would have been kind, but she was pretty sure the true story, that she had abandoned her mum's boat and best friend when they needed her most, could be inferred from whatever Valerie had told him.

'A bit,' Mason admitted, glancing at Valerie. 'Just in passing,' he added, 'when I get a coffee.'

'And this is Archie?' The dog was panting gently, still waiting to be congratulated for his find, or perhaps have it returned to him now it was clearly unfit for human consumption. 'Valerie said he was a bit of a terror.'

'*Summer*,' Valerie hissed.

Mason glanced at Valerie and ran a hand through his hair. 'Really? He's cheeky, but he's not usually this much of a pain – but then you've never had bacon at the café before. I was actually coming to ask if I could get a roll, but,' he looked at his dog, 'I guess that won't be happening now.'

'Why did you take a photo of him? Do you catalogue all his errors?'

31

Mason shrugged. 'I like taking photos. It's not Archie's finest moment, but it made a good photo.'

Summer shook her head and started to laugh, but Valerie put her hand on her arm.

'I think he got through to the back of the boat.'

'What?' Summer inhaled.

'I'm not sure the door was shut.'

'Mum's things.' She slipped past Valerie and hurried through the café, into the kitchen and then, without allowing herself time to think, pushed the door fully open and stepped into the living area. She turned the light on, blinked, and reached out to touch a shelf. There was no visible disruption by Mason's dog, because there was nothing to disrupt.

The room was bare. The furniture was still there, the sofa and the built-in cupboards, but the trinkets, the cushions, the photographs were all gone. Everything that had made the space her mum's had been taken. There was nothing of her left. Summer rushed ahead, into the berth. The bed had been stripped, the photo Madeleine had had above the headboard, of the three of them – Mum, Summer and her brother Ben – was missing. In the tiny bathroom at the end, the cabinet was empty, the towels and bathmat gone, no rubber duck on the basin.

It could have been any boat.

She went back to the living room, feeling the pinch in her nose that meant tears weren't far away. She hadn't wanted to come in here, but she had never imagined it would be completely stripped of her mum's memory. Mason was standing next to the sofa, looking slowly round him, rubbing the side of his face.

'Has he done much damage?'

Dazed, she shook her head. 'Where's Valerie?'

'There was a customer.'

'You need to keep your dog on a lead,' she said, shrugging past him.

Mason followed her. 'He's usually well-behaved. The bacon just got him over-excited.'

'Valerie,' Summer said, 'where are Mum's things? Why is it like that?' She heard the crack in her voice and inwardly cursed herself.

Valerie turned from the hatch, frowning. 'Ben cleared it out.'

'*What?* When?'

'Straight after the funeral. I know things were – you didn't want to come back here – and so I assumed you'd agreed for him to sort it out. We kept the kitchen fully stocked, for the café, but the rest he said he'd get rid of. I left you a message, I assumed you'd discussed it.'

'I had no idea. There were things . . .' She shook her head. Could she be angry at Ben? She'd never have dreamed of doing it so soon, but equally he would never consider leaving things this late to deal with. Summer had assumed that he and their dad had shown so little interest in the boat that they would never come here, and that everything would be preserved until Summer chose to look at it. And she hadn't listened to Valerie's messages. As with everything else, she'd chosen denial, and was now having to deal with the consequences.

'I'm sure Ben's kept the special things,' Valerie said, rubbing her arm. 'Why not give him a call? I know Maddy was happy that he did it, that her belongings didn't linger too long, dusty and unloved. It's ready for a new owner now, a new beginning.' Valerie gave Summer a pointed look. 'Maddy wants that more than anything.'

Summer stepped back, right into Mason, catching a whiff of citrus and vanilla aftershave before moving quickly away. 'How do you know that, Valerie? How do you know my mum agreed with Ben? She's dead! She can't agree, or approve, or disapprove of anything, however much you want her to.'

Valerie's eyes went wide, like saucers. 'But Summer, her presence—'

'Her presence isn't here,' Summer said, the anger stoking inside her, 'she's not here, Valerie. There isn't anything of her left!'

'I feel her.' Valerie held a hand to her chest. 'And if you'd just let me talk to her for you—'

'No!' Summer said. 'No, I won't. It's not possible.' She put her coat on too quickly, her hand getting stuck in the arm.

'Where are you going?'

'Home. I'm going back home, to my flat and my dog and my life. It's better now,' she said, gesturing around her, 'we've sorted some of it out. You'll be fine.'

'Summer,' Valerie said aghast, 'of course I won't. This place can't survive without you.'

'Sure it can.'

'You're coming back tomorrow, though?'

'Didn't you hear me?' Summer said, her gaze darting from Valerie to Mason, who was standing against the window, his face impassive but his eyes fixed on her. She felt a flash of embarrassment, knowing this was all wrong, that it wasn't Valerie's fault and she was coming across badly. It doused her anger, but didn't change her mind. 'I'm going back to my life,' she said quietly.

'Please come back,' Valerie said. 'I'm not against begging.'

'I could do with a bacon sandwich tomorrow,' Mason said, 'seeing as I didn't get one today.'

'You don't need me – you've got all the bacon.' Summer picked up her handbag and walked outside, closing the door behind her. In the dying light, she saw that Mason had tied Archie's lead to the side of the boat. She crouched and stroked the terrier, who looked up at her with big brown eyes and tried to lick her hand. 'That was cruel, wasn't it?' she said. 'Will you tell Mason I'm sorry, I didn't mean to snap at him.'

'You're forgiven,' said a voice behind her. She turned to see Mason in the doorway, almost smiling. 'I deserve the worst you can give, after what Archie did. The bacon's in the bin – let me buy some more tomorrow and I can cook for you, make it up to you.'

Summer stood and looked at him, finding it difficult to turn away. His voice was soft, with no hint of an accent. She could tell, from the way he spoke, that he was an infinitely patient person, but it was more than that. His hair was wild, his appearance on her boat had been shambolic, and he couldn't seem to control his dog, but there was something compelling about him, a directness and depth in his eyes that she found hard to ignore. She wanted to know more about him.

'I have to go,' she said quietly. She moved towards the towpath, her gaze drawn to a white box that sat against the deck wall. She opened it, her anger returning at the red velvet cake inside. She picked it up and thrust it at Mason. 'Here, enjoy – with the compliments of Jenny. Maybe you could take a photo of it before you eat it.' She looked up at the pub, but in the gloom could see nothing beyond the glow of the lit windows. She knew Jenny would be watching, though, delighting in her joke, which might as well have been a 'Get out of town' poster.

Leaving a bemused Mason standing on the deck of her boat holding a cake, Summer hurried back to her car.

Chapter 3

When Summer turned the key in the lock of her flat, forty minutes later, her anger had gone. Latte treated her like a long-lost friend, yapping and walking on her feet as Summer fed her and made herself a cup of tea. She curled up on her bed, Latte's small, warm body snuggled next to her, and called Ben.

'I thought you'd be fine with it. It made sense.'

'Why? I'm not fine with it, and it doesn't make sense.'

'She's been dead eight months, Sum. You wouldn't have wanted all her stuff to go mouldy.'

'So where is it?'

Ben sighed, long and hard. 'I got rid of it – charity shops, mostly. Dad wasn't that interested and you – well, you were a mess, an *understandable* mess,' he said before she had time to retaliate, 'so I just sorted it.'

'You didn't keep anything?' Summer pulled Latte on to her lap, hugging her white, springy fur against her. She'd got the puppy not long after her mother died and couldn't imagine not having her at her side. If she went back to the boat, Latte would be going with her.

'A few bits,' Ben said. And then, his voice softening, 'You've already got her compass though, right?'

'The compass wasn't there?' Summer closed her eyes. She loved her mum's compass, with its pearl and rose quartz inlay, its surface impossibly smooth and cool.

'You didn't take it, before?'

Summer shook her head, added a 'No.'

'It wasn't in her things, I swear. I searched, but then – I assumed you already had it.'

'So it's been thrown out with the rest of her belongings?'

'I – I'm sure I didn't,' he said. 'I wouldn't do that, not intentionally.'

Summer buried her head in Latte's fur. 'I know,' she muttered. 'I know you wouldn't.'

'It could still be somewhere on the boat. Maybe fallen down behind the sofa, anything. Check everywhere.'

'Sure,' Summer said, suddenly feeling exhausted. 'How are you, anyway?'

She listened as her brother told her about his life in Edinburgh, about his job at a solicitor's firm, his girlfriend, Vicky, who he'd recently moved in with. It felt so normal which, Summer guessed, her life had been up until that day.

'Look, Sum,' he said, 'I honestly don't think I chucked out Mum's compass. Have another look will you? And if I get a chance, I'll come down soon. See how you're doing.'

'You're not a bad brother, Blaze,' Summer said, managing a smile.

'I'll be a monster if you keep calling me that.'

'Like the Incredible Hulk? Blaze turns you into some kind of superhero baddie?'

'Don't push it, Sum.'

'Blaze is actually a great superhero name. I'm surprised you ditched it – think of all the girls you could have got.'

'I'm hanging up now.'

'Thank you for think—' she started, then heard the click as her brother ended the call. She lay on her bed, staring at the ceiling.

Her brother had never been the warmest person, and was much more formal and focused than Summer, his apple not falling far from his dad's tree, but he had remembered about the compass. He could have told her sooner about emptying the boat – he could have asked her, in fact – but, if she thought about it rationally, it was a horrible, impossible task that she now didn't have to go through.

She had her mum's boat, she was determined to find the compass, and she had all her memories. Now all she needed to do was pluck up the courage to access them, to move past the sadness that her mum was no longer there, and try and remember the good times. To do that, she knew she had to go back to Willowbeck.

The next day, Sunday, was also Valentine's Day. It was still cold, but the sun was making more of an effort, and Summer replenished her stock of rolls and bacon before making her way to the boat, Latte bouncing alongside her, delighted at the adventure. The narrowboat was dark and locked, Valerie not yet up and about, and Summer ferreted in her bag for the keys, wondering if her strop the previous day had been the last straw for her mum's best friend, and Valerie had finally abandoned the café, leaving it to sink in Summer's unwilling hands.

Summer flipped on the lights, took the brownies and scones out of the fridge and put them on the counter, and turned on the coffee machine. The place felt too empty without either her mum or Valerie alongside her, and she was glad she'd brought her furry companion with her.

She busied herself tidying up, wiping down the counters and putting some bacon on before starting a batch of cupcakes, while the Bichon Frise explored every corner of the boat. She selected a Bat for Lashes album on her phone, turned it up as loud as it would go, and sang along as she mixed the ingredients. She could bake a few basic things, despite not having the flair or imagination her mum had when it came to cooking, and in her experience people were delighted to have even the option of a scone or flapjack when walking or cruising past.

As the sun continued to rise, Willowbeck woke up around her. The willow trees bowed into the river, shivering as if in response to the icy water. Footsteps echoed as dog walkers and joggers used the towpath, the streetlights dimming as February sunlight took over.

Three swans glided serenely past the boat, their motion smooth, necks stretched out, then two narrowboats, one after the other, chugged slowly down the river, one helmsman shouting to the other about where they were going to moor up later that day.

At half past nine, Summer opened the hatch and flung open the door at the bow, where a fold-down plank acted as a bridge between the towpath and the café. The deck had a wooden bench that hugged the curve of the bow, and Summer's eyes fell on something on the floor, partly hidden beneath the seating.

Her immediate reaction was irritation, but this wasn't

another cake box. It was much smaller, and definitely inedible. Summer picked it up and, turning it over in her hands, realized it was a heart. A carved, wooden heart. She glanced around her, but it could have been there for days, dropped or thrown from the towpath or another boat. She ran her finger over it, its surface rough and unpolished, the carving crude, but full of artistic beauty. She could tell it had been done by hand. Making a final, slow turn and spotting nobody, she took the heart back inside and put it on the counter, next to the snowdrops that were already beginning to wilt.

Valerie appeared fifteen minutes later with a screech that shattered the quiet. 'Summer! Oh my goodness, you're back! I was worried someone had broken in.' She was wearing a grey dress with a hint of silver shimmer. Summer had chosen a long, sky-blue jumper over leggings and fleece-lined boots for her second day on the water. She embraced Valerie, and then introduced her to Latte, who had hopped off her chair and was already pawing at the older woman's feet.

'Oh, what an adorable dog. How old is she?'

'Six months,' Summer said. 'I got her after . . . as a bit of a companion.'

'Animals do so much for our wellbeing,' Valerie said, 'and she's perfect. Aren't you?' Valerie stroked Latte, and the little dog turned in circles, her tongue sticking out in delight.

'She likes you,' Summer said, smiling. 'Valerie, about yesterday—'

'I can't tell you how happy I am that you came back,' Valerie said, cutting her off.

'I didn't behave very well,' Summer said. 'I'm sorry I got so angry.'

'You were upset.' Valerie shook her head. 'I'm surprised

you coped as well as you did, your first day back. And here you are again!'

'It's just for today and then . . . who knows? I'm making some cupcakes, and I thought maybe heart-shaped cookies.'

'Hearts?'

'Valentine's Day,' Summer said quickly. 'I mean, it's all very Hallmark, but lots of people love it, and it might increase sales if we can add a bit of a theme.'

'I love your thinking,' Valerie said. 'I would never have come up with that.'

'I might not have either, if it hadn't been for this.' She showed Valerie the heart, watching her face closely, but the older woman seemed as perplexed as she had been.

'No local woodcarvers that you know of?' Summer asked.

Valerie shook her head. 'It could be from the gift shop, maybe? Someone dropped it, and it somehow ended up here.'

'Maybe,' Summer admitted. 'Whatever it is, it's—'

They were interrupted by the smoke alarm shrieking, followed by a thick waft of black smoke. Latte started barking, her small yaps drowned out by the alarm.

'Oh shit, the bacon!' Summer rushed into the kitchen, and found a smouldering frying pan of blackened remains. She took it off the heat and ran it straight under the tap, wondering whether the frying pan would be salvageable.

'It's all right!' Summer stepped back into the café, where Valerie was wafting the now-silent smoke alarm with a tea towel, just as Mason appeared in the doorway. He was wearing jeans and a black shirt that was only half done up, and he was frowning, his dark eyes creased from sleep. He seemed to take a deep breath before walking towards the counter.

'Wow, you're keen,' Summer said, trying not to focus on

41

the half-open shirt. 'I'm afraid you'll have to wait a bit for your sandwich – I burnt the bacon.'

'That's fine,' Mason said, giving her a quick smile. He seemed distracted, looking around him, his chest rising and falling as if he'd run from his boat to hers. 'You're OK?' He looked first at Valerie and then Summer, his brows lowered.

'Fine thanks,' Summer said, but Mason was peering past her towards the kitchen. 'Yeah, sorry about that. Did our alarm wake you?'

Mason shook his head, as if trying to shake an unwanted thought from his mind. 'It reminded me about the bacon – I said I was going to cook for you, remember?'

'I'm doing it for the café anyway. I'm one frying pan down, but if you pull up a seat and give me five minutes, then I can honour your craving from yesterday.'

Mason leant on the counter, his breathing back to normal. 'Sounds great.'

'What do you want to drink?'

'An espresso, please.'

'Straight to the strong stuff.' Summer turned to the coffee machine, but not before she noticed that Mason's feet were bare. Latte had noticed too, and before she had time to warn him the dog was licking his feet.

'Who's this?' Mason bent to stroke Latte, his face softening.

'Latte. So far she's not stolen any bacon.'

'But she is trying to eat my toes.'

'Yeah, sorry about that, she's got a thing about feet. Weird dog. Stop it now, Latte. Come on.' Latte looked up at her and then trotted to the front of the café, jumping on the farthest away chair and sitting with her back to them. 'Oh no,' Summer said, 'now I've offended her.'

Mason laughed. 'Your dog's a diva.'

'That's not fair.'

'Did you not just witness that? She's sulking.'

'Are you trying to tell me Archie doesn't sulk?'

'Of course not.' Mason leant against the windowsill next to the hatch, and noticed that his shirt was still half-open. Summer felt bad for not mentioning it earlier, but she hadn't wanted to embarrass him, and besides, he was in good shape, from what little she could see. He caught her gaze as he did up his buttons, and she gave a little shrug.

'I have to cook fresh bacon. Valerie?'

'What can I do?'

'No, do you want a sandwich?'

'Oh, well, that sounds lovely. But let me help.'

With the cupcakes and cookies in the large oven Madeleine had got specially installed when she bought the boat, and with bacon sandwiches made and coffee poured, Summer, Mason and Valerie settled at two of the tables, Summer opposite Mason. Latte sat in the final chair, though she took a bit of coaxing and a titbit of bacon to get over her sulk. Mason had returned to *The Sandpiper* to get his dog, and Archie was lying on the floor next to the table. Latte was peeping over the edge of her chair, her black eyes trained on Archie as if wondering whether he was friend or foe.

The hatch was open, the blackboard on the towpath advertising the same deal as yesterday, with the addition of a red chalk heart and the words '*Whether love, lust or nookie, feed your sweetheart a tasty cookie*'. Summer and Valerie were taking it in turns to serve customers, though so far all had ordered through the hatch. Summer thought that if they sat at a table, it would encourage people to follow their example.

'I can't believe you gave Archie bacon,' Mason said, shaking his head.

'I couldn't give Latte some and leave him out.'

'But he'll think he's won, that he's been given the spoils of his crime. How am I supposed to get him to behave now?'

'I'm not sure he was that well-behaved before,' Valerie said, grinning.

'Why did you come over this morning?' Summer asked. She wanted to add 'half-dressed', but she was sure Mason had seen her noticing his state of attire. His dark hair was particularly untamed, a single curl falling over his forehead as he ate.

'The alarm woke me and I couldn't just ignore it.'

'It was very kind of you to check on us,' Valerie said, adopting a gentler approach.

'I was coming to ask you to turn it off.' He grinned at them, and it was so disarming that Summer almost missed the tension in his shoulders. 'Seriously though, one thing I've learnt, living on a boat, is that you have to look out for each other. Life is much better that way. Great cake, by the way.'

'The red velvet cake? You ate that?'

'Only a slice so far. What else was I supposed to do with it?'

'It wasn't poisoned then?' Summer asked, giving him a rueful smile.

'Poisoned? I thought it was a present from Jenny, and for some reason – maybe because you were so angry with the world last night – you didn't want it, so you gave it to me.'

Summer sighed. 'Jenny is not the biggest fan of *The Canal Boat Café*.'

'Why?' Mason asked, sipping his coffee. 'Because it's competition?'

Valerie nodded furiously. 'Yes, exactly that.'

'You can't exist alongside each other? Surely you can never have too much cake.'

'*We'd* like to,' Summer said, 'but Jenny's not so keen.'

'So the cake wasn't a peace offering?' Mason ruffled the fur between Latte's ears.

'More a display of superiority. Next time though, it might well be poisoned.'

'Isn't that a bit melodramatic?' Mason asked.

'I wouldn't put anything past that woman,' Valerie said vehemently.

'Tell me about your birds,' Summer rushed.

Mason frowned. 'My birds? What has Valerie been telling you?' He folded his arms.

'Nothing!' Valerie said, her eyes widening.

'I mean your work. Valerie said you were a nature buff.'

'I'm a buff, am I?'

'Like a buff naturist,' Summer said, 'but the other way around.'

Mason raised his eyebrows.

'Not that you aren't buff,' Summer continued, flustered. 'I mean I haven't really seen enough to pass judgement, but—'

'Summer Freeman!' Valerie squealed.

Summer felt heat reach her cheeks, and hid her face behind her hands. 'Crap.'

'I'd forgotten about this,' Valerie said, waving her hands at Summer. 'This – this foot-in-mouth disease. Who wants a refill?' She didn't wait for an answer, but collected the cups and went to the coffee machine.

Summer looked at Mason. His chin was resting on his hand, his smile wide and unapologetic. Latte put her front paws on the table, desperate to be included.

'That wasn't how I intended that to come out,' she said.

'Well, I'm not a naturist,' Mason said, 'but I do spend a lot of time studying, taking photos of, and writing about nature. I guess nature buff is a good way of putting it, even if it could give some people the wrong impression.'

'Maybe sticking to wildlife journalist is better,' Summer said, pressing her hands against her cheeks.

'Maybe,' Mason said, shrugging.

Valerie put fresh coffee on the table in front of them and Mason lifted Latte on to his lap and away from the steaming drinks.

'Ever since I've known her,' Valerie said, 'Summer's had this wonderful ability to share her stream of consciousness with the world, without any modification or diplomacy, as if there are no walls up inside her brain.'

'I don't think that's fair,' Summer said.

'It's perfectly accurate,' Valerie replied, 'and I'm delighted.'

'You are?' Summer looked up at her.

Valerie nodded, her eyes bright. 'Yes. Because since I laid eyes on you yesterday you've been nothing but one big wall, until just now. It's good to have you back.' She patted Summer's shoulder. 'And you,' she said, pointing at Mason.

'Me, what?' Mason gave her a quick grin, but Summer could see he was nervous.

Valerie wagged her finger at him, and then, without saying anything, turned and disappeared into the kitchen.

'I'd like to hear more about your job and what you take photos of,' Summer said to fill the awkward silence.

'Everything,' Mason replied.

Summer grinned. 'A summary would be fine to begin with.'

'No, I mean I take photos of anything and everything – I try and capture unique moments, things that strike me as beautiful or unusual. Can I come back and take photos of Latte?'

'Are you going to put her in one of your magazine articles?'

'I wasn't planning on it,' Mason said, rubbing Latte's ears.

'Oh. She'll be disappointed, won't you?' Latte let out a yip, and Summer laughed. 'See?'

'Excuse me,' a voice called through the hatch, 'are you open?'

Summer got up from the table. 'I'd better . . .'

'Sure,' Mason said, standing. 'I should go and get dressed, for a start.'

'Your feet must be freezing.'

'Thanks for the sandwich. It was worth the wait.' He went to give his coffee cup to her just as she picked it up, and his hand landed on top of hers. She waited for him to take it away, but he didn't.

'Your hands are cold,' he said.

'It's February.'

'Valentine's Day,' he added.

'Come back for a cookie if you'd like to, they should be ready soon.'

'"Whether love, lust or nookie" . . .' Mason quoted.

Summer swallowed. 'It's just a rhyme . . .'

'Excuse me,' the voice called again, 'I'd like one of those cookies!'

'Sorry!' Summer pulled her hand away and, leaving Mason and his empty coffee cup at the table, and with her heart thumping in her chest, went to greet her customer.

The day was taken up serving a constant stream of customers – Valerie had been right about that – and baking, replenishing plates with fresh cakes and cookies, the whoosh as the coffee machine frothed milk for cappuccinos. Willowbeck was attractive even on a grey day, so with a whisper of winter sunshine and a hint of spring in the air, the water and the towpath were busy with boats and strollers. *The Canal Boat Café* was noticeable in its red and blue livery, Summer and Valerie were encouraged to their tasks by gentle yips from Latte, and on three occasions customers ventured inside the boat and sat at the tables.

The interior was barer than Summer would like: the ever-dirty windows needed to let in the light rather than fracture it, the bunting had to be replaced and the scratches on the tables repaired. It could be homelier, but the heating system was up to date, the café remained warm even when the hatch was open, and decoration could be worked on at a more leisurely pace.

As it got to five o'clock and the sun had almost bowed out for the day, Summer closed and locked the hatch, untied Madeleine's red and blue gingham apron and gave Valerie a hug.

'I can't come tomorrow,' she said softly.

'You can't?'

'I'm working on several commissions at the moment, and I can't afford another day away from the studio.'

'So this is it?' Valerie asked, her voice high with panic.

'No,' Summer said, drawing the word out. 'No, I don't think so. But I – let me think. Thank you, Valerie, for asking me to come back. I didn't think I'd want to, but . . .'

'You know it's where you belong?' Valerie's smile was hopeful.

'I've enjoyed myself,' Summer settled for. 'And it hasn't been as – as painful as I thought it would be.' She smiled, but the truth was, today especially, she'd been too busy to think about anything but who needed serving, what needed removing from the oven, and what had happened between her and Mason that morning. She hadn't failed to notice that he'd never returned for his cookie.

'You'll be back,' Valerie said. She was much more positive than she had been on Saturday, and she said the words with conviction. 'And in the meantime, I'll struggle along. But don't leave it too long.'

'I won't, I promise. Come on, Latte.' She clipped the lead on the Bichon Frise, and stepped out into the dusk.

Her feet echoed on the towpath, a sudden burst of laughter coming from the hill as someone opened the door of the pub. She found herself slowing as she passed *The Sandpiper* and could see that the lights were on behind the thin curtains. She gave an involuntary shudder, not of cold, but of longing.

There was nothing more magical than walking in the dark, staring into lighted windows and imagining the families, couples, conversations happening in that safe, snug world, locked away from the night. That feeling was magnified when she was on the river, both because the outside was more inhospitable, the icy depths of the water thrilling in their danger, and because she had never felt as cosy as she had curled up on her mum's boat on a cold winter's night, the woodburner flickering away as they watched a film, or talked over low music.

Now, she imagined Mason sitting at a desktop computer, large in the compact space, scrolling through photos, or reading a book, a glass of red wine at his elbow, his feet bare. She was surprised by the vividness of the picture that formed, the desire to see what the inside of *The Sandpiper* was like.

Each boat was individual, but all, in Summer's mind, were beautiful. A place where you could feel safe and calm. Mason's presence, she was sure, would only add to the effect.

As she got back into her car she thought of her mum's boat and how, behind the galley, it was just a shell. It wasn't right, the space being so empty and hollow. She didn't want to go back to the boat permanently. She didn't think she was ready, but as she drove to her flat the ideas were already brewing in her mind. Willowbeck and *The Canal Boat Café* were trying very hard to work their way back into her thoughts.

Over the next three days she worked solidly on her commissions; a sign for a new boutique, and one for a pub that had changed its name to The Daft Duckling, which made her laugh at least ten times a day.

She was part of an artists' cooperative that had a small gallery and studio space on the outskirts of Cambridge. It had been started a few years ago by a group of people she'd gone to art college with and who had offered her the opportunity to be involved at a time when she was struggling to sell her work and make contacts. Now there were around thirty artists involved, using the studio and holding exhibitions in the gallery. It was friendly, with the marketing and finances shared out equally, so she never felt under too much pressure.

She loved the attention to detail and being able to create things that she knew would last for years, and she got on with the other artists she worked alongside. But now, her concentration was wandering. She found herself coming up with cookie recipes, wondering which flowers would work best as table decorations as winter turned to spring, trying to decide which of the artists in the cooperative could source her the best fabric for new bunting. Even Latte, usually the picture of docility on a cushion nearby, was restless, sniffing around the studio, poking her nose into everything.

As Summer worked on her pieces and tried to keep her dog from becoming a fluffy canvas, her mind also drifted back to Mason. She had been in his company for less than an hour, but his serious face, occasionally lit up with the most transforming smile she'd ever seen, his dark eyes – even his bare feet – returned to her thoughts on a regular basis. Almost as regularly as she received a call or a text from Ross.

Summer sat back on her haunches, clutching her takeaway coffee cup in her hands, and appraised her sign. She'd nearly finished the 'Daft' and would soon start to flesh out the sketch of the duckling itself. She knew her work was good, but she wasn't being as meticulous as she usually was. Her phone beeped, and she sighed.

Ross owned an art supplies shop in Cambridge, one that Summer used often. His prices were good, his customer service excellent. She'd struck up a friendship with him over the course of the previous year, but he'd twisted things on their head by making it clear one night, when Summer was rushing in for more paint and he was about to close up, that he wanted more from their relationship.

His directness had caught her off-guard, mainly because Summer had never seen him as anything more than a friend. She'd never felt an attraction to him, had never seen any passion in him. He was nice, but he had no conviction – except perhaps about getting Summer to go out with him – and Summer couldn't imagine being with someone who lived their life on the surface, who didn't feel deeply about anything. She had remained firm, friendly, but adamant, right up until the point where her mum had died.

She closed her eyes now, thinking back to what had happened, how Ross had been there to comfort her, to listen to her, to hold her when that was all she wanted. One night, when Summer couldn't face going back alone to her flat, she had gone to the pub with him. She had felt safe and comforted, and she had let him come back with her.

She had known – even while it was happening – that it was a mistake, that it wasn't what she wanted, but she had needed to feel something other than the pain of losing her mum, and she had used Ross as a sticking plaster. After that night Summer had apologized, explained that she wasn't in the right place for a relationship, and that she just wanted to be friends. He had been understanding – too under-standing – and said that he was fine with friendship.

Summer knew that he wasn't, that he had chosen to stay close to her rather than lose her altogether, and she hadn't been strong enough to cut off contact completely. Partly, she felt guilty about the way she had treated him, and partly she knew that he'd be there for her without question. She had lost Valerie's friendship and the warm hub of people she knew in Willowbeck because she couldn't face going back there, and Ross seemed somehow to fill that gap. Summer knew it was wrong, but she knew it would be more hurtful to him if she backed away completely. She felt stuck, and while she was uncertain, Ross was the opposite. He remained as unwavering and as present as ever.

She politely declined his text inviting her to a local arts festival that weekend and began packing up her things, cleaning her brushes, setting the easel out of the way to let her sign dry. There was only one person who could help her sort through the muddle inside her head, and that was Harriet.

Whereas Summer had always loved the freedom that being on the water gave her, her best friend Harry was firmly rooted on the ground. As Summer pulled up to the picturesque white cottage, she smiled at Harry's ability to make the garden glow with colour, even in winter. The beds were full of blue and pink hyacinths, snowdrops and some early wild primroses. Harry had a wreath on her door all the year round, and currently it was heart-shaped and made of red twine, with sprays of white carnations and baby's-breath woven through it.

Harry opened the front door, her smile wide on her oval face, her mahogany brown hair falling glossily over her shoulders. 'Sum, come in. Kettle's already on.'

'Thank you,' Summer said, hearing the relief in her voice at the comfort that came from spending time with her best friend. She followed Harry into the large kitchen, simply designed in wood and cream, but with Harry's creations giving it a homely touch. Felt stars hung from the dresser, home-made, pastel cushions sat on the chairs, a small flock of crocheted sheep adorned the side by the toaster. A stack of paperwork and unopened envelopes was partly covered by a half-knitted hat on the kitchen table, and Summer moved the pile to one side.

'How are you, Harry?'

'We're good, good.' Harry nodded, taking something out of the oven, the delicious smell growing in intensity.

'What's that?' Summer asked, hurrying over to peer at the tray.

'Orange and cinnamon cake.'

'Wow, is it—'

'In your honour.'

'Where are the boys?'

'They've gone fishing.' Harry laughed. 'Greg showed Tommy one of those ridiculous shows on some obscure Discovery channel, trying to be all casual as if he'd accidentally come across it, and Tommy seemed genuinely keen. I don't think I've ever seen Greg look so pleased. I might lose them both to the river, which would be ironic.'

Summer smiled and rolled her eyes. Ever since they'd met,

Harry had teased Summer about her hippy mother, and hadn't been at all surprised after Summer's parents had divorced that Madeleine had bought the boat. Harry had often visited Summer at *The Canal Boat Café*, and accompanied her on trips up the river when custom was slow, but at the end of the day she had always been happy to get back to dry land and her solid, rooted home. Summer had never even managed to convince Harry to go camping with her, let alone give up her stability and her soft furnishings and try life on the water.

'I can't believe Greg's waited this long to take him,' Summer said. 'Do you think Tommy'll catch the bug as badly as his dad?'

'I guess it depends if they catch a fish.' Harry winced. 'We'll just have to see. He was meant to be going go-karting with some friends this morning, but we ended up having to cancel, so I hope it cheers him up.'

'No hope of getting him interested in crochet or baking?'

'Hey, there's lots of time yet,' Harry said, waggling her finger. 'He's only ten.'

They sat looking out over the country-cottage garden, a couple of sparrows fighting over one of the feeders, and Summer felt her tension drain away.

'So,' Harry said. 'Tell me. You didn't come here just for delicious cake.'

'But it *is* delicious.'

'Sum?'

'OK, OK. It's just . . . everything's complicated at the moment.'

'Are we talking about Ross?' Harry's voice was soft, tentative.

Summer shook her head. 'No, I mean, that's not changed. But it – it's my fault, I know that. No, this is the boat.'

'*The Canal Boat Café*?' Harry sat up, dark eyes wide. 'What about it? Are you thinking of going back?'

'I *have* gone back,' Summer said, 'that's the thing.'

'*Really?* When? Tell me everything. Are you OK? How did it feel?'

Summer sighed, added another sugar to her tea, and told her.

What felt like hours later, when Summer was entirely full of orange and cinnamon cake and empty of words, she waited for her friend to deliver her verdict.

'You know what I think,' Harry said, 'you've known what I think all along. That boat is your mum's legacy. It could be *your* café, Summer, *your* boat. It's a thriving, unusual, beautiful business, and it's yours for the taking. It's an amazing opportunity.'

'It's not quite so thriving now.'

'But it could be, if you put your heart into it.'

'But Mum—'

'Maddy would want you to do it, more than anything. You can make this your own, Summer. You can start again, with *Summer's* café. Your mum will always be there, in your heart, but she would want you to do it in your own way, not hers.'

'You sound like Valerie.' Summer laughed quietly and Harry gave her a sympathetic smile.

'That's who Valerie is. It's her way of coping, and she's only trying to help.'

'I know, it's just not how *I* cope. Believing that Mum's looking down on us, guiding us. She must know that saying things like that will never comfort me.'

'OK then, how *do* you cope?' Harry collected crumbs on the end of her finger.

Summer shrugged.

'By shutting yourself off from everything that reminds you of Maddy. But by doing that, Sum, you lose the good along with the bad. Don't you think you should try and let the memories back in?'

Summer felt the tears spring too easily to her eyes, the familiar well of grief open up inside her. 'But you know what I did,' she whispered, 'you know why it's so hard for me. How can I think of everything we did together, all the fun we had, without being reminded of that?'

Harry leaned forward and put her hand over Summer's. 'I don't know,' she said. 'But it will happen. Of course it will take time, but you'll find a way to forgive yourself. Maddy would never have blamed you – nobody blames you, except you.'

'But I can't shut me out, can I?' The tears fell, and Summer wiped them with the palm of her hand. 'I miss her so much. And I can't help but wonder, if it hadn't been for me, if it hadn't been for what I did, would she still be here now?'

Harry shook her head, and kept shaking, her gaze never dropping from Summer's. 'No. You have to stop thinking like that. It was bad timing, that's all. Terrible, tragic timing. But you're not responsible for her death, Sum. I'm not saying you haven't made mistakes – everyone has – but you have to move on from them. You need to tell Ross again, flat out, how you *don't* feel about him, and you need to get back on that boat and make it work.'

'It's a shell.'

'So fill it with things that make you happy.'

'I can't bake.'

'A, that's not true, B, I can help, and C – what will happen if you don't? No café can survive solely on someone else's Jammie Dodgers. That boat is *yours*, Summer. Embrace it. If

56

you don't, I think you'll be making a huge mistake – much bigger than anything you're worrying about now.'

Summer looked out of the window. 'Really?' She thought of the night her mother had died, thought of the evening she had ended up drunk and in Ross's arms, pictured the forlorn interior of the café when she'd gone back, Valerie's pleading, upset face. 'You think that I can turn it around?'

'I *know* you can, Summer. What's more, I think you have to. Just go back to any one of a hundred occasions on that boat with you and Maddy, Valerie, sometimes me and Greg and Tommy, and you know I'm telling the truth. That boat is your happy place – even if you're struggling to see it at the moment. Now, tell me, what are you going to do?'

Chapter 4

Summer arrived at Willowbeck early on Friday morning, just as the sun was coming up. Everything was still, and Summer's breath misted the air. Latte was quiet at her side, trembling with the excitement of being woken early and allowed to accompany Summer back to this strange, new place.

She walked up the path towards the water, passing the signpost, and stopped dead. One of the arrows had been replaced. The sign pointing to the pub now read '*The Black Swan Pub & Teashop*'. Summer gritted her teeth against a surge of anger. It could only have happened in the last week – Jenny's next move of attack. How could the pub realistically call itself a teashop just because of a few fancy cakes? She knew her mum wouldn't have stood for this, especially when *The Canal Boat Café* didn't have a signpost at all.

She stomped up towards the pub, and then realized she had no idea what she'd say. She needed to think, and that was exactly what she'd come here to do. She changed direction, passed *The Sandpiper* with a quick glance, fumbled her key in the lock, and opened up the boat.

She turned on the lights and the coffee machine, slipped off her coat and, waiting for the water to heat up, sat at one of the tables. Latte stood on the chair opposite, her front paws on the window, and barked at the towpath.

'Ssshh, Latte,' Summer said. 'Pipe down.'

Latte kept barking and Summer looked, her breath halting in her throat as she saw the figure approaching.

'What is he doing here?' She considered turning the lights off and hiding in the kitchen, but it was too late. Ross would have seen her car in the car park, even if he hadn't spotted her yet.

He raised a hand in greeting and climbed across the plank and onto the bow deck, then pushed open the door.

'Hey, Summer.'

'Ross.' Summer went to check the coffee machine. 'What are you doing here?'

'You said you weren't going to make it into the shop today because you had to come here, so I thought I'd join you.'

'It's still early.'

'You're an early riser,' he said. 'We both know that.' His short, chestnut hair was spiked with gel, a black, Diesel jacket open to reveal a slogan T-shirt that Summer couldn't quite read.

Summer nodded, swallowing down her anxiety. She had thought her need to come here would be a good – and not dishonest – way of putting Ross off, but she should have realized it would only encourage him.

'This is smart,' Ross said, appraising the café. 'I can't believe I haven't seen it until now. I mean, I get why, after your mum died, but before that. Why have I never been to Willowbeck before?'

'Do you want a drink?'

'Cappuccino would be great, thanks.' He moved slowly through the space, examining everything, his eyes lingering. He picked up the wooden heart and, giving Summer a quick glance, put it back down again. 'Does it feel strange to be back?' he asked.

'Of course,' Summer said. 'I hadn't imagined it, had never considered—'

'I must admit,' Ross said, leaning on the counter, 'I was surprised when you mentioned it in your text. From everything you told me, I thought it would be too hard.'

Summer frothed the milk. 'It's been different to how I imagined it,' she said, raising her voice over the sound of the machine.

'Different how?'

'It was lovely seeing Valerie,' Summer said. 'She needed help, and it reminded me of everything good about this place, what it used to be like, and that it's my responsibility now.'

'It's a long way away,' Ross said, accepting his drink with a smile that crinkled his eyes.

'It's less than an hour.'

'Yeah, but every day, Summer?'

'Well, I wouldn't be travelling if I—' She stopped herself.

'If you what? Moved aboard?' Ross gave a gentle chuckle. 'Come on, Summer. I was there, remember? I helped you deal with everything. Do you really think you're ready for the upheaval of moving your whole life to Willowbeck? What about the co-op, your work, your flat? You've never run a café before.'

'Yes, but the co-op's a business, I help run it, so it wouldn't all be completely alien to me. And I was here with Mum, so often.'

'Yes, but *with* your mum, not doing it all alone. Look,

60

Summer,' Ross reached out and took her hand, 'this is a big thing. You first came back here how long ago?'

'A week.' Summer tried to release her fingers, but Ross held them tightly.

He shook his head. 'It's not enough time. And is it really you? Just because your mum loved it doesn't mean you have to follow in her footsteps. You're an artist. I don't know anything about boats, but surely something like this would go for quite a bit? You could get your own studio.'

'I can't just sell it.'

'Why not?'

'I can't leave it like this, when it's floundering.'

'So put it in someone else's hands.' Ross took her other hand and held them between his.

'Ross—'

'Give yourself some more time, at least. It's a big decision.'

'I know. I just—' She turned at a skittering sound, and Latte started yelping, her high-pitched barks instantly joined by lower, gruffer sounds.

'Hello? Summer, are you there?'

Summer gasped. She hadn't noticed him walking past the windows, she'd been too fixated on what Ross had been saying, but now Mason was standing in the doorway, wearing a chunky navy jumper and scuffed jeans. His camera was in place around his neck, and his eyes were trained on Summer's hands, clasped between Ross's.

Summer wriggled out of Ross's grasp. 'Mason, come in. How are you? This is Ross.'

'Hi,' Mason said, holding out his hand.

'Nice to meet you, Mason.' Ross shook Mason's hand and Summer turned away, watching as Archie and Latte sniffed and pawed at each other, Latte's high-pitched barks expressing

61

her delight at seeing the Border terrier again, her earlier wariness gone.

'They like each other,' Mason said, following Summer's gaze.

'You sound surprised.'

'I'm surprised Archie's not trying to assert his authority now that Latte's less shy.'

'Just because he doesn't listen to you,' Summer said.

'Hey,' Mason grinned, 'Archie pays attention to me at least one time in five.'

'But not when there's bacon involved. Espresso?'

'Sure.'

'I could do with a top-up, too,' Ross said.

Summer took his mug and made the drinks, peering round the side of the machine at Mason and Ross.

'You live in Willowbeck, then?' Ross asked.

Mason nodded. 'I'm in the boat next door.'

'That's close,' Ross muttered. 'So you're a bit of a traveller?'

'Sometimes,' Mason said, shrugging. 'I feel settled in Willowbeck, though. It's good for work, and now with Summer here and the café on form, I'm not considering moving on any time soon.'

Summer's insides gave an involuntary flip and she hid her smile.

'We were just talking about Summer selling the boat,' Ross said.

'*What?*' Mason's voice was loud, and Latte and Archie both stopped fussing and looked up at him.

'Ross suggested it,' Summer said quickly. 'I haven't decided what to do yet.'

'But it makes sense,' Ross said, accepting a fresh drink from her.

'In what way?' Summer could hear exasperation in Mason's

voice. 'Summer, last weekend when you were here, I'm not sure I can explain what a difference you made. I'm not just talking about this,' he said, holding up his espresso cup. 'You bring a new lease of life to the moorings. This boat, and what it offers, is an important part of what Willowbeck is. That may sound melodramatic, but I know I'm not the only one who feels that way.'

Summer felt the warmth of his words, replayed the feel of his hand over hers only a few days before. But Ross, too, had made sense. Summer didn't know if she could make this her dream; and if she couldn't put everything into it, wasn't it better that someone else had that opportunity?

'Thank you,' she said, 'for saying that. I just need some time to work out what's best for me.'

'You know I'm happy to talk it through, Summer.' Ross downed his cappuccino, which Summer thought must still be too hot, and kissed her on the cheek.

Summer shook her head. 'I'm not sure—'

'I need to go and open up the shop, but I'll call you later. Nice to meet you, Mason.'

Summer watched him go. She could sense Mason's eyes on her, but he held the silence until Ross was out of sight.

'You're really thinking of selling the café?' His voice was soft, with no hint of accusation.

'It's just all so strange,' Summer said. 'I know Valerie wants me to come back, and I know the café can't survive if someone doesn't take it on properly, but I'm not sure I'm the right person.'

'From what I've seen, you are exactly the right person.' Mason moved close to her, and Summer held her breath. 'Don't decide right now – unless, of course, your decision now would be to stay. If you're thinking about selling, then think a bit longer.' His eyes flashed, breaking his serious expression.

'Oh right,' she said, smiling, 'so I'm allowed to think about it until I come to the right decision?'

'Exactly.' Mason slipped past her and put his empty mug in the kitchen.

'Customers aren't supposed to go back there,' Summer called. 'You're breaking the fourth wall! Anyway, why do you care so much?'

Mason whistled. Archie looked up from where he lay, snuggled up with Latte against the counter, then closed his eyes again. 'Archie, come!'

Summer folded her arms and watched Mason physically untangle his dog from hers. 'You were saying something about him listening to you?'

Mason sighed. 'This is obviously not one of those times. I care,' he said, changing the subject, 'because you have an espresso machine, and you make the best bacon sandwiches.'

Summer's throat dried out. 'Anyone could run the café.'

'I don't want anyone to run it, I want *you* to run it.' Holding on to Archie's collar, he looked up at her. 'I meant what I said, you're a welcome addition to Willowbeck, and I'd be sad to see you go. But if you and Ross want a life elsewhere, then—'

'Oh no,' Summer said quickly. 'It's nothing to do with Ross.'

'Then promise me you'll think about it,' Mason said. Archie struggled out of his grip and raced out on to the deck. Mason called after his dog and followed him out, and Summer felt Latte bump against her ankles.

'I promise,' she said, scooping the dog into her arms. 'I promise I'll think about it.'

After a quiet morning of baking and serving, Summer brought in the blackboard and pulled the connecting plank

64

on to the deck of the boat. She went through to the back, wondering how long it had been since it had moved from its mooring. It was probably over eight months ago, and the thought of her mum being the last person at the helm both steeled and scared her.

She went to the controls, disengaged the gearbox and opened the throttle slightly. She turned the key and checked that all the ignition lights came on – they did – and she turned the key further, closing her eyes in a silent prayer. It took a moment, but the engine burst to life, giving its deep, growly thrum. She set it on tick-over, moved slowly up the boat and tied a centre rope. Then she went through and untied the other ropes, the process that her mum had taught her coming instantly back to her. She untied the centre rope, stepped back on board at the stern, and took the engine out of tick-over.

Summer pushed away from the bank and slowly manoeuvred *The Canal Boat Café* away from its mooring, away from *The Sandpiper* and *Moonshine*, the wake of her boat reaching theirs. She steered out, straightened up, and took her boat slowly up the river, ducks swimming out of her way, the rich smell of vegetation reaching her despite the cold.

She'd forgotten how beautiful the river was. She passed beneath the brick bridge, keeping her steering as slow as possible. As she moved away from Willowbeck, the river widened and trees stooped over the water in their leafless nakedness; the landscape beyond was of fields and woods, no other sign of life there. A heron stood, motionless at the bank, poised for a silver flash of breakfast beneath the surface. Summer breathed in and out, filling her lungs with the river air, absorbing the peacefulness, the steady, gentle chug of her boat.

Latte sat close to her at the stern, a constant companion, unused to the boat's movement, the strange new way of being. Summer passed familiar signs as a stretch of towpath emerged to her left, the benches alongside painted different colours – purple, then yellow, then green. There was a tiny shack that, she remembered being told, had once housed a river warden, employed to look out for boatmen in trouble on the water and warn them about the upcoming locks. Now it was dilapidated, ivy snaking through the doorway and window, prising a hole between the body of the hut and the roof.

She passed another narrowboat painted different shades of blue, a man in a black windbreaker at the helm. He nodded at her, and she waved back, the smile coming easily. The river widened further and Summer steered her boat over to the towpath, slowed the engine and brought it to a halt. She tied up the central rope, and then secured it with ropes at the stern and the bow, attaching them to the mooring posts. She climbed up on to the roof of the boat, realizing first that it needed a good clean and then, soon afterwards, that she didn't care. Pulling the hood of her jacket up over her hair, she lay down, staring up into a sky of shifting grey clouds, passing quickly above her, the afternoon sun trying to peer through.

Summer tried to empty her mind, and as soon as she did, the questions came flooding in. Would her work suffer if she were responsible for the café as well? Could she really run it with help from Valerie, encouragement from Harry and Mason, and not much else? She didn't think she could do justice to the wonderful place *The Canal Boat Café* had become under her mum's vibrant management, but could she do something else, something that was all of her own making? Or was Ross right, should she sell up and move on? Was it too difficult, with Jenny so against her? She could have all the reassurances and supposed messages that Valerie was prepared to channel from her mum, but Summer had to be comfortable with what she was doing or, she knew, she would run away at the first hurdle. Was she strong enough?

She heard a high, familiar peeping sound and sat up just in time to see the flash of orange and blue as a kingfisher dived past on its way down the river. Summer smiled. Her favourite bird, and one that was almost commonplace on the quiet stretches of river. She never tired of seeing them.

The sight took her thoughts back to Mason and his passion for photography, his love of wildlife. She wanted to know more about what he did, she wanted to see his photographs, but to do that she had to be in Willowbeck, running the café.

'Excuse me?' A loud voice brought her out of her reverie. 'Are you open?'

Summer sat up, and looked at the towpath. A couple were standing, parkas zipped up, eyes narrowed against the cold.

'Sorry to disturb you.' The woman, in her forties and with long auburn hair, pointed at the side of her boat. 'Are you open? We could both do with a cup of tea, something to warm us up. We've been a bit ambitious with our walk and we might be blocks of ice before we make it back to our hotel.'

'Of course,' Summer said, pulling Latte to her and scrambling down to the deck. 'I don't have many cakes left,' she said, 'but I can do you a coffee or tea.'

'We should keep going,' the man said, 'or we'll get too warm and never want to leave. But a hot drink would be a marvel.'

Summer switched the café lights on and led the way to the counter, Latte close at her feet. 'It'll just need a couple of minutes to heat the water,' she said, switching on the coffee machine, 'please come in.'

'That'll give us a chance to warm up too,' the woman said, rubbing her hands together and looking about her. 'Are you anything to do with the café at Willowbeck?'

Summer stared at her. 'Sorry?'

'There's a café on a narrowboat a little way down the river, in a beautiful place called Willowbeck. Our friends live close by and they're always going on about how lovely it is. Apparently it's had a few problems, but they're hopeful it'll be back in the spring.'

'I, uhm . . . I'm usually moored in Willowbeck.'

The woman gazed at her, wide-eyed. 'You *are* that boat. I did wonder – they said the tables were painted blue. Have you moved on?'

'No, I'm just here for the afternoon. It's been a while since I saw this part of the river.'

'And we've interrupted you?' the man chimed in. 'We're so sorry.'

'It's not a problem at all. It's lovely to hear that the café's had such a good reputation.'

'Had?' the woman prompted.

Summer busied herself making the tea. 'There have been a few changes recently, and I need to make some decisions.'

'Well, don't leave Willowbeck, that's all I'll say. Jeff and Annie will be devastated if you close and we'll never hear the end of it.'

'They can't face the cakes at that pub on the corner,' the woman added. 'Apparently it's a strange cross between a bistro pub and a boutique patisserie. No charm, all a bit bland.'

'I heard the cakes were really good.' Summer tried to sound matter-of-fact.

68

'No point in good cakes if they don't come with a smile,' the woman said, gratefully accepting a steaming takeaway cup. 'I think this might be the most welcome cuppa I've ever had.'

Summer laughed. 'You're welcome to stay for a while. I've got a couple of cupcakes left, and it's warm in here at least.'

'We'd better be off, pet, or we'll want to move aboard.' The man shook her hand. 'We'll come and see you in Willowbeck though, with Jeff and Annie.'

The woman bent to stroke Latte, who was showing interest in them now that they were about to depart, and then zipped her coat back up.

'That would be lovely,' Summer said. She watched them go, bracing against the cold as they pushed open the door. 'And I can't very well let them down now, can I?' she said to Latte. The little dog looked up at her expectantly, and then settled on a chair and looked out of the window, one paw on the glass. 'At the very least, I have to get the café ready for spring, even if someone else is going to run it.' She went to the stern, started up the boat, undid the ropes and began the slow, cautious process of turning it round. She was going to take her mum's boat back to Willowbeck, and then she was going to start making plans.

Around two weeks later, Summer had reduced her necessary possessions to a large holdall and a cardboard box, and was giving her flat a final going-over, to check she hadn't left anything vital behind. Her plan was simple. Keep her flat for a few months while she went back to live on the boat. She and Harry had gone over it, how she could continue to work on commissions, leave her car next to the butcher's so she could get to the studio easily, begin to reduce her workload and, for the time being, open the café a few days a week.

Her best friend had even offered to do some baking for her, so she had a wider range of cakes to sell.

Harry was going to meet her at Willowbeck, and Summer was grateful for the moral support. What she hadn't told Harry was that, after a couple of months, she thought she would sell the business and the boat as one. Ross's plan made sense to her – she could give *The Canal Boat Café* the best possible start and then hand it over to someone else.

She closed her bedroom door, clicked Latte's lead on to her collar, and turned to the front door just as there was a knock on it. She opened it, and Ross thrust a bunch of flowers towards her. 'Surprise!'

'Ross.' Summer managed a smile. 'What are you doing here?'

'I know you said you didn't need me to be with you today, but I thought you might want some help.'

'That's really kind of you,' she said, 'but I'll be fine. Harry's going to be there.'

'That doesn't mean I can't be, too. All hands on deck, and all that.' He grinned, waited for her to take the flowers and then picked up her holdall. 'I'll follow you down,' he called, and instead of leaving her bag by her car, he put it in the boot of his Corsa.

'Crap,' Summer whispered. She put the flowers on top of her box, picked it up, took Latte's lead and double-locked the door. She'd told her landlady her plans, and Mrs Cumberland had been as matter-of-fact as ever, telling her that if she did decide to leave permanently then the notice period could be short: *There are always people looking for Cambridge flats, so it won't be empty for more than a moment.* Not that Summer had expected to be missed by her landlady, but it had felt a bit miserable to be dismissed quite so easily.

She'd been vague with Ross, told him that she was going to put her energy into making the café popular again, and had failed to acknowledge that she was considering selling it as he'd suggested. She didn't want to show anyone her hand until she was ready.

Harry's words were never far from her thoughts. She knew that she needed to be firmer with him, reiterate that they would never be anything more than friends – and perhaps decide not to see him at all – but she had planned to do that once she'd got the hurdle of moving on to her mum's boat out of the way. And now here he was, helping her. She looked at him in her rear-view mirror and he waved. She raised a hand, started the engine, and pulled away from the kerb. This was it; she was moving back to Willowbeck.

They were two days away from March and the sun was out, the sky a clear blue. Frost shimmered on the path and the signposts, and had turned the grass a pale, minty green, so Summer knew the night had been cold, the stars winking like ice. As soon as she stepped out of the car, she felt as if she'd put her face in a freezer. Ross pulled up next to her.

She checked the key to the boat was in her pocket, let Latte out on a long lead, and took her box from the boot, the spray of colourful carnations and baby's-breath still on top. Her arms trembled, and not just from the weight of her load.

'Right then,' Ross said, jumping out of the car and rubbing his hands together. 'God, it's cold. Will you be warm enough on the boat?'

Summer rolled her eyes. 'I've told you already, it's just like a house, except it's smaller and on the water – and you've seen it now.'

'But you have to empty the toilet.'

'Well yes, there's that, but I don't have to do it very often, and I just take it to a pump-out station. And I can watch television and get on the internet and even do exciting things like have a shower and blow-dry my hair. It's not like camping.'

Ross picked up Summer's holdall. 'The coffee was pretty good,' he admitted.

'There, you see, I'm all set up.' She led the way down the road, the stern of *The Canal Boat Café* and the red and gold of *The Sandpiper*'s bow soon coming into view. Summer took a deep breath and held it in. She bit her lip, as if somehow that would stop the swell of anxiety that was taking over.

'Summer,' a young, familiar voice called, and Tommy, Harriet's ten-year-old son, rushed towards her, waving a green net on a bamboo pole. 'Summer, we've been waiting!'

'Tommy!' Summer put the box down and hugged him. He'd grown since the last time she'd seen him; his dark hair was longer, scruffy in a way that suited him, and he had Harry's big dark eyes and Greg's long limbs. 'How are you?'

'Cool,' he said, stepping back, as if realizing that his enthusiasm at seeing her was distinctly *un*cool. 'Mum said I could do some fishing, but there's nothing here.'

'You've only been trying about three minutes,' Harry said. 'How are you, Sum?' She squeezed Summer tightly, then pushed her back to arm's length and looked at her. 'Ready to do this?'

Summer nodded, but Harry saw straight through it.

'Of course it's going to be hard,' she said, 'but look—'

'Harry! Great to see you.'

Harry gave Summer a quick glare, then turned back to Ross with a smile. 'Ross,' she said, 'how are you?'

'Not bad. I thought Summer could do with a little help settling in.'

72

'How thoughtful of you,' Harry said.

'Isn't that what we're doing?' Tommy asked, looking up at his mum.

'Sure, Tommy. We all are.' She ruffled her son's hair, and turned to a giant jute bag sitting on the towpath behind her. 'We brought a few things. Nothing useful, obviously, but hopefully they'll make it feel a bit cosier.'

Summer crouched and looked inside the bag, and Latte, determined not to be left out, put her nose in it. 'Harry, this is – did you *make* these?'

Harry laughed. 'I'm not going to spend money on this stuff.'

Summer pulled out a small cushion in cream and pale blue, embroidered with a kingfisher motif, and then two crocheted cakes – a Victoria Sponge and a Battenberg.

'For the café,' Harry said. 'I thought they'd be a bit quirky.'

'They're incredible,' Summer breathed. 'Knitted cakes.'

'Crocheted,' Harry corrected. 'And there's this.' She put her hand into the bag and pulled out a large square frame wrapped in tissue paper. 'I should let you unwrap it really, but I can't wait.' The two friends smiled at each other, and Summer helped Harry pull off the white tissue paper. When she saw what was inside, she couldn't do anything but stare at it.

It was a needlework sampler, similar to the one Tommy'd had above his bed since he was born with the alphabet on, and farm animals along the bottom. But this one had *The Canal Boat Café* on, blue and red, sitting on a calm river, with a willow tree stooping over the side. Above it, in boat-matching red and blue, and with her name in sunshine yellow, were the words: '*Summer at The Canal Boat Café*'.

Harry put both of her hands over Summer's, which were gripping the frame. 'This is yours, Sum. Enjoy it.'

Summer shook her head and swallowed. 'I don't know what to say.'

'Don't say anything. Let's go and put your stamp on your new home.'

'Mum did that,' Tommy chipped in. 'She made it specially for you.'

'I know,' Summer said, her voice a whisper. 'It's beautiful.'

'It's a bit girly,' Tommy asserted. 'But it's clever, because it's your name, and it's a season. It's like you're here, and so is sunshine and ice creams and stuff. Like that boat will always be a happy, sunny place with you on it.' He grinned and pointed at the boat.

'I think he's got a point,' Harry said, her eyes bright with pride.

'I think he's a plant,' Summer said quietly.

'Why else do you think I brought him?'

'And, uhm, what shall I do?'

Summer turned to Ross. 'It was so kind of you to bring my bags down, but you don't have to stay.'

'I'd like to, though.'

'Sure,' Summer said, nodding, and felt Harry kick her on the ankle. 'The more the merrier.'

Ross's uncertainty was replaced by a wide smile. He picked up the bag and followed Summer, Harry, Tommy and Latte on to the boat.

'I've made up some brownie mix,' Summer said, 'so I just need to put it in a tray and I can pop it in the oven. I'll stay out here to get it done, then I'll come through.'

Harry gave her an even stare. 'I'll do the brownies, you make a start.' She pointed at the door to the boat's cabin.

Sighing, Summer took her Tupperware container out of the cardboard box and handed it to Harry. She went through the galley and, squeezing her hands together, slipped through into the living area of the boat. She switched all the lights on, stared again at the bare walls, the brown leather sofa, the built-in shelves devoid of personality.

'Oh,' Ross said, coming up behind her, 'this is really neat.'

'You think?'

'It's bloody amazing,' he said, moving in front of her and walking to the end of the room. 'Swanky.'

'It's *swanky*?'

'Don't you think so? Get your bits and pieces in here, and it's going to look like one of those luxury yachts in James Bond films.'

'I think you're overselling it a bit.'

'I'm serious, Summer. I know you said it was like a house, with all mod cons, but I didn't imagine *this*. Wow.'

Summer watched him, his genuine surprise as he stared around the place that Summer had been thinking of only with a sense of foreboding. She felt a surge of gratitude, followed by a rush of excitement. It was hers. She could make her mark on it. She reached into Harry's bag, took out the kingfisher cushion and plopped it on the sofa.

'There,' she said. 'What do you think?'

Ross nodded, his cheek chinking with the one dimple that appeared when he smiled. 'I think it looks great. You'll have no trouble selling this place once it's all set up.'

They worked through the morning, fuelled by Summer's brownies, unpacking her bags, putting books on the shelves, her artist's palette clock on the wall, toiletries in the bathroom, clothes in the tiny wardrobe. The bed was only a small double, four-foot wide, so Summer had bought a new duvet and searched the shops for the ideal bedding. She'd fixed on a blue checked design, simple but cosy, and she knew it would go well with the wood walls and interior.

Valerie arrived at eleven, a successful morning of readings having given her a glow that made Summer feel guilty for dismissing her profession. She might not believe in what Valerie did, but her customers got something out of it, and surely that was all that mattered.

'I'm going to have a neighbour again,' she said, embracing Summer as she tried to make Valerie a cappuccino. 'And not just any neighbour, but Summer Freeman.'

Latte looked up at her, bounced slightly on her front feet, and let out a piercing yip. 'And you of course, Latte. I can tell you're going to demand a lot of attention.' She lifted the small dog up, and Latte licked Valerie's nose.

'That's true,' Summer said, smiling. 'I don't know what I did to make her such high-maintenance.'

'Spoiled her rotten, I expect,' Tommy said seriously.

'Thomas Poole,' Harry gasped, 'what on earth makes you say that?'

'That's what you say to me when I'm getting all high and mighty.'

Valerie laughed and put Latte on the floor. 'You're a walking phrase book, young man.'

'I'm imprinting, that's what young people do. That's why it's important to surround yourself with good people.'

'Where is he getting this stuff?' Summer asked.

Harry shook her head. 'A young head on old shoulders, or possibly too much grown-up TV.'

'More brownies,' Ross said, coming out of the kitchen. 'How much of this mix did you make, Summer?'

'Enough for a few days' worth. I'm hoping to open up after lunch, so I don't completely miss the weekend trade.'

'You really think you've settled in enough?'

'I think getting trade going again will help me settle in. My boat is called *The Canal Boat Café*, after all.'

'I like the name *Sandpiper*,' Tommy said. 'And it's all gold and red and black, like some kind of uniform. Who lives there, Summer?'

'Oh that's Mason,' Summer said, aiming for breezy. 'I don't know him very well yet, but Valerie does.'

'He's a nice chap,' Valerie admitted. 'He was pleased you were coming back and said he'd try and pop over, but I think he's out on a bird hunt.'

'He's a *hunter*?' Tommy said, his voice a mix of fear and admiration.

'Only with lenses,' Summer said, 'not guns. He takes photos of the wildlife and writes about it.'

'Like the fish?'

'I'm not sure he's into fish, but you can ask him if you're still here when he arrives.'

'I expect he'll be pleased to have another neighbour too,' Valerie said. 'At the moment his immediate neighbour is Norman.'

'I remember Norman,' Tommy said, his hand shooting up. '*He* does fishing, doesn't he? But silently, and all a bit grumpy, like he's annoyed with the fish or something. Or maybe it's 'cause there aren't any fish in this river.'

'Maybe you need to give it another go,' Summer said, putting her hand on Tommy's shoulder. 'I'm sure Norman catches things, even if he never seems that pleased about it. But he did let me give him a bacon sandwich the other day. I felt very privileged.' She raised her eyebrows.

'Good old Norman,' Harry said, laughing. She looked out of the window, her expression suddenly unreadable. Harry had spent a lot of time at Willowbeck with Summer and her mum, and Tommy and Greg had often accompanied her. It was Harry's first visit for months, too. Summer squeezed her hand. 'Thanks so much for all you've done.'

'Make the most of it, Summer. Your mum would be so proud.'

Summer looked around her. 'It depends if I can make it as successful as she did. But then, it seems I've got lots of help. I'm just going to trim these flowers and put them on the tables.' She picked up Ross's bouquet. 'You don't mind do you, Ross?'

'Whatever's best,' Ross said, looking up from his phone. 'They're for you, after all.'

'We'll have to head off in a moment,' Harry said, 'we're getting Greg from work.'

'I haven't seen him for ages, does he ever have a day off?' Summer laughed, but Harry didn't join in.

'There's a bit too much work to go around at the moment, and they need as many staff as possible.'

'That's good, isn't it?' Harry's husband, Greg, worked for a small landscaping company that worked across Cambridgeshire.

'Yeah,' Harry said, but she didn't sound convinced.

'He does still get time off, doesn't he?'

'Of course – they're just particularly busy at the moment.'

'So the company's doing well?'

A shadow crossed Harry's face, and she gave a little shrug. 'Come on Tommy, let's go and get Dad.'

'But I haven't caught a fish for dinner!'

'That's fine,' Harry said, 'we can catch some from Jimmy's Plaice this evening.'

* * *

Summer, Valerie and Ross kept going once Harry and Tommy had left. The tables looked welcoming with their bright bouquets, and Summer opened the hatch, put a tower of brownies on the counter and a batch of blueberry muffins in the oven. She wished she had some of Harry's orange and cinnamon cake to draw in more people, or some of the Florentines she made – something unusual but homely. Red velvet cakes were all very well, but they were a bit too boutique for Summer's liking – and it sounded like she wasn't the only one who felt that way. She wanted to be friendly, different but not too trendy.

Valerie piled a stack of freshly washed plates next to the coffee machine. 'I've got a couple of readings this afternoon, so I'd best be off.'

'Come back for a tea once you've done?' Summer tried not to sound desperate, but it was still February, the evenings drew in early, and she would be alone on the boat for the first time. She had her iPad, her Netflix subscription, and the Wi-Fi booster her mum had had installed almost as soon as she'd bought the boat, and the cabin was a far cry from the empty hull it had been that morning, but she still felt nervous.

'Perhaps we could brave the pub for dinner?'

'Really?' Summer baulked.

'We'll have to at some point,' Valerie said. 'Jenny needs to know you're here to stay.'

'What can I do now?' Ross asked once Valerie had left.

'You've been brilliant, thank you so much. And I – I wanted to talk to you,' Summer said, remembering Harry's words.

'Sure.' Ross sat at one of the tables, a puddle of coffee in the bottom of his mug. 'Shoot.'

'Right, Ross. Look, the thing is . . .' She sat opposite him, fiddling with the buttons on her long, navy cardigan, 'about what's happened between us, in the past. I—'

'Hello? Anyone home?' Summer stopped mid-sentence and looked up to see Mason push open the door. His black curls were more tamed than usual, he had a green khaki jacket done up to the neck over jeans and black walking boots, and the camera round his neck. Archie was close at his feet, and Latte jumped down from her chair and padded over to him.

'Mason, hi. How are you?'

'Bit chilly, but good otherwise.' His smile faltered as he saw Ross and he offered him a quick nod. 'Hi again. How's it going, Summer? This place is looking great,' he said, turning in a slow circle. 'Like a different café already.'

Summer stood. 'Can I get you anything? A coffee, tea?'

He shook his head. 'No thanks, I've got to head back and load up my photos. I just thought I'd welcome you back here, officially. I definitely think you've made the right decision.'

Summer moved from foot to foot, wishing Ross wasn't there. More than anyone else, she wanted to tell Mason she was considering selling the boat – she hated the idea of keeping it from him. 'I'm going to see how it goes. My friend Harry's helped make the cabin feel a bit more cosy.'

'I'm glad,' Mason said, smiling at her. 'For what it's worth, I think you'll settle in quickly. I remember when I bought my boat, those first few weeks living aboard felt strange – very different from being on land.'

'The bed's a bit narrow though,' Ross said.

Summer saw irritation flash across Mason's face and she closed her eyes. When she opened them again, Mason was turning away.

'Right. So, work. Come on, Archie, leave Latte alone.'

'Will you pop in tomorrow?' Summer called. 'My first full day on the boat.'

Mason turned at the door. 'I'm out all day tomorrow, but I'll be back on Monday. I promise I'll come and see you.'

'You will?'

'Scout's honour.' He saluted and jumped over the plank to the towpath. Summer watched him go, and realized she was grinning.

'He's quite persistent, isn't he?' Ross asked, his fingers drumming on the table.

'He's my neighbour,' Summer said. 'It's good to have him around; to have some people here who I can count on.'

'You can count on me, Summer, you know that.'

'That's what I want to talk to you about.' Summer took a deep breath and sat down again. 'I want you to know how much I appreciate you coming here today, and helping me settle in.'

'What kind of a friend would I be if I didn't?'

'You're a great friend, Ross. I mean that. But it's never going to be any more than that.'

Ross frowned and folded his arms. 'What do you mean?'

'I mean that I don't want a relationship with you, not anything more than what we have now.'

'I know that,' Ross said.

Summer swallowed. 'I don't think you do. It just seems like you're . . . some of the things you said. Mentioning the bed in front of Mason.'

'It's a narrow bed – you wouldn't deny that, would you?'

'No, but – you seem so – so willing to be here, all the time.'

'I'm your friend, and I've been here twice. Would you prefer me to act like I didn't care?'

Summer shook her head, frustrated. 'No, of course not. But I think maybe we need to be . . . I need to focus on making the café work.'

'I can help, Summer. And, maybe in time, well, you never know what could happen.'

Summer squeezed her hands into fists under the table. 'I know what's going to happen, and what's not going to happen – for me. Ross, I'm sorry, but I don't feel that way about you. That's not going to change.'

Ross stared at her, his smile fixed. 'Just take your time. This is all so new for you. It's only been a few months since you lost your mum, and now this. You need to find your feet here, decide what you're going to do. You may realize you love it here, against all your expectations. You might decide to stay for good – nobody knows what the future holds, or how they'll come to see things differently. Just know that I'm always here for you, as close – or as far away – as you want me to be.'

'Ross—'

'I should be getting back. Don't think about it now. Give me a call, even if you just need some company. It can't be easy being on the boat on your own, especially at night.' He came round to her side of the table and wrapped her in a hug. 'Just look after yourself, and call me *whenever* you need to. As you said, it's not even an hour away.'

Summer closed her eyes, her energy and resolve gone. She wasn't sure how, other than flinging herself at another man, she could get Ross to accept the truth.

Chapter 5

Summer's first evening was quieter than she had originally hoped for, but by the time she got to it, she was glad of the peace. She fed Latte, put a ready meal in the oven, opened a bottle of wine and selected an Einaudi album on her iPad. She lit the cabin with lamps, recreating the cosiness that she had always associated with her mum's boat.

She wasn't sure she could thank Harry and Tommy, Valerie and Ross enough for what they'd done that day, helping her get over her nerves, and turning the boat into somewhere she could call her own.

She still felt guilty about Ross, but she also felt weary. She'd said, again, that nothing would happen between them. She'd been prepared to say they could cut off contact entirely if that would be easier for him, but again he'd failed to accept it, and she was beginning to despair at ever being able to get through to him.

Her phone chimed and she picked it up. Harry was checking in, telling her that Tommy and Greg had been delighted with their fish and chip supper, even if it wasn't as fresh as Tommy had hoped, and asking about her first evening. Summer sent her a quick reply and closed her eyes, the glass of wine pressed against her chest. Even when the boat was moored up, there was a gentle swaying that she barely noticed unless she focused on it, but she knew she would miss instantly if it stopped. Her boat knocked gently against the concrete of the towpath, or Valerie or Mason's boats, when another narrowboat passed on the river, the sound hollow, almost melodic.

The magic of being on the boat was beginning to come back to her. It had always been a one-berth boat, the living space squashed because of the café space, but the sofa she was sitting on folded down into an additional bed, and Summer had often ended up staying. She was used to the sounds, the sensations, of being on a boat at night, entirely cocooned in her own world. She had forgotten how much she enjoyed it and now, even without her mum there, she felt calm.

That night, she climbed under the fresh-smelling checked sheets, turned out the light and closed her eyes. Only moments later, it seemed, it was morning.

Summer got up early, took Latte for a walk along the towpath, then opened up the café. It was a Sunday, so Willowbeck was busy and she worked solidly, baking and cleaning and serving. A few people ventured inside the café, enjoying the views of the river through windows that were much cleaner than they had been. Summer had found a coil of red, yellow and blue fabric bunting in different patterns at the bottom of the bag Harry had left, and she'd strung it up along the back of the counter. She planned to use it as inspiration and make some of her own.

Harry was by far the most creative person Summer knew, and could turn her attention to anything – textiles, food, jewellery, wood – and create something special. Summer's artistic talents were limited to sign writing and acrylics, but Harry seemed to have magic fingers and an eye for detail. They'd met at art college and Summer had always expected Harry to have a versatile career, perhaps owning her own shop or gallery. But Harry had met Greg at twenty, had Tommy at twenty-one and seemed content to raise her family and keep crafting as a hobby. But the previous day Summer had sensed that not everything was right with her best friend, and wondered if maybe she was beginning to regret not exploring some of the endless possibilities at her fingertips.

By the end of Sunday Summer was happily exhausted. She'd had no major disasters, only run out of cakes as a fresh batch came out of the oven, and joined forces with an old gentleman and his umbrella to coax an intrepid duck out of the café. She'd decided she would spend the first week on the boat and work out a strategy – which days were busier, on which ones she could close and go to the studio without losing too much custom. She'd finished her urgent commissions before moving on to the boat, and the *Daft Duckling* sign wasn't due until the beginning of April. She went to bed early, snuggling up in her berth and rocking asleep to the gentle lull of the river.

Monday was the twenty-ninth of February. Leap day. She peered out at the grey sky, Latte snuffling at her feet, impatient for her walk, and wondered if anything strange would happen. She had nobody to propose to, and she thought that was a pretty outdated custom anyway. She locked the boat up and strolled down the towpath, past the pub and under the bridge. She gave an involuntary shudder at the few moments of dank darkness and remembered, a long time ago, Valerie telling her and Mum a story about a ghost that appeared on top of the bridge, looking down into the water. Valerie's story was elaborate; she had names and dates, the ghost supposedly a woman who had been jilted by her lover and thrown herself into the depths of the river, but Summer just remembered thinking that it was a tragic event that had, over time, become a myth. She was sure nobody other than Valerie would admit to having seen the ghost.

Summer kept walking, letting Latte explore, enjoying the quiet of the towpath until her hands went numb. She turned and strolled back towards Willowbeck, waving at other boats as they passed, most helmsmen cheery despite the cold. She'd just gone back under the bridge when Latte started barking. For a moment, Summer worried that her memory had conjured up the ghost, but then a Border terrier raced up to Latte, both their tails wagging excitedly.

'Archie,' called a familiar voice, and Summer buried her smile into her collar and picked up her pace.

Mason was standing on the towpath next to his boat, exasperation on his face and a rolled-up magazine in his hand.

'So well-behaved,' she said.

Mason gave her a sheepish grin. 'There was a fly buzzing around, dozy and irritating. I was trying to coax it out of the door and Archie took the opportunity to break free.'

'At least he's not gone too far.'

'He never does. It's like he's testing me. Letting me know he could really cause trouble if I took my eye off the ball. He keeps me on my toes.'

'Perhaps better than nibbling them?' Summer pointed at Latte.

'Maybe,' Mason considered. 'How is life in charge of the café?'

'Not disastrous,' Summer said, grinning. 'So far, anyway. How was work?'

Mason nodded and crouched to stroke Archie, who had returned to him, and then Latte, who saw the opportunity

86

for some extra attention. 'It was fine. Not as interesting as I'd hoped – most of the wildlife was hibernating – but I got some good shots.' He lifted his camera, waited for Latte to look at him, and then snapped her.

'I'd love to see them some time.'

'You're more than welcome to come aboard *The Sandpiper* and have a gander.' They enjoyed an easy silence for a moment, and then Summer felt the atmosphere change. 'I know it's not been easy for you, making the decision to come back. Your mum's death wasn't that long ago, was it?'

Summer sighed and looked at the floor. 'It was last summer, and I wasn't sure I'd come back. I loved it so much when we were here together, I didn't think I'd ever want to erase those memories by creating new ones without her.'

'I can understand that,' Mason said softly. 'It's none of my business, but I think it's a courageous thing to do. And I also think that, even if it's hard at first, it'll be worth it.'

'You do?'

Mason nodded. 'Aside from the fact that this was your mum's boat, the water is a calming place to be. I've always believed that it has healing properties.'

Summer narrowed her eyes. 'In a mystical kind of way?' Maybe he had more in common with Valerie than she'd appreciated.

'No,' Mason said, matter-of-factly, 'in a natural way. Nature is healing. Nobody in the world could argue that going for a walk in the fresh air was bad for you.'

'Jane Austen might.'

Mason frowned at her. 'What?'

'Many a Jane Austen heroine has nearly caught their death from a hearty walk in the rain.'

'Well, more fool Jane Austen then. I bet it wasn't the walk

that nearly killed them, I expect it was all the romantic turmoil they were being put through.'

'An interesting theory.'

'I'm full of them,' Mason said, standing and stretching his hands to the sky. He was wearing a rusty red jumper, and it rode up as he stretched, revealing an inch of toned stomach. 'Are you doing bacon sandwiches today?'

'How can you be so fond of bacon and still—' she stopped, realizing that Mason had caught her looking at him, again. 'Never mind.'

'What?' His smile grew, hovering on the edge of kilowatt, and Summer swallowed.

'I can do bacon,' she said quietly. 'Give me half an hour to get the place in order and warm up the coffee machine.'

'Deal.' He lifted his camera again and pointed it at her, asking her a question with his eyes.

Summer breathed in, surprised by how nervous she felt having Mason's lens on her. But then he seemed to change his mind, gave her a quick smile and, lowering his camera, walked back to *The Sandpiper*, Archie soon leaving Latte and following behind.

As Summer stepped on to the bow deck, her breathing slowly returning to normal, her eyes fell on something nestled up against the wall. She crouched and picked it up, but not before Latte had sniffed at it, and quickly decided that despite the intriguing shape it wasn't something she was interested in. Summer turned it over in her hands, and then, realizing she was alone apart from a squirrel and a pair of mallards on the grass in front of the pub, picked it up and went inside.

Once Mason was leaning on the counter, tucking into a crispy bacon sandwich, Summer asked him about her new find. She'd placed it alongside the wooden heart and Harry's crocheted cakes.

'I found this,' she said, moving the wooden frog in front of him. 'It was left out on the deck.'

Mason looked at her, and then examined the carving. 'It's good craftsmanship, don't you think?'

'I do,' she nodded. 'Rough but beautiful, like a charcoal sketch.'

'Same as this one?' Mason picked up the heart.

'I'm sure of it. I found them in the same place and at first, with the heart, I thought maybe it had fallen off another boat, or out of someone's bag or pocket on the towpath. But now?' She shook her head.

'What do they mean? A heart, and then a frog?'

Summer shook her head again. 'Beats me. It's my own little mystery.' She had one theory, but she wasn't about to share it with Mason, because it was that he'd been leaving them for her. The heart had appeared the day after she'd met him, the frog just as she was moving on to the boat full time and was experiencing strange leaps of her heart at Mason's smile or a glimpse of his flesh. This seemed ridiculous, even to her, and was perhaps a sign that she was thinking about him too much, making connections where they didn't exist.

'And you're sure the wood's not poisoned?' he asked, raising an eyebrow.

'Ha ha. Jenny's threats are much more straightforward. *I'm baking cakes, look how good they are, now piss off.*'

'What is it with you two, anyway?'

Summer looked out of the window. 'She doesn't like the competition.'

'But you've hardly been here – how come she got so angry so quickly?'

'Because I'm a threat.'

Mason folded his arms on the counter, and rested his chin on them. He looked up at Summer and she fumbled with the cup she was drying. 'I've spoken to Dennis and Jenny quite a few times since I've been here,' he said, 'and they both seem perfectly pleasant.'

'How long have you been in Willowbeck? You weren't here last June.'

'Only since November. I'm usually much more mobile, but there's lots of activity at the local nature reserve and they're having a revamp. They want me to take photos for their new guidebook and they've got an arrangement with a wildlife magazine for a series of features over the next year or so, about the changing seasons, habitats, wildlife, so I've made this sort of a long-term temporary home.'

'And then you'll be off again?'

'Probably.' Mason sipped his coffee.

'Have you lived on boats all your life?' Summer tidied the cups and then leaned on her side of the counter.

Mason shook his head. 'Five years.'

'Why? What made you take to life on the water?'

Mason remained fixated on his coffee. 'Various things. I felt I needed to get away, have a simpler life. It's a good way of travelling, of getting closer to nature. It suits me.'

'Your boat's beautiful.'

'When I bought it, it was a wreck.'

'Did you do everything?'

'No, I'm not skilled like that. I took it to the boat builders and concentrated on getting it seaworthy, and then the other bits and pieces have followed over the years. It's not been as polished as this for very long. Anyway,' he said, poking her forearm gently, 'you've changed the subject. What's going on

90

with Dennis and Jenny? It doesn't quite fit. Come to the pub with me this evening.'

'What?' Summer's heartbeat ratcheted up a notch.

'It's not like he's Norman Bates.'

'No, I – I'm not sure I can.'

'Are you allergic to beer?'

'Jenny won't want to see me.'

'Well, she won't mind seeing me, so that'll dilute the effect.'

'Mason.'

'Summer?' He gave her one of his disarming smiles, and it transformed him. His seriousness was gone, he looked as warm and open as anyone she'd ever met. She wanted to know him, to delve more into the man who didn't mind that he couldn't control his dog, who trained his camera on everything, and spent his days hiding in bushes waiting for wildlife to surprise him. She realized that if she hadn't been worried about purposely putting herself in Jenny's way, she would be equally nervous that he had invited her to the pub, however casual that offer might have been.

'OK,' she said, the words coming out with more conviction than she felt, 'I'll come.'

Summer leafed through her tiny wardrobe looking for something to wear, but found she was trying to present so many different fronts with her outfit that it was going to be impossible. She wanted to be assertive but not aggressive in front of Jenny, and she wanted to look good, but like she hadn't made an effort in front of Mason. And what kind of outfit was anti-aggressive, anyway? Pale-pink wool? What, honestly, was she trying to do?

She chose a long, claret-coloured dress over tights and flat, knee-high boots, and put on some subtle make-up in the mirror over the sink. The bathroom looked cheery and lived-in, even if her mum's rubber duck was no longer there. She would have to find something else to adorn the basin with.

She gave Latte some dinner and then watched her go straight to her bed and curl up on the checked pillows. Latte knew she wouldn't be told off, because Summer felt guilty about leaving her for the evening. Summer stroked her, wondering how she was allowing herself to be worked-over so completely by such a small dog, and thought maybe it was time to stop teasing Mason about Archie.

He was waiting for her on the towpath. As she switched off the café lights he – and everything else – was consumed by darkness, and then she was lit by the pale yellow glow of a torch.

'It's not a long way,' Mason said, 'but I've tried to get back on my boat in the pitch dark, and even before a few drinks it doesn't always go well.'

'Thank you,' Summer said. 'I didn't think to bring mine.'

They walked in silence up the path that cut through the grass in front of the pub, and to the large wooden doors. Summer's insides were fizzing with excitement and dread, which wasn't an easy combination to stomach. Mason pushed the door open and held it for her, and Summer was engulfed by warmth and the smell of chips.

She remembered the interior well. It was beautifully done, with dark wood tables against cream walls, navy cushion covers and booths against the windows. Willowbeck was quite isolated, but there was a gentle thrum in the pub, locals and passers-by getting in a few drinks to soften the blow of the new working week. Mason walked up to the bar, steering Summer with him with the lightest touch on her arm.

'What would you like?'

'A glass of red, please.'

'I'll have a red wine and a pale ale please, Dennis.'

Summer looked at Dennis for the first time in over eight months and a rush of memories overwhelmed her. Dennis, it seemed, was experiencing something similar, because he was standing behind the bar, staring at her as if she was as unlikely an apparition as Valerie's ghost on the bridge. He was tall and stocky, with short, muddy brown hair and warm green eyes that were usually crinkled in kindness, but were currently fixed on Summer like laser beams.

Mason glanced between them, a puzzled smile appearing. 'Uh, Dennis?'

'Yeah – yes, sorry. Sorry, Mason.' He shook his head and turned towards him, his smile too wide.

Mason repeated the order, and Dennis poured the drinks. Mason carried them over to a table, and Summer was about to follow him when she heard her name.

She turned back. 'Hi,' she said softly.

Dennis shook his head. 'Jenny mentioned . . . but I never thought that – how are you?'

'I'm OK,' she said. 'You?'

He gave her a rueful smile and a tiny shrug of his shoulders. 'Things are good, really. Better, anyway. It's great to see you. You're back in Willowbeck?'

'On Mum's boat,' Summer said. 'I don't want to cause any trouble, but—'

Dennis waved his hand. 'Not your problem to deal with.'

'Jenny left a red velvet cake on my deck.'

'Probably just a knee-jerk reaction to the shock of seeing you. I doubt she'll do it again.'

'She seemed pretty angry.'

Dennis held up his hand to a young couple that had

arrived at the bar. 'She's overreacting. She's really got into baking the last few months and your return has made her feel insecure. I'll have a word, Summer. Try not to worry.'

'Thanks, Dennis.'

'Glad to have you back.'

Summer turned and scanned the pub. She saw Mason sitting at one of the booths, watching her, his eyebrows rising as she approached.

'Cake strategy meeting?' he asked.

'Sorry?'

'Are you working out a plan to divide and conquer the people of Willowbeck with your respective cakes?'

'Something like that.'

'Or not.' Mason shifted sideways in the seat so he was facing her, his knee brushing against Summer's leg.

'Why not?' Summer asked, trying to drag her thoughts back to the present.

'Because there was more going on there, between you and Dennis.'

'I haven't seen him for a while, that's all.'

'So he's not against you starting up the café again, like Jenny is?'

'I wouldn't say that. Thanks for the wine.' She took a sip. 'Mmm, lovely. Tell me about your work, about the reserve. What are you studying at the moment?'

Mason gave her a quick smile. 'Oh, all sorts,' he said. 'I'm quite good at observing behaviour – it comes with the territory. Dennis is fond of you, isn't he?'

'We got on, before,' Summer said, shifting uncomfortably, the wool of her dress scratching the back of her neck.

'What happened?' Mason asked softly.

'Water under the bridge,' Summer replied, meeting his

eyes for a second then looking away. 'And it's not my story to tell, anyway. Not now.'

'Sure,' Mason said. He nodded once, and something seemed to break, some bubble around them. Mason took a sip of his beer and raised his eyebrows. 'Want to hear about my current love affair with the redshanks?'

'Sounds intriguing.' Summer knew she had been let off the hook. But as she listened to Mason, watching how animated he became as he told her about his work, about the hours of sitting and waiting, the magical moment when he saw what he was searching for and frustration if his pictures didn't come out as he'd hoped, Summer felt flat. Part of her had wanted Mason to keep probing, to force her into telling him what had happened the previous summer. Harry had reminded her that she needed to move forward, and it still weighed her down like an anchor.

For the rest of the evening, Mason steered clear of talk about Dennis and Jenny. Summer learnt a lot about Mason's job and she, in turn, told him about her work as a sign writer, how she had, at one time, been intent on narrowboat art. At the end of the night he accompanied her back to the boat, the torch guiding the way, and waited until she was safely inside with the lights on, before returning to *The Sandpiper*.

The following day, the first of March, a wooden carving of a daffodil was waiting for her on the deck. Summer picked it up and put it on the counter next to the heart and the frog. She wasn't sure what her collection meant, or who was leaving them for her, but she was becoming more intrigued, knowing that the first thing she would do every morning was step outside on to the bow deck to see if she had a new gift.

Summer spent the next month throwing herself into life on the boat. She baked scones and muffins, cupcakes and brownies. She made bacon and sausage sandwiches with fresh meat from the butcher. She kept the tables furnished with fresh flowers, and she began working on her own bunting, to complement the beautiful string Harry had made for her.

She didn't go a day without seeing Valerie, and the customers kept her busy. Adam from the butcher's repaid her custom by coming in regularly for coffee and cake, and even Carole, who ran the gift shop, popped on board occasionally, elegant and impractical in tight pencil skirts. Summer started writing quotes and mottos on the blackboard above the counter and the A-frame outside, hoping it would add a friendly touch to the daily specials.

March was typically cold and damp, but Summer felt snug on her boat, and, most importantly, she was running the café. It was a small café, but it had a steady stream of customers. They ate her cake and drank her coffee, and quite often came back. Harry came to see her at least once a week and she always brought something more exotic than Summer had the imagination or the skill to make – tiramisu cake, cherry and almond flapjack, salted caramel tiffin. Her cakes would fly off the counter and Summer would feel as bereft as the customers when the last jewel of culinary pleasure was gone and she was back to offering fruit scones with cream and jam.

When Valerie remarked, one morning over bacon sandwiches, that Maddy was watching closely over Summer, she *almost* felt inclined to agree. Things were going well: Summer hadn't messed it up yet, she hadn't sunk the boat or bankrupted herself or accidentally put cyanide in the Bakewell tarts instead of almond essence. And she hadn't seen Jenny or Dennis again.

She hadn't returned to the pub with Mason, or anyone

else, and wondered if, after her encounter with Dennis, Mason had decided to leave that stickiness well alone. She had been reluctant to open up to him, so she couldn't blame him for not trying again. She also wondered if Ross's behaviour in front of Mason had given him the wrong idea. She still saw him regularly – when he wasn't working on the reserve he came in for bacon sandwiches or a slice of coffee cake – but he hadn't invited her further afield again. Their relationship had become strictly café-based, and Summer didn't feel entirely happy about that.

Easter was in late March and, without an offer or the inclination to go and see her dad in Cambridge, Summer found herself working as hard as ever. The long weekend meant Willowbeck, and the river, was extra busy – people tempted outside by family celebrations and the suggestion of warmer weather. Summer called in Valerie's help when things got too busy and the café looked like it had been decimated, with empty plates and crumbs everywhere, the dishwasher working overtime and the coffee machine making worrying noises.

It calmed down after Easter Monday and Summer felt the tension in her shoulders begin to ease although, inside, there was the niggling feeling that it would be busy throughout the summer, and she would have nobody to help her full-time. Before, she had been the help, spending most of her summers with her mum. She could remember the tables being full, inside and out, and a queue at the hatch, but Maddy was always so in control, so unflappable, that it had never felt unmanageable.

She was doing a sweep-down at the end of the day when there was a knock on the door. She'd already cleaned out the coffee machine, but she sighed and went to answer it. 'I'm really sorry, but we're – oh.'

'Hi.' Ross held up a hand in greeting. 'Long time no see.'

'Yeah,' Summer said, stepping back.

'Sorry to drop in unannounced, I had a spare evening and thought I'd see how you were doing.'

'No, it's . . . it's lovely to see you. What can I get you?'

Ross shrugged off his navy jacket. 'Tea would be great.'

Summer dipped into the kitchen and put the kettle on, running her hands down her black trousers. She hadn't heard from Ross over the last month, and while part of her had missed his friendship, she'd also been relieved that he had decided to make the clean break that Summer hadn't had the courage to instigate. Now, though, he was back, and so was the ache in her shoulders.

'Here you go.' She put two cups of tea on one of the tables.

Ross frowned and pointed behind her. 'We're not going back there? To your living . . . house bit, whatever you call it.'

Summer glanced behind her and laughed. 'It's really messy – I had no idea you were coming. We should stay out here.'

'OK,' Ross said slowly, 'but it feels the same as if we were having tea in my shop. This is your *business*.'

'The boat is my home,' Summer said. 'All of it. And this is a café, a place for drinking tea.' She sat back when Latte appeared, hovering at her feet and asking to be let up. The Bichon Frise jumped on to her lap and turned in circles like a cat.

'How've you been?' Ross asked.

'I'm good, great. Busy.'

'You look well. Rosy-cheeked.'

'It's hot work.'

'It suits you,' Ross said, his hand edging closer to hers.

Summer tried not to look at it. 'How's the best art supplies shop in Cambridge?'

'Same as ever,' Ross said, 'except I miss my favourite customer. She's not been in for a while.'

'Oh?'

'You, you dingbat. I miss you.'

Summer looked at him, wondering how to pitch her next words. She didn't have a chance.

'I've just seen Valerie, actually.'

'Oh?'

'She caught me on my way to you, offered me a reading.' He grinned, his eyebrows raised comically.

'What did you say?'

He shrugged. 'I said yeah.'

Summer sat back in her seat. 'I wouldn't have thought you'd be interested in any of that.'

'It's just a bit of fun, isn't it?'

'Not to her,' Summer said. 'She takes it very seriously. When are you having it?'

'I had it just now. She took me into her boudoir,' he said, leaning forward, his hands round his tea mug. 'Purple velour and satin and this thick, heavy smell of incense. I think it's designed to distract you.'

'Valerie's not a schemer.'

'No?'

'No, of course not. She believes in what she does, I'm sure of it. What did you think of the reading?'

Ross smirked. 'I dunno. She said some things that were on the mark, said I'd be seeing someone really important to me soon, someone who'd have something crucial to say to me.'

99

'Ross . . .'

'It was entertaining, but I don't know how much store I'd hold in it. What do you think? You've known her for years.'

'She was Mum's best friend.'

'But?' Ross finished his tea and, in a quick move that she didn't see coming, put his hand over hers.

'I don't believe it,' Summer said, unsuccessfully trying to slide her hand out. 'I don't know about the readings, but when she talks to people who've passed over?' She shook her head. 'I don't think people hang around after they're dead just to chat with the living. It makes no sense – how does she find the right people, are they all waiting in little compartments for their relatives to show up? And how does she get the information? Can she see and hear them talking to her, or do the words just appear in her head, and how does she know it's real? Why wouldn't a dead person be as untruthful as a living person? There are just too many inconsistencies.'

Ross was nodding, his face serious. 'Sure, sure. I totally get that. And Valerie's not upset that you feel that way?'

Latte nudged Summer's arm, allowing her to take her hand out from under Ross's, and she stroked her bouncy fur, smiling as the dog licked her hand. 'Valerie doesn't care what other people think. If she did, she wouldn't be in business. But she knows I'm uneasy with her mentioning Mum so often. Mum's dead, and it's been hard enough for me to accept that without Valerie muddying the waters.'

'Yeah, that sounds tough. *Ghostbusters* is entertaining, but when someone's talking about a relative or friend, it must—'

'*Ex*cuse me!'

Summer jumped at the loud voice coming through the hatch. She'd forgotten she'd left it open, the spring day warmer than she'd expected. 'Sorry, I . . .' she said, faltering when she saw who it was. 'Jenny.'

'With the joys of running a business comes the responsibility of making sure your clientele behave themselves.' Jenny was wearing a tight red jumper, her dark hair pulled back to reveal sparkly gold earrings that dangled to her jawline.

'Sorry?'

'These,' she said, slamming cardboard coffee cups, one after the other, on the shelf inside the hatch, 'are all over the grass outside the Black Swan. You need to do something about it. It's littering.'

'I'm sorry, I—'

'And rubbish on the deck too.' She slammed something else down, something altogether more solid. It was a wooden carving of a rabbit, its ears straight up, a rough wooden cottontail at its back. Summer smiled, despite herself.

'You think this is *funny?* Someone could have tripped and broken their ankle.'

Summer looked into Jenny's eyes, saw a flare of anger, and realized she wasn't going to be able to appease her. 'I'm really sorry, Jenny. I'll be much more vigilant in future, and I'll do something about the coffee cups.'

'You'd better.' Jenny turned and stalked back towards the pub. Summer heard her mutter something about 'trouble' loudly enough for her to hear.

She collected the coffee cups and took the rabbit back to the table. 'Not my biggest supporter,' she said.

'I'm sorry.' Ross wrapped his fingers round her arm and gave it a gentle squeeze. 'That side of things must be hard. You know I'm here for you, don't you?'

'Yes,' Summer said. 'I really do.'

Chapter 6

'Heart, frog, daffodil, rabbit.' Mason lined them up on the counter, moving a plate of rather lacklustre ginger cookies out of the way. 'What's the connection?'

'I have no idea,' Summer said, 'and I don't know who I can ask.' Archie looked up at them quizzically, his ears alert. 'Do you know, Archie?' The Border terrier gave a loud bark, his tail wagging.

'They're all to do with nature, except the heart. Well, it sort of is, but not as directly as the others.' Mason chewed the side of his thumb, his concentration intense, and Summer found herself scrutinizing him. He had glasses on today, black-framed, which somehow emphasized the intensity of his eyes. His jumper was dark grey, close-knit and snug over dark jeans. His 'grab a quick coffee if the machine's still on' had lasted for over half an hour, and it seemed he was as intrigued by Summer's unusual gifts as she was. 'Suspects?' he asked.

'Not a clue. Except it's not likely to be Jenny.' She had told him about her run-in yesterday, and Mason had nodded sympathetically.

'Not Jenny,' Mason said. 'And we are on the river. It could be anyone who passes on another boat, or on the towpath, leaving them on the deck – even throwing them – unnoticed. But why?'

Summer refreshed their coffees and, instead of sitting at one of the tables, indicated for Mason to follow her. She went through the kitchen and into the cabin. She gently adjusted Latte's position on the sofa, trying not to wake her, and sat down. Mason sat next to her, and Archie lay on the floor at his feet, his head on his front paws, his large brown eyes looking up at them.

'You've done a great job in here,' Mason said, appraising the snug space.

'Is it like yours?' Summer still hadn't followed up on his offer to go aboard *The Sandpiper* and look at some of his photos.

'Similar, but I've got a bit more space due to not also having to fit a café in. Come round whenever you want.'

'I'd like that,' Summer said. She held his gaze, and then looked away. 'With the carvings, I wonder if it's someone who knew my mum, who was a regular customer, and who's passed by and seen that the café is busy again.'

Mason put his coffee on the side table and turned towards her, resting his arm on the back of the sofa. 'I remember your mum,' he said softly.

'You do? But I thought you only came here in November?'

'But I've been on the water for five years. I've never stayed very long in one place before, and I've passed through Willowbeck lots of times. You're not the first Freeman I've got coffee from.' He gave her a gentle smile, his eyes searching hers, as if unsure how she would react to the news. 'I remember her constant energy, how she always had a kind word or a joke to share with everyone. Nobody got treated like just another customer. She remembered names, stories she'd shared with people.'

Summer swallowed and nodded, wishing that she could grab hold of Mason and experience his memories, remember her mum without the taint of guilt and sadness that always accompanied her own. 'You look nice in your glasses,' she heard herself saying instead.

Mason gawped. 'Th-thanks, I think. Sorry, if you don't want to talk about her I completely understand.'

'It's not that,' Summer said. 'Sorry. I get flustered, and then my words misbehave. I was thinking about Mum, and what came out was . . .' She gestured to his glasses. 'But I'm glad you met her. I'm glad lots of people met her, because it means the life that she lived, or at least the memories of it, will stay on in other people. She won't be forgotten.'

'I see a lot of her in you,' Mason said.

Summer looked for any signs that he was just pandering to her, but his expression was serious. 'I don't share jokes with everyone,' she said. 'And I certainly can't remember everyone's name.'

'No, but you're always kind and attentive, and I know you've got a fun side. I think it just needs a bit of coaxing. You've had a rough year.' Mason took a sip of his coffee, looking at her over the rim. She could see he was thinking, weighing things up. 'And I think you feel guilty.'

Summer's mouth started to dry out and the sensation continued through her body, everything seeming to freeze and solidify, like water turning to ice. 'What?' It came out as a whisper.

'I'm not trying to put you on the spot,' he said, 'but there's just something, something you're trying to run from. I don't know if it has anything to do with Jenny and Dennis, but I want you to know, Summer, that I can help.' He leaned forward and took her hand, the gesture so surprising that Summer felt she could barely breathe. 'I *know* what it feels like to—'

'Summer! Summer, where are you?' Summer flinched, the banging coming from the window behind her, and Mason let go of her hand. She turned and tried to unlatch the window, and Latte woke up and started yelping, high and anxious. Archie jumped on the sofa, and Mason gathered both the dogs into his arms.

'What is it? What's wrong, Valerie?' She opened the window, and saw that Valerie was crouched down on the towpath, her face red, her eyes wet with emotion. 'Oh God, Valerie, come in. I'll open the door.'

She moved to get up, but Valerie shook her head. 'No,' she said, 'don't get up on my account.'

'But I want to help.'

'Then you should have told me the truth from the beginning.'

'What truth?'

'That you don't believe anything I do has an ounce of credibility. That I trick vulnerable people for my own personal gain.'

Summer's mind started to whirr. 'But I don't—'

'Do you have any idea how much that hurts me? That Maddy's daughter, the daughter of my best friend, really believes that I'm fraudulent, that I'm that kind of person?'

'I don't think—'

'I thought we were friends. I thought we looked out for each other.' Valerie had her hand on the edge of the window, supporting herself.

'We do,' Summer said, 'of course we do. I haven't forgotten, for even a second, everything you've done for me.'

'And this is how you repay me? Bitching about me behind my back? I knew you found it difficult when I mentioned Maddy, how she's watching over you, but I had no idea how far it went.'

'Valerie,' Summer said, her heart racing, 'I have never, for one second thought that you tricked people, that's just not true. Come in and let me get you a coffee, and we can—'

'I don't want to talk to you, Summer. Not now. I'm beginning to wish I hadn't asked you to come back. Maybe it would have been better if Maddy's café closed down. It could have been a fresh start for everyone.'

'You don't mean that,' Summer said, but Valerie pushed herself up from the towpath and strode towards her own boat. Summer leaned out of the window, startling a young couple who were passing with a bag of bread ready to feed the ducks. 'Valerie, please!' But Valerie stepped on to *Moonshine* without a backward glance.

Summer slunk inside and closed the window. 'Shit. Shit, shit, shit!'

She put her elbows on her knees, her face in her hands. She thought back to the previous day, to Jenny interrupting her while she was talking to Ross. What better way to cause discord with the café than to get Summer's few friends in Willowbeck to turn against her? Jenny must have heard her talking, and then twisted her words beyond recognition. 'I should have known this would happen.'

She felt Mason's hand on her shoulder, the warmth of it through her light cotton top. 'Who told her?'

'Jenny,' Summer said. 'But none of that's true. I'm sceptical, but I don't think Valerie's a fraud. I was talking to Ross about Valerie yesterday, and Jenny interrupted us. She must have overheard and decided to use it against me. What am I going to do?' She looked up at him, reluctant to sit up fully and relinquish the warmth of his hand.

'Be honest,' Mason said. 'Tell Valerie that Jenny twisted your words, and that you don't feel that way. I know she doesn't want to hear it now, but she'll calm down, and you can make her listen to you.' He smiled at her, rubbed her shoulder. 'How often does Ross come over?'

'Ross?' Summer repeated. 'Oh, not very often. He runs an art supplies shop that I use, and he's just . . . he's been a good friend the last few months. But Cambridge isn't round the corner, and he's got his own life to lead.'

Mason nodded slowly. 'Good friends?'

Summer gave him a quick smile. 'Quite good friends. He has a habit of . . .' She wondered how to explain, without being unkind to Ross. 'He's quite protective of me, which I suppose is understandable because he was there when I was at my lowest, but I'm doing OK, all things considered.'

'Right,' Mason said. 'Friends. That's good to know.'

If he turned his megawatt grin on her now, Summer knew she would be helpless. She waited for it, holding her breath, wondering what it would be like to have his lips against hers, when Latte jumped off his lap and launched herself at Summer's top, yelping for all she was worth. 'What is it?' she sighed. Latte continued to yelp and paw, a frenzied bundle of white fur. Mason lifted their coffee cups out of the way and took them back to the kitchen.

'You're going?'

'I've got an article to finish,' he called. He stuck his head back round the doorway. 'Come out with me, to the reserve. Now the weather's improving, there's so much to see. You'll find the photos much more interesting if you've taken some of them yourself.'

'When?'

'Let me check the forecast, but some time in the next couple of days. We could go early and watch the sun come up.'

Summer's insides fluttered as she struggled to hold on to Latte. 'Sounds lovely.'

'I'll let you know. And talk to Valerie.'

She nodded, then listened to him walk back through the café and close the door behind him.

'Latte,' she said. 'Why did you have to interrupt us then?' Latte yipped, jumped off Summer's lap and ran into the kitchen. 'Oh, food,' she said. 'How did I fail to guess?' As she took out the pouches of dog food, holding them out in front of Latte so she could choose a flavour in an entirely pointless ritual that Summer still liked to go through, she started rehearsing what she would say to Valerie. She hoped the older woman would believe her, and wondered what Jenny could have said to her in the first place to convince her that Summer had really said those words.

Summer woke up the next day with a sense of purpose. It was a new month, and Mason had given her hope. Hope that she could fix things with Valerie, hope that maybe, the truth – as simple as it was – could work with Jenny too. After all, she hadn't done anything wrong, but she'd been damned by association. And Mason had invited her to go to the reserve with him; he wanted to share one of his passions with her. She dressed in black leggings, tan boots and a long, dark purple jumper, and tied her hair back from her face. She put on a short leather jacket, clipped Latte on to her lead, and left the boat. She could talk to Valerie and still be open by nine thirty.

The sun was bright and sharp, as if it was shining through crystal, and Summer squinted as she made her way down the towpath towards *Moonshine*. Her palms were sweaty, her chest tight with anticipation, but Valerie's heart was kind, she had to listen to her. She knocked loudly, but there was no answer. She gave it a few moments and then tried again. Was she too early? Was Valerie having an uncharacteristic lie-in, or did she know it was Summer at the door? Frustrated, her adrenaline fading, she started walking slowly down the towpath, Latte bounding at her feet, happy to be finally getting on with their walk.

When she returned, Valerie's boat was still dark and there was still no response when Summer knocked. She sighed and dawdled the last few feet to her boat, waving at a narrow-boat that drifted slowly past. 'Bacon sandwiches today, love?' the heavily bearded man called.

Summer realized she'd served him before, and that she knew his name. 'Hi, Barry – they'll be ready in about twenty minutes.'

'Great, I'll moor up.' He gave her a thumbs up, and Summer watched him manoeuvre towards one of the short-term moorings.

Latte tugged on her lead and Summer turned away from the river, and almost straight into Jenny. The older woman had her hair down, a black coat with a fake-fur collar over a long, cream skirt, and looked altogether softer than she had the last time Summer had seen her. Summer almost relaxed.

'Jenny—'

'This isn't going to work.'

Summer stared at her. 'What isn't?' she asked, even though she already knew.

'You being here, running her café. We're never going to get on, and so it's not going to work.'

'But we could try—'

'No. I will never forget what your mother did to me, to my marriage. I can forgive Dennis, and I know that he's sorry. He's making it up to me. But your mother, what *she* did, the way she worked on him, manipulated him into cheating on me, I can never forgive her.'

Summer closed her eyes. 'But I'm not her,' she said. The words felt like betrayal, but really, how could she stick up for her? She didn't believe her mum had manipulated Dennis, she knew that he had felt the same about Maddy as she did about him, but the rest of it was true.

'You're in her café,' Jenny continued, 'running it as she did. And you must have known.'

Summer swallowed, nodded, felt the tears pricking at her eyes. 'I did,' she said, 'towards the end. But it wasn't my place, it wasn't my secret.'

'You should have told me.'

Summer shook her head. 'I know what they were doing was wrong, but I loved my mum. I would never have betrayed her trust to tell you.'

'But you didn't approve of what they were doing.'

'No,' Summer said, swallowing again and again as the lump stuck in her throat. 'No, I didn't.'

'So you can appreciate how I feel. You can see why you have to go, to leave me and Dennis alone. We were fine until you came back.'

'The café was still here.'

'Barely. It was dying a slow and satisfying death.' Jenny folded her arms.

'Please, Jenny.' But Summer was running out of words.

This was the confrontation that, above all others, she didn't want to have. The one about how her beautiful, beloved, charismatic mother had had an affair with Dennis, and ruined Jenny's life – and then her own – because of it. She'd looked up to her mother more than anyone else, but she had never been able to come to terms with what she'd done. It had been a friction between them the last few months of Maddy's life, tearing Summer apart until it came to a head one day last June. It was a day that Summer couldn't think about without going cold.

'Please, Jenny,' she said again, 'can't we exist side by side like this? Life's too short to fight.'

'You know I'm right,' Jenny said, her voice calm. 'You know neither of us can feel peace while we're both here. I think it's why you stayed away all those months, and why I'm not the only one you're fighting with. I overheard you and Valerie last night – it's because the memories are too painful. And why struggle on here when you could make a fresh life, somewhere else?'

'You're responsible for the misunderstanding with Valerie,' Summer said.

'I don't know what you're talking about.' Jenny shook her head. 'You're losing it, Summer. Just admit it.'

Summer tried to think straight past the memories that were crowding back in, and Jenny took the opportunity to deliver the final blow.

'Dennis doesn't want you here, I don't, and if you're fighting with Valerie too, what is there to stay for? Why don't you go somewhere you're wanted? If that place exists.'

'Because I—' But Jenny was already leaving, walking in the direction of the pub's car park.

Summer picked Latte up and held her close, burying her

111

nose in her puppy's warm fur. She blinked and tried to still her trembling hands. 'Bacon,' she murmured, 'I need bacon, don't I?'

She walked slowly in the direction of the butcher's, and saw Norman sitting on his deck, a fishing rod in the water. 'S'right,' he said as Summer walked past.

'Sorry?'

Norman nodded his head in the direction of the pub. 'Her.'

'What do you mean? Right about what?'

'Fightin'. S'not good for the soul. I've done enough to last me a lifetime. You too. Don't fight wi' people. Stay away from the fightin'.'

Summer looked at him, his eyes meeting hers beneath the bushy eyebrows, the peak of his cap. Fighting was the cause of so much upset in her life, but was she entirely responsible? Was she going around seeking confrontation? She'd never thought of herself that way. She shook her head and forced a smile. 'Do you want a bacon sandwich?'

'If you're offerin'.'

'I am.'

She stocked up on bacon and took it back to the café. Climbing on to the deck, the toe of her boot kicked something. She crouched, picked the object up and held it to the light. It was another wooden carving, this one more intricate than the rest. It was a familiar object, a distinctive shape, but it took her a moment to place it. It was a jester's hat, with its spikes and baubles on the end. How did this connect to the others? Was someone saying that her being here, in Willowbeck, was a joke?

She made the bacon sandwiches, put cakes out and warmed up the water in the coffee machine, going through the motions. Mason didn't come to see her, Valerie stayed away, she served Barry and took a bacon roll to Norman, but her mind was elsewhere. She found herself staring at the Elvis quote she'd put on the blackboard the previous evening, inspired by Mason: *'Truth is like the sun. You can shut it out for a time, but it ain't goin' away'*. Summer believed in the magic of words, that by taking something out of your head and writing it down, you gave it power. It was why she loved being a sign writer, why she made the effort to write rhymes and slogans on her blackboards alongside her menu. She read the quote through again. It rang truer than ever now.

She had been shutting out the truth for so long. The truth of her mother's affair, and what had happened the previous June. She had thought, by coming back, she could confront everything and start again. But the anger was still there and Summer knew she hadn't confronted the one thing that was stopping her from moving forward – what she'd done on the day her mother had died.

Maybe Jenny was right. Maybe she couldn't have a fresh start in Willowbeck, maybe it was too steeped in the past. But she lived on a boat. Why did she have to stay here, why couldn't she be successful with *The Canal Boat Café* somewhere else, where nobody knew her or Maddy or their history?

As the day progressed, the idea lodged itself in her mind and she mulled it over, thinking through the pros and cons. Without Valerie's support, and with Jenny and Dennis against her, even Norman wading in on the argument, what did she have to lose? She tried to pretend there was nothing, but every time she thought of Mason's hand on her shoulder, the look in his eyes, the smile that floored her, she felt the doubt creeping in. But was one dinner at the pub, an offer of a walk, enough to stay for? And their friendship didn't have to end just because she was somewhere else along the river. He had a boat too. They could stay in touch.

She hardly slept at all that night and by the morning she had made up her mind. She had a quick shower, pulled on jogging bottoms and a checked shirt, and stepped out into the dawn. Willowbeck was sleepy and still, the water glassy, a robin singing into the quiet. Summer began the process of casting off; turning on the engine, tying on the central rope before releasing the others. She glanced at *The Sandpiper*, willing the engine sound to wake Mason, or Archie, unsure why she hadn't allowed herself to go and tell him she was leaving.

As she steered out into the middle of the river, the bow of the boat brushing against the willow trees, she felt the thrill of the unknown. Could she really start again somewhere else? Could she take *The Canal Boat Café* and make a success out of it, and a life for herself, away from Willowbeck? If someone here thought she was a joke, then she was prepared to prove them wrong. It was her boat now, and she was going to embrace the opportunities that it offered her. With a final glance at the gold and red of Mason's boat, safe and snug in its mooring, Summer engaged the throttle and powered *The Canal Boat Café* up the river, the cold, deep water shimmering in its wake.

Casting Off

Chapter 7

Summer was woken by the less than dulcet tones of Mumford & Sons blasting through the slightly open window of her cabin. Latte started yelping, her front paws pushing down on Summer's sternum. It was an effort for Summer to open her eyes, but when she did she saw that sun was streaming in through the window, which she'd left not only open, but uncurtained. For a moment she thought she was still in Willowbeck and that the music was the remnants of a dream. She wondered if it was too early to go and see Adam in the butcher's for a supply of bacon, and whether Mason was aboard *The Sandpiper*, and would come on to *The Canal Boat Café* that morning with Archie, his Border terrier, trotting happily at his feet. Summer found that she was smiling, and then Latte put one front paw on her cheek and started whimpering, and Summer remembered.

She wasn't in Willowbeck, and hadn't been for a week. She sat up, and with Latte snuffling and wagging her tail beside her, looked out of the window. Instead of the hanging willow

117

trees and the glimpse of fields beyond, Summer could see, across the wide river, a row of small cottages, each a different colour – white, then beige, blue and pale yellow – the front gardens tiny squares of grass or, in the case of the beige house, a riot of spring flowers. The towpath was already in use, a young man with a baseball cap walking an Irish wolf-hound, and a woman cycling past, her coat flying out behind her like a cape.

A little further up the towpath was the entrance to an alleyway lined with tall brick walls, and at the end of that was the market square of Foxburn. It had a fountain in the middle, a small but impressive town hall with a columned entrance, and an independent deli that had slices of home-made pizza in the windows.

Already, in her temporary mooring, Summer could hear the other boat owners waking around her, a couple shouting to each other, the low growl of an engine as one of the boats set off cruising for the day. Summer had counted twelve moorings, all full as spring started to bloom, a mixture of traders and visitors in short-term moorings, and residential boats. She'd been exchanging pleasantries with a white-haired couple called Una and Colin, who lived in a traditional green and red boat moored next to hers. It was called *A Seeker's Fortune*, and sported flowerpots bursting with daffodils along the roof.

Two days before, a gaggle of trading boats had moored up in Foxburn, including a narrowboat selling antiques, a sandwich boat which looked fairly up-market, with exotic fillings listed on the blackboard next to the hatch, and a navy cruiser with subtle silver accents and the name *The Wanderer's Rest* inscribed in silver on the side. Summer had no idea what happened aboard that boat, and as she'd walked past, she'd noticed that all the windows were covered with heavy, dark blinds. This group also included *Water Music*, the boat responsible for waking her with Mumford. It was moored three berths down from Summer, which she was quickly realizing was a little too close.

She had been waiting for her roving trader licence – something she'd never needed in Willowbeck, which was smaller, with room for only a few moorings. In the meantime, she had opened the hatch when she was on board, leaving a teapot and some bite-sized brownies next to a sign that said 'Help yourself – *The Canal Boat Café* will be opening soon.' She hoped that it would build some anticipation and ensure at least a few people came back when she was trading properly.

Her licence application had been approved yesterday, so after a week of exploring the area on foot, giving her boat a spruce-up, changing filters and clearing moss out of the window vents – and spending far too much time mulling over what had happened in Willowbeck – she could start running the café again.

But there was no fresh bacon from Adam at the butcher's, she was further away from her best friend Harry, who had been supplying her with top-quality cakes, and she had lost the regular customer base she was starting to build up in Willowbeck. Still, she had started there with uncertainty; she would just have to do the same here. Summer swallowed and pulled the duvet off, pleased that she'd worked out how to clean out the diesel boiler and get the heating system working efficiently. It was the beginning of April, and despite the brightness of the sun, it was still cold outside.

'Right, Latte,' she said, 'breakfast?' The dog jumped to the floor and followed Summer into the kitchen, her nose pressed against Summer's ankle, so it was hard to walk without tripping up. She wasn't the only one who was feeling unsure in this new place. Latte had jumped on her bed every morning for the last week, yapping, whimpering and pawing. Summer could see the little dog was unsettled, but she didn't know if that was because Latte was genuinely unhappy with the unfamiliar surroundings, sounds and smells, or because she sensed Summer's uncertainty.

But today was a new day, and she could start running the café again. She fed Latte, switched the oven on and, still in her pyjamas, started making a batch of brownies. She chuckled as a Bryan Adams song started playing outside, and a flurry of ducks flapped upriver, their legs skimming the surface of the water.

The owner of *Water Music* played an eclectic mix of tunes at all hours of the day, to advertise the second-hand vinyl, CDs and tapes being sold. Summer wondered how often that particular boat was asked to move on, and decided that, when she had a batch of fresh cakes, she would offer the owner some and try and find out a little bit more about their roving market. After all, much of her confidence in Willowbeck had come from the friends she had around her – Valerie, Mason and even Norman. She was determined that, if she was going to make things work somewhere new, then she should get to know her fellow boatsmen and women.

Whisking the brownie mix, she let her mind drift back to her last days in Willowbeck. Had she been too rash to untie her boat from the mooring and leave without telling anyone? Perhaps, but the decision to leave Willowbeck, to see what else the winding, sparkling river had to offer her, had been enticing. She had a fixed mooring there that she could return to at any time, but she had her roving trader's licence now, and with it the opportunity to prove that she could do this alone, in a place where nobody knew her, *The Canal Boat Café*, or her mum's history.

And yet, there were things she already missed badly about Willowbeck. She'd been a permanent fixture there for little over a month, but she'd come to rely on Valerie's encouragement and the cuddles with her silver tabby Harvey, Norman's gruff greetings, and Adam's cheery face whenever she went to stock up on sandwich fillings.

And she missed Mason. She didn't know him that well yet but already she felt his absence, as if no day was ever quite fulfilled, as if there was something she was always waiting for, just over the horizon.

Summer poured the folded brownie mixture, smelling so sweet already, into the deep tray, and slid it into the oven. She turned on the coffee machine, hoping that today she'd be making lattes and cappuccinos and hot chocolates, instead of just filling the teapot. In the cabin, she pulled on leggings, a soft green jumper, and her Ugg boots, then sat on the bed and opened Mason's text again.

She'd got it the day she left Willowbeck, the sender unknown until she'd read the message: *Summer, it's Mason. Valerie gave me your number. Where are you? We're both worried.* It had heartened her to know that, despite her anger, Valerie was still concerned about her, even though at that point she'd been gone for less than a day, and could have made the decision simply to go cruising. She'd replied, telling Mason she needed a few days' space and would be in touch.

Mason had accepted the explanation, but had reminded her that she'd agreed to go to the reserve with him, and told her that he was going to hold her to it. Since then they'd kept up a stream of messages, the subject matter light. Mason: *Archie just tried to catch a duck. He's a good swimmer, but now I have to clean out my cabin because it smells like mildew.* Summer: *There's a boat moored three berths down from me that has been playing music nonstop since nine a.m. I was fine with Adele and London Grammar, but they've moved on to S Club 7. How am I meant to cope?* To that one, Mason had replied that there was no teen pop playing in Willowbeck, but Summer had sent him a smiley face and left it at that.

This morning, her phone screen was blank, and Summer realized she couldn't spend her time mooning over Mason when it had been her decision to leave Willowbeck. She checked on the brownies and started a batch of scones, then turned on all the lights in the café and took the A-frame and her coloured chalks out into the sunshine.

To celebrate my first day, head aboard The Canal Boat Café, she wrote. *A free cup of coffee with a slice of my brownie – whatever you fancy, come and see me!* Back inside, she swept and mopped the café floor, then polished the counter and the tabletops until they gleamed. She rearranged her crocheted cakes and her wooden carvings, and then realized, with a pang of sadness, that unless the person who had been leaving her the trinkets had followed her to Foxburn, which in itself would be disconcerting, she wouldn't be getting any more. She didn't want the mystery to end and wondered if, now she wasn't there any more, they would be left on Valerie or Mason's boat. She would have to ask him next time she got in touch.

Latte started barking and Summer turned just in time to see a woman push open the door and stride into the café.

'Hi,' Summer said. 'Can I help?'

'I can have whatever I fancy?' She asked, and Summer

detected a hint of a Welsh accent. She looked a bit older than Summer, in her mid-thirties, with a rosy, round face and a short bob of black hair that was too vibrant not to be dyed. She wore a red silk shirt over jeans, and American flag Converse shoes.

'Sure,' Summer said, 'what can I get you? Latte, cappuccino?'

'I'd love some pistachio-and-rose-flavoured macarons please, and a chai-spiced latte.'

'Uhm, right. Well, I can do the spiced latte, but . . . how about a slice of brownie, warm out of the oven?'

The woman looked to the ceiling, as if she was thinking hard. 'All right. That'll have to do for now. Do the brownies have cherries in?'

'No, sorry.'

'Good, because I hate cherries.' She gave a triumphant smile and Summer felt a surge of relief that she'd met a modicum of the woman's approval. She slipped behind the counter and got a clean mug, while her new customer approached the counter and crouched to pet Latte.

'Oh, and can I have your dog? She's a real cutie.'

Summer frowned. 'No, I—'

'I'm kidding, kidding. But your sign is a bit misleading.' She was stroking Latte vigorously, the little dog squeaking in ecstasy at the attention. 'It says you can have whatever you fancy. Maybe you should add a "within reason" at the end, or something.'

Summer laughed. 'I'd love to be able to offer pistachio-and-rose – what was it? Macarons?'

'Oh God, they're divine. Seriously, if you start selling those then you'll have a friend for life.'

'I wouldn't know where to start,' Summer admitted.

'But you're a baker, right? So get a book. Brownies are lush,

I'm not about to turn one down, but a bit of variety never hurt anyone. That's what I tell my customers.'

'Do you run a café too?' Summer stiffened, wondering if this was an ambush and she was destined to have to spend her life cruising up the river, away from other bakers who didn't like the competition.

The woman stood and held out her hand. 'Not cakes, but I sell music – CDs, vinyl, a few tapes for the truly retro. I'm Claire, I own *Water Music* just down the way there. We arrived a couple of days ago, but I've not seen you on this part of the river before – there's not much I miss – and I've been waiting for you to open your doors so I could come and have a nosy.'

Summer shook her hand. 'So you're responsible for the Mumford & Sons alarm call.'

'And I'm not about to apologize for it. Variety is the spice of life. What's your name?'

'Summer. Don't you get complaints?'

'The odd one, but most people don't mind a mood-lifting tune here and there. And those that do complain are the ones who could do with it the most, but don't realize it. You're not about to start, are you?' Claire accepted a cup from Summer, blew on the drink and sipped it immediately. 'That's good.'

'I'm not going to complain,' Summer said. 'I'm as much of a rover as you, I could move on if it bothered me that much, but it doesn't.' She remembered her text to Mason, and felt sheepish.

'What are you doing here? The café's been around a while, hasn't it, but not with you at the helm?'

'You recognize it?' Summer asked, using the opportunity of getting the brownies from the kitchen and cutting them into chunks on the counter as an excuse to hide her surprise.

'Sure I do. As I said, I've not seen you along this stretch of the river before, but it's a small world. It used to be run by an older woman, Margie was it? Missy, maybe?'

'Maddy,' Summer said, hearing the gravel in her voice. 'My mum, Madeleine.'

'Oh, right.' Claire studied her. 'Yeah, you do look like her, the strawberry-blonde hair, big eyes. A bit more guarded though, but that's fair enough if you've not been doing it long. Did she hand it over to you?'

Summer sighed, trying to think of a less blunt way of putting it, and realized there wasn't one. 'She died.'

Claire gave Summer a kind smile. 'Sorry to hear that. Tough times.'

'Yes,' Summer said. 'It has been.'

They fell silent, Summer joining Claire in a hot drink and a slice of brownie, eating and drinking in a quiet that was already companionable.

'So, you're roving now? Not steady at that place down the river?'

'Willowbeck.'

'That's it. Beautiful, I always thought. Good access, but quite quiet, big green expanse near the pub, it's crying out for something.'

'What do you mean?' Summer asked, intrigued.

'I dunno,' Claire shrugged. 'It just seems so inviting, but a bit lacking in something.'

'Like *Water Music*?' Summer laughed. 'A blast of Bruce Springsteen at eight thirty in the morning?'

'Hey, nobody could argue about The Boss. But yeah, a bit of music wouldn't hurt the place. A bit of verve and vigour.' She nodded. 'Especially if you've gone, now. Pub still there?'

'Still there,' Summer said, grimly.

Claire narrowed her eyes. They were dark, almond-shaped, and gave Summer the impression that she was constantly being appraised, mulled over. 'You were competition,' Claire confirmed.

'We didn't exactly get on,' Summer said, thinking of Jenny's last rant.

'So you moved away?'

'I thought I could do with a change of scenery,' Summer clarified. 'It doesn't mean I'm not going back. I have friends there, but this is the beauty of living on a boat, and Mum and I used to travel up and down a bit. I don't think we ever moored here for too long. I don't remember the town square.'

'Foxburn,' Claire said, shaking her head, 'pretty as a picture.'

'But you only arrived a couple of days ago – you don't stay here?'

'Oh no, I move around with the others. There's a little clutch of us, traders on boats, me with my music shop, an antique boat and a sandwich boat and a barbecue boat, and we do a good bit of business sticking together, turning wherever we moor up into a kind of market. You fit right in, you know.'

'The sandwich boat wouldn't mind?'

'Ralph doesn't do cakes,' Claire said, 'more's the pity. But think of any sandwich filling – almost any – and he can do it for you. If not that day, then he'll source it for the next. Oyster and gooseberry, not saying that would be your favourite, mind, but if you fancied it, he'd take twenty-four hours and do it for you. And he'll tell you himself, offering that kind of service he's got no time for cakes as well. That's why I was so excited.' Claire smoothed down the front of her shirt and gave Summer a warm smile. 'If you really offered what you said, then I would be in heaven.'

'Macarons?'

'All cakes. I'm a cake fiend, and if you can branch out a bit, offer the same service with cakes that Ralph has built his reputation on with sandwiches, then we'd be unstoppable. Music, food, old bits of tat – what else do you look for in a market?' Claire spread her arms wide, and Summer laughed.

'I'm not sure I can grow my repertoire that much. My friend, Harry, used to bring me cakes to sell a couple of times a week. Orange and cinnamon, strawberry and banana, this amazing almond-and-toffee flapjack that I—'

'Oh God, stop. Stop. Where is this Harry? Is he single?'

'Harry's female,' Summer said, 'and it used to be such a short drive for her when I was at Willowbeck, so I don't know . . .'

'Get her back on side,' Claire said, urgency in her voice, 'or get her to send you all her recipes.'

'What?'

'I'm serious. That's what I'm talking about. The brownies? Delicious. But after a few days of brownies, I'm going to be craving something else. And so will the other river-folk. Boat owners and towpath trawlers like their variety, in case you hadn't realized. Get cracking.' Claire finished her latte, licked each of her fingers in turn and beamed at Summer. 'I think we're going to get on famously. What are you up to this evening?'

Summer opened her mouth, glanced behind her at the cabin, and shrugged.

'Well then,' Claire said. 'That's settled. I'll introduce you to some of the others.'

Summer watched her go, the red silk shirt shimmering like water as Claire sashayed to the door. She was larger than life, both in size and presence, and Summer felt as if she'd been torn through by a tornado – albeit a very good-natured one.

'Did I agree to anything?' she asked Latte, who was sitting on a chair, her face angled on one side, looking up at Summer. 'Did I agree to trying out different cakes, or to going out with her this evening or . . . or anything?' Latte continued to look at her. 'No, I didn't think so. But why do I get the feeling I don't really have a choice?'

Summer's first day trading in Foxburn was busier than she could have imagined, and she enjoyed the steady stream of customers and the almost carnival atmosphere as random music was blasted out from Claire's boat. Classical, opera – Summer recognized 'Three Little Maids' from *The Mikado* – some Kylie, Rolling Stones, the Goo Goo Dolls. Claire certainly wasn't imposing her taste on Foxburn, unless her taste was 'all music'. Summer could imagine that – already she admired Claire's desire to soak up everything, not to narrow her perspective. Summer was looking forward to spending time with her instead of finding another nineties film to watch on her iPad.

At first, her customers seemed happy with the range of treats Summer was supplying and continuing to bake throughout the day. She'd picked up the ingredients from the mini-supermarket in Foxburn square; as well as scones and brownies, there were cupcakes with vanilla icing, a lemon tray bake and an apple cake. It was a juggling act, serving and making sure the cakes didn't burn, but she'd researched and practised some of the recipes while she'd been waiting for her licence to come through, and had got the timings down to perfection. But then visitors started asking for more obscure things: Viennese fingers, oatmeal cookies, cheesecake, custard tarts. Summer had her suspicions, and so she began asking questions herself.

'Have you had a good day? Bought any music?' and 'You didn't happen to pop aboard *Water Music*, did you?' or 'I can't believe they were playing Marilyn Manson, did you go and talk to the owner?' Most of them confessed that, yes, they had visited her café after seeing Claire. A few tried to deny it, their eyes averted.

Less than a day into trading and Summer was the focus of a stealth campaign from someone she'd just met. Well, two could play at that game, but Summer wanted a bit more time before she launched her counterattack on Claire's musical preferences. As the customers asked for their 'favourite ever cake', Summer made a list of them. After all, if she couldn't call on Harry's expertise as easily, why shouldn't she listen to someone who would spend more money on her boat if she could branch out a bit? As the stream of customers slowed down, and the day grew colder, Summer vowed that she would spend time looking up some more exotic recipes.

At five, she locked up the café and moved through to the cabin, Latte bounding on to the sofa, bagsying her place. 'Not tonight, Latte,' Summer said, 'we're going out! Get your glad rags on.' Latte barked, her tail wagging, her paws slipping slowly towards the front of the sofa. Summer lifted her up and held her close, allowing the little dog to lick her cheek. 'Are you feeling happier?' she asked. 'Because I am.'

Her phone beeped, and Latte jumped out of her arms.

Summer picked it up, and saw that it was Mason: *Are you about?*

Smiling, Summer replied: *What does that mean? About where? I'm on the boat. What's wrong?*

Nothing, was the reply, and then a moment later her phone started ringing.

Mason would like FaceTime, it read on the screen. Summer panicked, wondering what she looked like after a day of rushing about and frothing milk, but realized she didn't have time to mind. She hit *accept*, and a grainy image of Mason filled her iPhone screen.

Summer gave a sharp intake of breath. There he was, smiling back at her, his dark hair unruly round his face. His eyes didn't have the same intensity as they did in real life, but seeing him still sent a flood of warmth through her.

'Hi,' she said, smiling nervously. 'What's this?'

'This,' Mason said, 'is an ambush.'

'What do you mean?' Summer sank on to the sofa, keeping the phone up in front of her, so her face stayed in the tiny screen in the corner.

'Oh, Summer,' said another voice, and Summer watched as Mason edged to the side of the picture and Valerie appeared, her eyes squinting at the screen. 'Oh look, there you are! Are you live?'

'Valerie!' It came out as a squeak.

'Summer, where are you? What are you doing? You have to come back!'

'I – I didn't think you wanted to talk to me.'

'I didn't. I was furious for the first couple of days, and then I came to my senses.'

Summer sighed, relief washing over her. 'You did?'

'You would *never* think that about me, Summer. Of course

you wouldn't. For someone who is usually open to so many channels, I got completely the wrong end of the stick.' Valerie shook her head, and the silver splodge of her earrings jiggled against her neck.

'Maybe someone tricked you?' Summer said, not wanting to mention Jenny, but curious to see if Valerie would.

'No, I misunderstood, or I heard it wrong. I'd had a bad reading, an unhappy customer and then – well, I must have taken it out of context. It's not your fault, but now I've sent you away.'

'I had to go,' Summer said quietly. 'Not just because of what happened between us, there were other things too.'

'OK,' Mason said, his voice even, 'but now you can come back.'

'I – I don't know. I think trying out new places is good for me – good for my confidence.' She puffed her chest out, hoping self-assuredness radiated out of the screen at them.

'Come back, love,' Valerie said. 'There's a big hollow space where your boat was, and every day more and more geese are coming and filling it, and squawking, and antagonizing walkers and pooing lots of green poo. We'd much rather have your boat.'

'I'll second that,' Mason said, and Summer watched him, frustrated that the screen kept freezing and pixelating, and she couldn't get a good image of him. She wondered if it would be weird if she asked him to email her a photo – maybe he took selfies as readily as he took other photos – but dismissed the idea instantly. 'Anyway,' he continued, 'you owe me a walk. I haven't forgotten.'

'Nor have I.'

'Where are you, anyway?' Valerie asked.

Summer glanced behind her, as if there might be a big sign outside the window that said Foxburn. 'Not far,' she said, 'but I've made a new friend.'

'Oh?' Valerie sounded disappointed.

Summer sagged back against the sofa and Latte jumped on to her lap and stuck her nose up to the screen.

'Oh, Latte,' Valerie said, her voice wavering, 'Oh, look at your beautiful little dog.'

'Archie's pining for her,' Mason said, edging a bit further into view. 'And when he's unhappy, he gets even more badly behaved – if you can believe that. Maybe you should come back for their sakes.'

Summer chewed her lip. Even now that Valerie had made the effort to connect with her, clearly seeking out Mason and his advanced technology to do more than just phone her, Summer wasn't about to turn her boat around. While she'd begun to settle into life at Willowbeck, the tension with Jenny at the pub had become too much, to the point where Summer had felt she needed fresh air, new sights, a different outlook. Willowbeck had become claustrophobic, and Summer needed space to breathe. Suddenly, the sight of Valerie and Mason jostling for space on her tiny iPhone screen, their images distorted, seemed like the most ridiculous thing in the world. She started laughing.

'What's so funny?' Mason asked.

Summer shrugged, trying to speak through her giggles.

'You, it's just . . . I don't know. Like you're technologically inexperienced relatives trying to have this really earnest conversation and it . . .' She shook her head, giving up.

'Hey,' Mason said, sounding affronted, 'I'm very good with technology. What I don't know about Photoshop isn't worth knowing.'

'I know, I know. It's just so weird.' Summer smiled. 'I wish I could see your faces properly.'

'So come back,' Valerie urged.

Summer nodded. 'Soon,' she said, and then, thinking of Jenny, 'I'll think about it, at least. But we should do this again.'

'What,' Mason said, 'so you can laugh at us some more?' She could just about make out a frown. She wanted to reach into the screen and pull him out, so that he was sitting beside her on the sofa.

'Why else?' Summer asked. They all fell silent, and she shifted angle. 'Valerie, I'm so glad you've got in touch. It's lovely to talk to you, and I really didn't mean to upset you. After everything you've done for me, I owe you so much.'

Valerie shook her head. 'It wasn't you, Summer. We miss you. It's like we've just got you back, and you've gone again.'

'I know, but I – I have to do this. It feels right.'

'Don't be away too long.'

They said their goodbyes, and Mason ended the call. Summer stroked Latte absent-mindedly, and wondered for the fiftieth time if she should go back. It was tempting, with the safety and security of Willowbeck and Valerie, and the intrigue, the pull of Mason, which was only getting stronger the more time they spent apart. But Foxburn had the potential to be interesting, Claire was going to introduce her to her friends, and Summer was keen to find out more about their lifestyle cruising the waterways. Besides, her friendship with Mason didn't have to end just because she was no longer in Willowbeck.

As if reading her thoughts, her phone beeped with a message from him: *Where are you? I promise I won't hunt you down and drag you back to Willowbeck.*

Summer grinned. *Foxburn*, she typed. *I'm not that far away, and I'm fine.*

You are! was his reply. *Weird seeing you in pixels, but better than nothing. M.*

She moved through her berth to the tiny bathroom, realizing she had no idea what time Claire was expecting her. But she felt a sense of adventure, of hope and of new landscapes. She hadn't burnt her bridges in Willowbeck, but she was already building new ones here. Maybe she could have the best of both worlds. Feeling happier than she had since she untied her ropes from the mooring in Willowbeck, Summer Freeman got ready to dip her toe in new waters.

Chapter 8

Summer strolled down the towpath, Latte on a short lead at her feet. So far, her dog had shown no interest in wanting to chase the ducks and geese that were an inevitable part of life on the river, but Summer wasn't taking any chances, and she hadn't yet tested whether Latte could swim. The boats she now knew were part of Claire's group of roving traders were moored up close to hers, and *Water Music* was sandwiched, appropriately, between *The Sandwich Shack* and *Doug's Antique Barge*. Claire's boat was traditionally painted in red and green, with a castles-and-roses design that was adapted to include musical notes, bass and treble clefs, all dancing around the words *Water Music*, painted in pale, shimmering blue. It had two large speakers fixed to the outside, allowing Claire to delight or distress anyone within a fifty-foot radius.

Summer stepped on to the deck and knocked on the door. Claire opened it and waved her inside as she fumbled with an earring.

'Can Latte come aboard?' Summer asked.

'Course.'

Summer walked through the cabin, realizing that Claire's boat was similar to her own, with a large section at the bow end set aside for her trade, and the living space squashed towards the back. Claire's cabin was a riot of colour, the sofa bright blue, a tiny kitchen with red cupboards and a black, granite-effect worktop. It was smart and sassy and individual, and it suited her perfectly.

'Can I see the shop?' Summer asked.

'How long have I been here, and my music hasn't enticed you in yet?' Claire flashed her a grin and ushered her through. Summer stepped into the music shop, and gawped.

Her first thought was that the boat must be close to sinking, with so much stuff on board. It was a treasure trove of music, vinyls cramming the small space, in boxes on the floor and on shelves built into the walls. Summer could make out only one window, and that was so surrounded by vinyls that she barely noticed the gleam of the street lamp outside. There was a tiny counter with a cash register in roughly the same place as the one on *The Canal Boat Café*, and a faint smell of dust mixed with another aroma Summer couldn't quite place.

'Wow.'

'Yeah, I know. Not exactly sharp and modern, and I do try, I promise you.' Claire ran her finger along the top of a row of LPs, and came away with a smudge of dust. 'Every spring and autumn I take myself off somewhere quiet along the river and I have a sort-out, try and neaten the place up a bit, but I always think, what if I get rid of this album or sell it on eBay, and then someone comes in looking for it the next day?'

Summer pulled out one of the LPs and looked at the cover. 'Even *Paradise Theatre* by Styx?'

'That has a laser etching on the vinyl. It's a classic.'

'Hhhmmm.' Summer wrinkled her nose and slid it back into place. 'I bet you get some really interesting customers in here,' she said. 'Do some people stay for hours?'

'Yup.' Claire folded her arms. 'And what would really help them spend more money in my shop is if there was the most amazing selection of cakes a couple of boats away, to fuel them with the energy to keep searching until they find their Holy Grail.'

'I *do* have amazing cakes. I think you said almost exactly that about my brownies. Latte,' Summer said, watching as her dog extended the lead as far as it would stretch and tried to climb into one of the bigger boxes, 'not in there.'

'We should get going anyway.'

'Where are we meeting the others?' Summer asked, feeling a prickle of nerves.

'Ah,' Claire said, flashing her a grin that was pure mischief, 'now that would be telling.'

They didn't have to go far, but Summer's heart skipped a beat when Claire stopped outside the narrowboat moored in the last berth, on the edge of where quaint Foxburn dissolved into thick, leafy countryside. It was *The Wanderer's Rest*, navy and silver, somehow subtle and ostentatious all at the same time.

Summer turned to Claire with wide eyes. 'Here?'

'Here. I bloody knew you would have noticed it. Everyone does.'

'The colours are unusual. My friend, Valerie, has a purple boat moored up in Willowbeck. She does readings – fortune-telling, astrology, that kind of thing.'

'Ah, well, you'll find a lot of magic on this boat too,' Claire said, and stepped aboard.

'Right.' Summer's anticipation grew, and she lifted Latte over the threshold and followed Claire on to the deck.

Claire knocked once on the door and pushed it open, and they walked into a fug of warmth, of low murmuring and an aroma of tantalizing spices. Summer blinked, her eyes adjusting to the space lit only by a couple of strategically placed lamps and a woodburner. Latte wriggled in her arms and yelped, and several pairs of eyes turned in their direction.

The room they were in ran almost the full length of the boat, and was bare of furniture save for a small, open-plan kitchen consisting of a fridge, a worktop and a hob. Behind that was a door, which Summer presumed led into the bathroom. The floor wasn't carpeted, but was strewn with large cushions and worn beanbags, on which people were sitting or slouching, eating out of metal takeaway containers.

'What is this boat for?' Summer murmured, trying to pick out faces she recognized in the gloom.

'It's for whatever you want it to be.' The man who approached was tall and slender, his walk almost a saunter, and his blue eyes latched on to hers. His ash-blond hair was a shaggy mop, and his beard gave the impression of being left untamed, but Summer thought it was probably carefully cultivated to look that way. He wore a loose-fitting shirt with a paisley pattern in blues and pinks.

'Summer,' Claire said, 'this is Ryder. Ryder, meet Summer.'

'Hi,' Summer said, 'is this your boat?'

'It is indeed,' Ryder said, swinging his arm wide. 'And at the same time, it's everyone's. A place we can all come together. We'll set off shortly, I think most people are here.'

'Where are we going?'

'A bit of night cruising,' Ryder said. 'Stories, music, whatever you feel like. You and your pup. You should come and meet Jas, he's got an Irish wolfhound.'

'On a boat?' Summer laughed.

Ryder looked at her seriously, and Summer held her breath, but then the smile was back, wider than ever. 'It takes all sorts,' he said. 'I once met someone who kept a pair of marmosets on his boat, called them Ethel and Eldred.'

'Has storytelling started already?'

Ryder flicked Claire a look as if to say *Where did you get her from*, and then snaked his arm around her shoulders. 'Come and meet everyone.'

Summer was introduced to Ralph, in his forties with wispy blond hair, who ran *The Sandwich Shack*, and Doug, slightly older and soft round the edges, with dark, heavily receding hair and a kind smile. He owned *The Antiques Barge*, and seemed slightly wary of Ryder, despite the younger man introducing him with what Summer thought was genuine affection.

'This,' Ryder said, his hand squeezing Summer's shoulder as they wove their way through the cushions, Claire following closely behind, 'is Jas. Jas, say hello to Summer and her candyfloss dog.'

The man scrambled to his feet, but Summer was distracted by the huge Irish wolfhound who, even sitting on his haunches, easily came up to her waist.

'Hi.' She held out her hand, and Jas shook it.

He looked mid-twenties, his black hair thick, but flattened on top as if it lived most of the time under a hat, his beard much neater than Ryder's. His eyes were attentive, and he had a gentleness about him that reminded Summer of Mason.

139

'Nice to meet you,' he said, 'and your Bichon Frise. What's his name?'

'She's called Latte. How about the bear you've brought with you?'

Jas glanced at his dog and laughed. 'This is Chester. He takes up a lot of room but he's very placid.'

'Can I?' Jas nodded and Summer stroked the wolfhound's nose. Latte struggled in her arms, and the large dog angled his snout up towards her. Summer watched them closely, but the overriding emotion was definitely curiosity, and Summer put Latte carefully on the floor. She padded forward to Chester, and the two dogs examined each other.

'The bear and the candyfloss,' Ryder said, watching them. 'It could be the start of a great love story.'

'Maybe you could tell it later,' Jas said, 'embellish it in the way that only you can.'

Ryder folded his arms and nodded. 'I might just do that,' he said. 'Once we're somewhere a little bit more . . . atmospheric. Time to get our cruise on.'

Summer glanced around her as Ryder sauntered his way towards the stern, thinking that the boat was already fairly atmospheric. She wondered if her mum had ever come across *The Wanderer's Rest* before. It was just the kind of place she would have loved.

Claire put a hand on her shoulder. 'OK?' she asked.

'Yeah. Great. I've never been anywhere like this before.'

'Ryder would take that as the biggest compliment. He's harmless, by the way. I know he comes across as an arrogant knob, and there's no denying he is that, but he's genuinely kind-hearted, and he opens his boat up for anyone who fancies a get-together.'

'So he lives here?'

140

Claire nodded. 'Pulls out a sleeping bag every night.'

'Or heads off to a local hotel,' Jas said. 'None of us are ever really sure.'

Claire laughed. 'Cynic.'

Jas spread his arms wide. 'Just calling it as I see it.'

'Right,' Claire said, 'let's get some of Ralph's Thai curry, and wait for the fun to begin.'

Once they had scooped curry into takeaway containers, and the boat had powered into action with a low, comforting thrum, Claire and Summer sat down on cushions alongside Jas.

'Where have you come from, Summer?' he asked, as he nudged Chester's nose out of Claire's dinner.

'Willowbeck. I've got a permanent mooring there, and I've been running the café for about six weeks. I fancied a change of scene,' she added, and felt Claire's gaze on her intensify. 'How about you?'

'I've been a liveaboard for two years,' he said. 'It's something I've wanted to do since before university. I travel with this lot, I'm a freelance writer, and I run a blog about life on the water.' He laughed when he saw Summer's surprise. 'Not all blogs are run by teenage girls, you know.'

'It's got quite a following,' Claire said. 'How many are you up to now?'

'Nearly twenty thousand. I think having Chester helps – who doesn't want to read stories about a giant dog living aboard a narrowboat? It's starting to make a bit of revenue through advertising, and the biggest struggle is keeping a steady signal so I can respond to the comments.'

'Chester's gorgeous,' Summer said, stroking his rough brown fur. 'And so calm.'

'Not much bothers him,' Jas laughed. 'Except, for some

reason, pugs. He gets really worked up by them, as if he thinks they're not a real breed of dog, but some kind of strange imposter.'

Summer nodded. 'I can see where he's coming from.'

'Says the woman with the dog made from candyfloss,' Claire said.

'Hey.' Summer put her hands over Latte's ears. 'Don't you start.'

'Yeah, Claire,' Jas said, 'if Ryder thinks you're on his side for even a second, he'll run with it and you'll end up being his permanent sidekick.'

'Ryder's OK,' Claire said, giving them a quick smile, and Summer saw the blush rise to her cheeks, despite the dim lighting. She tried to catch her eye, but Claire focused her attention on scraping up the residue of her curry with her plastic fork.

The boat juddered to a halt, and people began slowly getting to their feet, the chatter rising in volume.

'Where are we?' Summer asked.

'The fairy grove,' Claire said in a dramatic whisper. Summer looked to Jas for clarification, but he just rolled his eyes and handed her a blanket. They filed out of the boat, Summer keeping Latte's lead short.

'This way, fair maidens.' Ryder gave them a regal bow, and locked up the boat behind them.

Claire took Summer's arm as they stepped off the deck on to muddy ground. They were moored deep in the country-side, with no house or streetlights in view. The smell of vegetation was strong, the river a black hole, the air chilled but not perishing.

They followed the trail of dancing torch beams across an expanse of grass and into a cluster of trees. Summer could

142

hear Ryder's light footfall behind her and, ahead of her, some of the others began to hum a soft, rhythmic tune. She shivered, despite herself, unsure whether curiosity or fear was winning the battle inside her, a vision flashing through her mind of being tied to a makeshift altar in the middle of the woods. Claire, as if sensing her disquiet, squeezed her arm, and Summer pushed the thoughts away.

The torch beams were soon joined by other, smaller lights, and Summer realized there were fairy lights strung up in the trees. The line dispersed, and people began perching on tree stumps, or sitting on the dry, dusty floor. They were in a small clearing amongst the trees, the fairy lights surrounding the makeshift arena.

'The fairy grove?' Summer asked.

'That's not its real name,' Claire said. 'I don't think it has one. It's just somewhere Ryder's found, where we come when we're on this stretch of river, and with the circle and the lights . . .' She pointed upwards.

They sat on the ground and Summer wrapped the blanket around her shoulders, shooting a grateful glance at Jas. Someone had lit a fire in the middle of the clearing, its orange flames soon crackling and spitting into the darkness, and Ralph began handing out plastic cups and filling them with a dark liquid.

'What is this?' Summer asked, as she held out her cup. 'And on a scale of one to ten, how lethal is it?'

'It's home-made plum wine,' he said proudly, 'and I'd say it's about a seven.'

'Thanks.' Summer took a tiny sip and closed her eyes as the warmth hit her. It was sweet, and easy to drink once she got used to the burn, and so she put her cup on the floor, almost out of reach.

Ryder raised his glass and everyone followed suit in a silent cheers, but it was Doug who cleared his throat and started talking, his voice carrying easily across the clearing.

'A little way from here, running alongside the narrow, bubbling creek,' he started, 'is a road you never want to go down after dark, for fear of finding a Shucky Dog. Not like you, Chester,' he said, and the Irish wolfhound pricked up his ears, 'and as far as you can possibly get from the little lapdog over there,' he pointed at Latte. 'The Shucky Dog is a fearsome creature, and each and every one of you should be praying that you never come across one.' He took a sip of his drink, and then continued.

'When it comes, you may not even see it. There'll be a prickling on your neck, as if someone has walked up close behind you, and the rattling of chains, distant so as to be almost a figment, but just on the edge of your hearing. Listen.' He stopped talking and cupped his hand behind his ear. The small group, already quiet, fell completely silent, and Summer tried to still her breathing, could feel the tension in her chest. She strained to hear a sound, but prayed that it wouldn't be the soft tinkling of chains rattling together.

'Next,' Doug said loudly, making them jump and sending a nervous titter round the circle, 'you'll hear the breathing. A wet, heavy rasping as the hound, its mouth full of spittle, prepares to take its next victim. If you're unlucky enough to see it – because the Shucky Dog, ladies and gentlemen, is a harbinger of death – then it will be a flash of red eyes, a blur of thick black fur. Nobody has ever got a clear look at it, but a glimpse is all you need for death to chase you down. So heed my advice, stay away from the creek road, and if you hear heavy panting behind you or the clink of chains, pray that it's just a traveller, a lost boatsman who's strayed from the water. Don't travel down that road at night.'

Doug nodded once and took another sip of his drink. Summer raised her hands, ready to applaud – she could feel the hairs prickling on the back of her neck, and nobody, *nobody* could convince her to turn around right now and peer into the black woods behind her – but nobody else put their hands together.

Instead, an older man with white hair down to his shoulders, who Summer hadn't yet been introduced to, leant forward and began speaking.

The stories kept coming, some ghostly, some tragic, some funny and ridiculous, told in turn by members of the small group. Everyone had their own style, their own way of hooking their audience in. Ralph was blisteringly funny when he told the tale of a local theatre group who had, unbeknown to them, cast – and then spurned – a famous actor in a play, and the humiliation that followed. Jas told a creepy story about a boat that cruised the waterways with no helmsman, just a low wailing and the occasional flash of a face at the window, and Claire's story was musical, both in theme and in the telling, with snippets of folk songs littered throughout.

Summer was entranced, her face burning in the glowing fire while Latte snoozed in her lap. She laughed and shuddered and, on a couple of occasions, squealed aloud. She had no idea what the time was, but she would have been happy listening to the stories until the sun began to glimmer through the trees.

And then Ryder's eyes turned to her, the fairy lights casting shadows of his eyelashes on his cheeks. 'Summer, do you have a story you want to tell?'

She swallowed and reached for her cup, glanced at Claire who raised her eyebrows.

'I – I'm sorry, I've not done this before,' she said. 'I haven't thought.' She waited, her breath in her throat, wondering what Ryder's reaction would be.

'Of course,' he said, 'maybe next time?' His smile was full, his eyes finding hers out despite the shadows, and Summer felt a rush of relief.

'Next time,' she nodded. 'Thank you.' If there was a next time – and the fact that she was being allowed back was pleasing enough – she would be bold, she would find a story to tell.

When they finally stood, Summer found that her legs had gone numb, and Jas helped haul her to her feet. Back on the boat, with the warmth of the woodburner seeping into her bones, Summer felt her eyelids begin to drop. She forced herself to speak, in an attempt to stay awake until they got back to Foxburn.

'You have a wonderful voice,' she said to Claire. 'You must have music going all the way through you, like "Southwold" in a stick of rock.'

Claire laughed. 'There's nothing I'm more passionate about,' she said. 'Nothing that a tune or a song can't improve. Will you do a story, next time?'

Summer nodded. 'I'd like to.'

'For now, tell me about Willowbeck. What sent you north? Was it really just competition at the pub?'

'It was a variety of things,' she admitted. 'I hadn't been there that long. It took me a while after . . . Mum died to even want to see the boat. And then, in my absence, her best friend was trying to run it and fell into some difficulty. My intention was to go and get her back on her feet – not that

I thought that I really could – and then it . . . It sort of all came back to me. Why I'd loved being on the boat. Lots of it was to do with spending time with Mum, but not all of it.'

It had become clearer to her since she'd travelled away from Willowbeck. She had previously thought that if her mum had been running a café in a shopping centre or on a high street then she would have loved that, and had memories that were just as happy, but she was beginning to see that it was more than that. The river really was a magical, calming place to be.

'Once a water baby, always a water baby,' Claire said.

'Have you lived on boats all your life?'

'Not at all,' Claire said, 'though I've always grown up around narrowboats. I come from Brecon, and the Mon and Brec canal is stunning. We used to take trips on it all the time. We got to spending so much of our money on the day cruisers that the boatsmen ended up letting me and my brothers ride for free, as long as we helped with handing out teas and coffees, and did a bit of the tour-guide business here and there.'

'So you always wanted to be a liveaboard?'

'Not consciously. I fell into it after a relationship ended. I was trawling through the flat listings online, it was a bloody nightmare and I thought – why not? Why not do something different? The shop came later, when I realized how hard it was to find a residential mooring, and so a fixed place of work wasn't that easy either. It's haphazard, but I couldn't imagine not being on my boat. And there are nights like tonight, these get-togethers. Nothing's too formulaic or routine, and that suits me. What's next for you after Foxburn?'

Summer shrugged. 'I don't know.' Her visitor mooring was

for fourteen days, and after that she had to move on. The residential mooring at Willowbeck was never too far from her thoughts, though after tonight, Summer could see that there was so much more to explore, things that she'd never dreamed of.

'Don't think about that now,' Claire said. 'Think about the next week.' She held up a hand in greeting as Ryder approached, a bottle of local cider in his hand.

'Can I offer you ladies a drink? Help to warm you up.'

Summer shook her head, but Ryder sat alongside them anyway.

'Who's steering?' Claire asked.

'I've left Jas in charge. He's a better helmsman than I am anyway, especially in the dark. How did you find our little gathering?' He leaned in close to Summer. He smelt of apples and charred wood.

'It was fun,' Summer said. 'A bit cold and creepy in the woods, but I suppose that's all part of it.'

'Claire mentioned that you run a café on your boat?'

'I do.' In his company, her blackboard, her gingham apron and vases of flowers all seemed a bit tame. 'You should come aboard, have a coffee on the house.'

Ryder narrowed his eyes, but didn't respond.

'I'm going to help her branch out,' Claire said. 'Make a list of all the delicacies she should be baking.'

'Oh, I already have a list,' Summer said. 'It's the things customers asked me for this afternoon. In the time I was at Willowbeck, three people asked me if I made a certain kind of cake, and one of those was Jenny, who was just showing off about her own red velvet cakes.'

'I *love* a red velvet cake!'

'Don't side with the enemy,' Summer said. 'Anyway, the

point is, this afternoon *eight* different people asked for cheese-cake or fondant fancies or cream horns.'

'The people of Foxburn are a diverse lot,' Claire said, looking away.

'Don't think I don't know it was you,' Summer said.

'Don't pay any attention to her,' Ryder said. 'She loves sticking her nose in.' A look passed between them, not hostile, but definitely charged. Summer wondered if she should invent an excuse to move further down the boat and leave them to it, but then she felt the boat turn as Jas negotiated it into its mooring.

Summer said goodbye to everyone, receiving a quick hug from Jas, handshakes from Doug and Ralph, and a kiss on the cheek from Ryder, his beard soft against her skin.

'Until next time,' he said, leaning in the doorway of *The Wanderer's Rest*.

'Absolutely,' Summer replied, shooting a quick glance at Claire.

They made their way down the towpath, the glow of the streetlights hazy in a river mist that had descended while they'd been gone.

'Have I convinced you, then?' Claire asked quietly.

'About what?' Summer pulled Latte's lead closer as she strayed towards the water's edge. 'I prefer your folk songs to One Direction, definitely.'

'I'm with you there,' Claire said. 'But I was talking about the cakes. Try some new recipes – I'm sure I've got a baking book somewhere, but believe me, you don't want to try any of my muffins.'

'Excuse me?' Summer laughed.

'I'm a hopeless cook,' Claire said, regret in her voice. 'Total foodie, but put a bowl and a whisk in my hand and I'll use it as percussion.'

'So you're giving me all these instructions—'

'Suggestions.'

'Instructions,' Summer repeated, 'and you can't do any of this yourself.'

'I wouldn't have to ask you if I could, would I?'

'Fair point.' They reached *Water Music* and Claire got her keys out.

'You've enjoyed tonight?' Claire asked. 'I know they're a bit whacky, but they're a lot of fun.'

'I had no idea this kind of thing went on. I haven't laughed so much – or been so terrified – in ages. I feel like my mind's had a workout. Thank you for tracking me down.'

'For following the smell of brownies, you mean? Friendship is a mere side-effect of what I need you for.'

'So when you said suggestions . . .' Summer let the words trail off, and grinned.

'Yeah, fair enough. Nobody ever said I was meek. But give it a go – if I can't find this book then there's always the internet.'

'And Mason was content with simple bacon sandwiches,' Summer said, sighing.

'Mason?' Claire paused in the doorway.

'He was my neighbour in Willowbeck. He'd started to become quite a good friend.' She tried not to sound nostalgic, but wasn't sure she'd managed it.

'Ah, right,' Claire said, 'so he's . . . he's not happy you've gone, then?'

'We're still in touch. I've only been here a few days, but it's nice that he's not treating me as out of sight, out of mind.'

'The waterways are a pretty tightknit community. It's good you've still got friends there.'

'Can I ask,' Summer said, 'what's the deal with you and Ryder?'

150

'Oh,' Claire's eyes flashed, 'have you seen something you like there?'

'No, I – I sensed something, between you. But it's none of my business.'

'Curiosity's allowed,' Claire said. 'I've not exactly left you alone, have I? Ryder's a good guy, despite the act. I can't say I'm not attracted. But we're both part of the band of roving traders, and a relationship is always a risk. If it went wrong it might cause a rift, and I'm happy as part of this haphazard little crowd. I don't want to do anything to wreck that.'

'Who says it would?'

Claire gave her a wide grin. 'Don't throw logic into the mix. We've only just met and you're organizing my relationships.'

'You're organizing my café!' Summer protested.

'Touché. Right, I'm heading in. We can continue this battle tomorrow.'

Summer gave Claire a hug, waited while she bent to say goodnight to Latte, and then walked past the other narrowboats to her own. It was close to two in the morning, and *A Seeker's Fortune* was closed up, all the curtains drawn. She wondered if Una and Colin had ever met Ryder, or been involved in one of the storytelling evenings.

Foxburn was dark and still. Ducks and geese were asleep, the little cottages were all in darkness, and the boat owners who had been with her that evening were quietly climbing aboard their boats and closing their doors behind them. It was ridiculous, but the story about the Shucky Dog and Jas's tale about the ghostly narrowboat had left an impression on Summer, and she felt a sharp tug of fear at being out in the dark with only Latte for company. The little Bichon Frise wouldn't be a match for a snarling hound with chains and red eyes.

When Summer was safely under the covers, she sent a text to Harry, inviting her to visit. She had a proposition she wanted to talk to her friend about, something that could be beneficial for Claire, her café customers and her best friend as well. Summer turned out her light, and with the gentle lulling of the boat, the feel of Latte's warm body on her feet, and despite demon dogs and ghostly helmsmen hovering at the edge of her thoughts, she soon fell asleep.

Summer woke the following morning with grand plans. She was going to try and broaden her repertoire – maybe not as far as cream horns, because she was sure she didn't have the skill or the space needed to make French patisserie master-pieces – but she agreed with Claire that variety could only improve the café's reputation.

On the phone, Harry was enthusiastic.

'Of course you can do it, Sum, all you need is a sound recipe and perseverance.'

'But I don't have your magic fingers.'

'Come off it. Your signs are exquisite, and that's all done with your hands and an eye for detail. Add in a bit of taste and smell and you're there.'

'You make it sound so simple. Will you come and see me? We can talk it through, and maybe some of your magic will rub off on me.'

'I'd love to, I really would. I want to see this place, all these amazing new people you've met, but it's – I'm just a bit busy at the moment, a bit tied up with things. I'll see though – maybe I can come some time next week. I'll check with Greg.'

Summer paused. 'Are you OK, Harry?'

'Sure, fine. Why wouldn't I be?'

Summer pulled back the curtains in her cabin. The sun

was high and bright, as if it was also choosing today to be bold.

'You sound . . . evasive. As if you don't want to see me.'

'Summer, of *course* I do. Things are just hectic here, Tommy's getting mountains of homework and Greg's doing long hours. I'm sure I can come and see you soon.'

'You have to *promise*. Bring Greg and Tommy with you if you like.'

'We'll see.'

'I miss you, Harry.'

'Well you don't need to. We'll see each other very soon.'

Summer opened up the café. It was Friday, which, Claire had informed her, meant market day in Foxburn. There was a steady flow of people heading from the towpath into the market square and vice versa, which meant that, for the first time in ages, Summer had barely any time to think. Latte got overexcited and, when she almost jumped into a pushchair to say hello to the pudgy little boy who was sitting in it, Summer had to shut her in the cabin. She hated doing it, but she had no time to keep an eye on her, and Latte's affection wasn't always taken in the way it was meant, especially with people who weren't as fond of dogs as she was.

There were no requests for outlandish desserts or pastries, which made Summer think that Claire was being kept similarly busy, and by the time three o'clock came round, her feet ached and her countertop was almost bare. She must have made over fifty cappuccinos, and the sound of the milk frother was on repeat inside her head.

With the market packing up, the custom began to thin out. A blue and white narrowboat-for-hire called *The Blue Heron* moored in the visitor space beyond *A Seeker's Fortune*, and a group of men in their twenties, all wearing loud shirts and no jackets, jumped on to the towpath.

'Stag do,' said an older woman with a neat white bob and large, tortoiseshell-rimmed glasses, shaking her head and watching as they went past, jostling each other and laughing. She was sitting at the table closest to the counter, drinking Earl Grey and eating a scone. 'Why they think a narrowboat is the best way of letting off steam before marriage, I'll never know. I thought they all went to Eastern Europe these days, to shoot guns and drink vodka.'

Summer laughed. 'It's quite unusual, isn't it?'

'No dear,' the woman said, 'not around these parts.'

'Do you get lots of stag parties stopping, then?'

'Stags and hens, fortieth birthday parties.' The woman spread strawberry jam liberally on to her scone. 'Combining high spirits, alcohol and deep, murky water is award-winning stupidity in my opinion. And that poor boat.' She pointed in the direction of *The Blue Heron*. 'When you compare it to yours, or that antique boat further down, it looks like a wreck. And it's not as if your boats are private – you get people tromping on here all the time – but you don't neglect it, do you?'

Summer thought of the eight months she had abandoned it. 'Not any more,' she said.

'Exactly. Those hire boats are often kept only to the minimum standard. They become a blight on the river, and not just because of the people on board. My Terrence and I were liveaboards for twenty years, with a residential mooring near Northampton. We travelled a lot, all the way up the Grand Union canal and back on a regular basis.'

'It sounds amazing,' Summer said, leaning on the counter.

'And these parties weren't popular back then. Just other folk respecting the river, delighting in its beauty.'

'You're not on a boat now?'

'No dear, I have a little flat in Foxburn. I like to stay close to the water, but since Terrence passed, it's just me and Ginny.'

'Ginny?'

'Yorkshire terrier. She's got a gammy paw at the moment, otherwise I'd have brought her out. But she adores chasing the geese, and it's torture if I bring her to the towpath and she can't move properly.'

'The *geese*? She's brave for such a small dog.'

'Size has never been an issue for her,' the woman said. 'In her mind, she's a mighty bear.'

Summer laughed. 'My Latte would probably be chased by a duckling, she's so timid.'

'Oh?' The woman looked at her with interest. 'You have a dog?'

'A Bichon Frise,' Summer confirmed, and the woman's eyes lit up. 'It was so hectic earlier that I had to shut her away – not everyone feels comfortable having a dog onboard when there's food being served – but it's fairly quiet now. Hang on.' Summer slipped into the kitchen and opened the door to the cabin. Latte was asleep on the sofa, the sleeve of Summer's red wool jumper in her mouth. 'Come on, you,' Summer said. 'Come and say hello.'

Latte opened her eyes and looked dozily up, then rested her head on her paws.

'Please, Latte, come and meet a new friend.'

Latte sniffed and turned away.

Summer crouched and stroked her. Latte pretended to be asleep.

'Latte, you'll love her. She's really friendly, like a grandma, and she loves dogs, she's got—' Latte sat up, her ears suddenly alert. Summer listened, but couldn't hear anything, and then

155

Latte barked so loudly and so close to Summer's face that she almost fell backwards. 'Hey—' she started, but the little dog bounded off the sofa and through the kitchen, and Summer scrambled up and raced after her.

'Latte—' she called, bursting through the door into the café, and then stopped dead.

Latte was turning in tiny circles and yapping, directly in front of a Border terrier whose tail was wagging like a metronome set to the fastest beat and whose lead was far too long for the small space, and looked like it was wound around three table legs. Summer didn't need to follow the lead to see who would be attached to the other end, because Mason was standing next to the older woman's table, and they were both laughing at something he'd just said.

His scarf was wound tightly around his neck, his battered denim jacket was done up and his jeans were tucked into serious-looking walking boots. He turned and grinned at her.

'Hi,' Summer heard herself say, and then wondered if her boat had become untethered, because she felt like she might be floating away.

'You'll need a warm coat,' he said, 'and gloves, and maybe a hat.'

'Why?'

'Because I've come to take you out on our walk.'

'But I—' She glanced at the older woman.

'Oh don't worry about me, I'm off home before it gets too cold. I've been introduced to Archie, and I can see that Latte's otherwise engaged.' The two dogs were weaving in and out of each other, as if performing some complicated dance they'd spent months rehearsing.

'Are you sure?'

'I'll be back for another scone tomorrow, if you're still here.'

'I will be,' Summer said, smiling. 'It would be lovely to have a few regulars while I was in this part of the world.'

The older woman got to her feet, and Mason helped her to put her coat on.

'Goodbye, dear,' she said. 'It's a lovely evening for a walk, but Mason's right, you need to wrap up.'

Summer watched her go, and then turned back to Mason. She couldn't stop smiling. 'She knows you?' she asked.

'She used to be a liveaboard. I haven't seen her for a few years, and she was just telling me her husband died last year, that she's moved to a flat nearby.'

'I'm sorry. Did you know him well?'

'Not really. You meet a lot of people on the water – you must be finding that out by now – but, unless you stay somewhere for any length of time, you don't ever get to know them properly. But –' his eyes met hers in a way that made her shiver from head to toe – 'I'm not letting you slip away so easily. Are you up for a walk? I know I've sprung it – and myself – on you a bit.'

'It's a lovely surprise,' Summer said, wondering whether to hug him or kiss his cheek. In the end she did neither. 'It's so good to see you. And as long as you promise not to force me back to Willowbeck, then I'm game.'

Mason held his hands up. 'Why do you think I've brought the walk to you? This area's got a lot to see, especially in the late afternoons.'

'Give me a few minutes, and I'll close up.'

Chapter 9

Summer's cheeks were burning with the cold by the time Mason opened the wooden gate and stood back to let her through, but in her woolly hat, gloves and boots, the sting was pleasant, the fresh air freeing after a day spent on board her boat. The area Mason had brought her to was a ten-minute walk from the mooring at Foxburn, and Summer was amazed at how close the town was to the stretch of stark, open marshland.

After their enthusiastic reunion, Archie and Latte were quietly investigating, noses to the ground, determined to trip Summer and Mason up by crossing the path constantly, backtracking and changing direction.

'Dogs are allowed,' Mason said, 'but we have to stick to the pathways and bridleways, and shorten their leads.'

They were on a firm, gravel pathway, an expanse of long, unkempt grass to either side. Summer could see the glint of water in the distance, but around her the land was flat, with no hills or buildings breaking the skyline. The only other feature was a forest to their right, the trees plush with new leaf growth, the chatter of rooks drifting up into the air. Ahead of her was nothing but the long grass and the pale blue sky, no cloud cover to raise the temperature.

The dogs' leads shortened, Mason picked up his pace, making sure Summer was alongside him.

'What will we see?' Summer asked, her voice hushed, not wanting to disturb anything.

'There's a good flock of wading birds and geese on the lakes,' Mason said, 'and you get common tern here from Africa at this time of year. We might see a hobby, or a cuckoo, and if we're really lucky there might be an otter, though I'm not sure with the dogs around we'll have that chance.' Every few moments he brought his camera up in front of him, snapping pictures of the landscape. Summer noticed that he looked into the viewfinder, winking to get the shot, rather than at the digital screen – old school, despite all the technology at his fingertips.

'I feel completely unprepared – you've got your camera and binoculars.'

Mason tapped them. 'I do this for a living. I wouldn't be much good if I just squinted in the distance and guessed at what I'd seen. But you can use them too, as soon as we find something.'

'Thank you,' Summer said. She stole a glance at his strong profile, his gaze taking everything in, making sure he didn't miss something important. But when she looked away, she sensed him doing the same to her, and she had to bite back her smile. 'You didn't have to come and find me, you know.'

'I wanted to,' Mason said. 'You took off without saying goodbye and I – well, Valerie came to see me, and she was worried. Of course I knew she was upset, that she'd confronted you, but neither you or Valerie strike me as the kind to hold grudges, so I thought that you would have put that behind you quickly.'

'I tried,' Summer said, keeping her voice low, her eyes and ears alert for movement in the grass at either side. They were walking towards a large lake, the surface shimmering like patterned glass, ducks and geese sitting in clusters around the edges and on islands in the middle. 'I went to see Valerie, and either she wasn't there or she wasn't prepared to talk to me. And then I . . .' She stopped, wondering how much to reveal about what had happened with Jenny. She knew Mason got on with the Greenways – there was no reason why he shouldn't – and she didn't want him to have a bad opinion of Maddy, or of her, because of what had happened. 'I had another run-in with Jenny,' she settled on.

She waited for a response from Mason, but he kept walking, checking every now and then how far Archie had strayed, his camera going up to his face and back down almost unconsciously. 'Valerie told me,' he said eventually, and Summer's breath got stuck halfway between her chest and her throat. 'I hope you don't mind.'

Summer inhaled, but didn't trust herself to speak.

Mason glanced at her, his brows lowered, and then continued. 'She came to see me the day you took off, in a panic. She told me what had happened, how she'd accused you of calling her a fraud – which of course I already knew about – and then said that wasn't the only reason you might have left. I hope you don't blame her for betraying your confidence, or for getting me involved, but she asked for my help and I think she wanted me to have the full picture.'

'And you've always been keen to know the real story between me and Jenny.' She couldn't help it, the thought of Mason knowing, judging her, put her automatically on the defensive.

Mason stopped and turned to face her. 'That's not it. I didn't ask to know, Valerie volunteered the information. But, if I'm honest, I was worried too. After Valerie's accusations, and knowing how hard it had been for you to come back in the first place, I wanted to find out where you'd gone, to talk to you.'

'How much did Valerie tell you?' Summer asked.

'That Maddy and Dennis had an affair, and that Jenny found out shortly before your mum died.' His tone was apologetic, his dark eyes locked on to hers.

Summer swallowed and nodded. She wasn't sure even Valerie was aware of all the events leading up to Maddy's death, and Summer had only told the full story to Harry. 'It wasn't just Mum's death that made it hard to come back to Willowbeck,' she said quietly. 'I always knew Jenny wouldn't like me being there, but I didn't realize quite how much she'd take against me.'

'And in some ways I can see why she's upset,' Mason said, 'but you weren't a part of what your mum did, and I think that she should be able to see that you've gone through enough.'

Summer glanced behind her at the cry of a bird, and looked up to see a skein of geese flying in a V overhead. 'You don't have to defend me. I can see it from Jenny's point of view too.'

'So you left because you felt guilty? Summer, you haven't done anything wrong.' He reached out and took her hand, the contact dulled by two pairs of gloves. Summer felt the urge to rip them off, to feel the human warmth of his fingers around hers.

'I'm not sure that's true,' she said. 'It doesn't feel like I'm blameless.'

161

'I don't know the whole story, but I'm guessing it was a messy situation. All the lines get blurred, and sometimes you can feel guilty just because you weren't able to fix something, or solve it, when it wasn't ever possible for you to make a difference in the first place.' There was something in Mason's expression, a sadness that Summer didn't think was pity, but unsettled her all the same.

She turned and started walking again, refusing to let go of his hand. 'But that doesn't make it any easier,' she said.

'No, of course it doesn't. Letting go of guilt is one of the hardest things you can do.'

'And what if you *did* do something, and it turned out to be the wrong thing?'

'Were your intentions good?'

'Yes,' Summer said, her voice dropping to a whisper. 'Or at least, I thought I was doing the right thing.'

'And all of this has meant being in the same place as Jenny is too hard for you?' Mason asked, slowing as they approached the lake.

'It's made it hard for me to be in Willowbeck at all, regardless of Jenny's opinion.'

Mason caught her eye. 'I want you to be in Willowbeck,' he said softly.

'I – I don't know if I . . . it doesn't seem that easy.'

'What, dealing with the past?'

'Any of this,' Summer said. 'The whole liveaboard . . . the boat thing. When I was in my flat in Cambridge, working at the studio, it was easier. It was straightforward, and none of this – nothing about this – is.'

'Straightforward isn't always best,' Mason said, and Summer thought back to the previous evening's storytelling, to fairy lights in the trees and the home-made wine.

'Maybe,' she murmured.

'Some things are worth struggling for. You belong in that café.'

'I don't know . . .'

'And what about all of this, so close to your front door.' His grip tightened and he led her to the side of the path, where the grass was longer. He shortened Archie's lead even further, moved a few feet into the grass and crouched, pulling Summer down with him.

Summer laughed. 'Aren't there hides for this sort of thing?'

'Not here,' he said, 'and this is the best spot. Look.' He leaned his face in close to hers, so their viewpoints were almost identical, and pointed out the different species on the lake. He showed her redshanks and little grebes and the common tern he'd mentioned earlier. A blue heron stood, as still as a statue on one of the central islands, serene and powerful, the ducks and geese fussing around it. Mason pointed out a little egret, small and snow-white, hiding amongst the reeds at the edge of the lake, and they listened to the different calls, Summer laughing at the chirp of the sedge warbler that sounded like a musical toy gone wrong.

She began to feel overwhelmed. She was sure she would never remember the names or identifying features of the birds, and wondered if Mason would think less of her. But at the same time she loved listening to him talk, could feel the enthusiasm bubbling under the surface, admired the way he tempered it, so that his voice had a calm, even cadence when he pointed out the different birds to her. He was so close she could almost feel his words vibrating in her chest. And his camera kept flashing up in front of him, darting as quickly as the birds he was capturing.

It soon became no longer about the wildlife, but just that

she was here with him, and he cared enough to take the time to show her. The sun moved overhead, the temperature started to drop and Summer felt herself freezing, losing the feeling in her feet. She didn't dare move, she didn't want to shatter the moment.

And then there was a sound she recognized, high-pitched, almost lost on the air currents. She thought she'd been mistaken, but she looked at Mason, and he smiled.

'Kingfisher,' she murmured. They turned back towards the lake, and a glimmer of orange and emerald blue skimmed low across the surface of the water, landing on a depth marker in front of them. 'I love kingfishers,' she whispered, and saw Mason nodding out of the corner of her eye.

'Single birds all have their own territory and move closer together the nearer it gets to the breeding season.'

'Not mates for life, then?'

Mason shook his head. 'They often only get one year – they don't live very long. And lots of the young die quite quickly. Their feathers get waterlogged when they're learning to dive, or the parents drive them out before they know how to fish. Lots of them drown.'

'Oh God,' Summer whispered, 'that's so sad, Mason. Why did you tell me that?'

'Because it proves how miraculous it is when you get to see one, like this, right in front of you. A rare thing,' he said, and Summer could hear the awe in his voice.

'I'd never thought of it like that,' she said, 'about it being a privilege to see one.' Either the kingfishers were there or they weren't, and she enjoyed watching them when they were. But with just a few facts, Mason had given her a different perspective. It was tragic, but it also showed her what a miraculous thing nature was, how things survived against so many odds.

Summer took the opportunity to edge closer to him, on the pretence of seeing what he saw, and pointed at a row of large black birds sitting on a fallen tree that was protruding from the water. 'Tell me about them,' she said. 'Are they cormorants?'

'Yes,' he said, 'similar to – but not to be confused with – the shag.'

'Oh.' Summer felt her cheeks flush. 'No, we definitely shouldn't confuse them.' She risked a glance at Mason, and saw that he was smiling, his eyes bright in the slowly descending sun. He turned properly to face her, their noses almost touching, and she could feel the warmth of his breath against her face.

'Shags are north, and coastal, and wouldn't be found here.'

'Right,' Summer murmured.

'And they're usually alone, whereas cormorants stay in groups.'

'Ironic, really,' Summer said, unable to take her eyes from his.

'Great divers,' Mason added, all hints of a smile gone. He was searching her eyes too, and Summer felt warmth spread through her, fighting against the cold that had lodged itself in her bones.

'They are?'

Mason nodded, his breath hitching in his throat, and Summer felt herself go still, in anticipation of what would happen next.

'Excuse me,' a loud voice said, 'but is that your dog? The one currently embroiled in an argument with the signpost?'

'What?' Mason stood abruptly. 'Oh, shit. Sorry – thank you.'

The man who interrupted them, who was tall and very

165

thin, with a telescope almost as big as he was, gave Mason a withering look and strode away from them down the path.

Archie had managed to wind his lead around the base of a signpost in such a way that his head was stuck against the wood, which he'd been trying – unsuccessfully – to chew through as a means of escape. Latte was sitting next to him and only yelped when Mason and Summer approached.

'We're only over here, why didn't you tell us?' Summer asked Latte, crouching to stroke her. 'I thought Archie's lead was as short as possible,' she said to Mason.

'It's an old lead, and I think the retractable mechanism is broken. I need to get a new one.'

'You do,' Summer said, watching as Mason tried to untie Archie, while the Border terrier made the task nearly impossible by moving the moment he had an inch of wriggle room. The more Mason worked, the harder Archie struggled, and when Mason finally untied a section and Archie bolted free, Mason fell forward, almost landing on his nose on the gravel walkway.

'Shit.'

Summer rushed forward, struggling not to laugh. 'Are you OK?'

'It's not me I'm worried about,' Mason said, sitting back on his haunches and checking his camera and binoculars. 'That was nearly a very costly fall.' He dusted gravel off his palms. 'Grit in the lens would not make for magazine-worthy photos.'

Summer held her hand out and he took it, and she pulled him up to standing. 'Thanks,' he said, giving her an embarrassed smile.

She grinned back. 'You and that dog are hopeless.'

'Yeah well, we'll get there one day.' Mason tied the lead

around and around his hand, so that Archie was only able to move about a foot from him. 'Heading back?'

Summer nodded, though her stomach twisted with disappointment. 'Are you going back to Willowbeck tonight?'

Mason glanced up. The sun was fading, the sky on the horizon a glowing yellow, the midnight blue of night far above them, with the turquoise of dusk in between. The brightest stars were beginning to appear, winking like beacons in the expanse of blue. There was a flurry in the trees as birds began to find roosting posts for the night.

'I'm not so keen on night cruising,' he said, 'so I think I'll stay until tomorrow.'

Summer's heart leapt. 'Evening plans?'

He turned to look at her. 'I hadn't thought that far ahead. You?'

'Just me and Latte. Now that you've come all this way to show me this beautiful place, the least I can do is cook you dinner. You and Archie.'

'Bacon sandwich?' he asked, raising an eyebrow.

'Oh, I think I can do better than that,' she said. 'If we're quick, the deli might still be open.'

With bags from the deli, Summer and Mason walked along the towpath in the dusk, the dogs worn out and subdued at their feet. 'Where's *The Sandpiper*?' Summer asked.

'In the last visitor mooring, beyond that *Blue Heron* boat.'

'Your friend was telling me that it's a stag party,' Summer said. 'Apparently that's quite a common thing on the rivers.'

'Yup,' Mason said, 'and results in a lot of unintentional swimming.'

'Have you had to rescue anyone, then?' Summer asked, putting her key in the lock.

Mason ran his hand through his hair. 'A couple, though not on my own. I like a drink as much as the next man, but it's risky to take it too far close to the water. People think that falling in is a laugh, but it's often much colder than you think, and it's the shock that'll cause more problems than anything. And believe me, trying to haul a full-grown man, who's drunk a keg of beer, to the side of the river and then get him out, isn't easy.'

'It sounds like a nightmare. Let's keep our fingers crossed our services aren't called on tonight, though at least you have experience of rescuing people. I'd be hopeless – I'd probably make the situation worse.'

She laughed, but Mason was staring into the water, as if he were mesmerized by the ripples on the surface.

'Mason?' She touched him lightly on the arm and he looked up, startled. 'Come in,' she said gently. 'Make yourself at home.'

He blinked and nodded, then followed her inside.

She led the way through the café and into the kitchen. The dogs scampered ahead into the living space and Summer dumped the bags on the counter and took off her coat and hat. 'Put your coat on the sofa. Can I get you a drink? I've got wine.' Summer checked in the cupboards, and opened a bottle of red. She unpacked the shopping, got out a bag of small potatoes and two thick rump steaks and began slicing tomatoes. She looked up, and saw that Mason was leaning on the doorframe, watching her. He'd taken off his coat and scarf, and his binoculars.

She smiled and tucked a strand of hair behind her ear. 'I'll just let the wine breathe a bit,' she said. 'You can put some music on, if you want.'

'Can I help?' Mason asked.

Summer shook her head. 'There's not much to do. Water on for potatoes, grill on for the steaks. It's a one-person job.'

'It looks delicious. Are you sure there isn't anything I can do?'

'You could go and see if the dogs are behaving themselves.'

'You mean Archie?' Mason raised an eyebrow.

'I mean together,' Summer said, grinning. 'Archie's a bad influence on my puppy.'

'Archie's a bad influence on *me*,' Mason said, reaching forward and taking an olive from a pot on the counter. 'I'll go and see what they're up to.'

Summer busied herself with preparing dinner, and found that, despite the long day, and the long walk, she was full of energy. The boat was much warmer than the April evening outside, and her cheeks were flushed even before the wine. She felt giddy, her mind replaying moments out on their walk, Mason's face so close to hers, his concentration as he pointed out the different types of geese, his awe at nature's miracles and the rareness of a kingfisher. Things survive against the odds, and maybe that was what Summer and *The Canal Boat Café* were doing. Maybe she was stronger than she'd imagined she could be.

'They're both wiped out,' Mason said. 'Shall I?' He poured the wine and handed her a glass. Summer turned and leaned on the counter, and they clinked.

'Thank you for coming,' she said. 'I've not been lonely here, but I have had a really lovely afternoon with you.'

'So have I. I'm just sorry I can't stay longer. Work calls.'

'Is your reserve very different from where we were this afternoon?'

'Not so much,' he said. 'It's more cultivated than where I took you – we wouldn't be able to take the dogs on to a

169

reserve – but as you can see, the wildlife in open countryside is often just as impressive. Where I'm working is more marshland than meadows, and it's got a couple of trails through the woods, so the habitat's a bit more diverse. They've been expanding, and they're keen to maximize publicity. They're hopeful of getting common cranes to stay on the reserve. They've been successful introducing some pairs into Norfolk, so it's not impossible.'

'Cranes,' Summer said, frowning. 'They're like herons, aren't they?'

'Not too dissimilar, though they're bigger, and much rarer. I'll show you some photos later, if you like.'

'I would,' Summer said. She sipped her wine, unwilling to turn back to her dinner preparations, wishing they could talk all night. Mason glanced at the floor, suddenly nervous, and then lifted his camera up, just as he'd done on the towpath in Willowbeck. Summer held her breath, waiting, wondering how having your photo taken could feel so intimate, especially as Mason spent so much of his time capturing things on his camera. She tried not to be self-conscious, but the thought of him looking at her, studying her through the tiny viewfinder made her stomach flutter.

'Mason . . .'

'Do you mind?' he asked softly, looking at her over the top of his camera.

'No. Though I thought you wanted to take photos of my dog.' She laughed nervously.

Mason took several photos, then lowered his camera and took a step towards her. 'Latte's a poser, she knows when the camera's on her and makes the most of it. But you . . . Look.' He turned, so he was leaning against the counter next to her, and began scrolling through the photos. 'You'll be able to see them better on the big screen, but even so.'

Summer looked at the photo.

It was her, wine in hand, leaning against the counter. She couldn't see anything remarkable in it, though her face had a look of clear contentment, her eyes alive in a way she hadn't noticed in the mirror recently. It had been a long time since she'd had any photos taken of her. The last few months hadn't seen many occasions for happy snaps, and the camera roll on her phone was taken up with images of her work – first her signs in various states of completion, and then, more recently, the café, and photos of Latte. 'It's me,' she said, unsure what else she could add.

'I know,' Mason said. 'But . . .' he sighed, 'it's hard to explain. Maybe I shouldn't try to, maybe it only matters to me.'

'What does?' She turned to look at him, but he was staring at the photo on the screen. He was frowning slightly, as if he was searching for something he couldn't put his finger on, and Summer felt herself being similarly captivated by him. His jacket discarded, he was wearing a thin black cotton jumper, a tiny gap between the hem and the waistband of his jeans, as if it had shrunk in the wash. She knew the staring was quickly becoming a compulsion to touch, and she didn't know if she was ready for what that might lead to.

A knock on the door forced her out of her reverie. Mason, too, seemed to start, and gave her an uncertain smile as she went to answer the door.

'Claire!' She bit back the disappointment, and invited her inside.

'I popped by earlier, but you were out. Ryder's keen to get

171

you back on *The Wanderer's Rest*, and I wondered if you fancied it tomorrow evening?'

'It sounds great,' she said, thinking that she would have to set time aside to prepare a story. 'Do you want a drink?'

Claire shook her head. She was wearing a turquoise wrap-around dress, her black hair impossibly glossy, and Summer felt a sudden twist of envy. She turned as Mason came into the café, following the sound of voices.

He exhaled sharply when he saw Claire, and the two of them stared at each other. Summer knew that, at that moment, she was as good as invisible.

'Mason,' Claire said, the word steeped in curiosity, 'I wondered if I might see you.'

'Claire, hi.' He tried to smile, but Summer could tell it was an effort. 'How are you?'

Summer glanced between them, and the envy solidified into something deeper.

Chapter 10

'You two know each other?' Summer asked, trying to keep her voice light.

'From a few years back,' Claire said. 'It's good to see you, Mason. You're keeping well?'

Mason ran his hand over his face and glanced at Summer. He looked shocked, his gaze almost accusing, as if Summer had planned the encounter, knowing it would be unwelcome. 'I'm fine, thanks. You?'

Claire nodded, her smile suddenly weak. She seemed like a different person to the bubbly, bolshie woman of the previous day – or even a few moments ago. It was as if she'd had the confidence sucked out of her. 'I'll be off, Summer. Just came to ask you about tomorrow.'

Summer nodded, incredulous. 'OK,' she said. Almost before she'd had time to say goodbye, Claire had turned and walked off the boat, leaving Summer and Mason standing in the dimmed café. 'Let's have dinner,' she said, trying to inject enthusiasm into her voice.

They ate at one of the tables in the café, rather than on

their knees on the sofa, but even though the setting wasn't as cosy as she would have hoped, Summer didn't think it was responsible for the change in atmosphere. Mason had become quiet, closed off. He cut into his steak, moved his potatoes around his plate, and kept glancing up at Summer, though not holding her gaze.

She talked about how busy the café had been, and he told her how Norman had almost bitten his head off for trying to take a photo of a pair of Egyptian geese that were sitting on the stern of *Celeste*, but in all the silences, and the hollow laughs, were unspoken words about what had just happened. Summer wanted to tell him about *The Wanderer's Rest*, the glade where they'd sat and told each other folk tales. She wanted to know if Mason knew about it, if he'd been involved in anything similar while he was more nomadic, but she didn't want to bring Claire up in case it sent him even further into his shell.

Mason eventually broke the stalemate. He sighed, drained his wine, and while he was refilling both their glasses, asked her how she knew Claire.

'She found me,' Summer said, watching him carefully. 'She came to introduce herself and told me how I should be offering a wider variety of cakes. She took me to meet some of the other roving traders last night. She seems nice.'

Mason nodded gently. 'She is. She said that she expected to see me?'

'I mentioned you, how much of a friend you've been to me. Do you mind me asking how you know her?'

Mason frowned, his fingers running up the stem of his glass. 'We knew each other a few years ago. We were moored up alongside each other, and – as you know – she's good at introducing herself. We were friends,' he said, though he didn't make it sound like that was a good thing.

'And then you became more than that?' Summer added, almost in a whisper.

Mason shook his head. 'No. It never . . . never turned into anything else. It wasn't long after I'd moved on to my boat, and I . . .' He rubbed his eyes. 'It was never going to happen.'

Summer leaned forward, trying to get him to look at her, but his eyes wouldn't meet hers. 'Are you OK?'

He nodded and looked up. Summer was startled by how anxious he seemed. 'I think you should come back to Willowbeck,' he said. 'Come back with me, tomorrow. Not just for my sake, but for Valerie's.'

Summer gawped. 'What?'

'I know I said I wouldn't, but—'

'Yeah, you did. You promised me you wouldn't do this.'

'I know,' Mason said. 'But after tomorrow, who knows when we'll see each other again?'

'I might come back, I don't know yet, but Mason, I need to be able to make up my own mind. After all that's happened, I need to see if I can do this, run this café away from Jenny and Ross and Willowbeck, and then . . . maybe I'll feel confident enough to come back. But not yet.'

'There's nothing I can do to persuade you?' He smiled, but it seemed hollow, as if he wasn't all there.

'Mason,' Summer sighed, 'why are you doing this? What's wrong? What happened between you and Claire?'

'Nothing. It was just a blast from the past that I hadn't expected.'

Summer swallowed back the lump in her throat. Their perfect afternoon was disintegrating. She wanted there to be trust between them, she wanted to get to know Mason, but this seemed like a step backwards. 'You don't have to tell me, of course you don't—'

'There's nothing to tell,' he shot back, his eyes flashing with a sudden anger.

Summer gasped and sat back in her chair.

'Shit,' Mason murmured, 'shit, I'm sorry, Summer. I'm so sorry. Maybe I should go.'

She nodded, even though it was the last thing she wanted. But whatever had spooked him, whatever seeing Claire had done to him, he wasn't prepared to talk about it, and Summer didn't think the evening could be saved. She knew she'd done the same with him, keeping the real reason for her friction with Jenny a secret, not wanting to be judged by him, and he had left it alone. She wanted to tell him there was nothing, nothing he could tell her that would make her dislike him. But she saw how weary he suddenly looked and knew she had to let it go for the moment.

'Thanks for dinner,' he said, getting to his feet. She did the same, clearing the plates away while he extracted Archie from whichever cosy spot he'd found to curl up in. The dog trotted obediently to the door, and Mason hesitated, turning back to face her.

'I'm sorry,' he said again.

'For coming to see me?' She gave him a quick smile. 'I've had a lovely time. I've missed you, Mason.'

He raked a hand through his hair, then stepped closer. Summer moved towards him, and gave him a tentative hug, her breath hovering in her throat as she felt his warmth through his jumper. Mason put his hands on her back, his head almost on her shoulder, his hair tickling her cheek. It was as soft as she'd imagined, the feel of his arms round her as comforting, though she could sense the tension in his shoulders. She closed her eyes, breathing him in, indulging in the sensation of being so close to him.

She wondered what it would have been like if Claire hadn't knocked on the door, if the tension would have been fuelled by a different emotion. She wanted him to be here, with her, and until the interruption, everything had felt right. Now, it was strained, almost as if they'd gone back to being strangers.

'I'll see you soon?' he said, stepping back to look at her.

'Of course.' She watched him go, and then, feeling a familiar knot in her stomach that for a few, blissful hours had been lifted completely, she gathered Latte into her arms and crawled into bed.

When she woke the following morning and stepped out on to the towpath, *The Sandpiper* was already gone. Summer went back inside and busied herself with her maintenance checks. She tested the oil and bilge levels, checked the bilge pumps were all working, and that the fuel tank filters were clear. When she went to turn on the coffee machine, Claire was waving at her from the bow deck. Summer beckoned her in and Latte went to greet Claire's flip-flop-clad feet, snuffling around them as if they were bowls of high-quality dog food.

'Get off, Latte,' Summer chided.

She made two cappuccinos and they sat at a table looking out on the river, which today was grey and swirling below heavy cloud cover.

'Mason still here?' Claire asked, staring resolutely at her coffee.

'No, he's gone back to Willowbeck. He seemed a bit shaken by your visit.'

Claire looked at Summer, her eyes narrowed. 'How much do you know about him?'

'Not that much,' she admitted. 'But he's been kind to me,

and he's made the effort to stay in touch since I came up here.'

'You like him?'

Summer chewed her lip, and watched as a grey and pink narrowboat called *The Laughing Gala* glided slowly past, the ripples of its wake jostling gently against the side of their boat. 'I do,' she said, 'but I have a feeling you're about to tell me something that's going to put me off for life.' She tried to smile, but saying the words had gripped her with despair.

Claire's smile was equally weak, and though she shook her head, she didn't jump to refute Summer's claim. 'I met him a while back, almost five years ago now. He'd not long been a liveaboard, and he was pretty green about it all. God, his hair?' Her eyes widened with amusement. 'He used to be so smart, so tidy, and we told him it wouldn't last.' She shook her head. 'Well, he's grown into it, hasn't he? Boat life. He looks well.'

'You were close?' Summer prompted.

'We got friendly. He seemed great, easy to get on with at first, but then you get so far and . . .' She sighed. 'I'm not really talking for me, here.' She winced, and Summer steeled herself, ready to hear the worst. 'My friend Tania fell for him pretty hard,' Claire continued. 'He was kind, but a little bit mysterious. I remember she said he was like an exotic puzzle that needed to be cracked. Everything about him was tempting, all sunbeam smile and irresistible body in tight T-shirts, but with a bit of intrigue thrown in. And at first he seemed to like her too, he was warm and considerate, they started a relationship, and I don't think it took long for Tania to fall in love with him.'

'So what happened?' Summer was cross with herself for sounding so desperate, but she couldn't help it. This story was as compelling as any she'd heard the other night, and this time she was invested in the outcome.

'He took off,' Claire said, her gaze apologetic. 'Hardly a word spoken – no argument or possible cause that Tania told me of. She was devastated.'

Summer chewed her lip. 'Do you think she could have been holding something back? Something that caused them to break up, that she was ashamed of or unwilling to reveal, even to you?'

Claire sighed and swirled her coffee. 'I know that would be nice, the best-case scenario, and of course I can't know all that went on, even from Tania. But from the way she was afterwards, she . . . God, I don't know, Summer. She was heartbroken, and shocked more than anything, as if it was completely out of the blue. I'd told her not to fall for someone so enigmatic – I thought he had all the makings of a classic bad boy – but if you're presented with a cream doughnut and told not to eat it, what are you going to do?'

'Eat the doughnut,' Summer murmured.

'Exactly. I'm not saying this to put you off, Summer, but I think you should know the truth. From what I know of him, he puts on a good show, but he's as cold as ice cream, and nowhere near as sweet.'

Summer stared at the froth at the bottom of her cup, trying to digest Claire's words. She couldn't imagine, for a moment, that was Mason's style, but she had to admit she didn't know him very well, and she couldn't ignore the way he'd changed after Claire had appeared. 'He followed me up here,' she said, only half talking to Claire.

'Maybe that suits him. If you're up here, he can woo you, then disappear back off to Willowbeck when he's had enough. Sorry – that sounds harsh, but I'm just . . . I'm butting in, aren't I?' Claire reached out and squeezed her hand. 'He may have changed, or there may have been more to what happened between him and Tania. I'm just telling you what I know.'

'And he changed after he saw you,' Summer admitted. 'He seemed so – so withdrawn. He definitely had something on his mind.' She spooned the coffee froth into her mouth.

'Hey,' Claire said, her voice gentle, 'don't do a complete U-turn because of what I've said. Everyone's complicated, and I can't deny he's even more of a looker now he's settled into his boating skin, scruffy and tousled and ripped.' She raised her eyebrows. 'Just be a bit cautious, that's all.'

Summer nodded and swallowed. 'Sure,' she said. 'He's gone now anyway. I can put him out of my mind, concentrate on the café and getting to know people here.'

'And the fairy glade!' Claire said, giving Summer an appraising look. 'You don't have to get involved if you don't want to. All stories need an audience, so if you're more comfortable just listening then don't worry.'

'No, I – I'd like to.'

Claire grinned. 'Good on you. I have a feeling you'll be good at weaving a few tales, once you get going.'

'I'm not so sure,' Summer forced a laugh, 'but it'll take my mind off things.' She wasn't sure she'd ever be able to think of anything else, except the way Mason had snapped at her, apologized and then wrapped his arms around her, or how different it might have been without Claire taking Mason back to the past, to memories he clearly wasn't comfortable with. He had never come across as cold before, and Summer wondered which was the work of fiction: Claire's story about Mason and her friend Tania, or Mason himself.

In the end, Summer didn't have much time to think about Mason because, despite the weather being grey, it was still a

Saturday in early April and Foxburn was alive with people. She couldn't remember a stretch of river being as busy. The traffic was constant, the visitor mooring spaces all full, and, while the café had a steady stream of people, Summer often found herself out on the deck, watching as narrowboats tried to navigate past each other without scraping paintwork, waving to the helmsmen, offering drinks and cake if they looked like they were pausing, even for a few minutes.

A couple in one of the colourful houses opposite the moorings put deckchairs in their front garden and, with a jug of Pimm's and tatty paperbacks, set up for the day. Summer couldn't help grinning at their perseverance, even though they both had thick jumpers on and the man had a blanket over his knees. Latte was enjoying the sights as much as she was, always barking when another dog went past. One boat had a mini Schnauzer at the bow, front paws on the deck seating so it looked like a masthead, and another had a glossy black Labrador swimming alongside, managing – at least while it was in Summer's view – to keep up with the boat. The helmsman was constantly checking on him, shouting things like 'Good work, Leo' and 'Keep going, my son', as if the dog was training for a Channel swim.

Nobody in Foxburn seemed shy about coming aboard *The Canal Boat Café*, and Summer did as much business inside as she was doing through the hatch. It was as if the village was willing spring to bloom, and thought that if they acted as if it had properly arrived, then the weather was bound to take notice. Summer thought that was a good attitude to have. Harry was coming to see her in the next couple of days and she hoped her friend would be enthusiastic about her idea. If it worked, then *The Canal Boat Café* would hopefully see even more custom coming her way.

Summer turned up at Claire's that evening with Una and Colin, who had been keen to join the folk night. Claire, Jas and Ryder made them feel welcome, and on the journey to the forest they tucked into falafel wraps, zingy with raita and chilli salsa.

As they sat in the circle with the fairy lights twinkling above them, Summer's palms prickled with sweat. She had never been much of a public speaker, and had always hidden behind her creations, her signs and her artwork. Along with Una and Colin, there were a few other unfamiliar faces, and she realized the group changed from day to day, Ryder accepting anyone and everyone on board his boat. With this in mind, she expected the stories to be similar, retellings and adaptations of the tales she'd heard before, but every single one was different.

Ryder, who was wearing a shirt in a bright, grassy green, and who looked at home in the leafy surroundings, turned his blue eyes on Summer. 'Do you have something for us?' he asked.

Summer nodded, and realized her mouth was completely dry. She tried to swallow, and took a long sip of the home-made wine that Ralph had once again produced.

'N-not far from here,' she started, leaning forward, hoping her voice would carry, 'a few hours down the river, there's a small, brick bridge. Even at dusk, it looks innocuous. Its arch is elegant, the low walls ensuring a beautiful view of the river and the surrounding countryside as you walk across it. It's a bridge for lovers to pause on, for friends to cross on their way to the pub.'

She glanced at her audience, a thrill running through her as she realized she was holding their attention, nobody whispering to their neighbour or making shapes in the earth with their fingers.

'But walk beneath it,' Summer continued, 'take those few, short steps in the gloom, with its dank bricks overhead, and you get a different sensation altogether. A feeling of foreboding, of dread and of heartbreak.' She gave a flicker of a smile, and then told the group the tragic story of Elizabeth Proudfoot – Valerie's ghost – who was supposed to haunt the bridge at Willowbeck.

'She was young and beautiful,' Summer said, 'with porcelain skin and black hair, too precious for her father, a local estate owner, to bear. He thought that by keeping her confined to their large estate, she would be safe from unwanted advances, but the gardener fell sick and his son, Jack, took over. He saw Elizabeth walking through the gardens every day – and was captivated. When her father realized Jack's attraction to his daughter, he sent him away. Elizabeth heard rumours from the maids that her father hadn't just sacked Jack, but had killed him by drowning him in the river. And what her father didn't know,' Summer continued, pausing for dramatic effect, 'was that Elizabeth had returned Jack's affections, and that they'd been meeting in the apple orchard, away from the large windows of the main house. She was devastated.

'One spring evening she stole away from the estate and made it down to Willowbeck and the bridge over the river. It's not a high bridge, but with stones in the pockets of her white dress, and with nothing inside her but a desire to join her love, Elizabeth threw herself into the water. She was discovered the next day, a look of serenity on her pale face. The saddest thing is that Jack hadn't been killed, but had moved to the next village, desperate to work out a way of being with Elizabeth. To this day she haunts the bridge, her white dress flowing behind her, searching for Jack, though she's destined never to find him below the surface of the water.'

It had taken her a lot of time and frustrating online research, going from site to site, but eventually she had found the story, a brief mention of the historical details. Valerie's tale was that the woman had been jilted by her lover, but it seemed the truth was even more tragic than that – rumours had led to Elizabeth's fateful decision, when in reality Jack was still out there, waiting for his chance to be with her. Of course, Summer had used her own imagination to embellish the story, but it was grounded in truth.

When she'd finished, Una and Colin gave her wild, enthusiastic applause, and the more seasoned members of the group nodded approvingly. Doug held up his cup and gave her a beaming smile and Summer felt the warm glow of acceptance.

As they made their cautious, torchlit way back to *The Wanderer's Rest*, Ryder fell into step alongside her and rested his hand on her shoulder.

'Impressive story,' he said. 'You held us in the palm of your hand.'

'Even you?' Summer asked, laughing.

'Especially me,' Ryder said, his low voice dropping even further, his hand squeezing her neck.

'Oh,' Summer murmured. She glanced behind her, looking for Claire.

'You're a real find, Summer. And I think we have a lot in common.'

'I'm not a shell on the beach,' Summer said, rolling her eyes. 'You haven't *found* me.'

Ryder laughed, the sound echoing through the darkness. 'Too right. Sorry. Very patronizing of me.'

'What do we have in common, anyway?' Summer asked.

'We're both children of hippies. I can see that in you a mile off, even if you're fighting against it.'

'I'm not fighting against anything,' she said, 'I'm just trying to do what's right for me.' Latte yipped at her feet, as if in agreement, and a moment later Chester loped up alongside her, closely followed by Jas. Summer gave a quiet sigh of relief.

'*Great* story, Summer,' he said.

'I was just telling her how much I liked it,' Ryder added.

'Yeah, I bet you were. Summer, I want to hear more about your haunted bridge on the way back. I'm all over the ghosts on the waterway and it would be a good story for my blog.'

'You're not taking us back to Foxburn?' Ryder asked.

'Not this time, buddy,' Jas said, slapping him on the back. 'A man should be the king of his own castle, and I reckon a bit more practice at night cruising wouldn't do you any harm.'

As they climbed on board the narrowboat, Summer gave Chester a long, grateful hug. She hoped Jas would see it for what it was, and the look they exchanged told her he did. He had rescued her, even if Ryder wasn't a serious threat. Summer wasn't in a position to accept anyone's advances, and definitely not from someone Claire had expressed an interest in.

As they walked back down the towpath, Claire linked her arm through Summer's.

'Good night?' she asked.

'Definitely. I never knew telling stories could be so exhilarating.'

'They're an eclectic bunch, but we make a great team. It would be nice having someone to even things out a bit,' Claire said. 'Maybe someone a bit more . . . feminine.' She shot Summer a glance.

'What?'

'The visitor moorings only last for fourteen days, and you've got less time left than we have. What are you going to do after that?'

Summer floundered. 'I – I really don't know.'

'So come with us. You've got your roving trader licence now. We're heading north, further up the river to a place called Tivesham. Not quite as busy as here, but it's got its own feel. I've been looking for somewhere I can put on a music festival.'

'What?' Summer asked, her mind whirring at the invitation, unable to keep up with Claire's stream of thoughts.

'The boating community's so friendly, everyone offering whatever they can when it's needed – whether it's sandwiches or their maintenance skills or just their time helping out. There are lots of these little villages with their pubs and their green spaces and wide towpaths – a festival would be perfect. We can have storytelling, dance, theatre, and of course it has to have a musical element. I know a few people in the business, and I'm keen to organize something this year. I'm scouting venues, and Tivesham seems like a good place to start.'

'A proper music festival? With bands and crowds and glow-sticks?'

'Nothing too big or fancy. Just a few bands, mainly local, some great food – including cakes.' She jabbed Summer in the ribs. 'We'd advertise it through word of mouth all along the river. You've seen that we can create an atmosphere. What could be better?'

'Sounds great,' Summer said, nodding, though her mind was almost entirely on what Claire had said before that. Go with them, become part of their troupe of roving traders, and head further away from Willowbeck.

'Hey,' Claire said, as they stopped outside *Water Music*, 'you don't need to decide yet. We've got a few days. And I know you have a lot to think about.'

Summer nodded, let Claire peck her on the cheek, and then walked with Una and Colin back to their boats. The towpath lights created golden, wavering pools on the black surface of the water, the colours of the narrowboats muted in the darkness.

Summer lay awake, staring at the low ceiling of her cabin, Latte's gentle snores comforting at the end of the bed. She focused on the rhythmic lull of the boat, the gentle clonking of the heating system, the tick of the boat's shell moving and settling around her. The sounds were comforting, reassuring. She'd got used to them, they were part of the fabric of her new life, and she knew she'd miss them if they weren't there.

She'd only just moved away from Willowbeck, and she'd known the visitor moorings were much more time-limited, but to keep cruising off into the distance away from where her mother had been so happy, and away from Valerie and Norman, away from Mason? She closed her eyes.

She'd heard nothing from him since their beautiful walk, and then the awkward dinner, the tension-fuelled ending. Was Claire right? Had Mason got so close and then manufactured the argument so he could detach himself from her? What would be the point? They hadn't slept together, and she still couldn't believe that was his only motivation for getting to know her. What Claire had said didn't sit true with her. She enjoyed his company, she was sure he enjoyed hers, and the chemistry between them was undeniable. She liked him enough to want to find out more, but if she kept moving further and further away, would she be able to do that?

* * *

187

When Harry arrived on Wednesday afternoon the sun was warmer, hinting at things to come. Blackbirds pipped and sang as they burrowed for twigs and leaves in the undergrowth, industriously preparing their nests, and the river sparkled, glimmering with a new clarity under the blue sky, flashes of silver as shoals of minnows passed below the surface.

Summer felt the heat on her cheeks, and took her friend to the market square. They went to the deli and picked up giant slices of home-made pizza covered with sun-ripened tomatoes, mushrooms, grilled chicken and artichokes, and sat on a bench to eat them.

'This is beautiful,' Harry said, gazing at the town hall and the fountain, occasionally drifting faint sprays of water in their direction in the breeze. 'Why aren't we on the boat?'

Summer shrugged. 'I fancied a change of scene – I've been working all day and I thought the fresh air would be welcome.' She gave Latte a scrap of chicken. 'And I'm sure this one was about to go stir-crazy.'

Harry laughed. 'Latte? She's a cushion dog. Sofas and beds and comfort.'

'You'd be surprised,' Summer said. 'Since becoming a live-aboard, leading a slightly more rugged lifestyle, and of course since getting to know Archie—' She stopped, turning away on the pretence of sipping her tea.

'Archie?' Harry asked. 'Isn't that Mason's dog? Is there a blossoming romance that I don't know about?'

'What?' Summer jolted, spilling hot tea over her hand. 'Shit,' she whispered, wiping it off with a napkin.

Harry was watching her, her long dark hair falling over the collar of her red jacket. 'I was going to say between Archie and Latte, but now I'm wondering if I've hit on something else.'

'That isn't why I wanted to see you,' Summer said.

'It is,' Harry said, 'even if you tried to pretend it wasn't.'

Summer narrowed her eyes, trying to be annoyed.

'So, you and Mason, then?' Harry asked. 'It distresses me that I've only met him in passing.' Summer had introduced them once in Willowbeck when Harry was on her way in with a fresh, delicious tray bake, and Mason was on his way out with a bacon sandwich. 'So I need you to tell me in extreme detail.'

'First I need to talk to you about something,' Summer said.

'Yes, this. Come on, Summer.'

Summer knew it was futile to resist, so she told Harry everything. The FaceTime, the walk through the countryside – which had, in only a few days, taken on an ethereal quality in Summer's mind, like it was part of a fairy-tale – and then the bump back down to earth with Mason asking her to come back to Willowbeck and Claire's revelation about the side to Mason that Summer hadn't seen.

Harry listened in silence, her expression barely changing as Summer confessed how close they'd got, and how charged it felt, how she couldn't be mistaking the signals, and then Claire's suggestion that he was a womanizer, that he disappeared each time he got a notch on his bedpost.

'You don't believe that, though?'

Summer shook her head. She'd done so much talking her pizza had begun to wilt. She scoffed it down, listening as Harry gave her opinion.

'Right, so he saw Claire and something about that relationship – or the memory of her – upset him. Could it just have been a bad time for him generally? What I don't get is why seeing her made him pressure you about going back to Willowbeck with him.'

'After promising he wouldn't,' Summer added, mumbling through a mouthful.

'Right. So either he realized that afternoon that he couldn't live without you, which is a possibility by the sounds of the chemistry—'

'But why didn't he say that?'

Harry shrugged. 'Because he's scared? Because nothing's really happened between you yet and he didn't want to commit himself? But you're right, if he was asking you to go back with him, then he's already committing to you. Or maybe he was worried that Claire was going to spill the beans about something, and he wanted you to move away from her.'

'About him being a womanizer?' Summer asked.

'Possibly.' Harry frowned. 'But Claire only has Tania's word to go on. It's not like she's experienced "Mason the bad boy" quite first-hand. Sure, she would know how her friend felt, but even so, Mason's reaction to seeing her seems a bit extreme. If it was Tania, I could maybe understand it.' She drummed her fingers against her lips. 'Unless Claire's not giving you the full picture, either to save your feelings or because she doesn't think she knows you well enough.'

'She's asked me to become part of their band of roving traders.'

'Right,' Harry said, pointing at Summer. 'So . . . I don't know. It's a pickle. He's really not sent you so much as a text since it happened? Have you sent him one?'

Summer shook her head. She knew what her friend was going to say and so she jumped in with a change of subject that would hopefully prevent those words from being released into the spring air.

'How would you feel about baking cakes?'

190

'How is that going to solve the Mason thing?'

'It's not. It's going to solve the problem that my cakes are . . . well, they're OK, but they're not that inspiring.'

'That's not true!' Harry said. 'But I'm sorry I haven't brought you anything for the last couple of weeks – things at home have been manic. I have got an apricot and pecan Victoria sponge in my car though, I'll get it for you on the way back.'

'You *have*? Oh God, that sounds amazing. This is what I'm talking about. If I put your apricot and pecan cake next to my fruit scones – does it have apricot jam in the middle?'

'And cream,' Harry said.

Summer rolled her eyes. 'Wow. See, no competition. This is what I need. I need better variety, and I need quality. Just think how much more custom I'd get, how the reputation of the café would go up. *Cakes by Harry Poole*,' Summer said, moving her hand out in front of her as if imagining the sign, '*they're bound to make you drool.*'

Harry laughed. 'Oh, come on.'

'The rhyme needs a bit more work, but isn't it a great idea?'

Harry's smile faltered. 'I – I don't know,' she said.

'Why not? I know it's a slightly longer journey, but I won't always be in Foxburn, and we can sort out the logistics.'

Harry rested her elbows on her knees. The bell in the local church started ringing, and pigeons scattered into the air from the trees in the churchyard.

'I've got a part-time job,' she said.

'What?' Summer asked. 'Why? Where?'

Harry hid her eyes behind her hands. 'Greg's job is . . . they're losing work. The company's struggling and there's not enough to go around. He's put himself forward for everything, tried to show he's worth keeping – they took on every contract they could get, which was why he was working so much, but they've all been short-term and the regular business is being swallowed up by this new company that's started up in the area. They've got more money, rates that Greg's company can't compete with, and they're vicious, stealing all Greg's existing clients without mercy. There's not been talk of redundancies yet, but it's looking likely.'

'Oh, Harry,' Summer said, putting her hand on her friend's back. 'I'm so sorry.'

'And of course I don't mind working, I can fit in lots of hours when Tommy's at school, but . . .'

'Where are you working?'

'A local café.'

'The bastards, how dare they get your cakes?' Harry looked up and Summer grinned at her.

'I'm just a waitress,' Harry said.

Summer gawped. 'No way. Do they know you bake?'

'They were looking for a waitress.' Harry shrugged, and Summer felt a lump in her throat. This was not like her confident, rational friend. Surely she would have told the café the benefits she could bring to them, and so make the most of the opportunity?

She gripped Harry's hand. 'So bake for me instead. Not like you have been, once a week as a huge favour for your best friend in the world, but properly, as a business partner. I'll pay you for everything, pay for your mileage to travel to wherever I'm based on the river. We can work out new recipes, the quantity we'll need, all those things. Will you think about it?'

'Wow,' Harry whispered. There were tears glistening in her eyes. 'I'll think about it, Sum, it's an amazing offer.'

'I was going to ask you before I knew about Greg. It's not a pity proposal, Harry, I thought *you* could help *me* and make some money doing something you're so good at and – I think – something you love.'

'I do, I do,' Harry said. 'I just . . . It's all so confusing at the moment, and Greg is feeling really . . .' Harry turned away, and Summer put her arms around her.

'No pressure,' Summer said. 'I know we'd make a brilliant team, that's all. Just think about it.'

'Of course I will,' Harry said, 'and thank you.'

Chapter 11

Tivesham turned out to be a middle ground between Willowbeck and Foxburn. Without Willowbeck's quaint beauty or Foxburn's bustling vibrancy, it had several moorings, the most appealing with fields on one side of the river, and the towpath running alongside a park on the other. There were benches, a large expanse of grass and a derelict bandstand that Claire was intent on using in her music festival.

Summer had agreed to try the life of a roving trader and had cruised out of Foxburn the day after her meeting with Harry. While Claire and the other traders had time left at their visitor moorings, Summer's time was running out, and Claire had managed to get the band of boats to move on earlier so that Summer could accompany them.

They'd ended up stopping at a smaller mooring en route, when a passing helmsman told them the local hotel was full of American tourists keen to soak up idyllic English river life and Claire thought they could be tempted by her music, Summer's cakes, and probably some expensive antiques too.

After that, they'd cruised on to Tivesham and had been

there nearly a month. It was bigger than anywhere Summer had been so far and, with several different moorings, had allowed them to stay in the area more than fourteen days while Claire and the others investigated the potential for their festival.

They were enjoying steady custom, with footfall along the towpath and cruisers taking advantage of the plentiful berths to stop and soak up what was turning into a warm and sunny spring. The storytelling and folk-music nights had continued in the derelict bandstand, Ryder patiently stringing up the fairy lights each time they went, the atmosphere just as electric and, Summer thought, slightly less scary for not being in the middle of a forest.

Claire had an acoustic guitar to accompany her singing, Jas played the tin whistle, and Ralph produced something that looked to Summer like an accordion but which, he informed her, was called a melodeon. Not to be left out, Ryder and Summer took makeshift drums along with them, and Summer had discovered that her best brownie tray made a satisfying noise when played with an acrylic spoon.

She'd got the measure of Ryder as they'd spent more time together, and while she could see why Claire was attracted to him, there was something about him that she found unsettling. His trade turned out to be sourcing anything that people wanted but couldn't get hold of. He seemed to have a network of contacts he could call on at a moment's notice to find a cheap engine part or a particular brand of trainers. He was a typical dodgy market trader, only with a hipster vibe that perhaps made him seem more legitimate to his customers. Summer had vowed never to buy anything from him, and wanted to tell Claire that *he* was a bad boy, *he* was the one to be wary of, and that Mason didn't even come close. They were becoming close friends, but even so, she wasn't sure Claire would appreciate that observation.

She'd got into a routine at the café, opening every day and baking in the evenings so that she could focus on serving customers while she was open. She hadn't been to the studio for weeks, and while she was in touch with Harry almost every day, Harry had yet to make a decision about her proposition. In the meantime, Summer was selling bacon rolls, inferior with supermarket bacon, and trying to build her cake repertoire with Claire's guidance and recipes from the internet.

Valerie had bought herself a tablet since Summer had moved away, and they often exchanged emails and phone calls, Valerie updating her on Harvey's latest feline escapades, or the plight of a boat that had been tied to the towpath opposite the residential moorings while the owner tried to patch up a leak. *It seems to be getting lower and lower in the water*, Valerie had written, *and I wanted to tell the couple I'd done a chart and that it'll all work out, but I wasn't sure they'd be keen. If only you were here with your café, I'm sure they would have spent a fortune on muffins.*

One thing that was guaranteed with Valerie's communications was a plea that Summer come back to Willowbeck. Summer always told Valerie that she was thinking about it, and in truth she was. She couldn't deny that travelling with Claire, spending time with the other boat owners, was giving her a new lease of life, but she also believed her time at Willowbeck wasn't over, that in some ways – although she was reluctant to think of it like this – it was calling to her.

One evening after Summer had finished baking, and with her limbs satisfyingly weary from a day of hard work, she took a glass of white wine and a notepad and climbed up to the roof of her boat with Latte. It was near the end of

May, the light was only just beginning to dim and the early summer breeze was gentle and delicious. A robin sang loudly in a tree next to one of the towpath lights, believing he'd found a brand-new sun. Summer looked out over the expanse of park, its greens fading to shadows, and a couple of late dog walkers, a jogger in a luminous pink top running down the towpath. Latte stayed close at her side and Summer relaxed, comforted by the feel of the dog against her thigh, and the soft glow of the other boats moored alongside her.

She scribbled the heading *Willowbeck* in her notebook and started to list all the reasons to go back. Firstly there was Harry: if she was near to Cambridge and Harry's cottage, then the cake-making partnership was a real possibility, which would help both the café and Harry's family. Summer was rushed off her feet keeping the café and the boat going all on her own, and if Harry worked with her, she wouldn't have the pressure to bake every evening as well.

She'd surprised herself with how she'd taken on the challenge of looking after the boat, getting the hang of seeking out the small leaks that were becoming more frequent now she was cruising more often, and patching them up with putty she'd bought at the nearby chandlery. She cleaned out the boiler regularly, had so far avoided diesel bug building up in the filters, and had, with Jas's help, found and repaired an exhaust leak in the engine. She had convinced herself she could be a solo liveaboard, but that didn't stop her missing her Willowbeck friends.

There was Valerie, who was the main reason she'd ended up back on the boat in the first place, and who she missed, despite her insistence that Maddy's presence was watching over them all. And while she was enjoying being part of Claire's troupe of floating traders, roving wasn't the most settling way of living. Once they'd run out of time here, they would have to move on again, so that Summer felt as if she was constantly running away from something – and hadn't she done enough of that already? There was one person in particular she didn't want to run away from. Since their aborted evening, Summer had been in touch with Mason by phone, but it didn't feel right, and she wanted to clear the air in person.

It had been a relief when, a few days after Mason had left her boat so abruptly, he'd texted her: *Sorry about the other night. I was caught off-guard, and I said the wrong thing. I should never have asked you to come back. M.* After that she'd phoned him, but it had gone straight to voicemail, and she hadn't been able to find out what 'caught off-guard' really meant, except that it was to do with seeing Claire.

After that he had sent her a photo of Archie with, she assumed, what had once been a bath towel torn to shreds in his mouth. He'd written: *As you can see, all the work I'm doing on Archie's behaviour is really paying off.* She'd laughed out loud and sent him a photo of Latte sitting on the café counter in response, telling him she was sad that her dog would rather be sold to a customer than stay with her.

Their relationship had slipped into an easy back-and-forth, always skimming the surface and never testing the deeper feelings that were developing. She knew that couldn't happen until she saw him, and, along with Harry's plight, it was her strongest reason for wanting to go back to Willowbeck. She sipped her wine and looked up. The stars were beginning to show, their clarity in the dark sky breathtaking, their reach so endless that she could imagine gazing at them forever, watching for the glimmering streak of a shooting star.

Moments like this were the best thing about living on a boat. The water was quiet around her, she had companionship, knowing her new friends were only a few feet away, snug on their own boats, and she had an unsullied view of the stars winking down on her. She knew that Mason would appreciate the view, and she wished he were with her. She felt a surge of longing, an ache in her chest, and so, with the wine working its way into her tired mind, she returned to her messages.

Sitting on the roof looking at the stars, she typed. *Wish you were here. Xx*

She felt nervous – could she really say that when there was so much unresolved between them – but it was entirely true, and they couldn't ignore what had almost happened in Foxburn. Maybe this was the first step towards talking about it.

It wasn't until she'd climbed down and was beginning to give in to sleep that she got a reply. *It's a good night for it*, Mason's text said. *Not the same place, but the same stars. M. PS. My roof is filthy.*

That weekend was the late May bank holiday and Summer was busier than ever, with a small fairground taking root in the park. The café was packed, and while Summer was elated at the custom, cracks were beginning to show in her one-woman business.

She didn't have time to clear the tables in between each sitting, which meant crockery was being moved to the side of the tables and she soon ran out of clean cups. But the cookies, muffins, brownies and scones she'd baked were popular, and she'd even attempted some rose-and-pistachio macarons. They didn't look as beautifully uniform as the recipe she'd found, but they tasted delicious and had allowed her to write a new note on her A-frame: *Stuff in a muffin, swoon at a macaroon, or try a gooey brownie with your coffee, juice or tea. Happy Bank Holiday!*

She'd started to pick out a few familiar faces in the weeks she'd been in Tivesham, and she realized that was something else she missed about Willowbeck – the regular customers, the cheery hellos and knowing what drink to make as soon as someone appeared in the doorway. She kept hoping to see the old woman who'd told her about stag parties and her dog Ginny, but then she remembered she wasn't in Foxburn any more, and that, if she wanted this new lifestyle, she would have to get used to a continual stream of new faces.

When she finally closed the café doors at six o'clock, she could barely feel her feet. She loaded the dishwasher, silently thanking her mum for kitting out the boat with all mod cons, and slumped on to her sofa. She could hear shouting from the fairground and toyed with the idea of asking Claire if she wanted to go on the dodgems and get some candyfloss, but she felt too comfortable to move. She leaned her head back on the sofa, closed her eyes and then, just as sleep was calling her, was jolted awake by a loud knock on the door.

Claire was standing outside, a figure in darkness behind her on the deck. Summer squinted, but couldn't make out who it was, her heart suddenly in her throat at the thought that it might be Mason. She opened the door and the figure moved into the light, and Summer's heart sank.

'I found this one wandering around on the towpath,' Claire said. 'He told me he was looking for the café with the cute owner.' She smirked, and then frowned when Summer didn't smile back. 'Are you all right? You look exhausted.'

'I'm fine,' Summer said, waving her away. 'Just been rushed off my feet. I'm sure you have too. Ross, what are you doing here?'

'Hey, Summer,' Ross said. He was wearing a pale-blue hoody, his face slightly tanned. 'You're looking great.'

Claire gave him a strange look and squeezed Summer's arm. 'Leave you to it?'

Summer nodded and stepped back, ushering Ross in. 'I'm afraid I don't have much to offer this evening, I've been so busy.'

'I know,' Ross said, 'bank holiday. I've brought provisions.' He held up a bottle of wine and a plastic bag, the scent of Chinese food wafting towards Summer and making her stomach rumble.

She gave him a weak smile, found plates and glasses and asked him to set up at a table in the café. Latte stayed close to her feet, whimpering occasionally, even once Summer had fed her a tin of her favourite dog food. 'What is it, Latte?' she asked, her tiredness and Ross's unexpected presence making her irritable.

The little dog pawed at her leg and Summer lifted her up, giving her a hug. 'I know,' she whispered, 'I don't want him here either, but how can I turn him away?' The dog appraised her with her big, dark eyes. 'You're right, I should just tell him to go, but I can't deal with an argument tonight.'

She washed her face and looked at herself in the bathroom mirror. She had dark circles under her eyes, but her cheeks had taken on a golden glow in the sunshine, her hair gaining natural highlights. She tried to imagine how she'd be feeling if it was Mason who'd just turned up at her door with dinner, and her stomach somersaulted. Silently cursing Ross, as well as her own weakness, she went to join him.

'How did you find me?' she asked, once they'd sat down and the food was served. Summer tried to keep her voice light. She didn't want to sound accusing, but she wasn't entirely comfortable either. As with Mason, Ross had stayed in touch with her via text, but she'd never given him her location.

'It's a funny thing,' Ross said. 'I was just messing about online, and now that I know someone who's living on board a boat, I browse some of the narrowboat websites. I came across this blog written by a guy named Jas – I think his name is – and he mentioned *The Canal Boat Café*. It was a stroke of luck, really. I knew you'd headed up the river, but this gave me the actual location. I thought you might be feeling a bit out on a limb.'

'I'm not,' Summer said, wondering whether to be worried or impressed at how he'd managed to track her down. 'I've made some good friends – you met Claire – and it was my decision to leave Willowbeck in the first place, to try somewhere new.'

Ross shrugged and smiled, either not picking up on – or choosing to ignore – her discomfort. 'Are you enjoying it?'

'Yes,' Summer said, 'I am.'

'It doesn't seem a great area. I didn't feel that safe walking from the car park. Aren't boats pretty vulnerable? How good are your locks?'

'Ross,' Summer said, putting her fork down. 'Why did you come? Because if you're just here to undermine my decision—'

'Hey, hey.' Ross held his hands up. 'Not at all. God, I'm sorry. I'm just – I haven't seen you for a while, and I care about you – I've been worried. I've been down to Willowbeck too, Valerie really wants you back, and I've seen some of your friends from the co-op in my shop. They said you've not been there, you haven't started any new projects, and the way you took off – it's just not like you, Summer. I came to see if you're OK.'

'Shit, the co-op. I should get in touch with them.' Summer rubbed her temples.

'See, you're not OK,' Ross said, his voice softening. 'I know I said you looked great, and you always do, but you look tired too, Summer. You're taking on too much by yourself, and I think you really need this,' he indicated the table. 'Let someone else look after you for a change, rather than doing everything alone.'

'I'm not alone,' Summer said. 'Claire's only a couple of berths down.'

'You know what I mean.' Ross gave her a gentle smile. 'It's taking its toll on you, and you need someone to talk to.'

'I just need a good night's sleep. It's bank holiday Monday tomorrow, so it'll be busier than ever.'

'I can help,' Ross said, shrugging. 'The shop's closed tomorrow, so I can be here and clear tables, wash up, whatever you need.'

Summer chewed on her spring roll and looked at him. She was tempted by the offer. There was nothing she'd love more than someone to help her, just to get her over the hump of bank holiday, to take some of the pressure off. But – other than the insinuation that he would want to stay in Tivesham rather than drive back to Cambridge – she knew that it would be a mistake. If she allowed him in this far, then things would get even more complicated.

She shook her head. 'That's so kind of you, Ross, but I'll be fine. I need to prove to myself I can do this on my own.'

'I wouldn't get in the way, I wouldn't even speak.'

'I know, and it's a generous offer, but I just need an early night and then I'll feel as fresh as a daisy. This, though, is a real treat. Thank you.' She smiled at him, and watched as his perma-grin faltered slightly.

'I've not seen much of Mason at Willowbeck. You were friendly with him, weren't you? I don't know, but he might have moved on.'

Summer shrugged, not willing to be drawn in and knowing

that, wherever he was, he had told her he was looking at the same stars as her.

'How's the shop?' she asked. She listened to him update her on work, the gigs he'd been to recently, an art festival in Peterborough, his constant, cheerful chatter somehow reassuring, reminding her of the way he had helped her through the worst time of her life. Whatever was happening with Ross now, she had to remember how much he'd been there for her, unwaveringly, and that reminded her that it was almost a year since her mum had died. The thought shocked her, and she choked on a mouthful, turning away to cough.

'Are you all right?' Ross asked, stopping mid-flow.

Summer nodded. 'Just a bit of rice down the wrong way.'

Ross gave her such a penetrating gaze that Summer felt the urge to run away from him and the café and into her cabin.

'I know it's still hard,' Ross said, 'and I know that you're desperate to show the world you can take this all on, but you have to give yourself a break. Why make it extra hard by moving away? This is nothing like Willowbeck. There were beer cans on the towpath, a bike wheel left chained to a lamppost after someone nicked the rest of the bike, and the fair in the park looks a bit dodgy to me. Claire – your friend – was telling me that she'd planned on hosting a music festival here, but has been really discouraged by the area.'

'Really?' Summer asked. She hadn't caught up with Claire in days.

Ross nodded. 'You're on your own, Summer. And you're exhausted.'

'Which is why I need to go to bed,' Summer said, trying to inject forcefulness into her voice. 'I'm sorry, Ross, and thanks so much for coming, but I can't stay up late.'

Ross pushed his plate away from him. 'That's fine. I just

wanted you to see a friendly face. And if you decide, as late as tomorrow morning, that you need help, then I'll be here. I'll always be a car ride away.'

Summer stood and hovered, waiting for him to do the same. She insisted he take the rest of the wine back with him, pressing the bottle into his hands. At the door he turned and wrapped her in a hug that she hadn't prepared for. She pressed her hands against his chest, trying gently to push him away, thinking how different it felt being inside Ross's arms to the tentative hug she'd had with Mason. Even though they'd left on uncertain terms, that embrace had been charged with feeling that was, in this case, entirely lacking.

'Stay in touch, Summer,' Ross said, bending to kiss her on the cheek.

'Thanks for coming.' Latte barked at him, and Summer wondered fleetingly whether it was a bark of goodbye or good riddance.

Bank holiday Monday dawned to sunshine. Summer had slept well, and she had meant what she'd said to Ross – she wanted to prove that she could tackle the café's busiest days on her own, just as her mother had done for years on the days Summer wasn't with her. She had packets of bacon and rolls, extra cakes and scones, along with some more macarons waiting in the kitchen, and was confident they would last through the day. She showered, dressed in jeans, a black T-shirt with an owl on it and a pair of super-comfy Skechers, and tied her hair in a ponytail. She was ready.

She opened up the bow door and let the warm summer air snake through the café, then sighed as she noticed the litter that had blown on to her deck from the fairground. There were empty coffee cups, popcorn bags and beer bottles, a discarded cuddly monkey that someone must have won and then got bored with, and endless bits of newspaper. Summer found she was actually tutting, just as her mother used to, as she put on gloves and found a black sack, and started tidying the deck. She threw most of it away, and then decided that the cuddly monkey could go in the washing machine and then sit alongside the wooden objects – her other deck-found treasure – and the crocheted cakes on the counter.

She crouched, leaning beneath the deck seating to get the last bits of rubbish, and then, turning to grab hold of a paper bag that was trying to blow into the river, noticed that the wood on the door below the lock had been scratched, the red paint missing. Summer frowned and ran her gloved hand over it, feeling a sudden chill. She glanced up at the park, but the fair seemed silent now, the marquees zipped up, stands boarded and shuttered until later that day.

Trying to brush away her unease, she went back inside and opened up. Everything was clean and sparkling, all her crockery and cutlery within easy reach. She'd ordered more takeaway cups and had bought freesias to decorate the tables, which she combined with some handpicked forget-me-nots to make attractive displays. She made herself a coffee, drank it while it was still too hot, and with Latte at her feet, went to put out the blackboard.

Come and rest your feet, allow yourself a treat, it's nice to be afloat, in the café on a boat.

It wasn't her best, but it would do. People would, at the very least, chuckle at the childish rhymes – wasn't that what Jenny had called them? She might well be right, but it hadn't seemed to put people off so far.

Ten minutes later, an incredibly tall man with a smile that stretched right across his face bent his frame inside the café, a girl of about four tottering along with her hand in his, her white-blonde hair in pigtails. 'Hello,' he said, 'are you open?'

'Of course,' Summer said. 'What can I get you?'

The man appraised the menu above the counter, chose a selection of macarons, a coffee and an orange juice. As soon as Summer turned to the coffee machine to grind the beans, the door opened again to reveal an older couple, sunhats on even though it was only just after nine. Summer smiled and asked them what they wanted.

It had begun.

The day was as busy as she'd imagined, and despite all her preparations and foresight, she had almost run out of cakes by four o'clock. She was tired, but she'd spent most of the day smiling. She didn't know if it was her involvement with Claire and the storytellers that had boosted her confidence, or if it was just that she was truly beginning to inhabit the role of café owner, but she was enjoying the interaction with the customers more with each passing day, and had found her own stories start to slip in to the conversation, no longer simply taking down orders and exchanging pleasantries.

The custom dwindled as the music from the fairground got louder, and people began gravitating towards the games and rides, taking advantage of the sunny evening.

'I'm not happy with their music choice,' Claire said, pushing open the door just as Summer was tucking the blackboard back behind the counter.

She looked as tired as Summer felt, her dark hair plastered to the sides of her face. 'I thought you embraced all music,' Summer said.

'I do, but only when I've chosen it.' Claire grinned. 'My boat is like an oven. Do you have anything cold?'

'Coke, lemonade, elderflower?'

'That one,' Claire said, flopping into a seat. 'Jas and Ryder fancy going over to the fair later. I told them that they were mad, and that I wouldn't be up for a helter-skelter even if I hadn't been working all day.'

'I'm almost tempted,' Summer said, bringing two bottles of elderflower to the table. 'But I might fall asleep in the waltzers. Let those pretty young things enjoy themselves, and we can put our feet up in front of the iPad.'

Claire laughed. 'God. Are we old?'

'No.' Summer shook her head. 'Just busy. Which is good, but . . . Ross mentioned you're not sure about holding the music festival here any more?'

Claire wrinkled her nose like a rabbit. 'It's got the space, as you can see, but I'm not sure it's the idyllic venue I thought it was. It's got no character, no little houses or fairy groves like Foxburn.'

'But would residents really want a music festival so close?'

'True,' Claire sighed. 'I just . . . I don't feel that inspired by the place. It might be back to the drawing board.'

'My deck was covered in litter today, and Ross said a bike had been stolen. And the music from the fair is a bit over-whelming – I keep thinking I can hear it even when the rides are closed.'

'The fair's moving on tomorrow,' Claire said, pouring her drink into a glass and taking a long sip. 'And litter's going to happen with any kind of event or festival, but there should be someone responsible for clearing up. Why has Ross been feeding you tales?'

'There wasn't a bike wheel missing the rest of the bike?'

'There may well have been, but that's a common enough sight just about anywhere. Who is Ross anyway, just a friend?'

Summer nodded. 'Quite a persistent one,' she said.

Claire's eyes widened, and she smirked. 'Ah. I get you. Sorry if I made things awkward by bringing him to your boat last night.'

Summer waved her away. 'You weren't to know. He's been a good friend, but he won't take a hint. He's determined to be there for me, even when I tell him I'm fine.'

'He's not a patch on Mason, then?'

Claire said the words so softly that at first Summer thought she'd misheard. She shook her head, looking down at the table.

'I'm sorry about what I said,' Claire said. 'It wasn't my place.'

'You were only telling me what you know.'

'You're still in touch with him?'

'A little bit.'

'And I don't need to ask if you still like him, because that's obvious.'

Summer sighed. 'I'd like to get to know him better,' she said. 'Not that I'm ignoring what you told me, but I need to find out for myself. And whereas Ross's help has at times seemed suffocating, it never feels like that with Mason.'

'That tells you everything, then. I'm pleased for you, Summer.'

'Pleased that I have a crush?'

'Pleased that you've maybe found someone. That's hard enough anywhere, let alone living on the river. I won't give you any more lectures.'

Summer looked at Claire, at her dark, messy hair, her expression never too far from cheeky. In the short time she'd known her, she'd found a good friend. 'Lectures are always welcome, as long as you're OK with me making up my own mind.'

'I'd be disappointed if you didn't.'

'So can I say something to you, too?'

Claire opened her arms wide. 'Shoot for the moon.'

'Ryder,' Summer started tentatively, watching Claire stiffen. 'He's a bit . . . manipulative. Charming, undoubtedly but . . . in my opinion, he's a classic bad boy.'

'One hundred per cent,' Claire nodded.

'And you're still interested?'

'I've known him a lot longer than you, and I *know* there's more to him. It's just hard to crack the surface. And as long as I know what I'm getting into . . .'

'Unlike Tania, you mean? Mason gave the impression of being serious about her, and then turned out to be the opposite.'

'That's the thing. As long as both of you go in with your eyes open, I don't see any harm in it.'

'What if you *think* your eyes are open, but then they turn out not to be?' She thought of Mason again and how, according to Claire's experience of him, she'd read him entirely wrong.

Claire sighed. 'That is a quandary I'm too tired to deal with right now.'

'Fair enough,' Summer said, smiling and pushing thoughts of Mason to the back of her mind. 'Now, let's blow off this funfair business and watch a film. I know it's a lovely evening, but after serving customers all day I'd be very happy to hibernate.'

'Done,' Claire said. 'Give me five minutes to tell the boys we're being the ultimate party-poopers, then I'll be with you.'

Chapter 12

Summer said goodbye to Claire at about midnight and had almost forgotten her weariness in her friend's company. Despite the awkwardness over Mason, she felt entirely comfortable with Claire. She was funny, confident, and sometimes brash – and in no small way reminded Summer of her mum.

She cleared up the wine glasses, snuck a bit of salami out of the fridge and gave some to Latte, then brushed her teeth and crawled into bed. The night was warm and she had the window open a crack, despite the fairground still going strong, the shouts and screams and waltzer music reaching her easily. Latte settled down in the crook of Summer's arm, and she closed her eyes.

She didn't know how long she'd been asleep, but suddenly Summer was wide-awake. It was pitch black in the cabin, and the sounds of the fairground had gone. Latte was standing on the bed, her small paws digging into Summer's thigh, and Summer could tell that she was alert. Her heart missed a beat and she leant up on her elbows.

'What is it, Latte?' The dog whimpered, jumping when Summer reached out to touch her. She was shaking.

Slowly, licking her lips, Summer reached for her phone. She pressed the button that illuminated the screen and saw that it was nearly three in the morning. The air coming in through the window was cool, licking around Summer's neck and shoulders. She hesitated, and when she couldn't hear anything, rested her head back against the pillow.

'Settle down, Latte.'

The dog didn't listen, just pawed at her and continued to whimper. As her eyes got accustomed to the dark, she saw that Latte was looking towards the bow of the boat, in the direction of the kitchen and the café. The little dog couldn't see beyond the cabin, but she was aware of something – something she was unhappy about. Goose pimples prickled on Summer's arms.

And then there was a loud bang and the sound of glass breaking, and Summer's heart was no longer thrumming, but banging. She brought her legs up to her chest, dislodging Latte and making her bark.

'Sssshhh, Latte,' she whispered desperately. 'Sssssshhhhhh.'

The banging continued and Summer recognized the sound of chair and table legs scraping across the floor of the café. She thought of the money from the till, which she removed and secured in the safe in the living area every night. She heard more glass smashing and a low, murmuring voice. She fumbled for her phone and, about to dial nine-nine-nine, realized she had help closer at hand. Her fingers shaking and her palms sweaty, she dialled Claire's number. The noises were unrelenting, seeming to get louder and closer all the time, competing with Latte's unrelenting barking.

Claire picked up on the fifth ring, her voice thick with sleep.

'Summer?'

'I think someone's on my boat,' she whispered. 'In the café.'

'Fuck,' Claire said, suddenly alert. 'Get out of there. We're coming, and I'll call nine-nine-nine on the way.'

Her heart pulsing in her throat, making it difficult to swallow, Summer climbed out of bed and pulled jogging bottoms and a jumper on over her pyjamas, her hands moving clumsily, as if she was doing everything submerged in sand. She grabbed hold of Latte and slipped through the cabin, through the tiny bathroom, to the door that led to the engine and then the stern of her boat.

The night air was cool, the water a black, bottomless hole, and the stern deck felt rough against the soles of her feet. Summer was consumed by fear. She felt the chill and the heat of it rushing through her, the taste of it in her mouth, thick and immovable, but she tried to even her breathing, tried to think clearly through the panic.

She crouched on the stern deck next to the tiller, afraid to step on to the towpath in case whoever was inside saw her and followed her out. Behind her, she heard another loud thump, the sound of metal clattering, and thought they must be in the kitchen, perhaps searching for the takings. Shivering, and with Latte whimpering against her, Summer squeezed her eyes closed. Should she be brave and confront them? She could barely stand, she was shaking so much.

There was a shout from the bow end, a voice she recognized, Claire's, and then Jas's and Ryder's, all calling out, loud and incoherent, making as much noise as possible. The light in the boat next to hers came on, and there were more noises from inside, the sound of someone moving quickly. For a horrifying second, Summer thought that they would try to get out past her, but then the commotion at the other end

213

got louder, and she heard Claire shout 'Come back here, you fucker!' Footsteps echoed on the towpath, more than one pair, and then she heard her name.

'Summer! Summer where are you? Are you OK? They've gone, Jas is after them.'

Grabbing on to the tiller, Summer hauled herself up. She stepped shakily down on to the towpath, and Claire, wearing a grey polka-dot dressing gown, rushed forward and embraced her and Latte.

'Oh God, are you all right? Fucking hell.'

'I'm OK,' Summer said, exhaling, her voice weak.

'Shit,' Claire murmured. '*Shit.*'

Summer pressed her face into Claire's shoulder. She could hear other people opening doors, coming off their boats to see what was happening, muttering, exclaiming, voices anxious or hazy with sleep. Summer pulled away from Claire when the sound of sirens cut through the air. Doug, Ryder and some of the other boat owners were clustered around them on the towpath, and Ryder put his hand on her shoulder. There were murmurings of reassurance and kind, apprehensive smiles, as everyone tried to offer her comfort without being sure what had really happened.

The two PCs, both male and, Summer thought, probably younger than she was, were calm and confident. Claire explained what had happened, that Jas had gone after the intruder down the towpath, and one of the policemen followed, even though Summer thought they must be long gone by now. The other encouraged Claire to take Summer on to her boat and, once they were all seated, and with coffee Summer could tell was laced with something much stronger, asked Summer questions.

She went over what had happened – waking up and hearing the intruder, calling Claire before making her way to the stern

214

– but she didn't have much to tell. She explained what was on board, where the safe was and where the keys were, and after a while the policeman left to investigate Summer's boat.

'Are you all right?' Claire asked, feeding Latte some cold cuts of beef from her fridge. 'It must have been such a shock.' Ryder hovered in the doorway. His swagger was gone, his expression one of genuine concern.

Summer nodded and sipped her coffee. She was still shaking, despite the warm clothes she'd pulled on, her teeth chattering constantly. The adrenaline was fading, but it left behind a cold wedge of fear that had appeared the moment she'd realized there was an intruder on her boat. 'It – it was scary,' she said. 'I didn't know what was going on, and then when I worked it out, I didn't know what to do. I didn't want to be trapped on board with them,' she said, her voice wavering dangerously.

'You weren't, you weren't,' Claire said, her voice soothing. 'You got out. You're safe.'

She poured more brandy into Summer's mug, but added no more coffee. The knock on the door made Summer jump, and both policemen appeared, followed by Jas, wearing a T-shirt and shorts, his trainers undone on his feet. His forehead was shimmering with sweat and he was panting. When he caught Summer's eye, he shook his head.

'Sorry, Summer, I didn't get him.'

'That's OK,' Summer said, but it didn't feel like it was. She didn't want the intruder to be out there, now that he knew the lock was broken, that he could gain access to her boat any time he wanted.

'We've looked over the boat,' the fair-haired policeman said. 'The lock's been broken and a couple of windows have been smashed, but from the list you've given us, nothing has been taken. He didn't get into the safe.'

'There is a fair bit of superficial damage, though,' the other policeman added.

'We can deal with that,' Claire said, with bravado. 'No worries.'

'We'll dust for fingerprints and we'll board up the door and windows, so you won't be able to go back to the boat tonight. We've got your statement, and Jas's, and we'll ask the other residents here if they heard or saw anything. The best thing you can do is try and get some sleep.'

Summer nodded, but she couldn't focus on what the policemen were saying to Claire, and watched in a daze as her friend showed them to the door. Claire, Jas and Ryder carried on talking, but she felt too exhausted to listen. She pulled her phone out of her pocket. It was nearly half four, almost time for the sun to come up.

'You can get in my bed,' Claire said, after Ryder and Jas had gone back to their boats. 'Do you want me to call anyone for you?'

Summer shook her head and pulled her knees up to her chest, wondering what her mum would have done, how she probably would have confronted anyone who tried to damage her beloved café, how she would have shrugged it off afterwards and used it as an excuse to redecorate.

'Hey, hey, Summer,' Claire said, sitting next to her on the sofa, 'shhhhhh.'

Summer hadn't realized that she was crying until she felt the wet on her cheeks. 'Sorry,' she murmured.

'What for? You've been through an awful experience.'

'I should just get on with it,' she murmured.

'Like hell,' Claire said. 'Please will you go and get some sleep?'

Summer shook her head. 'I'm fine here.'

'Right,' Claire said, sighing. 'Well, let me get you a blanket.

And can I borrow your phone a sec – I need to let the others know Jas is back safely, and I'm not sure where mine is.'

Summer unlocked her phone and handed it to Claire. She closed her eyes and an image of the dark, glistening water as she crouched on the stern deck came back to her, along with the panic of not knowing whether to stay or go, listening to the sound of someone ransacking her boat, and the café that she'd taken so much care over recently. She imagined the freesias and forget-me-nots amongst broken glass on the floor and swallowed down a sob.

Claire reappeared and covered her with a large, fleecy blanket, putting her phone on the sofa next to her. 'You're sure you don't want my bed?' she asked.

Summer shook her head and curled up under the blanket, bringing it up to her chin. Latte snuggled in close and Summer fell into a fitful doze, her body alert to every sound and every movement. She thought she heard voices, but her eyelids felt heavy and unwilling to open, her shoulders rigid with tension.

'Where is she?' the voice said, and Summer knew she must be dreaming because Mason was miles away, but it was Mason's voice, edged with anxiety.

'How bad is the boat?' said an older, deeper voice, and Summer recognized Dennis's calm tones, felt a flash of fondness for him, despite everything that had happened between him and Mum. Willowbeck was creeping back in, and Summer felt comforted by it. She turned over and tried to get comfortable, pulling the blanket up further, and heard Latte yip and jump off the sofa, leaving a cold patch where she'd been.

'Summer?' It was Claire now, gently shaking her awake. She forced her eyes open, turned to look at Claire and gasped when she saw the two figures behind her, crowded into the compact living area.

Mason and Dennis looked down at her, their faces tight with worry, the effect slightly dulled by Latte yipping happily in Mason's arms and trying to lick his chin.

Summer scrabbled to sit up, throwing off the blanket. 'What are they doing here?' she whispered. 'What's going on?'

'Now, don't be cross with me,' Claire said, her hand on Summer's knee. 'After what happened last night, I used your phone to call Mason. I thought you'd want a friendly face – not that I'm not friendly, but you've known him longer.' She glanced behind her. 'I thought he'd be reassuring.'

Summer swallowed. 'Hi.' She raised a hand in greeting.

'I had to come,' Mason said, 'after Claire phoned me and told me what had happened. How are you? Are you all right?'

Claire stood and slipped into the kitchen, and Dennis followed her, asking if she needed a hand making the tea.

'It's not even six o'clock,' Summer said, glancing at her phone. 'I can't believe you came straight away. I'm sorry Claire phoned you.'

'I'm not,' he said, sitting next to her on the sofa and setting Latte down. Archie was hovering in the doorway, but trotted forward to greet the Bichon Frise now that she was at his level.

'I'm sorry you've had to go through this,' Mason continued. 'I needed to see for myself that you were OK. *Are* you OK?' He squeezed her arm, and Summer felt a shiver of emotion at his kindness. He looked sleepworn, his hair all over the place, the grey T-shirt and dark jeans slightly creased, his dark-rimmed glasses masking his tiredness.

'I'm fine,' Summer said, 'except . . . I'm not, not really. I was so scared,' she whispered, the words tumbling out of her in Mason's presence. 'I felt like he was getting closer and closer to the cabin, that he was going to confront me and I would be trapped, that he could do anything . . .' She swallowed and coughed.

Mason leaned in, his arm squeeze becoming a hug, his citrusy-vanilla scent washing over her. 'It's OK now,' he said, 'you're safe.'

'But there's this wedge, right here.' She pulled back slightly and pressed her hand against her chest. 'It won't go away. Every time I close my eyes, I can see the dark water and I can hear him, moving among my things, on my mum's boat, getting nearer to me, and I feel like I can't breathe.'

'I know,' Mason said quietly.

Summer looked at him, at the dark brush of stubble where he hadn't had a chance to shave, the lines at the corners of his eyes, the intensity of his gaze overwhelming.

'It won't go,' she murmured.

'It will,' Mason said, reaching up to brush a strand of her hair away from her face. 'Not for a while, admittedly, but it will go.'

'How do you know?' Summer asked.

'It's unbearable at first,' he said, ignoring her question. 'It feels like it's crushing you, the weight of the memory, the fear, but it will go. It's only been a few hours, and being on the water will help.'

'But that's where it happened,' Summer said, though already thoughts of her own pain were being diluted by her curiosity, by how Mason could be so sure of how she was feeling. 'I know you said the water was calming, but how can it be, after this? How can I go back on to my boat?'

'Because we'll fix it. We'll fix the damage that's been done and soon you'll go back to being you, confident and happy and in charge of your café. Don't let one dickhead ruin this for you.'

'Is that what you did?'

'What?' Mason asked, his fingers still hovering at the side of her face, the light touch feeling like a burn.

'When you . . . felt like that. Did you turn to the water for comfort?'

He nodded gently, though suddenly she felt like he was somewhere else, and it was his reflection, pale and insubstantial, in front of her. 'I did,' he whispered.

'And what happened?'

'I've been here ever since.'

They sat in silence until Claire and Dennis returned with the tea, the four of them crowding into Claire's small living space, Latte and Archie in the centre, lapping up the attention. Summer was relieved to see that Latte didn't seem traumatized, and had greeted the Border terrier as enthusiastically as ever.

'We'll check out the damage,' Dennis said, glancing at Mason. 'You don't have to come, Summer, if you don't want to.'

Summer shook her head. 'I'll need to face it some time and I'd rather do it while you're both here.'

'Right you are,' Dennis said. 'And then will you be coming back with us, to Willowbeck?'

Summer gawped, unable to respond immediately. She could sense Mason watching her closely, though he didn't say anything.

'We'll be moving on from here in a few days,' Claire said. 'Tivesham hasn't been a great experience, to say the least, but there are much better places, friendlier and safer.'

'None safer than Willowbeck,' Dennis said cheerily.

'I'm not sure I can come back,' Summer murmured. 'What about Jenny?'

Dennis shook his head. 'You leave Jenny to me, love. Just because she's been aggrieved doesn't mean it's right for her to keep taking it out on you. I can have a word with her, and you've got a permanent mooring, haven't you?'

Summer nodded.

'But you can't head back just because this has happened,' Claire said, 'otherwise you're letting them win. Keep going with us, Summer, we'd be lost without you. I mean,' she sighed, exasperated, 'of course it's up to you, and you've had a shock, I know that, but I'm not sure how you'd be any safer in Willowbeck.'

'But you know everyone there,' Dennis said calmly. Summer stared at him, wondering why he was suddenly so intent on her coming back, when she couldn't do anything for him other than make his life more complicated with Jenny.

'Maybe I should see the boat first,' she said slowly. 'I – I don't know if I can think about that yet.'

'Are you sure you want to go now?' Mason asked. 'You could get some more rest.'

Summer gave a little shudder, but she stood before she lost her resolve. 'I'm sure.' She forced a smile, then strode out of Claire's boat and down the towpath towards *The Canal Boat Café*.

The door at the bow deck was boarded up, just as the policeman had said it would be, and so she led the way through the boat from the stern, feeling a slight flush as Mason, and then Dennis and Claire, followed her through her berth, where she'd discarded the covers in fear the previous night. She slowed as she reached the living space, but nothing seemed too out of place apart from the sampler that Harry had made for her, which was at a slight angle on the wall. The safe was behind it, and Summer moved it aside to check it was still locked after the police had investigated.

She stepped over the threshold into the kitchen and came

to a sudden halt, as if her blood had frozen to ice. Every implement, every spoon, whisk, knife and plate, had been hurled on to the small floor space. It looked more like a moment of madness than a methodical search for precious goods.

'Shit,' Mason breathed behind her.

Speechless, Summer took a step forward and felt Mason grip her shoulder. 'Careful,' he said, 'you haven't got any shoes on.'

Summer went back to the berth for her Skechers, and by the time she returned, shutting Latte and Archie in her cabin to protect their paws, the others had moved ahead of her. She picked through the mess on the kitchen floor and stepped into the café. This time her gasp quickly became a sob, and Mason straightened from where he'd been picking up bits of broken vase, concern etched on his face.

'Summer,' Claire said, 'I'm so sorry, but it looks worse than it is.'

Her towpath A-frame had been broken in half, and the counter swept clear as if by an angry arm; everything was on the floor, cake domes and crocheted cakes and wooden carvings. The coffee machine, at a glance, seemed OK, but coffee grounds and beans had been thrown across the floor, mingling with flowers and broken glass and upturned chairs and tables. The bunting had been pulled down, and her burglar had written a filthy word in red chalk across the blackboard. The cash register had been broken into and flung on the floor along with almost everything else.

Summer leant against the counter, her legs unsteady beneath her, and Dennis held her by the shoulders in a way that was both comforting and forceful. 'You'll be fine, Summer. It's a blip, a pretty grim one, but a blip nonetheless. All of this can be fixed — the window and the door and the till. Don't look at the whole, look at how easy it is to fix each part.' He got a damp cloth from the kitchen and wiped the blackboard clean. 'There,' he said. 'Ready for a new message.'

Summer nodded faintly, trying to feel the weight of Dennis's convictions. He gave her arm a quick squeeze and went back to picking up chairs.

Claire headed towards the kitchen. 'I'll get the dustpan and brush.'

'If you can find it in all that mess,' Summer said, offering her a faint smile.

'That's the spirit,' Claire said brightly. 'And I think you need to check on the coffee machine, because if it's not broken we're going to need espressos. I think we're all pretty much running on empty, isn't that right, boys?'

Neither of them answered, and Summer turned towards Mason in time to see Dennis gripping his shoulder, giving him a similar pep talk, though his voice was quieter, Mason nodding weakly in response to whatever he was saying.

Summer waited until Dennis had gone to look at the damage to the bow door, and then tiptoed through the mess towards Mason, feeling the crunch of broken glass beneath her feet. His face was pale and his dark eyes, usually so full of warmth, seemed distant. It was as if Mason was a mirror of the fear she felt, the terror of realizing she wasn't alone on the boat, the panic, all logical thoughts of escape deserting her. She was certain, at that moment, that his words about the wedge of fear, the memories fading, had been spoken from experience. She could see that Mason was struggling to hold her gaze, that he was desperate to turn away, but couldn't.

'I think Dennis is right,' she said softly, stopping in front of him. 'I think this can all be fixed, and that I can get the café running again soon enough. It looks bad now,' she said, gesturing around her, 'but once we start mending and righting things, it won't feel so bad any more.'

Mason nodded, his Adam's apple bobbing.

'And I think this,' she said, putting her hand against her chest again, 'will go too. It feels pretty scary right now, but I know that the memories will fade in time, and so will the fear.' She held his gaze. 'What happened to you, Mason?'

He sagged against the side of the boat and shook his head. Summer wanted to reach out to him, but she wasn't sure whether he would find it comforting or intrusive. She felt guilty that what had happened to her could cause him so much pain, so instead of physically reaching out, she did what she thought was the next best thing.

'What if I come back to Willowbeck?' she asked. Claire was sweeping up behind her and she heard the sweeping stop, so she moved closer to him. 'Do you want me to come back?'

Mason ran his hand over his jaw. 'I didn't think you were ready,' he said, 'and I was wrong to ask you, before.'

'I was defensive,' Summer said. 'I shouldn't have got angry. But now this has happened, everything's different. I don't want to be afraid, and I never felt afraid in Willowbeck. I was frustrated – with Jenny, with Valerie's insistence that Mum is still there, with Archie's bacon-stealing tendencies,' she continued, trying to raise a smile out of him, but it didn't work. She swallowed, wondering if it no longer mattered to him, if she'd left it too late, been away for too long. 'What do you think I should do?' she continued. 'Do you think I'm being a coward if I come back to Willowbeck, avoiding complications, my tail between my legs, or do you think it's the right thing to do?'

Mason sighed. 'You know what I think, Summer. But this

has to be your decision, and I don't want to force you into making one you'll regret.'

'You're not forcing me into anything.'

'I only came up here to check that you were OK. I was lucky, it would have taken too long on the boat, so I went to Dennis and woke them up – I've probably joined you in Jenny's doghouse – and he didn't hesitate. He drove me straight here.'

'Why are you telling me this?' Summer put her hand on his arm. His skin was warm, his muscles tensed.

He shrugged. 'I want you to know, Summer, that I care about you. But I care about you enough to let you do what you have to, even if that means never coming back to Willowbeck. I can't hold on to things forever. Life isn't like that – so much is out of our control. Maybe it's all down to fate.'

Summer narrowed her eyes. 'Have you been spending a *lot* of time with Valerie while I've been gone?'

This did raise a smile, and Summer felt a glimmer of hope.

'Maybe this is all part of it,' he said, 'taking the rough with the smooth, so that you believe in yourself and know that you can face the odds. You've got Claire here, and the other traders. It could work, it could be where you belong.'

'But . . . ?' Summer's gaze danced over his curls, followed the lines of his strong eyebrows, his lips. She was desperate for a 'but' from him.

Mason smiled and took her hand, and Summer knew that he wasn't going to help her.

It seemed as if she had lived a lifetime in the last twelve hours, her evening in with Claire a fading memory. She forced herself to relive the events of the early morning, the darkness and the noise and the fear, and the overriding thought, after it was over and the shock and cold was settling in, that the one person who could make her feel better was Mason. Not Claire or Valerie – though of course they were good friends – or even a longing for her mum to be there with her, but the scruffy, charming, captivating nature buff.

And now he was here, and he wasn't the assured person she had thought she was beginning to know. He had closed down after seeing Claire, and now, in the face of her devastated café, he seemed as shell-shocked as she was. But, far from putting her off, Summer realized she only wanted to know him more, to understand him and, if she could, to help him the way he had already helped her.

'Right,' she said, squeezing his hand and then letting go. 'Right, I think I know what I need to do. But first, I'm going to fix the bunting.' She hefted her damaged cash register back on to the counter and lifted the forlorn bunting, smiling when she realized that it hadn't been broken, just dislodged. Stretching on to her toes, Summer tied it back up above the blackboard, the black surface, still damp from where Dennis had cleaned it, glistening invitingly, waiting for a new menu and a new message.

Already, Summer knew what she was going to write on it.

A new message for a new direction – either north, further up the river with Claire and Jas, with *Water Music* and *The Wanderer's Rest*, or back to Willowbeck, to Valerie and Norman and Mason. There was no longer any doubt in Summer's mind as to which direction she would choose: she only wished she had her mum's compass with her to help guide the way.

226

Chapter 13

By the time Summer passed under the familiar brick bridge, just before Willowbeck, she could barely keep her eyes open. The journey down the river, from Tivesham back to *The Canal Boat Café*'s original home, had taken several hours, and the weather was hot and turning humid, almost stiflingly unpleasant. Sweat was running down her back, and she could feel the tightness of her skin on her cheeks and forehead where the sun had been hitting it for much of the day.

Latte and Archie were curled on the deck at her feet, their playfulness long since extinguished in the heat, their small bodies panting, Summer and Mason checking that the water bowl was always topped up. Summer was finding the gentle chug of her narrowboat increasingly soporific and couldn't wait to have a cool shower, slip into some fresh, loose clothes, and curl up on the sofa. But, she realized, she was lucky. After everything that had happened, she had escaped relatively unscathed. Tomorrow, the cleanup for *The Canal Boat Café* would begin, and Summer could start to put the nighttime break-in on her boat behind her.

Mason appeared with two cold bottles of lemonade from the café's fridge. 'I've put the money on the side table next to the sofa,' he said.

'You didn't need to do that,' Summer said, gratefully accepting the bottle and taking a long swig. 'You didn't need to do anything you've done, and you certainly don't have to pay for your refreshment while you're doing it.'

Mason shrugged and leaned against the boat, giving her a lazy smile. Summer knew he must be as exhausted as she was. His movements were without their usual energy and he'd replaced his black-framed glasses with sunglasses, so she could only guess at how tired he looked beneath them.

'Do you want me to take over for a bit?' Mason asked. They'd shared the steering all the way down the river, Mason refusing to leave Summer and go back in the car with Dennis. Summer had accepted his offer immediately, not wanting to be alone on the boat yet.

'I don't think it's worth it now,' Summer said, as they emerged from under the bridge and into the slightly narrowed river, the willow trees in full leaf, green and shivering above the blue water. Summer inhaled, her pulse increasing as the moorings came into view. There was Valerie's purple boat *Moonshine*, and the Black Swan on the hill, its picnic tables full of families and couples, groups of friends with pitchers of beer in the summer afternoon. Ducks and geese wove their way in between the tables searching for a spare chip or corner of a sandwich.

'Here we are,' she said, unsure whether it was relief, excitement or dread that was making her feel suddenly jumpy. 'Home sweet home.' She began the slow process of turning the boat round, negotiating it back into her residential mooring between *Moonshine* and Mason's boat, *The Sandpiper*. The visitor moorings were all full, the towpath as busy as the pub garden, with people enjoying the sunshine. Summer had a flash of memory, to the last days she had been here with her mum, the busyness and the heat, the almost carnival atmosphere. It was getting close to the anniversary of her mum's death, but she wasn't prepared to think about that now.

'I'll get ready with the ropes.' Mason disappeared, leaving Summer to focus on the manoeuvre, waiting while a yellow narrowboat called *Sunny Spells* chugged past.

'A café eh?' the helmsman called. 'Could have done with you this morning. Late night last night, and an early coffee would have been welcome.'

'Sorry!' Summer called. 'I'm back now.'

'Just as we're off.'

'You'll have to make a return visit, then.' Summer grinned.

'Might well do that,' he called and gave her a wave as he headed in the direction they'd just come from.

Summer tried to concentrate, keeping an eye on each part of the boat as she turned it slowly round. She was aware that lots of the pub visitors were watching with interest, ready either to applaud or laugh depending on whether she made it back into her mooring, or made a huge mess of it and ended up parked across the river, stopping the other boats from passing. A couple of months ago she wouldn't have felt remotely confident, but being with Claire and the other roving traders, moving from one mooring to another, had given her invaluable experience, and she slid *The Canal Boat Café* into its mooring with barely any to and fro. Mason hopped on to the towpath and tied the ropes, flourishing his hands in Summer's direction when a group of friends sitting at one of the pub's picnic tables gave them some half-hearted applause.

231

Summer turned off the engine and gulped down the rest of her lemonade. Mason joined her, and the dogs, perhaps sensing the sudden stillness of the boat, woke up and raised their heads expectantly.

'That,' Summer said, leaning against the boat, 'was a very long day.' She turned to look at Mason. 'But I couldn't have done it without you. Thank you so much for all your help, for coming to my rescue.'

'It was the least I could do,' Mason said.

'Why? You don't owe me anything.'

Mason shook his head. 'I'm not sure, after our walk, the way we left things . . .'

Summer hesitated. She wanted to clear the air properly, but wasn't sure she'd do the subject justice when she was so tired.

'At least now we'll have a chance to talk. If you want to?'

'I'd like that. What will you do now?' He didn't say it, but Summer knew he was talking about the wrecked café, the inevitable clearing-up process. After Summer had made the decision to move back to Willowbeck, she had contacted the police. With very little to go on, they said she was free to move on, that they'd be in touch if they had any news. Claire, on the other hand, hadn't been quite so relaxed about Summer's decision.

'I'm not going to do anything tonight,' Summer said. 'I'm going to have a shower and then find some food. How about some chips at the pub?'

Mason pushed his sunglasses on to his head. 'Really?'

'I need to thank Dennis, and now that I've made the decision to be a permanent fixture in Willowbeck, I need to face Jenny head on. Not to confront her, but I need to be assertive, to prove my place here. I want us to get on,' she said. 'It's going to take a while, I know, but I'm determined to do it.'

'I'm all for that,' Mason said. 'And I've probably got some making up to do myself, after beating their door down in the middle of the night.'

'Which is also down to me,' Summer reminded him.

'You didn't ask to be burgled,' he said, his voice softening. 'But I did feel helpless, having no wheels of my own, unable to be with you as quickly as I wanted without help from elsewhere. I'm lucky Dennis was so accommodating.'

'And I'm lucky that I ended up with two knights in shining armour. I'm really grateful for you coming, for being there, for travelling back with me. I've lived my life fairly independently for a long time and I guess you don't realize how alone you are until something like this happens. This has made me see that I'm not on my own at all – you, Dennis, Claire . . . Valerie too. Amongst all this, it's the most heartening thing.' She felt a swell of emotion and swallowed it quickly, putting it down to tiredness.

'The boating community looks out for each other,' Mason said, 'but on a personal level, I'm glad that I was able to come.'

'Even if you did have to see Dennis in his pyjamas.'

Mason gave her a sideways look. 'I'm pretty sure he doesn't wear any.'

Summer laughed and screwed her nose up. 'Stop there, please. Right, shall I meet you at seven? I'll ask Valerie too.'

'Done.'

Summer watched him click his fingers at Archie. To her surprise, the disobedient Border terrier sprang up immediately and bounded after him on to the towpath. Summer started laughing and Mason looked at her, eyebrows raised innocently.

'What?' he asked.

'Have you drugged him?'

Mason grinned and stepped on board *The Sandpiper*, his dog close at his heels.

After one of the most satisfying showers of her life, and feeling much fresher and almost awake, Summer stepped off the stern deck and on to the towpath, Latte alongside her. The pub seemed busier than ever, the humid weather making people seek out cool beers and the breeze coming off the river. In denim shorts and a black vest top, and after a day under the full force of the sun and its reflection bouncing off the water, Summer was looking forward to spending the evening in the shade of the pub.

She knocked on the door of *Moonshine* and it took only a few moments for her mum's best friend to fling open the door, her face a picture of surprise as she saw Summer standing there.

'You're back!' Valerie squealed, flinging her arms around Summer, wrapping her in the musty scent of incense. 'When did you arrive? Why didn't you tell me? Summer,' she held her at arm's length, her smile wide and sparkling, 'this is wonderful.'

'It is . . . it's a long story,' Summer said. 'But I was wondering, will you join me and Mason for some food at the pub? Outside, if we can find a table.'

Valerie narrowed her eyes. She was wearing a long, sleeveless green dress, the fabric with a faint shimmer, her skin pale, her red hair tied away from her face. 'You're voluntarily suggesting we go into Jenny's domain? What happened to you out there on the river?'

Summer laughed. 'A lot happened, and I'll explain it all while we eat. Will you come?'

'Wild dogs couldn't keep me away. Not you, Latte,' she said, crouching to give the Bichon Frise a hug.

'I think Latte is as ferocious as a teddy bear,' Summer said. 'I'll see if I can find a table.'

There was one at the top of the hill, set snugly up against the wall of the building, with a good view of the narrowboats and the river. Summer tied Latte's lead to the table leg, and moved the large water bowl within her reach. She'd left Valerie getting ready and there was no sign of Mason yet, so she sat and waited, not wanting to leave Latte alone while she went inside. When Valerie arrived, she went to order the drinks, silently berating herself for the nerves she felt as she pushed open the heavy wooden door.

The interior of the pub was deliciously cool and Summer approached the bar. She'd hoped it would be Dennis or one of the other staff members there, but she'd spotted Jenny's dark hair and upright frame almost as soon as she walked in. She took a deep breath.

'Jenny,' she said, keeping her voice even and, hopefully, bright.

Jenny's expression was wary but, Summer noticed with a small glimmer of hope, not downright angry. 'Summer, I heard you were on your way back. I'm sorry about the break-in, that can't have been pleasant.'

Summer knew she was gawping and struggled to respond. 'Thank you,' she managed. 'It wasn't nice, but I'm very grateful to Mason and, of course, Dennis, for coming to find me, especially in the middle of the night.'

Jenny nodded and gave her a quick, cold smile. 'What can I get you?'

Realizing that Jenny wasn't yet ready for chitchat, Summer ordered wine for her and Valerie, and one of the local ales for Mason. 'Are you doing food this evening?'

'Of course.' She handed Summer a menu. 'We're cooking until nine, and we've got an excellent range of desserts if you want to indulge your sweet tooth. Lots of cakes, all freshly cooked. I've had more baking time than usual today, due to being woken up at an ungodly hour. You have to find your silver lining anywhere you can, I suppose.' She gave Summer another tight smile and Summer returned it, her shoulders dropping slightly.

'Thanks,' she said. All was clearly not forgiven, and she wondered how long Jenny's half-truce would last. It seemed she needed to thank Dennis for more than just pitching up to rescue her. Summer took the menu and her tray of drinks into the evening sunshine. She sat next to Valerie and they clinked glasses.

'How did it go?' Valerie asked.

'It was only mildly chilly,' Summer said. 'I think Dennis has told her to be nice. I'm not sure it'll last, but if I keep making an effort – who knows?'

'Stranger things have happened,' Valerie said.

'Have they?'

Valerie sighed. 'No. Not even in my life.'

Summer laughed, knowing Valerie was alluding to her readings and ghost sightings, the side of her life that Summer couldn't quite grasp, and which had, not too long ago, been the cause of their falling out. That Valerie was prepared to make fun of herself showed Summer that she had truly relaxed and Summer wondered what the cause could be. Was it the presence in Willowbeck of a red and gold and black boat, and its laid-back occupant? Mason seemed to make friends everywhere he went – and she was sure he had a calming influence on more people than just herself. Except she was also beginning to realize that his easy humour was hiding something, and she was eager to find out what it was.

But she had time for that. She was back in Willowbeck, surrounded by her friends, and she needed to focus on working hard as the summer flourished and the warm weather brought customers to the café. She thought of Claire, the way she had been reluctant to let her go, agreeing that the decision was Summer's but telling her in no uncertain terms that she wasn't happy about it.

'You belong on the river,' Claire said, when Summer had told her what she'd decided.

'Willowbeck is on the river,' Summer said. 'You should come.'

Claire had shaken her head. 'We're travelling north for now. You should be with us – I've got so used to having you as part of our party, being able to gang up on the boys. Things are going to be boring without you.'

'Your life will never be boring,' Summer had said. 'And we'll stay in touch.'

'I'm going to send you new recipe ideas all the time, and when I do make it to Willowbeck, I expect to get a taste test of each and every one.'

'Righto.' They had hugged, and Summer had known that, even if she wasn't travelling with Claire and *Water Music*, they would continue to be good friends and, hopefully, see each other often.

She gazed out at the river, the Canada geese waddling between tables, not shy about stretching their long necks up, seeking out scraps of pub food, customers laughing or exclaiming angrily. Summer found she was smiling.

'So,' Valerie said, 'are you going to tell me about your adventure? What made you come back here? Last time we spoke you were enjoying cruising up the river with Claire and her friends.'

'Ugh,' Summer said, resting her elbows on the table. 'There was a bit of an incident.' Had it really only been that morning? The day seemed so different, it was as if she was in another country, instead of just a few miles away. Sunshine and laughter and the shimmering blue of the river, so different to the black depths she had crouched close to while someone ransacked her boat.

'An *incident?*' Valerie's voice was sharp. 'What happened?'

Summer shifted on her chair, took a sip of her wine, and told her.

Valerie stayed quiet, but her eyes grew wider, her body more tense as Summer spoke, tension returning to her own shoulders as she recounted the noises that had woken her, her desperate call to Claire and then creeping towards the stern, the noises following her, and her feeling of being trapped as she wondered whether jumping on to the towpath would expose her. She sipped her wine, trying to quench the dryness in her mouth, and finished her story with Mason and Dennis showing up, the way they had all – Claire included – helped her when she went back on to the boat to face the damage.

'Summer, my dear,' Valerie said, 'was this really only last night?'

Summer nodded.

'You're incredible. I hope you'll forgive me for saying this, but I cannot imagine the Summer I greeted in February bouncing back from something so horrendous quite so quickly. That you're sitting here now, maybe looking a little

238

tired, granted, but as smiley and sparkly as you are, is a testament to your strength. It's the Maddy in you.'

'It is?' The thought had crossed Summer's mind too. She had been asking herself, as she approached every decision about the café, and about life on the river: *what would Mum do?* But to hear Valerie say they were similar was, to her, proof that maybe she *could* be as bold and as bright as her mum had been.

'There is a lot of her in you,' Valerie continued. 'So, so much, in your eyes, in your smile, and in your determination.'

'I'm discovering that you have to be proactive and deter-mined living on a boat,' she said, trying to defuse the emotion that was building up. Her tiredness meant she was already on the edge of an unnecessary sob, and Valerie's words were taking her closer. 'When I think of the things I had to do in my flat – change a light bulb, hoover, take the bins out – it was all so easy. On *The Canal Boat Café*, a weird noise usually means taking things apart, repairing, cleaning things out. It's like the boat's another person, and a very high-maintenance and temperamental one at that.'

'And yet you're smiling,' Valerie said.

Summer shrugged, and then gave a wide wave as she watched Mason hop off *The Sandpiper* and scan the grass for them, Archie eager to get ahead of him and amongst the geese.

'I am,' she said. 'I love it. When I saw the café this morning after the break-in, I was devastated.'

'Understandably.'

'Not just because it meant a lot of work, but because someone had harmed *my boat*, they'd hurt her, and I hadn't been able to protect her from it.'

'Oh, Summer,' Valerie said, 'you're turning into a true river creature.'

'Like an otter?' Summer laughed.

'Who's an otter?' Mason asked, sliding easily on to the bench. He was facing Summer, and she could see where the day spent under the sun had brought out a few light freckles along his cheeks. His glasses were gone, his hair was damp and extra curly from the shower, and he was wearing a faded orange T-shirt and grey shorts. While the tiredness was evident as a few extra lines round his eyes, he too seemed more relaxed to be back in Willowbeck and at the end of their unpleasant adventure.

'*I'm* an otter,' Summer said. 'Valerie said I was a river creature, so I picked otter. Water voles are cute, but I hope that, now at least, I'm a bit bolder than a vole.'

Mason nodded, and held his beer up in silent thanks, before taking a long sip. 'Otters are impressive. They like their own territory though, so apart from when they're breeding they're pretty solitary. I can't imagine an otter inviting every other creature along the river into their holt for cake and bacon butties.'

'You're taking us a bit too literally, Mason dear,' Valerie said.

'All I'm saying is that you're much more sociable,' Mason said. 'More like a lapwing.'

'What are they like?'

'They're beautiful birds,' Mason said, and then stopped, his eyes meeting Summer's and holding her gaze. 'And they live in large flocks. But they're becoming rarer in the UK.'

'Something to be treasured, then?' Valerie asked, reaching over and squeezing Summer's hand.

'Not to be taken for granted,' Mason agreed. 'Thank you for the beer.'

'Doesn't it feel like the most delicious, most welcome drink you've ever had?' Summer said. 'Just like the shower I had when we got back. I'm savouring everything that's not hot and sticky and tiring. Not that I don't love cruising up the river, but it was a bit of a struggle after last night.'

'I don't know,' Mason said, 'maybe you would have got cold feet if you hadn't done it straight away. If Claire had helped you to mend the café, maybe you would have carried on with them.'

'I could have waited,' Summer said, 'but I didn't want to. I was ready to come back here. Even if the break-in hadn't happened, I was beginning to get tired of roving, of feeling unsettled.'

'I thought you loved the lifestyle with Claire and her friends?' Valerie asked.

'I did, I'm not at all sad that I did it, but I don't know – this just feels right.' She swept her arms wide, taking in Willowbeck's idyllic summer vista, the cheerful, chatting people, the gentle riverside hum. When she thought back to Foxburn, and Tivesham, she realized they weren't a patch on Willowbeck. 'It was time to come back. This is where I belong.'

This time when she said it, she meant it wholeheartedly. She was even sitting at one of the pub tables – she'd purposefully gone into Jenny's territory – and it felt OK. She lifted her glass, and Mason and Valerie clinked theirs with hers.

'I think it's chip time,' she said. Archie looked up, his eyes alert. Summer laughed. 'That's not up to me, Archie. That's up to Mason.'

'Or Archie,' Valerie said.

Mason tried to look affronted, but he was smiling. 'Want some help?'

Summer shook her head. She thought the more she went into the lion's den, the less fear the lion would hold for her, and would maybe begin to get used to her too. But this time Jenny was nowhere to be seen and she ordered the food from Dennis.

'I can't thank you enough,' she said, leaning over the bar to give him a peck on the cheek. 'You and Mason really saved the day.'

Dennis brushed her compliments off, but she could see the glimmer of pleasure in his eyes. 'We weren't there when it happened.'

'I know, but you came straight away. You made me face up to things, you wouldn't let me wallow in self-pity for long.'

'Self-pity does nobody any good, and you just need to be shown the light at the end of the tunnel. In your case, it's a grim-looking tunnel but it's pretty short.'

'I'm going to start the clean-up tomorrow,' Summer said. 'Mum would have used it as an opportunity, someone telling her to do a bit of renovation. I'm going to do the same.'

Dennis nodded, his smile sad, his eyes bright. 'You do that,' he said softly. 'I'll bring your chips out to you when they're ready.'

Summer thanked him and turned away.

'And, Summer,' he said, and she turned back. 'You've got a good one there. Mason,' he added when she frowned. 'He's a top-notch bloke.'

She wanted to tell him that she didn't really have him, that she didn't know *what* they had, but instead she just nodded and smiled, and gave Dennis a thumbs up which, a moment later, seemed ridiculous.

'Summer,' Valerie said as soon as she appeared, 'you're going to need to make a birthday cake!'

Summer trailed her hand along Archie's warm fur and then sat back down. 'Why?'

'Because young Mason here is turning thirty-five.'

'Wow!'

Mason laughed. 'It's not *that* old.'

'I thought you were younger.'

'My dashing good looks?' Mason flashed her a grin and Summer's stomach responded with a backflip.

'What kind of cake?' she asked quickly. 'Chocolate, coffee, Victoria sponge?'

'How about red velvet?'

Summer gasped and hit him on the arm, Mason's words taking her back to the first day they'd met, when Jenny had provocatively left a red velvet cake on Summer's deck, and Summer had given it, angrily, to Mason. 'You'll end up with no cake if you keep going like that!'

'Sorry, sorry. It was irresistible.'

'Stop complimenting her cakes.'

Mason rolled his eyes.

'We *are* about to eat her chips,' Valerie said.

'That's different, I don't cook chips.' Summer grinned and sipped her wine. 'When is your birthday?'

'The tenth of June,' Mason said. 'But honestly, don't worry. I don't do anything any more, I don't know why I mentioned it.' He ran a hand absent-mindedly through his quickly drying curls, and bent down to stroke the dogs.

While he was distracted Valerie made wide-eyes at Summer and Summer gave her a thumbs up, this time feeling that the gesture was justified. There was just over a week to go, and Summer thought that was enough time to plan something special. Her own birthday – her thirty-first – had been in October, and it had been the first time that she hadn't felt like celebrating much, with such an important person missing.

She wondered what had made Mason give up on birthdays, whether it was just his solitary lifestyle on the river, or something more. Surely if they did something small, with just the few boating residents of Willowbeck, then he wouldn't mind – he would know that there were people who cared about him. Summer wanted to show him how true that was.

Dennis arrived with their cheesy chips and gravy and they dug in, Mason and Summer both quickly realizing how ravenous they were. The bowls were soon empty and Summer was licking her fingers, but Archie and Latte seemed disappointed with their meagre pickings, and Latte put her paws on the bench, asking to be let up. Summer obliged, and Latte licked her cheek.

'I'm sorry, Valerie,' Summer said suddenly, 'I haven't asked you how things have been here.'

'Your adventures have been much more interesting than mine,' Valerie said, laughing. 'But everything's been running smoothly here. Harvey keeps me on my toes, Mike's a very obliging lap cat, and my client list is as strong as ever. I've been keeping busy, but I didn't have a premonition of your break-in,' she said, frowning slightly. 'I believed you were well and happy, in good hands.'

'I don't need to be in anyone's hands,' Summer said, 'I'm fine. But maybe I was . . . too far away for you to know what was going on.' She shrugged, knowing how lame that sounded. She had no idea how it worked.

'I should have known,' Valerie said. 'I wish I'd been able to be there for you.'

'You're here now,' Summer said. 'And I had Claire and the other traders, and then of course Dennis and Mason.' She

244

looked at him, realizing how much emptier and more hollow she would have felt if he hadn't turned up, if she'd made the journey back to Willowbeck on her own.

'Mason,' Valerie said, 'you're a treasure.'

Mason shrugged and Summer saw colour rise to his cheeks. 'Does anyone want another drink?'

He hurried inside, barely listening to their orders, and Summer found herself laughing. 'He's not great at taking compliments, but I really don't know what I would have done without him.'

'He's taken quite a liking to you,' Valerie said. 'That's as plain as day.'

Summer bit her lip. She hoped that was true, but she couldn't shake Claire's words, the knowledge that he'd broken Claire's friend's heart, the way he'd backed off when Claire had appeared and he'd, in a sense, been found out. But she was back in Willowbeck, *The Canal Boat Café* alongside *The Sandpiper*, and so she had all the time in the world to get to know the real him.

A wind shivered around her and Summer looked up to see that the perfectly blue sky was being swallowed by churning grey clouds. The humidity was still strong and there was a smell of rain in the air.

'I think there's a storm on the way,' she said.

'About time too,' Valerie said. 'This humidity's been creeping up mercilessly for days now.'

Summer gave an involuntary shudder. She loved the sound of rain pounding on the roof of the boat and the surface of the river, the flash of lightning. She felt anticipation deep down in her stomach, a sense of hope and excitement, a future at Willowbeck with her café and the people she loved around her.

When Mason reappeared with the drinks, Summer gave him her biggest grin. She couldn't help it.

'What?' Mason asked, laughing. His eyes crinkled at the edges, dark and sharp despite his tiredness, and Summer had to drag her gaze away.

'I'm happy,' she said. 'This is how things should be. I know Jenny and I have still got some working out to do, and that the café's in a state, but everything else is right. Summer at Willowbeck is beautiful – and before you make a joke, I'm *not* talking about me.'

'You could be,' Mason said quietly, and now Summer couldn't look away. His gaze went right through her, and she could see intent there. Was he really a love rat? Was this all part of his game? Summer couldn't believe it.

It was only when the first, fat raindrops fell on to them, one dropping into her wine, and sudden, deafening thunder crashed through the air, that they looked away from each other.

A mad panic followed, people rushing from their picnic tables, jackets on heads, half-full glasses clutched against them, squeals and shouts, half of consternation, half of childish glee, at the sudden thunderstorm. Summer, Mason and Valerie were closest to the door and so made it inside quickly, though Mason had to stop and shoo a Canada goose out of the doorway, the large bird hissing at him and flapping his wings. Latte and Archie scampered in ahead of them, Latte yelping at the geese.

They sank into a booth in the far corner, the pub quickly filling up, people tracking water on to the floor and shaking their damp hair. Dennis looked stunned, a pint paused in mid-pull, and for a few moments the sound of the rain bashing against the windows drowned out all other noise.

The pub seemed gloomy under the sudden, intense cloud cover until someone flung on all the lights. A moment later, lightning flashed intensely white and the following thunder sounded directly overhead, eliciting squeals from some of the customers.

'You were saying something about summer in Willowbeck?' Valerie said ruefully.

'I was,' Summer said, getting her breath back and wiping water off her face. 'Isn't it wonderful?'

They all agreed it was.

Chapter 14

The following day, Summer woke with her head full of plans for the perfect birthday celebration. She would bake a cake, get some balloons and a couple of bottles of prosecco, and decorate the café. She could imagine it with streamers, sparkling confetti on the tables, the warm breeze wafting in through the open windows, carrying with it the scent of summer flowers. They could even sit on the tables on the towpath, as long as the weather was good.

It would be small and select – Mason, obviously, and Valerie and Harry and Tommy, Greg if he was around, maybe even Norman. She desperately wanted to invite Dennis, and wondered if it was something Jenny would stretch to. After all, Mason's friendship with them shouldn't be compromised just because he was also friends with her.

She stretched and wriggled her toes, and Latte jumped on to the floor with a little squeak. There was no yapping, as she'd done every morning when they were roving. Summer looked at her fur-ball dog, her little pink tongue and her wagging tail, and knew that the Bichon Frise was happy to be back here too. Summer wondered what Latte would think of balloons, and how pretty they would look bobbing up to the low ceiling of the café, and then she remembered.

There would be no party in her café, there would be no *café* in her café until she had fixed the damage. The door, the broken vases and cups, the cash register, all needed mending or replacing.

'Ugh.' Summer pulled the duvet off, showered and dressed and went into the galley. All the kitchen implements that had been on the floor were now on the counters, and though Claire had swept the floor, nothing was in its rightful place. She fed Latte, finding her bowl under a pile of tea towels, and loaded everything she could into the dishwasher. At least it was an opportunity to give everything a deep clean.

In the café, Summer gazed around her, feeling a waver of uncertainty, a glimmer of defeat, and then exhaled, shaking her head. Bright sunshine was streaming in through the windows, picking out all the damage. At least the vases and flowers were gone, the detritus on the floor cleared away, but there were the bigger repair jobs to take care of.

Summer turned on the coffee machine, thankful that the most expensive and crucial piece of equipment had foiled the burglar. She could still offer tea and coffee through the hatch while things were being fixed, and then remembered that her beloved A-frame had been broken.

With a strong, sugary coffee, Summer sat at one of the least damaged tables and made a list. Her mum had gone to a wholesaler in Cambridge when she needed to stock up, and Summer knew she could easily replace the vases, the broken crockery, the cash register and the A-frame. The broken door and window wouldn't be so easy, and she had no idea who her mum had used when she needed repairs – she was sure Maddy had a small address book, but Summer thought that must have gone when her brother, Ben, cleared everything out.

Summer grabbed her bag, put Latte's lead on and locked up the boat, leaving through the engine room at the stern as the bow door was still boarded up. As she got closer to the car park, she realized that her Polo had been sitting there for a couple of months, unused, and that the parking charges had started again at the end of March. Her insides recoiled at the thought of the parking fine she would have to pay, and as she approached she saw a white ticket on the windscreen. She walked up to it and, taking a deep breath, looked down to see what the damage was. It read:

Permit Approved. Ask at Willowbeck Butcher's.

Summer grinned and hurried round to the front of the row of shops. Adam looked up as soon as she walked in. 'Thirty rashers of bacon, young Summer?'

'Not today, today is just a huge thank you for sorting my car out.'

Adam waved her away. 'It's no bother. I knew you'd gone, but didn't think you'd want to abandon your little car, even if she is on the rusty side. I've got a proper permit for you out the back, but didn't want to break in to put it on the dashboard. Then it really *would* have looked abandoned.'

'I appreciate it.'

'You're back again?'

Summer gave him a rueful smile. 'It was good to get away for a while. But it helped me to realize that, as beautiful and interesting as the river is, my home is here.'

Adam chuckled. 'Of course it is. Nobody can resist Willowbeck's charms for too long.'

'And I will be back for bacon, I just need to do a bit of repair work first. But you can expect good, steady custom from me from now on.'

'Glad to hear it.'

'And let me know how much the permit is. I'll pop in later with the cash.'

Adam waved her a goodbye and, to Summer's surprise, her little car started first time. Latte sat on the passenger seat as Summer chugged through the vibrant countryside towards Cambridge. It felt strange driving these familiar roads after such a long time, strange even to be at the wheel of a car, instead of the tiller. But she had the window open, the radio on and, while the café was looking forlorn at the moment, Summer knew that some elbow grease and a bit of investment would soon make it as right as rain. After all, she and Valerie had fixed it once before – there was nothing stopping them doing an even better job this time.

The wholesaler met all her needs and she emerged with a boot full of crockery and vases, balloons and bunting, a state-of-the-art cash register and, her most exciting purchase, a new, sturdy A-frame and a set of chalk marker pens. Summer was already imagining the beautiful words she could write, the messages that would entice customers into sampling her cakes and coffee.

Back on the boat, Summer set to work, packing away her new items, setting the cash register on the counter. Licking her lips, a fresh coffee at her side, she got out her chalk pens and wrote a message, savouring every moment, using different chalks and drawing a steaming cup of tea in the bottom corner. *No tables today, we're blowing cobwebs away, but I'm still serving drinks, so come and get your latte.* Summer knew she could put the tables out on the towpath, but she had so much to sort out inside that she thought doing both would be counterproductive.

Before she put the new sign out and opened up the hatch, she walked up to *The Sandpiper*. It was nearly eleven – she had spent far too much time at the wholesalers – and she assumed Mason would have been long up. Their evening at the pub had been fun, relaxed and comfortable, so why did she feel so nervous? She hadn't yet been on board his boat, and her heart was in her throat when she knocked on the glossy, black doors.

She didn't have to wait long for Mason to open them. In his glasses and a scruffy khaki T-shirt and jeans, he looked irresistibly crumpled.

'Hi,' he said, surprise in his voice.

'I'm sorry to disturb you. If you're busy I can come back later.'

'No, it's fine, come in.' He stepped back, inviting her forward. Summer stepped inside and, before she'd had a chance to look around, was greeted enthusiastically by Archie. She stroked the Border terrier and he looked up at her expectantly.

'I'm sorry, I've left Latte on my boat. I didn't think I'd be long.' She gazed around her, her mouth falling open. The inside of Mason's boat was beautiful, and unusual. It was decked out in white oak or alder with black and red accents, and was obviously done to a high standard. She was standing next to a small kitchen table, and beyond that the galley was open, with black, marble-effect counter tops, the line of the cupboards curved, like a wave. Behind that was the living space, where she could see a sofa, a television built into a cupboard against the wall, and a large iMac on a tiny desk. Everywhere she looked, there were curves. The large,

252

rectangular windows were interspersed with portholes, there was a curved edge to the desk and round, red cushions on the black sofa. The floor was wood, apart from in the galley where it was black and white checkerboard.

Summer had always known that her living area was squashed, because the café took up half the space, but it had never really sunk in until she saw how spacious the other residential boats seemed. This, though, was something else. It exuded space, light, and calm.

'Wow,' she breathed. 'Your boat is stunning.'

'It's been a long time coming, but I'm finally happy with it.'

'Where do you put your muddy walking boots?'

Mason laughed. 'That's your most pressing question?'

'It's beautiful, so full of character, so – so perfect.'

'And I'm not?' He grinned. 'Do you want a coffee?'

'Yes please,' Summer said, but she was thinking of the famous *Bridget Jones* line. *I like you, very much, just as you are.* She trailed after him, taking in the tiny touches of detail, a sheep-shaped kitchen timer on the counter, a Kilner jar full of bone-shaped dog biscuits, with a label on it that said 'Archie' in case he got confused and ate them himself. There were small framed photos on the slanting walls: a muntjac deer in the mist, neck and head alert, looking straight at the camera; a swan taking off from the river, its body elongated, wings spraying flecks of glistening water; a close-up of a robin, its breast impossibly red, the detail of the individual feathers as intricate as lace.

'These are yours?' she said.

'They are.' Mason spooned coffee into the cafetiere. 'Sorry, I don't have anything as sophisticated as a machine,' he indicated, boiling the kettle.

'I'm surprised you have anything other than instant.'

253

He looked affronted. 'Do you really think that little of me?'

'You just spend a lot of money on my espressos.'

'Coffee's never the same at home, you know that. Although, you're probably the exception.'

'I do have the means to make a good coffee.'

'How's the café? Do you want any help fixing it up?'

'That's what I'm here about, actually,' she said. She watched as he poured water into the cafetiere, stirred it, and put the lid on. The smell of the coffee mingled with his usual citrus and vanilla scent. 'I wondered if you could give me the name of someone who can fix my door and windows, and maybe help with the table repairs too?'

'Of course,' he said. He went to his desk, and started rifling through papers. Summer followed him, and noticed a few signs of his scruffiness creeping in amongst the showboat. There was a pile of photography magazines on a side table, the page corners bent over, one left open with a large marker-pen circle round one of the articles. Two different jumpers were strewn over the back of the sofa and an empty glass was on the floor, a dribble of red wine left in the bottom. A box on the sofa looked like it was full of rolls of film, and Summer wondered where he got them developed, grinning at the thought he hadn't entirely embraced the digital age.

'Here you go,' he said, handing her a piece of paper. 'This is where I got most of the work on *The Sandpiper* done. I knew nothing about boats when I bought her, and they're keen to teach you, so I ended up being able to do quite a bit in the end. They're not too far away, and Mick, the guy I dealt with, might come out to you if it's a quick job. Tell them that I recommended them to you.'

'Thank you, I really appreciate it. I need the café up and

running as quickly as possible in this weather.'

'I'm sure they'll do you a quick turnaround.' Mason slipped past her and poured the coffee, and they leaned on the kitchen counter, side by side, sipping their drinks.

'This is the most beautiful boat interior I've ever seen,' Summer admitted. 'I mean, compared to the café, and then – I don't know if you've been on *Moonshine*, but it's all fabrics and dark corners.'

'That's because it's Valerie's office, where she sees customers all day. And you have people tramping in and out of yours. Your cabin's as nice as this.'

Summer laughed. 'No, it's not. You don't have to be kind. Was your house like this, too, before you moved on to the boat? Beautifully designed, attention to all the little details?' She ran her hand along the curve of the cupboard, and felt Mason sigh beside her.

'Not really,' he said. 'This was – it was a clean break, buying *The Sandpiper*, becoming a liveaboard, and I wanted to make the effort, to make it a home. And, to be honest, I also treated it as a project, working closely with the boat-builders to design the interior, doing research about the best features, heating system, gadgets. And then, towards the end, working alongside them to get it finished. It was a good distraction.'

'From what?' Summer thought of Claire's friend, and wondered if she had been a distraction too. She brushed the thought away.

'From some unhappy memories,' Mason said, giving her a quick glance. 'But I'm glad you approve. I'm sorry it's taken this long for you to see it, but you're always welcome. You should come and have a look at the photos I took that day in Foxburn.'

255

'I'd love that,' she said. 'How about a week on Friday? Let me cook you dinner in your beautiful galley, and you can show them to me.'

Mason turned towards her, raising his eyebrows. 'That sounds like an ambush.'

'What do you mean?'

'Do you think that by leaving out the date, I'll conveniently forget that a week on Friday is my birthday?'

Summer laughed. 'Isn't it a nice way to spend it, having your dinner cooked for you? Unless of course you've got other plans.' She felt herself flushing slightly at the thought he might have somebody else to spend his birthday with.

'No plans,' he said, narrowing his eyes at her. 'I'll think about it.'

'Good. You don't have to go all out, but I think you have to recognize the day you came into the world, even with something small. I'd like to recognize it,' she added quickly, gulping down the last of her coffee. 'I have to get back to Latte and my wreck of a café. Thank you for the boat-builder's details.'

'Do you want help?'

Summer shook her head. 'There isn't much else to be done until the door and windows are repaired. Thank you, though.' She gave him a quick wave and then opened the door, squinting as the sunlight assaulted her eyes. As she left, she noticed a pair of muddy walking boots sitting on a carrier bag next to the door.

She dawdled back to her boat, letting the summer breeze caress her skin. She would have loved Mason's help, but she wasn't just repairing the café, she was planning his surprise party. It would be small, nothing flashy or impressive, with less than ten guests – unless you counted the geese. But it would show Mason how much he was thought of, and it would show her gratitude for all that he'd done for her. She needed a fully functioning café before she could do anything, so first she had to call Mick.

Mick arrived later that afternoon, and Summer was worried he'd break the boat apart rather than mend it. He was at least six-foot-three, wearing a bright red T-shirt and with a scruffy, wiry brown beard that could have housed a nest of blue tits. He reminded her of Desperate Dan from the comics she used to read when she was small, but he had kind eyes, and his handshake was solid and warm.

'What happened here then, love?'

'I had a break-in,' Summer admitted. 'They didn't get away with anything valuable, but they've messed the place up a bit.'

Mick nodded and turned in a small circle, his body stooped. 'Nothing that can't be fixed pretty sharpish.'

'Oh, really?'

'I can measure up, bring you new windows and replace the door with a better one, more secure – it was about time to replace this one anyway,' he said, running his finger down the back of the door, which was still boarded up. 'Won't take me long, I reckon.'

'And the tables?' Summer showed him the damaged furniture.

Mick ran his hand over these too, and Summer thought they looked like Hobbit furniture next to him. 'I can take 'em now, love, bring 'em back tomorrow with the windows and doors.'

'*Tomorrow?*'

'Unless that's too soon for you, love.' He grinned, or at

least Summer thought he did – it was hard to tell behind the beard.

'That would be incredible. I had no idea you could fix it all so quickly.'

'We're a bit lighter in the summer, people cruising rather than mending. If it was winter, I wouldn't be able to give you a look-in for weeks.'

'Well then I'm very grateful they broke in during the summer.'

'Yup,' Mick admitted. 'Let's thank the burglar for their consideration.' Now she did spot the grin, and she resisted the urge to reach out and hug this huge, weird man who was going to help her get her café right much sooner than she had imagined. 'You said Mason recommended me to you? Is he in?' He pointed in the direction of *The Sandpiper.*

'He was this morning,' Summer said.

'I'll give the old Lothario a look-in. Come back for the tables in a while, if that's all right?'

Summer told him it was, thanked him again and waved him goodbye. She tried not to think too hard about the nickname Mick had for Mason, or where its origins might lie.

Mick was good to his word, and the following day returned with mended tables and the new windows. He also had a new door, painted a glossy, pillar-box red.

'It's beautiful,' Summer said, her voice full of awe as she caressed the wood.

'I'll just pop 'im in,' Mick said, 'get 'im all set up for you.'

Summer worked at the hatch, serving the Thursday strollers tea, coffee and cookies, while Mick removed the broken windows and replaced them. It was extra hot today, the humidity returning, and Summer thought there was another storm on the horizon. She kept the large man topped up with strong tea and choc-chip cookies, wondering if she should also offer him a massage, the way he was stooping to get her boat repaired. She wanted to ask him what had led him to boat repair when he couldn't really stand up in one, but thought better of it.

He finished just as the families at the Black Swan's picnic tables were being replaced with couples and groups of older friends. Summer had the money ready – Mick wasn't cheap, but it was worth it to have the café beautiful again and, Summer knew, more secure.

'Anything else, just give me a bell.'

'You've been wonderful, and so quick. No wonder Mason recommended you.'

'He's all right, that one,' Mick said, nodding thoughtfully.

'Even if he is a bit of a Lothario.' Summer laughed, but it sounded awkward, not at all relaxed as she'd intended.

'Ah, speaking from experience.'

Summer blushed furiously and shrugged. She shouldn't have gone down this route; she shouldn't have tried to go fishing for details.

'He's come round though,' Mick continued, oblivious to her discomfort, 'a bit like *The Sandpiper*.'

Summer raised her eyebrows. 'Oh?'

'Started out as a wreck, but now he's much more settled. Bit of a Steady Eddie, whereas before . . .' Mick shook his head, gazing off into some distance Summer couldn't see. 'Still, can't blame 'im, can you? After what happened. Anyway . . .' He snapped back into the present, grabbed Summer by the hand and gave her a bear-paw handshake.

Summer saw him out and then went back to her new bow

door, running her hand over the red finish. It was beautiful, almost like a little piece of *The Sandpiper* had been delivered to her as a present from Mason. Mason the Lothario, Mason the Steady Eddie. What *had* happened? Summer couldn't spend her life wondering. She could either ask him, or wait for him to tell her, for their friendship to reach that level of trust. There were still things he didn't know about her, after all. She needed a distraction, something to take her mind off the thoughts going round in her head. The trouble was, her distraction *was* Mason, and his impending birthday. Sighing, she gave her new door a kiss, and glanced quickly around to check that nobody was watching. Latte looked up at her, her head at an angle, a look of utter incredulity on her little doggy face.

The tenth of June, Mason's birthday, dawned as humid as the previous week had been. There was no sign yet of a storm to break the sultry atmosphere, and Summer had noticed a listlessness in her customers as well as herself. Everyone was doing things as slowly as physically possible, people lingering longer at the tables inside, where a minimal but welcome through-breeze came from the windows on either side, and a stream of customers wanting cold drinks and ice creams from the hatch, so that Summer's stock ordering became frantic in response.

Summer knew that she was in the best place possible, that being on the river was much better in this weather than a café in the centre of Cambridge. Latte was also lethargic in the heat, sleeping a lot and, occasionally, staring at the water as if she'd like to jump into it. She hadn't done it yet and Summer tried keeping her as cool as possible, taking her for walks early or late when the day was at its coolest, and almost following her around with the water bowl.

She had everything prepared for that evening. The cake was made and in the fridge, balloons filled with helium were bouncing about in her cabin, and she had streamers to decorate the tables. She'd started work on a present for Mason – a small painting of a kingfisher – but with the short notice, she hadn't had much time to work on it and knew it would be several weeks before it was ready. She'd invited Valerie and Adam from the butcher's, and Harry was coming with Tommy and Greg. She'd also asked Norman, and left a note for Dennis and Jenny at the pub, but wasn't holding out much hope of hearing from the occupants of either *Celeste* or the Black Swan. Even if there were only a few of them, Summer was sure it would be fun.

When she closed the café at six, the balloons and streamers and confetti would come out, along with the bottles of fizz and the cake, and Summer would coax Mason off his boat on a pretence, though she hadn't yet decided what that would be. She knew he'd be there, because she'd invited herself to have dinner with him on *The Sandpiper*. She felt slightly reluctant to share him with anyone else, but hopefully, if the party went well, there'd be more opportunities for just the two of them to spend time together.

Still in her summer pyjamas, pale yellow shorts and vest top, Summer went to turn on the coffee machine. At first, her bare foot registered only cold, and she frowned and looked down. Then she realized that the cold wasn't just cold, but wet, and that there was a layer of water floating happily on the surface of the café floor. She didn't realize she'd shouted aloud until Latte appeared, did a small dance in the water, and then ran and hid behind Summer, yelping furiously.

'Argh! What is this? Am I *sinking*?' she screeched at Latte, but unsurprisingly the little dog was unable to answer her and simply added to the noise by yelping at her.

Summer ran back through her cabin and jumped on to the stern deck. She banged on Mason's door, startling a young man who was passing on a bicycle. Latte was at her heels, her yelping reaching an almost inaudibly high pitch.

She thought she heard a voice from inside, and then the door opened and Mason was there, his face a mix of concern and sleepiness, his eyes crinkled. The quickest glance told Summer that he was only wearing shorts, and that he was incredibly toned, but she didn't really have the time to get distracted.

'Summer,' he yawned, 'what is it? Are you OK?' She caught his eyes quickly flicker over her legs, bare below her tiny pyjama shorts, before meeting her gaze.

'My boat's full of water,' she rushed. 'The café – am I sinking?'

'Shit,' Mason said, suddenly alert. 'Hopefully not. Two secs.' He disappeared inside and Summer held on to Latte, who was as desperate to see inside *The Sandpiper* as Summer had been. A few moments later he appeared again, a white T-shirt over his shorts, his feet still bare. 'Archie, stay.' He shut the door and followed Summer back to her boat and through the cabin, giving her a quick, puzzled glance when he saw the balloons, and then into the café.

'Crap,' he murmured.

'Am I sinking?' Summer asked again. 'Please tell me I'm not.'

Mason shook his head. 'I don't think so. I think maybe one of the pipes has burst. Hopefully it's that, otherwise you may have a leak in the hull.'

'I can't have! That – that would be awful, wouldn't it?'

'It's probably a pipe. Let's say it's a pipe.'

'OK, I like your optimism. What do we do?'

Mason looked at her, then rubbed his face with both hands. 'We call Mick,' he said.

'Good plan.' Summer quickly found her phone and called the boatbuilder. He was cheery and helpful, but Summer's heart sank when he told her he couldn't get there until lunchtime.

Summer told Mason the bad news.

'Right,' he said, appraising the café, his hand worrying his hair, making the curls even more unruly. 'Right. Well, we can find the leak, then when he gets here, it'll be a quicker job.'

'H-how do we do that?'

'We take up the floorboards.'

Summer gawped. 'Us?'

'Yes,' Mason said, his voice defiant.

'OK,' Summer said. 'What do we need?'

'Screwdriver and chisel.'

'I'll get my toolbox.' As Summer hurried to the engine room to get her tools, she had time to realize that Mason's surprise was ruined. Even if they managed to get the boat fixed, he'd seen the balloons. Summer had no idea how serious the leak was, how costly it would be, but it was unlikely that they could go ahead with the party now or even open to customers today – not to mention the long-term impact it might have on her business. Swearing to herself, she picked up her toolbox and made her way back to the café.

Chapter 15

Summer didn't think she'd ever been more flustered in her life. They'd moved the chairs and tables to the back of the café, closest to the counter, and were focusing their attention on the bow of the boat, which was where Mason thought the leak was likely to be. They were prising up the floorboards one by one, Mason taking care not to break them as he chiselled them out, exposing the pipework and the bilges beneath.

'Why is she doing this?' Summer asked, as she helped lift one of the floorboards out of place.

'Who?' Mason looked up, frowning. There were beads of perspiration on his forehead, his curls tightening into ringlets in the humidity.

'My boat,' Summer said. 'All I've done recently is repair her.'

'The break-in wasn't the boat's fault,' Mason said, his voice straining as he worked at a floorboard edge with the chisel. 'And we don't know what's happened here yet.'

'I think you're a bad influence,' Summer said.

'Me?' Mason said sharply. 'Why? What have I done?'

'I think *The Canal Boat Café* has seen how gorgeous *The Sandpiper* is and she's jealous. I think she keeps breaking so I'll have to keep repairing her, until she's up to the standard of your boat.'

'My boat's not that great.'

'Your boat is a James Bond boat.'

'Which film was that? I can't imagine any director thinking that a narrowboat chase would get hearts racing, even if Bond did break the four-mile-an-hour speed limit.' Mason peered down into the bilges. 'If I can just find out where it is . . .' His voice trailed away until he emerged, wiping his forehead with a blackened hand.

Summer stared at his dirty forehead, and his complete obliviousness, and tried hard not to laugh. 'It was something Ross said, that my boat was like one of those swanky yachts in Bond films. Mine doesn't come close, but yours does.'

'I object to the word "swanky" in any situation, and definitely about my boat.'

'It's beautiful,' Summer said dreamily, and then looked around her at the water and the cavern they were opening up in her boat, as if they were gutting her. They were both sitting in the water, shorts soaked, and Summer may have been laughing at the smudge on Mason's forehead, but she probably looked as bad. *The Canal Boat Café* and *The Sandpiper* were complete opposites right now. Summer sighed and bent over to where Mason was looking.

'I think it's down there,' he said, pointing. He reached up and got the torch from the windowsill, and hovered its beam over the pipework below them.

Summer thought she could see where Mason was pointing,

at the underside of one of the pipes that looked as if it had cracked. 'So it's fixable, and it's not the hull.'

'Exactly, and I'm sure Mick can repair it in no time.'

'And we're definitely *not* sinking?'

Mason glanced around him. 'Doesn't look like it.'

'That's a huge relief,' Summer said. 'Phew. *Phew*, puppy.' She picked Latte up and hugged her. The dog's paws were damp, and when she put her down, Summer realized she had little dirty paw prints stamped across her yellow vest top. She sighed, looked up and saw that Mason was smirking.

She folded her arms.

Mason gave her an innocent smile.

'Don't say anything,' she warned.

'Wasn't going to utter a word.'

'What on earth are you two doing? What's happened to the floor? Are you wearing your *pyjamas*?'

They both looked up to see Valerie standing in the doorway, her hair an orange mane around her face.

'My boat's leaking,' Summer said. 'We've been on a leak hunt.'

'Good Lord! You're soaked.'

'So's the café,' Summer said grimly.

'I'm going to take some photos and send them to Mick,' Mason said, 'that way he'll know what to bring with him when he comes.'

Summer pulled herself to standing and, skirting around the hole in the floor, went and sat on the bow deck with Valerie. 'I think tonight's ruined,' she said.

'Is that what you're really worried about, when your boat's in pieces like this?'

'I wanted it to be perfect.'

'It's not raining as far as I can tell,' Valerie said, looking up at the cloudless blue sky.

'Wow, are you a fortune-teller, Valerie? That's amazing.'

Valerie gasped. 'What's got into you, you cheeky thing!'

'Sorry,' Summer said, rubbing her eyes with her wrists. 'This has been a surreal morning.'

'It's a good thing Mason was there to call on.' Summer thought she detected more weight to Valerie's voice than usual, but decided it wasn't something she wanted to probe.

'I thought I was sinking. I'm so glad I'm not sinking.' She put her head in her hands.

'Mick's on his way,' Mason said, appearing in the doorway. 'He knows which pipe he needs to bring, and it should be fixed today. But you'll need to leave the floorboards up and all the doors and windows open as long as possible, to dry everything out. He said it's a good thing it happened in the summer. It would have been much harder to deal with if it was cold.'

'What a considerate leak,' Summer said, 'just like the burglar.'

Mason and Valerie exchanged a confused glance, and Summer repeated her conversation with Mick from the previous week.

'I can't really even serve from the hatch until everything's dried out,' Summer said. 'And – oh my God, Mason, I haven't even said happy birthday! Look what I've made you do on your birthday!'

'I did have a glimmer of hope earlier, when there was such an early knock on my door, that maybe someone had sent me a huge present.' He sighed dramatically. 'Instead I had you screeching that you were sinking. It's not been the best start.'

'I'm so sorry,' Summer started, and then saw that Mason was grinning at her. 'You don't mind?'

'Happy to help,' he said.

'Again,' Summer added.

'Again,' Mason echoed. 'Are you still on for dinner later? I can cook now you've been thrown into disarray.'

'N-no, that's OK,' Summer said, shooting a quick glance at Valerie. 'Let me do that. I'm sure I can work something out.'

'OK.' Mason shrugged, then lifted his T-shirt and wiped his grimy face with it, exposing his toned stomach above the shorts. 'Give me a shout when Mick gets here and I'll give him a hand.'

'Thank you,' Summer said. 'What are we going to do?' she asked, once Mason had gone. 'We can't have the party on my boat any more.'

'So we'll get your outdoor furniture on the towpath and have it there instead.'

'Unless there's a huge thunderstorm,' Summer said, giving Valerie a rueful smile.

Valerie raised her hand up to the sky. 'I predict there will be none, and as I'm a fortune-teller, you can count on me to know what the weather's doing.'

'Touché,' Summer grinned. 'We'll just have to make sure we tie the balloons very tightly on to the chairs.'

'Why's that?'

'Because they're filled with helium.'

'Ah,' Valerie said. 'Good point.'

While Mason and Mick worked on repairing the pipe, Summer took Latte and Archie for a long, slow walk up the river and across the fields, into a small, cool patch of wood. She wanted to help, but it was such a small space and she knew she'd just get in the way. She took time to enjoy the glorious summer day, making sure she kept the dogs hydrated, and listened out for bird sounds and any signs of wildlife. Her walk with Mason seemed like years ago, so much had happened since then, and she knew her knowledge was still very limited. But she recognized the songs of a blackbird and a robin, the birds hiding amongst the trees, away from the heat of the sun. It reminded her of her time with Jas and Ryder, of the stories in the woods on cooler nights, the crackling fire and the fear and the suspense. It might be bright sunshine beyond the trees, but under the canopy there was a stillness that was almost otherworldly.

When she returned from her walk, hot but relaxed, the dogs trotting placidly alongside her, Mason and Mick were replacing the floorboards.

'Is it OK to put them back, then?' Summer asked, peering into the café from the doorway.

'We've pumped out the bilges,' Mick said, 'so you'll just need to air this place for the rest of the day, and tomorrow too, and all will be right as rain.'

'You've come to my rescue, again!'

'Not a bother,' Mick said, standing and wiping his hands on a cloth.

Summer couldn't help it. She flung her arms around him, squeezing tightly. 'Thank you,' she said.

'Not a bother,' Mick repeated, his voice suddenly quiet and unsure.

Summer pulled back, and then, because she couldn't hug Mick and leave out Mason, she flung her arms around him too. 'Thank you, Mason,' she murmured into his neck. He smelt of oil or grease, and of wood, and his body was warm and much firmer than Mick's. She felt his arms go round her, hugging her awkwardly. She inhaled, and wondered if she could get away with running her hands through his hair. She quickly decided not.

'You've spent your birthday crawling around in muddy water and yanking up floorboards for me,' she said, reluctantly unwrapping herself from him. She noticed how dirty his hands were, and realized that he hadn't embraced her properly because he didn't want to mark her clothes.

'I didn't have any other plans,' Mason said. 'Not until tonight, anyway.' His smile was hesitant, as if he was aware her hug was more than just a thank you, as it had been with Mick.

'I'll be off then,' the boatbuilder said.

Summer paid him, briefly wondering if she should offer to set up a direct debit, and watched him head back to his van.

'Shall I come about seven?' Summer asked, hoping Mason still didn't suspect anything, and that he'd forgotten about the balloons in the excitement of dealing with pipes and bilges.

'Sounds good,' Mason said. 'It might take me that long to get cleaned up.'

'The favours I owe you are beginning to stack up,' Summer said. 'I don't know how I can ever repay you for all of this.'

'I think considering all the bacon butties and espressos, we're pretty much even.'

'That's too generous,' Summer said. Mason took Archie's lead and led him back to *The Sandpiper*. It was mid-afternoon, the day was still sweltering, and Summer thought she had time to mop up the café and give the drying process a helping hand before she set up the al fresco birthday party. She'd been set off course, but again she had to remind herself it could have been a lot worse, with her boat, her café and her entire life sitting on the riverbed. She'd had all the help she could ever have hoped for, and now there was even more reason to show Mason how grateful she was.

Everything was ready. Summer and Valerie had set out the tables on the towpath, covered them with streamers, and tied the balloons to the chair backs with triple knots. On her sturdy A-frame Summer had written: *It's Mason's birthday, hip hip hooray, but the café is closed for the rest of today.* Harry, Greg and Tommy appeared at about six thirty, Tommy in a smart red shirt and dark shorts, his hair reaching his collar. Harry looked beautiful in a peach-coloured dress, and Greg was all smiles, though when Summer peered closely she could see the tiredness around his eyes.

'Harry, you gorgeous thing!' Summer embraced her friend. 'Thank you so much for coming!'

'I couldn't miss getting to meet Mason properly,' she said, 'and of course seeing you again.'

'Glad to see you've got your priorities straight,' Summer grinned. 'And I'm back in Willowbeck. For good.'

'I can see that,' Harry said. 'Which means that . . .'

'We can think about going into business together. Unless of course you've got something else, or the café—'

'No no, there's nothing else. Let's talk about it properly. And I promise this isn't a pitch, but I've brought this to add to the celebrations.' Harry handed her a large tin and, holding it against her, Summer popped the lid. It was a huge, triple-layered cake with pale green icing. She looked at Harry quizzically.

'Pistachio cake,' Harry said. 'I've got some ice cream too. It's in a cold bag, but it needs to go in the freezer quickly, if you've got room?'

'I'll do that,' Valerie said, taking the bag from Harry. 'I'm going to get Tommy a lemonade anyway.'

Summer thanked her and turned back to her friend. 'How's Greg?'

'He's hanging in there,' Harry said, glancing towards where her husband and son were peering down into the river. 'But the work's so infrequent now he's looking around for something else, and so far it's not been the most buoyant of job markets.' Her large brown eyes blinked away sadness and she gave Summer a weak smile.

'I'm so sorry.' Summer rubbed her arm.

'Anyway, tonight's a celebration. What time does the guest of honour arrive? I'm desperate to talk to him.'

'When I go and get him.'

'Which should be now,' Valerie said, reappearing with a bottle of lemonade. 'He's probably seen all the kerfuffle out of the window anyway.'

'He saw the balloons this morning.' Summer regaled Harry, Greg and Tommy with the leak story, waved as Adam and his son, Charlie, made their way over from the butcher's, and then, wiping her hands down her blue sundress and cursing herself for being nervous, approached *The Sandpiper*.

Latte had accompanied her to Mason's front door and Summer turned to the little dog before she knocked.

'What do you think, Latte? Will he be delighted, or mad?' Latte cocked her head on one side, and Summer crossed her fingers, then rapped gently on the wood.

Mason opened the door, his smile wide, the blue of his shirt as dark and deep as the midnight sky. His hair was tamed into neat curls, his feet bare below the hem of his jeans. Summer inhaled.

'Summer, you look lovely. Come in.' He stepped back and gestured inside *The Sandpiper*, and Summer bit her lip, hovering in the doorway. Mason's smile faded. 'What's wrong? Has something happened – your boat—'

'No, no, my boat's fine,' Summer rushed, 'I wondered if you could come outside, just for a moment.'

He frowned. 'Sure. Archie – stay.'

'No, bring Archie.' It came out as a squeak. The dogs were touching noses, their tails wagging madly, Archie skittering backwards and forwards on the spot.

'OK,' Mason said, drawing the word out, and Summer realized she'd got it all wrong. She'd made him anxious and suspicious, because *she* was feeling anxious, whereas if she'd just said he should come and see how well the boat was drying out, then it would have been easy.

'Sorry, Mason, I—'

'What is it?' He stepped closer, and Summer caught his familiar scent, the vanilla reminding her of the icing on the cupcakes she'd made the day before.

Summer thought, in that moment, that she would happily leave everyone else to the party and stay here with him. But she couldn't do that, not when everyone had made such an effort. 'I've messed this up.'

'What?' He was looking down at her, a curious smile playing on his lips.

Summer took a deep breath. She took his hand and, ignoring the fact that he had no shoes on, pulled him on to the deck and out on to the towpath. 'Happy birthday,' she said quietly.

The small gathering on the towpath cheered, and Summer felt Mason squeeze her hand and then let go.

'Happy birthday, Mason!' Valerie said, clasping her hands together.

Harry and Greg clapped, and Tommy scooped a load of streamers off one of the tables and threw them vaguely in Mason's direction. Summer thought briefly that she would need to grab those before Jenny caught sight of them and gave her another reprimand for littering.

Next to her, Mason inhaled, and Summer closed her eyes, waiting for the expletive, or for him to turn and storm back on board his boat. But the breath turned into a laugh, and she risked looking up at him. His eyes were wide, bright, and – along with the confusion – she saw genuine happiness.

'Hi,' he said, giving a vague wave to everyone. 'I had no idea.' He turned to Summer. 'I had no idea,' he repeated. 'Did you do all this?'

'Me and Valerie and – well, all of us, really. Didn't you notice the balloons this morning?'

'The balloons? I—' He slapped his hand to his forehead. 'I did. But I'd completely forgotten about them. I can't believe you've taken the trouble to do all this.'

'Come on, enjoy.' She took his hand again and pulled him into the centre of the small crowd, letting everyone offer him their own birthday wishes.

'Fizz?' Valerie mouthed. Inside, they took out the bottles of prosecco, the sandwiches and nibbles that Summer had put together. They poured the prosecco into glasses and handed them out, and then, with everyone looking at her expectantly, Summer realized that, as the organizer, everyone was expecting her to say something. In all her planning, this was not something she'd considered.

The evening was beautiful, the water like shimmering glass beneath the clear blue sky, a faint breeze whispering down the towpath, making the streamers wave and the

274

balloons bob. It couldn't be more perfect. She could do this, for Mason's sake.

Her heart pounding unhelpfully in her throat, she swallowed. 'I just brought everyone here to—'

Quack. She looked down. Four ducks were waddling at her feet, their beaks angled up at the tables of sandwiches.

'Shoo.' She flapped her free hand. 'Shoo, ducks.'

Quack.

Tommy ran at the ducks, his arms out, and they scattered a few feet away then turned and waddled back. Summer rolled her eyes, and realized several mouths were twitching. Tommy had his head down, ready to charge again like a raging bull and Harry put her hand on his shoulder.

'I don't think there's any point,' she said. 'They're too determined.'

Quack quack, went the ducks.

Summer tried to suppress her own smile. 'Right,' she said, 'if the ducks want to join in, that's fine. In fact, it says what I wanted to say, but probably more eloquently. Mason, I haven't known you for very long.' She risked a quick glance at him. He was looking at her, his warm eyes giving her confidence, but also threatening to derail her with their intensity. 'But you have already become a good friend, and not just because you're always there when I have a crisis – a break-in, or an impromptu paddling pool in the café. You've shown me things about the river, and about nature, that I could never have imagined. You're patient and kind and funny, and I'm not the only one who has nice things to say about you. I know I'm speaking for everyone when I say that we all care about you, Mason. You're a – a good person.' She knew it was a lame ending, so she raised her glass and said, loudly, 'A toast! Happy birthday, Mason!'

Everyone raised their glasses and echoed her sentiment. The prosecco was cool and crisp and welcome on such a hot day. Summer had never worked out how bubbles could be so calming, rather than making her more jumpy and nervous, but she was glad of them.

They took the clingfilm off the food and everyone tucked in, falling into easy conversation, standing on the towpath rather than sitting at the tables, as if Summer's outdoor furniture had become a typical kitchen-at-a-party. Tommy ran down the ducks once more and then gave up, and Summer noticed him throwing small chunks of bread in their direction, so that soon the four ducks had become at least fifteen, and included a couple of Canada geese as well.

'Happy birthday, Mason,' called a woman with a pair of miniature schnauzers, and Mason looked up, his mouth full of sandwich, and frowned at Summer.

Summer pointed at the message on the A-frame, and Mason nodded in understanding, just as he was ambushed by Tommy, who asked him about his hunting, and whether he'd ever done it with guns, and what he thought of fishing and whether he'd ever caught any fish in the river.

Summer joined Harry at one of the tables, topped up their glasses and gave her friend a long look.

'How are things really?' she asked.

Harry smiled, her gaze drawn to the table. 'We're getting by,' she said. 'The café's been good to me, offering me a few more hours, and it's not horrible working there.'

'But your fingers are getting itchy?'

'Itchy?'

'Your wonderful, creative fingers,' Summer said, covering them with her hand. 'You can be doing more, you *should* be doing more.'

276

'I'm still doing lots of crochet.'

'Are you selling it?'

Harry shook her head.

'So what about my idea?' Summer asked softly. 'I really want to make the café unique, to set it apart from other eating establishments,' she nodded her head in the direction of the pub, 'but apart from the fact that my skills are sorely lacking, all I've done recently is fix up my boat. You can create masterpieces with a click of your fingers.'

'I'm not the fairy godmother,' Harry said, laughing softly.

'You really bloody could be, for me and *The Canal Boat Café*.'

'My cooking isn't that great.'

'Your modesty is going to get irritating soon,' Summer said. 'Look, I'll do you a deal. If anyone has a bad word to say about your pistachio cake – once I've unveiled it as the pièce de résistance – I'll stop asking.'

'No, I – I want to do it,' Harry said. 'I do.'

'So what's the problem?'

Harry shrugged, and Summer thought she knew exactly what her friend's problem was. Just as Harry had known that Summer would be happy if she gave her mum's boat a chance, Summer could see that her friend's confidence had been knocked by the situation she found herself in. Although it wasn't her fault, and they'd just been undone by circumstance – the failing fortunes of Greg's job – Summer knew that Harry felt responsible for not keeping their small family unit running perfectly. Harry's self-belief had been dented, and Summer knew that she could help get it back.

'One month,' Summer said.

Harry looked up. 'What?'

'If your pistachio cake gets positive feedback – and I'm

not including people who don't like nuts, they don't count – then we'll try it on a one-month basis. I've drawn up a business plan.'

'You *have?*'

Summer nodded. 'It's just a starting point. I'll give you a copy and you can go through it, make any changes you think it needs, and then come back here and we can iron out the details. You should stay the night and we can have a proper catch-up – I've got the pull-down bed I always used to stay on.'

'You really don't have to do this, Summer.'

'It's not a favour to you. I want to do this for me, and you, and for the café. Come and have a night on the boat. Get Greg to look after Tommy and take a night off.'

Harry rested her chin on her hand, and laughed.

'What?' Summer asked.

'You,' Harry said. 'You seem happy. Happier than when I saw you in Foxburn. And this – this determination, business plans, ideas for the café. It's great, Summer. I knew that you'd flourish being back on the boat. But I'm not sure it's just about that, is it?'

Summer felt her cheeks redden. 'I don't know what you mean.'

'Your blush tells me you do,' Harry said. 'And he seems lovely, though I've not spoken to him properly yet. I'm going to take a leaf out of my son's book and corner him against one of the boats.'

Summer laughed. 'I still don't know enough about him.'

'About what Claire told you?'

Summer nodded.

'But that's the point of getting to know someone,' Harry said. 'It's not an instant download, is it? One button press and you know everything there is to know about Mason. It's gradual, and that's part of the fun. Don't worry about what Claire said. Make up your own mind about Mason *now*, not what he was like five years ago.'

'You're probably right,' Summer said, glancing in Mason's direction. He was laughing at something Charlie, Adam's son, was explaining, his glass empty, Archie lying across his feet. Summer couldn't help but smile. 'I think it's cake time,' she said, forcing herself to look away. As she got up from the table, her best friend gave her a knowing smile.

The party broke up gradually, Summer joking that it was as soon as all of Harry's pistachio cake had been eaten. She gave Greg and Tommy a hug goodbye, and handed a copy of her business plan to Harry. 'One night soon, here on the boat. Promise me?'

Harry sighed, but she was grinning. 'I promise,' she said. 'I'll wait until I have my shifts at the café, and then I'll speak to Greg.'

'About what?' Greg had one arm wrapped around Tommy, who was blinking furiously in an attempt to look like he wasn't remotely tired.

'I want to get your wife on my boat for a night, to have her to myself.'

Greg looked down at Harry. 'And what's the problem? Sounds good to me.'

'We have to work it out – there's my shifts at the café, Tommy—'

'Don't worry about that,' Greg said. 'I'm sure the two of us can do *one* night without burning the house down. You go. Have some time off. God knows you could do with a break.'

'Thanks, Greg,' Summer said, grinning. 'See, no excuses now.' She embraced her friend and planted a kiss on her cheek, and then watched them walk back to the car park, looking like a perfect little family. She wanted to help Harry see that was still the case, and that their hardship only meant that was *more* true, not less.

Valerie was clearing glasses and plates off the tables, swaying gently and humming to herself, and Mason was talking to Dennis. Summer's heart leapt, and she approached slowly.

'Here she is now,' Mason said, and Dennis turned.

'I'm so sorry I couldn't make it down earlier,' Dennis said. 'Friday night in the pub, we're rushed off our feet. I heard it's been a good night, though?'

Summer nodded tentatively. 'I think everyone's enjoyed themselves,' she said, glancing at Mason.

'I've had the best night,' he said, 'truly.' He was holding a bottle of prosecco, and Summer wondered briefly if he'd been swigging out of it, until she realized the label wasn't the same as the one on the bottles she'd bought. 'I have low expectations for my birthday these days, and this was so thoughtful. You didn't have to, Summer.'

'I wanted to.'

Mason shook his head. 'And with all you've had to deal with . . .'

'But you helped me sort it out so quickly. If it wasn't for you, I would never have been able to go ahead with this.' She tugged on one of the balloons, and Latte barked. 'So you really only have yourself to thank.'

Mason frowned and rubbed his forehead. 'I am not thanking myself for my own surprise birthday party – I can't even get my head around the idea. I think we should take the prosecco Dennis has brought us and finish off the evening in style. Dennis, will you join us for a glass?'

Dennis glanced towards the Black Swan, started to thumb behind him, and then shrugged. 'Oh, what the heck, one glass won't hurt.'

'Great. Let me go and get some clean glasses.' Summer found Valerie in the galley, rinsed four glasses and dragged her back outside.

The four of them sat at one of the outdoor tables, watching the setting sun turning the water golden. There was still a gentle hum from the picnic tables, the warm evening encouraging people to stay out as late as possible, and there was a strong scent of freshly mown grass in the air.

The silence was easy, comforting, and Summer was almost reluctant to fill it. She was sitting next to Mason and could feel the warmth of his body close to her, knowing that a few inches to her right and their thighs, their arms, would be touching. She sipped her drink, feeling the burst of bubbles anew after hours of refreshing others' glasses, and serving food and cake.

'This is very near to perfect.' It was Valerie who said it, her words softened at the edges by the alcohol.

Three heads nodded in agreement. Latte snuffled at Summer's feet. She glanced down, and started to laugh.

'What?' Valerie asked. 'What is it?'

Summer tried to stem her laughter by breathing deeply, and hiccupped. She looked at Mason. 'You've spent your whole birthday party with bare feet. On the towpath. There could be anything – duck poo, cigarette butts . . .' Another laugh overtook her, and she put her hand on Mason's knee. 'I'm so sorry, I don't mean to laugh.'

'Well, clearly you do,' Mason said, his eyes slightly

narrowed. 'But if you remember, you forced me off my boat without giving me time to dress properly. It felt rude to leave my own party to go back and put my shoes on.'

Summer looked at him, studying his face for signs of irritation, but could find only warmth. Of course his job and the hours he spent outside meant that he couldn't be too bothered by a bit of dirt, but then she pictured his immaculate boat.

'You're full of contradictions,' she said, before she could stop herself.

'How come?' he asked softly. 'Where do I contradict myself?'

Summer opened her mouth, and then realized she didn't want to explain, and that the first contradiction, about how he could be so scruffy and tidy all at the same time, inevitably led on to the second one; how could he be so warm and open and attentive to her, and capable of the behaviour Claire described? Could someone really change so completely? She shook her head.

'Happy birthday, Mason.'

'That's not an answer.' He put his hand over hers, where it still rested on his knee.

She grinned at him.

'Maddy appreciated a good sunset,' Valerie said, 'though she'd probably be dancing on the tables with her prosecco rather than sitting at one.'

Dennis chuckled. 'Too right. Maddy wouldn't let a party end until there really was no other choice.'

Summer closed her eyes.

'You OK?' Mason asked quietly.

Summer nodded. 'It's nearly a year since . . .'

'God,' Dennis said, 'it is, isn't it?'

'The eighteenth of June,' Valerie added. 'A week tomorrow. Not a day any of us will ever forget.'

Summer shuddered. The date had been creeping closer and Summer had been increasingly aware of it, but in her attempt to remain positive she had been pushing it as far back as her thoughts would allow her. Now though, it seemed to loom large. Should she mark it? It seemed grotesque to mark the anniversary of losing someone so close. The start of grief, of sadness, and in Summer's case, of guilt. Not something to be celebrated.

'Here we are,' Valerie continued, 'marking something wonderful. The birth date of someone we all care about, and it's so close to a contradictory anniversary, the passing of someone who we loved, who we miss every day. Beginnings and endings – you can't escape them. You just have to be thankful for the time in between.'

'Too right,' Dennis muttered quietly.

Summer stared into her drink, feeling a hollowness that she soon recognized as fear. She didn't want to cope with the memories, the reminder, the anniversary. She let the others chat around her, but she could sense Mason's awareness, his glances in her direction. When the darkness was complete, Dennis insisted on putting the last table and chairs back on board *The Canal Boat Café*, and Summer offered to walk Mason back to his boat.

'It's about ten feet,' he said, but he put his arm across her shoulders and they walked in step back to *The Sandpiper*.

'You're not looking forward to the eighteenth,' he said quietly. 'Will you do anything?'

Summer shook her head. 'I don't think so. I'm dreading it, but I don't know how I'll feel until it arrives. The café will be busy, so that'll be something. A June Saturday in

Willowbeck will take my mind off it. Anyway,' she said, 'it's still your birthday.'

They stopped on his deck, Archie pawing gently at the door until Mason opened it and let him in. 'It's been the best one I've had in a long time. Thank you.'

Summer could feel the gentle lull of the water beneath her feet. She looked up at Mason, his face in shadow, and felt a shudder run through her. 'It was my pleasure,' she said, her voice dropping, as if the moment required quiet.

Mason reached out and slipped a strand of her hair away from her face. Summer could feel the tension, the anticipation between them, could picture herself leaning up to kiss him, slowly, lingeringly, on the lips. She wanted to, almost more than anything, but something was holding her back. Claire's words, the need to find out more about him before she let him fully in. She'd made the mistake of giving in too soon in the past, and she had her wits about her this time.

She kissed his cheek, pressing her lips against his skin for longer than necessary, breathing in the faint vanilla scent. His arm went briefly round her waist, and Summer had to fight against the desire to stay there, to press herself as close to him as she could.

'Goodnight, Mason,' she said, pulling away.

'Night, Summer,' he murmured.

She could feel his eyes on her as she walked back to her boat, her heart thudding loudly in her chest.

Chapter 16

Summer had expected the anniversary of her mum's death to be cloud-filled, grey and heavy. At the very least, she expected the humidity to be stifling. Instead, she was greeted with a perfect summer's day, the water sparkling under the sun's watchful eye, and a breeze licking through the boat. Summer had been out the day before and had bought the largest bunch of yellow roses she could find. They were her mum's favourite flower, and she used them in the vases on all the tables, and along the counter at the front of the café. With the remaining few, she climbed up to the roof of her boat and scattered them about. This, she told herself, was her own way of dealing with the day, and the best thing she could do in her mum's memory was keep the café busy and bustling all day.

She opened up, and within minutes she had people at the hatch asking for coffee and bacon rolls. She got to it, frothing the milk for cappuccinos, beckoning people inside with a wide smile when they hovered at the bow deck, wondering whether to take a chance on the inside tables. As lunchtime approached, and with Summer happily busy, a familiar figure appeared in the doorway and walked slowly towards the counter. Summer's heart did an unhelpful little skip and she found herself smoothing her apron down automatically.

'Hey,' Mason said.

'Hi,' she breathed. 'Did you find your eagle?'

Mason grinned, his face lighting up. He'd taken *The Sandpiper* down the river in a hurry the day after his birthday: a white-tailed sea eagle had been spotted travelling through Suffolk and up towards Norfolk, and Mason had been determined to face the wrath of Norfolk Broads boatsmen by taking his narrowboat into their waters in order to get a glimpse of the rare bird. Summer knew all this because he'd called her the evening after his party, explaining why he'd left so suddenly. He hadn't mentioned their moment on the boat that night, though the unspoken reason for the call was that he didn't want her to think that he'd been running away from it. They'd ended up talking for over an hour, Summer curled up on the sofa with Latte at her side, and the hoot of an owl from one of the riverside trees punctuating their conversation.

'So you did,' she said, his grin infectious.

'It was magnificent.' He rested his elbows on the counter. 'Its wingspan is huge, soaring on the high air currents. I wish you'd been there.'

'You do?' She automatically turned to the coffee machine and started making an espresso.

Mason nodded. The time he'd spent at the helm of his boat was evident by the darkness of his skin, the spread of freckles across his nose and cheeks. He was wearing a white T-shirt, making his tan even more pronounced. 'I've got photos – lots and lots of photos. Come and look at them.'

'I'd love to,' she said, 'how about later today?'

Mason narrowed his eyes. 'Are you sure you want to . . . today?'

She passed him an espresso cup on a miniature saucer. 'I am.' She was touched that he'd remembered, and would tell him so later when there was no risk of her emotions bursting out of her in front of the customers.

He stood aside, sipping his coffee while she served tables and kept up with the steady stream of people at the hatch; then, realizing she was too busy to have a conversation, gave her arm a quick squeeze. 'Come round whenever you're ready. I'll be there.'

Summer smiled and waved him goodbye, and then covered a hot chocolate with squirty cream and hundreds and thousands for a little girl who had come in with her grandfather. The girl gave a suitably impressed gasp as Summer put the drink on her table, and Summer felt a wash of contentment. This was what her mum had lived for. *This* was how she could honour her memory.

Trade began to die down at about five as people drifted in the direction of the pub or their back gardens for barbecues and bottles of beer. Summer's feet ached and her shoulders were tired, but happily so. She'd earned the aches and pains, running her mum's café – *her* café – all by herself, keeping her emotions in check, being professional and friendly. And now she could reward herself with a perfect evening. Looking at photos with Mason, on board his beautiful boat. She didn't care that she'd invited herself so soon; she wasn't bothered about how it might look to him. She wanted to do it, and, thinking back to Harry's plight, she knew that her friend wasn't the only one who needed to focus on being more confident and determined.

She cleared the tables, taking plates and cups out to the galley, filling the dishwasher. When she emerged back into the café to find a figure standing in the doorway, she thought she must be dreaming. He was tall, dressed in black trousers and a pale blue shirt, his sleeves rolled up to the elbows. His hair was heading towards red more than Summer's own strawberry blonde, but his eyes were the same as hers.

'B-blaze,' she said, 'what on earth?'

Irritation flashed across his face at the mention of his birthname, the one that Maddy had given him, and which he'd replaced with Ben as soon as he was able to. He brushed it aside and smiled at Summer as he moved down the central aisle of the café towards her. 'Summer. God, you look wrecked.'

'Lovely to see you too! I'm fine. The café's busy, it's summer and it's hot and it's . . . what are you doing here?' But she knew, already, and it made little wings of panic flap inside her.

'It was Valerie's idea,' he said.

Summer came out from behind the counter and she let her brother give her his usual, stiff embrace. 'What was?'

'This memorial, for Mum. By the river, here – Willowbeck.' He looked at her, his mouth gaping as if she was mad, or a complete stranger rather than his little sister. 'Sum?'

'I – I don't know – Valerie didn't mention it.' Summer turned in a slow circle, as if somehow she'd find the answer – a note on the counter, a message written on the blackboard, but Blaze – Ben – was nodding.

'She said not to mention it to you. I thought it was because you'd be sensitive about it, before the day, but she's taken it a step further, hasn't she? She hasn't told you at all.'

Summer blinked, shook her head, and untied her apron. 'No,' she said.

'Because you wouldn't have wanted this.' Ben dropped his voice. 'You want to brush today under the carpet.'

'Yes please, if I could that would be great.' She knew her voice had become small and high, almost childlike, and hated herself for it.

'Come on, Sum, Dad's here. Your friend Harry, too. We're all here for you – for Mum, of course, but for you too.' He put his arm around her. 'It'll be good to do this.'

'Will it?' Summer said, thinking that it had been a while since she'd even spoken to her dad, let alone seen him.

'Show me what you've done with the boat,' Ben said. 'If it's anything like the café then I'll be suitably impressed.'

'What?' Summer forced out a laugh. 'My brother being impressed at something I've done? Not a chance.'

'A very small chance,' he said.

Summer showed him her cabin and Ben made all the right noises, though she hardly heard him. Her brother and her dad, here in Willowbeck on the anniversary of her mum's death. She should have expected it – should have expected *something* was going on when there'd been no contact from them in the lead up to the date. Summer couldn't expect everyone to want to mark it alone, as she had done. Ben told her they were waiting at the pub and Summer said she'd get changed and join them.

Wearing a short purple dress with white flowers on it, and with her hair tied back from her face, Summer climbed up the grass in front of the Black Swan. Valerie and Harry were at a table with their backs to her. Opposite were her brother and her dad, the latter's greying hair receding, his dark eyes sharp and, Summer had always thought, a little bit unforgiving. But he smiled as she approached, and his hug engulfed her as if she was long lost which, in a way, she supposed she was.

'Summer, you're looking well. I've been hearing nothing but good things about your work down here, and how well you're applying yourself to running Madeleine's café.'

'It's Summer's café now,' Harry said brightly.

'Both of theirs, perhaps,' Valerie said tremulously. Summer knew today would be equally hard for her mum's best friend, and that maybe she'd been selfish in hiding away, refusing to acknowledge the significance of the date.

Ben poured her a glass of wine from the bottle sitting in an ice bucket on the table and they all clinked glasses.

'So,' Summer said, 'what's the plan? If there is a plan. I hadn't realized that . . . this was happening. Not that it isn't lovely to see you all, of course.'

She smiled, sipped her drink, looked at her family, again aware how out of place it all felt without her mum to complete the square. She had felt a mild jolt of surprise when Ben had mentioned her dad had come too, but while he and Madeleine had been divorced for seven years before Maddy died, they had remained on speaking terms, and she was sure her dad also partly thought it was the right thing to do for her and Ben.

'We thought we'd just go down to the river and say a few words,' Harry said. 'Wasn't that your idea, Valerie?'

The older woman nodded, looking hesitantly at Summer. 'I'm sorry, Summer. I wasn't sure how you would feel.'

'You could have asked me,' Summer said, but she kept her tone calm. She felt blindsided, but not angry. It was good to see her dad, even better to see Ben, but she was entirely unprepared.

'I know,' Valerie said, 'and I know I should have. I don't know what I was thinking, really. That if you didn't have time to talk yourself out of it, that maybe it would be better, that you could just . . .' She looked helplessly at Ben and he took over.

'I didn't realize Valerie hadn't even mentioned it, but it makes sense. It took you a long time to come back here in the first place, after Mum died.'

'I'm happy now, though.'

'So if she'd suggested this to you, you would have been up for it?' He gave her a kind smile, and folded his arms along the wooden table.

Summer shrugged. 'Maybe,' she said. 'No. Probably not, I . . . I don't know. Why bring it up? Why take time out to remember the day we lost her?' She could feel a thickness form in her throat, and knew this was *exactly* the reason she hadn't wanted to do this. She didn't want to fall apart now.

'Because we all loved her,' Valerie said, her thin fingers gripping Summer's, 'and it's important to remember that. Come on.'

Summer followed her dad and brother down towards the water. Harry looped her arm through hers and gave her a squeeze, but Summer found herself glancing in the direction of *The Sandpiper*. Could she go and get Mason? He'd met her mum – he'd told her that – but had he known her well enough? They turned away from the boats, towards the small brick bridge that marked the edge of the narrower part of the river. It was quieter here, out of sight of the boats and the pub's picnic tables. The towpath wasn't empty, but it seemed more peaceful.

Summer saw that Ben had a bunch of roses too, red and yellow, their blooms full to bursting with colour and scent and life. He untied the bouquet and began handing the roses out to each member of the party. Summer took hers and stared at the river, at the surface breaking into concentric circles where water boatmen or fish were disturbing it, a few green leaves following the current, lying on their backs as if they were sunbathing.

She remembered a day the previous year, not long before it happened, when it had been as hot as this. She and her mum had closed up the café, ordered two pints of lager from the pub, and sat on the edge of the towpath, their feet and ankles in the water. Summer hadn't known, then, about her mum and Dennis, but her suspicions had been starting to grow, and there had been a slow tension building between mother and daughter for the previous few weeks. She couldn't remember what they'd said, but that evening, under an electric blue sky and a burning sun, and with the bubbles of beer inside her, Summer had laughed more than she'd done for weeks before – and like she hadn't done since.

Her mum wasn't innocent, but she was her mum, she was the person Summer looked up to, and at that moment, she realized that she missed her more than anything.

'Right,' Ben said, clearing his throat and turning to face the water. 'Just to say that . . . that we miss you, Mum – Madeleine – all of us do, and that we think of you always. Here goes.' He thrust his arm forward, projecting a red rose, and then a yellow, into the river, as far out as he could manage. 'There.' He nodded, decisive, but Summer could hear the telltale roughness in his voice. He looked strange, too smart and stiff to be standing alongside the river and throwing flowers into it, but she knew her brother's words were heartfelt.

'Goodbye, my darling Maddy. Thank you for always shining down on us and keeping us safe. Not a day goes by when we don't think of you, or laugh at the warmth of your memory. You're in our hearts.' Valerie stepped forwards and

292

threw her own flowers in. Harry did the same, and then Summer's dad. Summer wondered, for a moment, if he'd say anything, but he didn't, just stepped forwards and crouched, his body slow and stiff, laying his roses on the surface of the water, as if they were made of crystal.

Summer inhaled and took a step towards the water's edge. She closed her eyes and pictured herself and her mum sitting side by side, their feet in the cold water, then her mum behind her counter in the café, the gingham apron on and smudges of chocolate cake on her cheeks as she laughed at something a customer had said, and then the last image – the one that Summer could never banish – of her mum's eyes wide with shock and hurt, her calling Summer's name and Summer storming through the café and flinging the door open and then shut behind her. The last sight she had of her mum, before the hospital.

'I'm sorry, Mum,' she said, kneeling on the towpath, embracing the tears as they fell down her cheeks. 'I'm so, so sorry about what I said. I never meant to hurt you. You're my hero.' She threw her red rose into the water and it drifted downstream, following the path of the others, its petals trailing in the water. 'I love you, and I hope I'm making you proud.' She threw the yellow rose in, watching its progress through her tears, wondering if Valerie was right, that Maddy *was* looking down on them, watching this awkward ceremony. At that moment, she hoped she was, and that her mum could see how sorry she was, and how much she missed her.

Latte's nose nudged against her hand and Summer lifted the little dog up and buried her head in the white, soft fur. Latte licked her cheek and the tears that were still falling. She felt a hand on her shoulder and knew that it was her brother's.

293

'Come on, sis. You did good.' He held out his hand and Summer took it, let herself be pulled upright, and followed the small party back to the pub.

'I'll get a bottle of wine,' Ben said. 'I think we could all do with a drink.'

Summer's eyes went again to *The Sandpiper*, and she thought of her plans with Mason. She wasn't late yet, but she soon would be, and while she desperately wanted to spend time with Mason, she knew she couldn't abandon her family. Her brother had come all the way from Edinburgh and she hadn't seen her dad for months. Besides, at that moment she would be the least fun company ever, and might end up putting Mason off her for good. She pulled her phone out, and sent him a message: *I'm so sorry, something's come up. Can we take a raincheck? I'm free tomorrow. xx*

The reply was almost instant. *No problem. Tomorrow's good. Hope you're OK? M.*

Summer sighed, the simple question making her brain hurt, unsure whether to answer with a breezy 'fine' or say something close to the truth. In the end she left it, putting her phone back in her bag and giving full attention to her family, choosing chips and gravy from the menu when they ordered food.

She sat next to her dad and asked him how he was, listened to the bland stories about his college, where he was a teacher, too professional to reveal any interesting tales about fellow teachers or students. He was close to retirement and Summer got a strong sense that he was dreading it and the lack of purpose he'd be faced with.

'Are you going to write that book you've always thought about?' she asked. 'You could now, you know.'

He gave a quick chuckle. 'I'm not sure I'm cut out for it, Summer. Fenland history isn't on most people's reading lists these days. It's all thrillers and sporting biographies and those YouTube superstars.'

'I'm sure lots of people who live here would be fascinated,' Summer said. 'And if you don't try, you won't know, will you?'

'Speaking from experience,' he said, giving her a solid stare, an almost smile. 'I think I could learn a lot from you, Summer. What you've achieved over the last few months. The courage it's taken.'

Summer was shocked by the words, the pride he was conveying, his knowledge of the effort it had taken to come back to her mum's boat, and her chip hovered in mid-air, halfway to her mouth. 'Dad,' she managed.

'I'd like to hear more about it. Not today maybe, not right now. But why not come and stay for a few days, when business is a bit quieter.'

'I'd love to. Thank you.' He clinked his glass against hers and Summer sat in shocked silence for a while, thinking that he had never reached out to her before, that it had always been her making the effort, arranging visits, calling him. Was it the fact that she'd stopped doing that over the last few months that had forced him into action? Had he realized that he was missing out on his daughter's life?

'Did you find Mum's compass?' Ben asked, pulling her away from her thoughts.

Summer shook her head. 'I've looked everywhere. Unless Mum had some secret panel somewhere to keep it safe – but wouldn't she just have used the wall safe?'

Ben looked angry. 'Maybe I did throw it out . . . But I'm sure – I'm *sure* I didn't. It was in my mind the whole time I was clearing out that boat. I'm so sorry, Sum.'

'It's not your fault,' she said, 'it's just one of those things.' But she felt the quiver in her bottom lip all the same.

'It's not lost,' Valerie said.

'It isn't? How do you know?'

Valerie leaned forward and put one hand over Summer's, and one over Ben's. 'I just know. It's not lost, and it will be found. It's important.'

'It was one of my favourite things of hers,' Summer agreed. 'It holds memories.'

'No, I mean that finding it will be important. I can sense it – it'll teach you something, Summer.'

Summer stared at Valerie, trying to read her face, trying to understand her strange, mystical beliefs. How could she know that – where did the knowledge come from? She glanced at Ben and he gave her a shrug.

'Well,' he said, his voice unsure, 'that's all right then. Great to know it's not gone for good.' Summer could only nod in response.

When they left, Harry driving Ben and their dad back to his house in Cambridge, it was close to nine o'clock. Summer felt exhausted and wrung out, like she had nothing left inside her. She took Valerie's arm and escorted her back to *Moonshine*.

'Dennis should have been here,' Valerie said. 'He should have been part of it.'

'I think that would have been hard, for him and for Jenny. I'm sure he's thinking of her in his own way.'

'We shouldn't exclude him,' Valerie said.

'We don't. We just need to strike a balance, that's all.' Summer gave Valerie a hug, waited until she'd made it on to her boat, and then strolled along the towpath, Latte at her heels. The outside lights of the pub reached down to the river and there was a bold moon out, giving everything a surreal, whitish glow. Summer stepped on to the bow deck and hovered at the door, her key poised. She glanced again at her watch. Nine fifteen. It wasn't unsociably late, and after wishing that she could hibernate all day, she'd been flung into the midst of friends and family. Now, the thought of going back to her boat and spending the rest of the evening with just Latte and her memories for company felt hideous.

Taking a deep breath, she stepped back on to the towpath and made her way along to *The Sandpiper*. The lights were on inside, and she reached up and knocked before she could lose courage.

She thought she heard a 'Coming', drift towards her from inside, and then the door opened.

'Hi.' Mason didn't seem surprised. 'Rough day?' His dark eyes met hers easily, and his smile was so kind, and he looked so relaxed – in a navy T-shirt and his trademark jeans – that Summer had to resist the urge to step against him and lean her head on his chest.

'It was good,' she said. 'Unexpected, but better than I thought. Can I – I'm sorry, it's late and I've already stood you up tonight, so—'

'Of course.' He let her in, turned to the galley and got a glass out of a cupboard. 'Actually,' he said, pouring red wine into the new glass and topping up his own, 'how about some fresh air?'

'What do you mean?'

He pointed up at the ceiling. 'There's a pretty spectacular moon out, probably a good star display.'

Summer leaned against the counter and grinned. 'The roof?'

'Shall we?'

'Lead the way.'

Latte and Archie explored every corner of the roof of *The Sandpiper*, peering over the edges and sniffing the odd leaf or twig that had landed there and not yet been blown off by the breeze.

'It's clean up here,' Summer murmured, sitting down with her back to the towpath, looking out at the dark water.

Mason sat next to her, his body close, but not touching. 'I cleaned it. After the last time, when you told me you were looking at the stars, when you were with Claire and the others, and I came up here, I pretty much ruined a T-shirt. I had to boil-wash it three times before all the muck came out. So there you go,' he added.

'There I go what?' Summer glanced at him.

'Not as immaculate as you thought.'

'Nobody could have a go at you for a grubby roof,' Summer said. 'But it surprised me, how you spend most of your time wandering through fields or mud or across beaches, dog in tow, and then your boat is so beautiful and polished.'

'It's my home,' he said. 'And my life. Being a liveaboard means that it's even more important, that I spend even more time there. Haven't you found that?'

'What do you mean?'

'When I was on land, living in a house, leading a normal-ish life, I wasn't moving between just work and home. There were dinners out, drinks, galleries and exhibitions and parties. Home seemed like somewhere to eat and sleep and spend the occasional evening, but here, on the river . . .' He shook his head. 'Maybe it's just that my life has changed. I've narrowed my field. Maybe it has nothing to do with living on a boat, maybe it would always have been like this, even if I'd bought another house.'

Summer sat very still. This was the first time he'd spoken about his past, about life before *The Sandpiper*, and she didn't want to say anything to interrupt his flow. 'Were you a photographer then, too?' she asked, carefully.

He nodded. 'Yes, but my focus wasn't on wildlife. I was freelance, picking and choosing the best jobs, trying to build a reputation. But it's so competitive, so difficult to get noticed.' He took a sip of his wine. 'In the end, you start chasing the money. You do any job that pays, telling yourself you'll do that one to get by and find another one you really care about, but it's hard to resist the money, and then it doesn't matter what you're capturing. I quickly began to lose pride in my work, and I was so focused on getting the jobs that I started missing out on everything else.'

'Was that when you decided to change your life? Did you always want to photograph nature?'

He moved his head slightly. Summer thought it was a shake, and then he turned, stretched his legs out and lay down along the boat. She put her wine down, and lay next to him. Latte trotted up and lay in the warm space between them, her short body elongated, her front paws stretched up towards their heads.

'Honestly, I hadn't thought about it,' Mason continued. 'We had bird feeders in the garden, and that's as far as it went. But when I bought *The Sandpiper*, I knew I would still have to make money as a freelance, but that I'd always be on the move, not just in London. My first week on the boat, I was sitting on the deck with a beer – it was February, so it was freezing, but I didn't care. I noticed a heron, partly hidden by bushes on the bank, waiting for his dinner. He was so close to me, so still, and I remember thinking he looked prehistoric. I went inside and got my camera, thinking the movement would disturb him and he'd be gone, but it didn't. It was as if he wasn't real . . . and yet he was more real than anything I'd seen, and then when he moved, darting into the water, emerging with this huge fish, I couldn't believe that I was able to watch it, to be so close.

'I downloaded the photos and scrolled through them, and I just knew. I didn't want to go back to fashion shoots and carefully arranged set pieces for magazines. I wanted to photograph wildlife. I wanted to capture life – and not posed, preprepared, polished-to-the-last-detail life – but real life.'

'I get that,' Summer whispered. 'I get what the draw is, the excitement of seeing these creatures just going about doing their own thing. It's like being in a different world, away from streets and towns and hubbub and televisions and shouting and cars and . . .' She breathed out, focused on the cluster of stars above her. 'It's like being here with you. It's just you and me and the dogs, the river and the sky. No distractions.'

'None,' Mason said, and Summer heard a roughness in his voice that hadn't been there before.

'Do you mind, talking about your past?' She thought back to his words after her break-in, how he'd spoken with such conviction and looked so upset when he'd seen the damage in her café.

'I don't speak about it very often,' he said. 'It feels strange. It almost doesn't feel like it was mine – it's as if I'm talking about a distant relative, or a film I saw once. But a few things recently have brought some memories back.'

'Does it make you sad?' She turned her head towards him. He was staring up at the sky, his lips pressed together, his face white beneath the bold moon.

'I have a lot of regrets,' he said eventually. 'Things I should have done but didn't. I was too wrapped up in myself and then . . . it was too late.'

'For what?' She saw his Adam's apple bob, and then he turned on his side so he was facing her too. He smiled, but to Summer it looked sad, full of memories and loss, a smile that wasn't quite in the present. Summer knew how he felt.

'For me to make amends,' he said. 'But it's something I'm working through. I'm in a good place now. My work, the river, Archie, *The Sandpiper*, and for the last few months, being in Willowbeck. They all help.'

'I'm glad,' Summer said, wondering whether to push, deciding not to.

'Tell me about today,' he said. 'What you did to remember your mum.'

This time there was no hesitance, no 'only if you want to'. He was challenging her, but in a way Summer knew she needed to be challenged. Mason, it seemed, knew it too. She told him about her brother and her dad turning up, how Valerie had organized their visit without telling her, which at first she thought was the worst idea possible but, actually, turned out to be a good thing.

'It was hard,' she said, 'saying goodbye to Mum all over again. Actually saying the words, acknowledging it in front of other people. I love words. But they have power, either spoken or written down, whether they're serious or silly.'

'Your blackboard rhymes,' Mason said.

'They're not too serious, are they? I could always make them a bit more light-hearted.' Mason laughed, and Summer felt his breath on her face. 'Ever since Mum died,' she continued, 'I've tried my best to keep everything inside – don't speak about it, skirt around the issue. But then, of course, I did nothing but think about it, and the thoughts had nowhere to go except round and round. I still don't like doing it, but I'm beginning to realize that speaking about it is better than not, that it helps to release emotions, and untangle things that get knotted up inside.'

'Maybe you could write your thoughts down,' Mason said.

'What?' Summer screwed her nose up. 'Like a diary?'

'I don't know,' Mason sighed. 'You said words had power written down too. Maybe it would give you the opportunity to put everything down, to get it out, but not in public. A middle ground. Maybe, if you did that, then talking about her wouldn't be so hard.'

Mason's idea had conjured up a picture of an immature teenage diary, with hearts on the cover and a tiny gold lock and key, but it wasn't the worst idea she'd ever heard. It was, when she thought about it, a sensible – and thoughtful – idea.

'Maybe,' she said, 'but I like talking to you. Maybe you could be like my diary, my sounding board.'

'You really want to open up to me? Not Valerie, or Harry?'

'Harry knows everything,' Summer said. 'I don't know, maybe I wasn't being serious, but I can talk to you. I *like* talking to you.'

'That's good. It would be a bit awkward if we were just lying here in stony silence.'

'You're not a stony silence kind of person,' Summer said, stroking Latte as the little dog pawed at her face.

'I'm not?' Mason leant up on his elbow, spotted Archie lying down at the edge of the roof, peering down into the dark water and then, seemingly satisfied, lay back down again.

'You're a warm silence person.'

'Like a portable heater?'

Summer laughed. 'They're never quiet. I mean that you're easy to be around, whether we're talking or not. And I feel a bit bad.'

302

'About what?'

'That we've not paid nearly enough attention to this.' She pointed upwards, and Mason's gaze followed her hand, up to where the stars winked down on them.

'It's not the best night after all,' Mason said, 'the moon's being too overbearing.'

'I bet that would be a good photo. You don't have your camera,' she said, suddenly noticing. 'Why don't you have your camera?'

'I didn't think to pick it up. Besides, I'd need to set it up properly to get a good photo of the moon. Slow shutter speed, tripod.'

'Not an impulse photo, then?'

Mason shook his head, his gaze still on the sky above them. Summer wriggled slightly, adjusting her position, and Latte, annoyed at the disturbance, got up and went to see what Archie was looking at. Mason glanced at her, then lifted his arm and beckoned Summer closer. Summer shuffled across the roof towards him and rested her head on his chest. He wrapped his arm around her, his fingers grazing along her bare arm. She was still in the dress she'd worn to her mum's goodbye, but despite the late hour it wasn't cold. She pressed her bare leg against Mason's jean-clad one, and stared up at the stars.

Neither of them spoke, but after the day's emotions, the conflicting thoughts whirring around in her head, Summer felt that this was the perfect way to end it. She couldn't say she felt calm – anything but – but her heart wasn't thudding out of fear or anxiety. She turned her head, her ear against Mason's chest, and found that his heartbeat was faster too.

Chapter 17

They watched the sky, the blinking, shimmering stars, and Summer found, as she always did, that the more she looked, the more she saw. Despite the moonlight, the stars fought their corner, and Summer could see some constellations she recognized – although she didn't know their names – and smaller, paler clusters, almost blurring into clouds. Star clouds. She got used to the feel of Mason's hand resting on her waist, his presence infinitely comforting.

'This was a good idea,' she murmured. 'This is perfect.'

'It was your idea, originally,' Mason said, 'I just stole it from you.'

'Well done me, then,' Summer said, smiling into his chest.

'You're full of good ideas. I haven't bothered to celebrate my birthday properly in years, but what you did for me was just right. I had a lot of fun, and I know you put a lot of effort into it. It was good to meet your friends – Harry and Greg and Tommy.'

'Sorry if they cornered you.'

'They didn't, and I got on with them. Tommy's got a lot of character.'

'He has – he's very curious.'

'I think he thought I was some kind of hunter. It took a while to explain to him that my only weapon was my camera.'

'He's just got into fishing. Greg's a big fan, and he's encouraged that Tommy's as enthusiastic as he is.'

'And Harry makes amazing cakes. That was definitely the best birthday cake I've had. I was disappointed that it was so popular – I could have lived off cake and ice cream for another week.'

'I'll get her to make you another one. I'm hoping she'll do some more baking for the café, on a regular basis.'

'You're not happy with what you're doing?'

'I'm not the best baker. Harry's a genius when it comes to cakes.'

'Oh I don't know about that,' Mason said softly.

Summer laughed. 'You've just told me how wonderful her pistachio cake was. You don't need to butter me up.'

'Well, you definitely make the best bacon sandwiches. I can say that with absolute, unbiased certainty.'

'You're very kind.'

'And you're the best company,' he said.

Summer heard the change in his voice, the shift to something more serious. Her heart skittered as his hand moved from her waist to her shoulder, and then he ran his fingers through her hair. She put her hand on his chest and looked up at him. The moonlight cast him in relief, his cheeks and forehead pale, his eyes in shadow, but she could feel him looking at her, the way it made her limbs tense in anticipation.

She parted her lips and Mason moved his head down, his own lips pressing against hers.

Warmth rushed through her, chasing the shudder, and she felt her whole body come to life. She pressed against him, returning the kiss, tasting red wine. She closed her eyes so she could focus on the feel of him, his hand cradling her head, his lips soft, the slight brush of stubble as his jaw grazed her skin.

She had wanted this, she realized, since the first moment she had met him. She had wanted it, and now it was happening it was as good as she'd hoped. The connection was there, it was real and it was exhilarating, and it made her want more. But her mind wouldn't rest and thoughts crowded in, trying to muscle in on the moment: Claire saying he was colder than ice cream and not as sweet; Mick calling him Lothario; her mum's face as Summer had stormed out of the café, a year ago today. She squeezed her eyes closed, trying to dispel them, and they came faster. *Be cautious*, Claire had said. But hadn't Summer waited long enough, hadn't she got to know Mason well enough?

She pulled back slightly, breaking the kiss, found Mason's eyes and looked hard into them. His breathing was elevated, his dark eyes as intense as flames, burning right through her. How could he be a womanizer? She had seen nothing but honesty and kindness from him.

'What is it?' Mason asked, his voice a barely there whisper.

'I – I don't know.'

'You're frowning. I'm sorry if I – if you didn't want—'

'Of course I did,' she said. 'Couldn't you tell?' She tried a laugh, but it sounded as if she was clearing her throat.

'So what's wrong?' He thumbed a strand of hair away from her face, then glanced behind him as Archie came up and put his head on Mason's shoulder, whimpering softly.

'Perhaps it's time to go inside,' Summer said.

Mason nodded, holding her gaze. 'Sure. It'll start to get cold soon.'

He sat up, and Summer felt the space between them immediately. He shuffled to the edge of the boat and then hopped down. Summer passed him the wine glasses and then gently hefted down Archie, and then Latte, into his arms. Mason put them on the deck and the dogs raced around, having a moment of madness after being on the roof.

Summer slid over to the edge of the boat and lowered herself down, careful not to let her dress ride up. Mason was there to catch her, his arms around her, helping her to land safely on the deck. Summer felt her body respond to his touch, keener now that she had some experience of how good it felt. Their faces were close, but Mason's look was questioning.

'This has been perfect,' Summer said, fighting with her urge to kiss him again. She wanted to, but she didn't want the thoughts to come back. She wanted to be free to enjoy being with him, she wanted to be sure. 'You've made today so much better than it could have been.'

'I'm glad,' Mason said. 'And I'm sorry if—'

Summer put a finger to his lips. 'Sorry isn't allowed,' she said. 'It was perfect.'

Mason raised his eyebrows. 'You didn't seem sure, a moment ago.'

'I am,' she said. 'I – at least, I nearly am. But I don't want to rush things. I've got it so wrong in the past, and I just don't want to . . .' She shook her head, sighing at her inability to articulate her feelings. 'Can I come and see your eagle photos? Tomorrow, maybe, if you're around.'

'I'll be here,' Mason said.

307

'Good.' She bent to stroke Latte, getting the dog's attention, and stepped off the deck on to the towpath.

'Summer?'

'Yes?'

'You would tell me, wouldn't you, if I was . . . misreading things?'

'I would,' Summer said, 'but you're not. You're not, I just – like you, I have to work through things.'

Mason nodded, and to her relief Summer saw him smile, a warm, genuine smile that broke out through the night-time shadows, and reached her almost as if his hand were running up her arm. He understood her hesitation; he knew that it wasn't as simple as two people being attracted to each other.

She made her way back to *The Canal Boat Café*, thinking that either Claire's story about Tania was missing some truths, or Summer was the worst judge of character ever. Mason was genuine, she was sure of it. He might still be keeping things from her, but she was just as guilty of doing the same with him. It wasn't instant download, as Harry had said, and tonight they had taken another step towards getting to know each other. She just had to make sure she didn't allow her physical desire to race ahead of her emotions. She couldn't bear the thought of getting it wrong and making an enemy out of Mason – he was already too important to her for that.

Summer found she couldn't sleep at all that night. When she closed her eyes she saw a slideshow of stars and the moon, Mason's face turning to her on the roof of the boat, the way he'd looked up as he spoke about his previous life. He'd begun to let her in, so she should do the same. She shouldn't be letting Claire's outdated warning – as good a friend as she was – or the nickname used by someone she'd met only a couple of times, win over the reality of being with Mason. But she was still wary. She'd got things so wrong with Ross, and she didn't want to make another mistake that would haunt her.

The following morning continued the run of beautiful, clear skies and fresh summer heat. Summer iced some lemon drizzle cake and opened the door, hatch and windows of the café as wide as they would go. She'd got through the first anniversary of her mum's death. It felt as if it was a milestone, that she was automatically stronger just for having passed that date, and that she could treat this day like a fresh start. Maybe it was fate that Mason had come to her now. Maybe she was meant to make things work with him, to get over the hurdles and run into his arms at the finish line.

She found that she was beaming as she worked, as wide and brightly as the sun, and the morning flew by. She welcomed in a group of two families who filled all twelve seats inside the café, and the outdoor tables were permanently busy. The coffee machine squealed and frothed, people adhering to the adage that a hot drink was refreshing on a hot day, and she ran out of Magnums before lunchtime. Barry, one of the regular helmsmen who often stopped for a drink, cruised past on his boat, and she gave him a takeaway coffee, bacon roll and slice of coffee cake, and then stood and watched as a family of swans, with six downy grey cygnets, swam past in a haphazard line. The season was in full flush, full bloom, and here on the river Summer felt that she was in the best place to enjoy her namesake.

When she closed up at half past six, her planned trip back to *The Sandpiper* firmly at the forefront of her mind, she hurried along the towpath towards Valerie's boat, *Moonshine*. She wanted to thank her properly for organizing the memorial, albeit surreptitiously. She wanted to be kinder and more open to Valerie, to start letting those closest to her in.

As she jumped on to the bow deck, she saw movement inside, and realized that Valerie must be finishing with one of her clients. She hopped back down to the towpath and was greeted by Harvey, Valerie's adventurous silver tabby. She crouched and stroked him, his body flattening out under her hand, his purrs loud and approving. His big green eyes looked up at the sound of voices behind them, and Summer turned to discover that Valerie's customer was none other than Ross. She felt irritation sweep through her, certain that he was about to get in the way of her talk with Valerie and her night with Mason. But she wasn't going to let him – not today.

'Summer!' Ross's grin showed off all his white teeth. He was wearing green khaki shorts and a blue T-shirt with a cartoon 'Kapow' speech bubble on it. 'You're looking very lovely, but then I guess you must be feeling pretty at home.'

Summer glanced in the direction of her boat, and Ross laughed. 'I meant the season. Summer in summer. It has to be your favourite time of year.'

She was sure they'd had this conversation before, but Summer played along. 'It's beautiful, but I love autumn just as much. Summer was my mum's favourite season, though.'

Ross nodded, his smile replaced by a solemn expression. 'Valerie was telling me what you all did yesterday, to remember her. It sounds like it went well, but it can't have been easy.'

'No.' Summer felt herself shutting down. 'It was tough, but it was worth doing. I . . .' She looked at Valerie, 'I was actually coming to say thank you, for what you did. For taking the trouble, and for contacting Ben and my dad and Harry. I know I was shocked to begin with, but I would have

310

been regretting it now, if I hadn't done anything to mark it. Instead, I . . .' She glanced at Ross, not wanting him to know how refreshed she felt. He would either laugh at it, or jump on it and try and make himself a part of her fresh start. 'I'm so pleased we did it. Thank you, Valerie.'

Valerie stepped on to the towpath, her thin dress in shimmering gold and yellow catching on the slight breeze, and put her arms around Summer. Summer relaxed into the hug, her head against Valerie's shoulder and her red hair tickling her face.

'I'm glad you saw the good in it,' Valerie said, 'and that you understand why I did it that way. It was Maddy's idea, actually.' She stepped back and looked at Summer seriously, and Summer resisted the eye roll.

'I'm not sure if—'

'I don't mean keeping it quiet from you. I mean the roses in the river.'

Summer frowned and lifted up Harvey who was slinking around her ankles, craving attention. 'She told you to do that?'

Ross folded his arms over his chest, and Summer could see a smirk playing at the corners of his mouth. Summer's irritation surged again – why was he getting readings from Valerie if he didn't believe in it, if he was going to ridicule her?

Valerie gave a soft, sad smile. 'A friend of hers, Warren, do you remember him? He used to be a lock keeper, but passed through Willowbeck regularly on his days off. He died a couple of years ago. I think he was in his early seventies, so it was terribly sad, but not tragic. Maddy only heard about it in passing, from another boatman, and she didn't really know him well enough to attend the funeral, so she said

311

that she would do her own thing for him. She got a huge bunch of white roses and threw them, one by one, in the river, while she told me stories about him. It was such a simple way of saying goodbye and I thought, for Maddy's memory, to remember her, that was what we should do.'

Summer smiled, relieved that Valerie hadn't told her a story from beyond the grave, and touched that her plans had been based on her mum's own, thoughtful ceremony.

'Thank you,' she said again. 'It was good to see Dad and Ben, too.'

'They've missed you, you can tell.'

'I should be better at staying in touch with them.'

'You're doing a good job, Summer. Look how the café's thriving under your influence. God,' Valerie laughed, 'was it only the beginning of the year when it was falling apart under my care?'

'That's not fair,' Summer said. 'You already had another job.'

'So did you,' Ross said, pointedly, reminding Summer of how long it had been since she'd worked on a commission, or even visited the other members of the cooperative. 'And weren't you going to sell *The Canal Boat Café*?'

Summer narrowed her eyes. 'Things change – you never know what's going to happen. I remember you saying something very similar to me, not too long ago.'

Ross grinned at her and scratched the back of his neck. 'Can I talk to you, Summer?'

'Sure,' Summer said, keeping her voice even, steeling herself for the inevitable, circular conversation. 'Let's get a table outside.' She gestured towards the pub.

'Things OK with Jenny, then? That's a surprise.'

'We've agreed to leave each other to it,' Summer said. 'She

312

has to accept I'm back here running the café, and I have to get used to her not wanting anything to do with me, which is fine – much better than sinister cakes appearing on my boat. It's working so far.'

'I'm glad,' Ross said. 'What do you want to drink?'

While Ross went to get their drinks, Summer headed back inside to get Latte, knowing she'd want to enjoy the sunshine, and thinking she could take the Bichon Frise for her evening walk afterwards, before she went to see Mason. She smiled at the little skip inside her tummy, and thought that, if she could just get through the next hour with Ross, then she was all set up for a perfect evening of Mason, his boat and his photographs – she hadn't yet decided which of those was the most beautiful. Her step was light as she went to meet Ross on the grass, Latte bounding along at her side. The day was full of promise, and Summer was prepared to let herself enjoy it.

It was a perfect summer's evening, the other tables at the pub busy with chatter and laughter, everyone relaxed, nobody too serious or solemn. They had come to enjoy the warmth of the late sun, and the picture-perfect English view next to the river. Summer couldn't imagine a more beautiful spot. The only place, she thought, where there might be the smallest semblance of tension was at the picnic table she was now seated at, and most of it was coming from her.

'Is this becoming a regular thing for you, having readings with Valerie?'

Ross shrugged. 'Would it be a problem if it was?'

'No, not at all. I just . . . I didn't think it was the kind of thing you were in to, that's all. What do you go for? Astrology, palmistry, clairvoyance?' Summer knew that Valerie used several methods, including tarot cards and tea leaves, as well as the stars, hands and her spiritual vision. That was the one that Summer most associated with Valerie's assertions that Maddy was watching over them, though in truth it could have been any of them.

'She varies the readings,' Ross said. 'I think that her inner sight guides it all, but she did look closely at my palms today. She spotted a few interesting things, actually.'

'Oh?' Summer wasn't sure she wanted to hear about this. There had to be another agenda with Ross, and while she couldn't bear the thought of rejecting him completely, she didn't want to spend too long with him – she had to get ready to see Mason.

Ross nodded and sipped his beer. 'I know – I remember you said that you didn't believe in this stuff, and I totally get that. But I really do think there's something to it. You get on with Valerie, don't you?'

'Of course I do. She's a good friend, but I . . . we can believe in different things, can't we?' Summer sighed, angry with herself for becoming defensive so quickly.

Ross, as usual, wasn't remotely rattled. 'Of course – I just think it's odd. Anyway, she predicted good things for the business, a possible expansion opportunity, which is interesting because I looked at a vacant shop the other side of Cambridge a couple of weeks ago.'

'Wow,' Summer said. 'You're going to buy another shop? You'll have to employ some more staff.'

'The rent seems pretty reasonable, and Cambridge is full of creative people. I would have thought some of the artists at your co-op might be looking for a bit of extra cash to support their artistic endeavours.'

'That's true,' Summer said, pushing away the guilt at not

having been in touch with them for so long. She was sure Ross could work out how she was feeling and was saying this deliberately to push her buttons. She wondered if he'd really had a reading at all, or had just been having a cup of tea with Valerie, and was now making all this up.

'Summer? Are you OK? You're away with the fairies.'

'I'm fine.' She gave him a quick smile, and decided to be bold. 'Ross, look, of course it's up to you what you do—'

'That wasn't the main thing Valerie said, though,' Ross interrupted, his voice loud, cutting her off.

Summer took a sip of her drink and squeezed her hands into fists under the table.

'She said that I would need to watch out for someone, that I'd need to be ready to pick them up off the floor, and that it wouldn't be the first time.'

'Ross, I don't believe—'

'I'm sure she was talking about you,' Ross said. 'She gave me such a pointed look. She said that it was my role to look after this person, even if they didn't think they needed it.'

Summer's irritation flashed into anger. 'She could have been talking about anyone. And anyway, you know I don't believe in it.'

'But *I* do,' Ross said. He pressed his palms flat on the table; there was no attempt to put his hand over Summer's, or squeeze her arm. 'I have to take her words seriously, or what's the point of going?'

Summer didn't have anything to say to that, so she just shrugged and checked that Latte was happy at her feet. The little dog was snoozing in the sunshine, one ear folded back as if she was listening to their conversation. A seagull had landed on the roof of *The Sandpiper*, and Summer wondered if Mason could hear it, if Archie was going mad inside at the tantalizing sound of something he could be chasing.

'Valerie said,' Ross continued, sighing, 'that someone close to me was about to be fooled, that they were about to be hurt, very deeply, at a time when they were only just getting back on their feet.'

'Why isn't this reading about you?' Summer snapped, not wanting to hear any more.

'It *is* about me. It's about what I have to do, what my role is.' Ross's open, easy face suddenly looked angry and Summer sat back, shocked. He was always happy around her, always relaxed in the face of her moods. Summer wondered, for a brief second, if what he was telling her was the truth.

'Sorry,' she murmured.

Ross shook his head. 'You are always so quick to point out how OK you are, Summer. Ever since last year, ever since we slept together, you've been like a porcelain doll with a fixed smile, not willing to admit to any weakness or sadness, and now I'm coming to you with this and you're doing everything you can to bat me away. Are you saying there's no prospect of you being hurt by anyone? That you're untouchable?'

Summer shifted on the bench. 'It's not really your business.'

Ross ran a hand through his short hair. 'Fine. You don't have to tell me anything, of course you don't, but I can't be blamed just because I care about you. Valerie said that this person I care about, this person I'm supposed to look after, is walking into the path of a Lothario.'

Summer froze, her intake of breath loud between them. Ross was giving her a steady look and Summer felt as if her insides were beginning to disintegrate. She tried to blink away her disbelief, tried to get her thoughts in order so she could work out what had just happened. Ross had a motive to put her off Mason – he had been suspicious and jealous of him since the beginning – but how had he known Mick's nickname for him, the one that, along with Claire's story, was niggling away at her?

'Summer,' Ross said kindly, 'are you OK?'

'Sure,' she said, flapping away his concern with a hand.

'You look pale – have you been getting enough rest?'

'Why do I need rest?' she snapped. 'I'm not eighty – or two! I'm a thirty-one-year-old woman and I have lots of energy. I don't need more rest than anyone else!'

'I just meant have you been working too hard, running that café all by yourself? Your boat was broken into in the middle of the night – the psychological effects of that will last much longer than you think.' He was back to unflappable, knowing that he'd got to her, that he had the upper hand.

'I need to go now, but thanks for the drink.' Summer had barely drunk any of her wine, so in an attempt to look like she wasn't flagging, or in need of rest, she gulped the rest down in several long swigs.

'Already?'

'I'm busy this evening,' Summer said.

'Oh?' Ross raised an eyebrow, but she could see the tightness of his lips, the inner irritation that he didn't want to reveal leaking out, like a glass with a crack in it.

'Thanks again,' she said. 'Sorry I can't stay longer.'

'You're always rushing off,' he said, 'always busy. I miss spending time with you, Summer, real time.'

'Maybe if you didn't just keep turning up—' she said sharply.

Ross held his hands up. 'I know, I know. I'm sorry. Let's plan something for when you're able to take some time off.

There's a Jeff Koons exhibition coming to Cambridge soon. How about that? We could make a day of it.'

Summer chewed her lip and wished she hadn't drunk her wine so quickly. The acid was burning its way down her chest. 'I'll think about it.'

'Think about it seriously,' he said, putting his hand on her arm. 'I miss you, Summer.'

She nodded quickly, wondering if it was possible for her to be any more noncommittal without being downright rude. 'I have to go. Thanks for the drink.'

'Any time,' Ross said. He stood and gave her a quick hug, and then sauntered off in the direction of the car park. Summer stared after him for a couple of minutes and then stomped towards her boat, Latte moving slowly at her feet after being unceremoniously woken from her doze.

It meant nothing, she told herself as she got Latte's dinner ready, banging drawers and kitchen implements. It was Ross being his usual, interfering self. He'd gone to see Valerie, had a cup of tea with her, and then pretended he'd had a reading to spook her into staying away from Mason. She could clear it up in a moment by going and asking Valerie the truth. But then, why had the word 'Lothario' come up? Was Ross just hedging his bets, hoping to put her off, unaware that he'd sailed so close to the wind? Pitching Mason as a womanizer was the simplest way of making him seem undesirable to Summer, so maybe he'd just landed on the name out of chance. But he could have said anything – *Casanova*, *heartbreaker*, *bad boy*. Lothario was very specific and it made Summer feel unsettled, like maybe the words *had* come from Valerie.

She'd picked out her outfit for the evening before she'd started work: cut-off jeans and a royal blue vest top, with a hint of lace around the hem and neck. She looked at it now, sighing, not moving as quickly as she could when Latte jumped on to the bed and stood proudly on top of the cut-offs.

Valerie could have heard Mick refer to Mason as Lothario – he wasn't the quietest man she'd ever met, he was doing his work in summer, when windows were open and sound carried on the still air. But if Valerie had heard that – through her own, mortal ears as opposed to divine intervention – then why had she passed it on to Ross? Was she trying to put Summer off Mason indirectly, using her profession to get the message across? Summer didn't really believe Valerie would do that. She wasn't a fraud and she was Summer's friend. Except, Summer thought, running a brush through her hair, the curls around her temple refusing to settle, Valerie had been underhand about her dad and Ben arriving, had organized the memorial *for her own good*. Was this also for Summer's own good? And if that was the case, what did Valerie know about Mason that made her want to put Summer off in this way? Why couldn't she come out with it directly? Was it because she didn't want to hurt Summer's feelings and inadvertently show her that she didn't trust her decision-making?

'Shit, Latte.' She sat on the side of the bed and let her dog walk on to her knees. 'It could be coincidence, couldn't it? It could just be that Ross or Valerie used a word and it's more accurate than they could have imagined.'

She hoped it was Ross. She hoped that he had wanted to spook her by bringing up the break-in and was trying to put her off Mason because somewhere, in some part of his brain, he thought he still had a chance of getting together with her – showing concern for her wellbeing, wanting to be the one to look after her. Either of the other explanations – that Valerie was consciously trying to dissuade her, or that Valerie's inner sight knew about Mason – didn't bear thinking about, because both of them ended with the truth that, to Mason, Summer was just another notch on his bedpost, even if he was playing a longer game to get her there. She pulled on her outfit, her nerves squashing down the excitement that had been bubbling happily all day. So much for her fresh start, she thought, as she lifted Latte into her arms and locked up the boat.

'Hey,' Mason said, opening the door with a casual smile. He was wearing a black T-shirt and grey shorts, the skin on his legs almost as tanned as his arms, his feet bare as usual. His dark eyes met hers and Summer found she was staring at him more closely, trying to read his thoughts. He frowned and gave a nervous laugh. 'You can come in, if you want to.'

'Hi,' Summer said, 'sorry, sorry. Thank you.' She stepped on board his beautiful boat. It was cool and fresh and smelled of delicious, slightly spiced food. The galley windows were open, and the summer breeze licked into every corner, tugging slightly at her hair. 'Have you had a good day?' She wanted so much to detach him from Claire's warning and Ross's weird prediction, and look at him objectively.

Mason nodded, and got two bottles of beer out of the fridge. He opened them and handed her one. Summer clinked her bottle against his and sipped, the bubbles refreshing after the tang of the white wine.

'You?' he asked. 'It looked relentless in the café today.'

'It was,' she nodded. 'And you – did you do any . . . bird-watching?' She closed her eyes, angry that she could no longer even make small talk with him. After the previous night, and her confession that she could be comfortable in his presence even when they weren't talking, she felt like they were grating against each other, and it was all her fault.

'Not today,' Mason said, moving towards his desk and beckoning for her to follow. He gestured for her to sit in the compact leather desk chair, while he perched on the edge of the sofa. She sat, beer in hand, and felt her senses respond as Mason leaned over her to reach the mouse. His skin smelt of lemons and his dark curls glistened, as if they were still damp from the shower.

She wondered if he was as nervous as she was after their kiss last night, the *what happens next?* that hung in the air between them. She wished her nerves were pure anticipation and not the wariness that was beginning to block everything else out.

'I've been sorting through my photos,' he said, 'and not just the shots I took of the eagle. I thought you might want to see some others, including some that I took that day in Foxburn.'

'I'd love to,' Summer said, 'but don't you want to sit here and have better control of the computer? You look uncomfortable leaning over like that.'

He flashed her a grin. 'Guests get the proper chair.'

'Guests? So you bring lots of people in here and show them your pictures?' She knew she sounded defensive, but the words were out.

'Only if I really like them,' Mason said, and then glanced behind him to where Latte and Archie were tussling good-naturedly on the floor, 'or if their dog is firm friends with mine.'

'Ah, so you pick your friends based on how much they can stop your dog causing mischief? If I hadn't had Latte, would you have even given me the time of day?'

Mason sat up and turned towards her. Their knees were almost touching, and he was so close that she could see the flecks of gold in his dark irises. 'I don't just want you for your dog and your espressos,' he said, his face serious.

'But you . . . you . . .' Summer's voice trailed off and she licked her lips.

Mason cupped her face with his hand, his thumb rubbing along her cheek. 'I want you,' he said, answering the question she couldn't get out, 'in my life. Having you here on board *The Sandpiper* is a good start.' He searched her eyes, let out a barely there sigh, and dropped his hand.

'What?' Summer asked, the single word noticeably shaky. She took a quick sip of beer and tried to calm her breathing. 'What's wrong?'

'I don't want to take things too far,' he said, 'if you're not ready.'

'But I – I—'

'You're not ready,' he said, and this time there was no question in his voice. 'So let's just look at some photos.' His smile was wide and warm, with no hint of frustration, and Summer found it impossible not to smile back. She'd unconsciously wheeled the chair across the floor, away from the sofa and the computer screen, and Mason took hold of the arm and wheeled it back again. 'But I don't bite,' he said, 'and you need to see these properly.'

Summer nodded and focused her attention on the screen.

'I've picked a selection,' he said, 'but if there's anything you're interested in that isn't here, or you just want to browse then that's fine – though there are a few thousand photos.'

'Thousands?'

'I've been doing this job five years,' he said.

'What about your photos from before that?' Summer asked. 'The non-nature ones? The fashion and magazine shoots?'

It might have been her imagination, but she thought she sensed him go very still, the mouse pointer hovering over a folder called *Summer.*

'I don't have them here,' he said. 'There's not enough room on the hard drive for everything. So, here we go.' He clicked open the folder and then selected the first photo, which popped up and filled the whole screen.

Summer, confused a moment before by the change in Mason's demeanour, was immediately transfixed by the beautiful photograph. It was of a blue, curving river next to a wide, raised bank, with golden-green fields beyond, on which a couple of cows were grazing. A windmill, its white sails reaching up towards the sky like open arms, broke the horizon, but it was the light that Summer was mesmerized by. It was white gold, pure and perfect, as if she could drink it. She realized she was doing that now, trying to drink it in.

'It's stunning,' she murmured. 'Where is that?'

'Norfolk,' Mason said, 'on the broads. I don't get down there too often because the waterways aren't suited to narrowboats, but they have some great reserves, and some beautiful views.'

'You took this?'

Mason laughed. 'I haven't invited you round here to show you a bunch of photos by other people.'

'Why is the light like this?'

'It was just after dawn, in summer. You don't see that quality of light at any other time.'

'It's like a fairy-tale.'

'Lacking a castle or a princess, I would have thought.'

'The princess could live in the windmill. She wouldn't care about a castle if she had that view.'

'Maybe,' Mason said, reaching forward and clicking on to the next photo, 'but you should see it on a damp, grey October day. I'm not sure the princess would be particularly happy then, especially if she was called Summer.'

'Hey,' Summer said, laughing, though her eyes were once again drawn to the image on the screen, this time an incredible close-up of a spider's web, its dew-covered strands glistening like silver thread. A spider sat in the very centre of the web, creating an almost perfect sense of symmetry. 'I wasn't saying *I* was the princess.'

'Weren't you?' Mason gave her a sideways look.

She glared at him for a second, and then turned back to the screen. 'Where was this taken?'

'About a ten-minute walk down the towpath from here,' he said. 'This one's recent.'

'How long did you have to sit there to get the shot?'

'A couple of minutes,' he said. 'Patience is important in my job, but on this occasion I didn't need it.'

Summer nodded. 'Patience,' she repeated quietly. Did his patience allow him to reel in his female catches too? Show them just enough care and attention, and then dump them unceremoniously afterwards, cruising off to a different part of the river to start again? Summer stared at the spider, thought of the flies that would fly headfirst into its trap, and drummed her fingers on the table. She couldn't keep wondering about him if she wanted to have any kind of a relationship with him – even friendship. This was ridiculous. *She* was being ridiculous.

'Summer? Hey, are you in there?' Mason tapped her fore-head gently with his fist, and Summer jumped. 'Are you OK? I asked if you wanted another beer.'

'That would be lovely, thank you.'

Mason put his hand on her arm, pushing the chair aside so he could slip past. Summer felt a jolt of electricity, a fizz of delight at his touch, her senses clearly ignoring the doubts in her brain. She had to end the ridiculousness right this moment. She followed him to the galley, pausing only to stroke Latte and Archie, who were engaged in a quiet doggy conversation on the floor in front of the sofa.

'Mason?' she said, and then stopped. She had no idea how to phrase her question; she just knew she had to ask it.

He got two beers out of the fridge, handed one to her and leant against the counter. 'Summer.'

'Can I ask you something?'

'Sure,' he said. 'Shoot.'

'Right.'

His eyes were narrowed slightly, curious but on edge. Did he think she was going to ask about his old life? In a way she was. In a way, she was asking the worst thing possible.

'Mason, have you had a lot of girlfriends?'

The words left her mouth and drifted into the narrow, airy space, and Summer saw Mason's curiosity turn quickly into surprise. 'What?'

'I just wondered, and . . . and now I realize this question would have sounded a lot less weird if it was part of a wider, more general conversation. I'm sorry, it . . . it – I should never have asked.'

'You can ask whatever you want,' he said, but his voice had an edge to it that hadn't been there before. 'And I guess it depends what you call "a lot".'

Summer shrugged, realizing she had no idea what her parameters were.

'What's this about, Summer?' Mason sighed and slipped past her, sitting on the sofa and patting the seat next to him. 'Is this why you backed off after our kiss? Because you have this impression of me as some kind of Don Juan, getting through as many women as I can find along the waterways?'

Summer fidgeted, staring past him and back at the spider on the computer screen.

'Where has this come from?' He ran a hand through his curls and turned sideways on the sofa, one leg, bent at the knee, resting on the cushion.

Summer copied him, but stared at the sofa, at his bare, tanned leg and the dark hairs covering it. 'It was something Claire said,' she admitted, 'when I was travelling up the river, after you'd come to see me and she'd seen you on my boat. She asked about us, and I – you were so different after you'd seen her, and then the next day she told me—'

'She told you what?' Mason asked, his voice sharp.

'About Tania.' Summer winced, and forced herself to look up at him.

She watched realization dawn on his face, his eyes widening with what looked like a mixture of sadness and understanding. 'So she *did* tell you.' His voice was quiet, but hard.

Summer nodded. 'Is that why you were suddenly so keen for me to come back to Willowbeck? So she wouldn't have the chance.'

Mason leaned forward, his elbow on his leg, a hand over his mouth. Latte chose that moment to jump on to Summer's knee with a little squeak. She kissed her on the nose and then put her gently back on the floor. When she turned back to Mason, he was hiding his head in his hands.

'That whole thing was such a mess,' he murmured. 'Tania, I . . .' He gave an angry sigh. 'I treated her so badly, I know that. It was unforgivable, but at the time . . .'. He looked up, and Summer was shocked at the emotion in his eyes. 'I wasn't in a good place, and I got things really wrong. But Summer, that's not what I do – I don't wait for people to get close to me and then leave them. It happened once, but I never meant to hurt her.'

Summer swallowed. 'But you did try to persuade me to come back to Willowbeck, so that Claire wouldn't be able to tell me what had happened.'

Mason grimaced, his handsome face crumpling. 'We didn't know each other well then, but already – I thought if you had a bad impression of me so early on, then there was no hope. And I really wanted there to be hope.'

'You did?'

He nodded.

Summer swallowed. 'Can I get a glass of water?'

'Sure, I'll—' He went to stand, but Summer put her hand on his shoulder.

'I can get it.' She went into the galley and found a glass, ran it under the cold tap. Her heart was pounding. He'd admitted what had happened with Tania, but he looked genuinely upset. Surely he was telling her the truth – he cared about her as early as Foxburn; already, he had wanted there to be a chance for them. But he had tried to hide his past by forcing her back to Willowbeck – shouldn't he have just come clean then? She leaned on the counter and sipped her water.

'Summer?'

She looked at him on the sofa, suddenly so forlorn, so world-weary, like he had been in her trashed café after the break-in. She was sure it was connected – what happened with Tania, the way he talked about his past. There was something there, something that had shaped him, had perhaps even made him move on to the water.

'Are you OK?' she asked. 'Do you want some—' she started, but her words got stuck and she froze, a cold chill shivering over her, making the hairs on her arms stand up.

On the wall was a small photo in a wooden frame. It was of Mason standing in front of a narrowboat, but it looked as far from *The Sandpiper* as you could get, with faded green paintwork, small, old windows and patches of rust showing through. Mason looked different – his skin was paler and his hair much shorter, the curls cut into submission. His face was pensive, and he had a haunted look about him, as if nothing in life was certain. But it wasn't the photo that had made Summer freeze. It was what was on the kitchen surface, below the photo.

'Summer, what's wrong?' She barely heard him. She reached out and touched the compass, tracing the smooth round shape, the rose quartz cold against the tips of her fingers. She had seen this compass, held it so many times, and now, suddenly, after months of missing it, here it was.

Mason had reached her without her noticing, and she jumped as he touched her arm.

'What's this doing here?' Her voice sounded strange, as if she was being strangled.

'This – the compass?'

'My *mum's* compass.' She looked up at him, and his eyes widened.

'What?' he whispered.

'What's my mum's compass doing here, on your boat?'

Mason gawped, his lips moving but nothing coming out.

'Did you take it? Did you see it on my boat and take it?' Her heart was pounding, and so was her head, struggling to take things in, struggling to deal with Mason's stunned reaction.

'No, I – of course not. I—'

'Did Archie steal it? You were both on the boat before I'd moved aboard. Archie got into the kitchen and stole the bacon, and then you followed me into the cabin. Did you think that you could just *take* it? Did you think I wouldn't notice because, back then, I didn't want to be there?'

'Summer, no! No, of course I didn't. I wouldn't do something like that. Shit, Summer, I had no idea it belonged to your mum.' He put his hands on her shoulders and she flinched backwards, her arm going out and hitting the glass of water, sending it flying across the floor. Both dogs yelped, and Summer stepped backwards, clutching the compass.

'I – I have to go,' she murmured. 'Latte. *Latte.*'

'Let me explain, Summer.' Mason walked towards her, oblivious to the water and glass shards on the floor and his bare feet, his arm reaching out to her. 'Just sit down for a minute and I can tell you everything.'

'Everything? What, about why you couldn't be honest with me about Tania, and about why Mick calls you Lothario, and why you have my mum's compass in your kitchen? And why you found it so hard to deal with my café after the break-in, and why you can be *so certain* what fear is like? Are you going to tell me all of those things?' She was close to shouting, she knew, but she couldn't help it. Her breathing was fast, her hand gripping the compass tightly, its cold hardness slick in her sweaty palms.

'Yes,' Mason said simply. 'Yes, I'll tell you everything. Please, Summer, please come and sit down.' She stared at him, at his dark curls and his eyes that were so direct, so intensely focused on her that she felt she was burning where she stood. He seemed suddenly calm, as if he was resigned to it – to what had to happen next. Archie and Latte were both looking up at him expectantly, sensing the atmosphere, knowing that all wasn't well. Summer looked into Mason's beautiful dark eyes, felt her mum's compass in her hand, and felt the sting of tears at the corners of her eyes.

'I have to go,' she said. 'I can't . . . I can't do this now.'

She turned, calling to Latte again.

'Summer, wait!'

She rushed out of the door, the Bichon Frise at her heels, bounding along as if it was part of a game. The sunlight was still bright, and momentarily stung her eyes. She refused to stop, even when she thought she heard Mason following her, and raced along the towpath to her own boat. She flung the door open and locked it behind her, not stopping until she reached her berth. She sat on her bed, her knees up to her chest and her arms around them, as if she could hold herself together. Her phone chimed next to her and Latte sniffed it, but Summer ignored it. She heard banging on the door, could hear Mason calling her name, and she wondered, for a second, if she should let him in, let him explain everything.

She held the compass out on her palm, her eyes drinking in its beauty, feeling the connection to her mum, the way she would always make Summer navigate whenever they unmoored *The Canal Boat Café* and took it along the river. How could it have ended up on Mason's boat? She wanted to know, she wanted him to tell her, but at that moment she couldn't listen calmly.

He'd admitted that he'd treated Tania badly, and Summer

felt nervous about what he would tell her, about the way it would make her feel about him. She needed to calm down, she needed space, and then, in the morning, she would go to him and she would ask him to explain. She had trusted Mason easily, almost immediately, but since then the doubts had started to seep in, crashing against her attraction to him and threatening to dislodge it.

He seemed prepared to tell her, to let her fully in, and if he did that, then Summer should tell him everything too. About Ross, what had happened between them, and about the night her mum had died. Summer crawled into bed, Latte on her feet, and though her head was still pounding, and her eyes stung with unshed tears, she felt a sense of relief, and of hope – the same hope that Mason had held for them. She would talk to him in the morning, they could tell each other everything, and start again with a clean slate – a clean blackboard on which to write new words.

She woke the next day, dressing hurriedly and leaving Latte eating breakfast on board *The Canal Boat Café* while she stepped on to the towpath and into the bright sunshine. But the mooring next to hers gaped emptily, the water that she shouldn't have been able to see sparkling in the early morning light. *The Sandpiper* was gone, and with it, so was her hope. She had left it too late. Fumbling with her phone, her hands shaking, she dialled Mason's number, squeezing her eyes closed as it went straight to voicemail.

With a lump forming in her throat and her hands clenched tightly against the anger welling inside her, cursing her own stupidity, her ridiculous exit from Mason's boat the night before, Summer almost missed the curved, wooden object nestled next to the door on her bow deck.

She crouched and picked it up. It was a sun. A fat, round sun, with wavy rays sculpted out from the centre, giving it a cartoonish air. It was beautiful and tactile, felt comforting in her hand. *Was* it Mason? Had he gone, but left behind a ray of hope for them?

Summer drifted back into her boat and went through the motions of opening up the café for the day. She placed the sun alongside the other wooden items: the heart, frog, rabbit, daffodil and jester's hat. What did they mean? Were they talismans?

Summer knew she had made a huge mistake. She should have let Mason talk to her instead of storming off his boat like a schoolgirl in a strop, thinking that her confusion, her suffering, was more acute than his. But she had to believe that there was a glimmer of hope. She turned on the coffee machine, opened up the hatch to sunshine and the liquid trill of a robin. She could feel the weight of her mum's compass in the pocket of her dress, and slipped her hand inside to clutch it for a moment.

Mason was gone. He might have left Willowbeck for good, but that possibility was too heartbreaking for Summer to consider. Over the course of the last twelve hours she had managed to convince herself that they would have an emotional reconciliation and fall into each other's arms. She hadn't bargained on him disappearing, too hurt by her anger or by the memories that she was forcing him to drag up again, to stay around and work it out with her. She had also, during a mainly sleepless night, realized the strength of her feelings for him. She was sure there was a simple explanation for why he had her mum's compass, and there was nothing he could tell her – short of a murder confession – that would dilute her affection for him, the weight of feeling that was growing into something she was too scared to give a name to.

Summer thought back to their night looking up at the stars, only a couple of days before, and how he'd told her to write her feelings down, not to keep them locked up inside. She picked up her red chalk marker and wrote, in large, bold words along the top of the blackboard above the counter: *Come back, Mason. I'm sorry, and I believe there's hope for us, too.*

It didn't rhyme. It wasn't electrifying or witty or original, but it was the truth. Summer closed her eyes and hoped that, now the words were out in the open, written down for anyone to see, they would have power. She had to believe that she could get in touch with Mason, or that he would come back to Willowbeck. She picked up the wooden sun and held it against her chest. She had to hold on to that ray of hope.

Chapter 19

Summer Freeman's eyes went to the watch on her wrist on an increasingly frequent basis, as if the passing of time was against her. It was a sunny June day, the longest day of the year, and *The Canal Boat Café* entertained an almost continuous stream of customers. Some arrived on boats, pausing in Willowbeck's visitor moorings for a few hours, taking in the idyllic country feel of the riverside village, coming to Summer for coffee, bacon sandwiches and slices of cake, or the Black Swan for a pint and a bowl of steaming, salty chips. Some stopped on their way along the towpath, popping their noses in at the hatch, seeking Summer out and asking for a cappuccino or a bottle of lemonade, or one of the choc-chip cookies she'd put within tantalizing reach.

When a man who looked to be in his late thirties, wearing a three-piece suit and silky blue tie despite the weather, asked for an espresso and a bacon sandwich, Summer found herself narrowing her eyes defensively. It was ridiculous – it wasn't an uncommon order, but it was Mason's, and Mason wasn't here. The customer had fair hair, spiked with too much gel, and green eyes. Maybe he saw her firing irrational anger in his direction, because all of a sudden he seemed to lose his swagger.

'Nice day for it,' he said, glancing at the blackboard behind her.

'It is, isn't it?' Summer replied. And then, because she felt bad, added, 'Are you on your way to work?'

He glanced down, as if wondering whether he'd accidentally dressed in civvies and her question wasn't stupidly obvious. 'Yes,' he said, and the small talk dried up. But as she handed over his takeaway cup and the bacon roll, already leaking ketchup onto the paper bag, he looked her straight in the eye. 'I hope Mason comes back,' he said, and gave her a quick nod.

'T-thank you,' Summer said to his retreating back, and looked at the message she'd written on the blackboard. She wondered how many other customers had read it, whether they thought she was mad or if, in the spirit of the people who travelled and lived on the waterways, word would reach him that she wanted him back. Maybe, if he wasn't prepared to answer his phone, the old-fashioned route of word of mouth would work instead. A few months ago she couldn't have imagined putting her feelings out there for everyone to see, the words bold on her blackboard. But now she wasn't afraid of what people thought, or what they would say. She was more afraid that Mason wouldn't return to Willowbeck and the words made her feel like she was doing something to bring him back. She hoped they would have power.

As she served, cleaned tables, stacked the dishwasher and got fresh batches of orange and chocolate muffins out of the oven, flashes of the previous evening came back to her. Mason leaning close to her at his computer; the photo of the windmill on the Norfolk broads; her mum's precious compass nestling on his kitchen counter below an old photo of him with the wreck of his boat, before he'd turned it into a masterpiece; Mason reaching out to her, his eyes hooded with sadness, walking through the broken glass on his floor to try and stop her from leaving. She wondered if he'd cut his foot, whether he still looked defeated, as he had done when she'd accused him and then refused to listen to his explanation. She squeezed her eyes closed, hating that she had hurt him, knowing that she had to find him and apologize, then try and make up for what she'd said.

Summer wrapped her hand around her mum's compass, her skin caressing the cool, smooth surface, and when she opened her eyes again her best friend Harry was standing in front of her holding a cake tin.

'Harry!' Summer squeaked. She took the compass out of her pocket. 'You're like a genie. I rubbed this, and you appeared!'

Harry laughed, a flash of confusion in her big brown eyes. 'You weren't expecting me?'

Summer stared. 'Oh God, you're staying, aren't you?'

'Yes, I thought – well, we arranged it at Mason's party, that we'd go through your business plan, and I've brought a few samples.' She held out the tin, but she was no longer looking at her best friend, but at the compass that Summer was cupping in her palm. 'You found it! Where was it?'

Summer stared at her, wondering where to start.

'What?' Harry asked. 'What is it?'

'Harry,' Summer said. 'I am *so glad* that you're here.'

They sat on the seating on the bow deck of *The Canal Boat Café,* with Harry's cake tin and a bottle of white wine in between them, Harry's short, caramel-coloured dress finding the evening breeze, its hem lifting gently. Summer's folder, with her business plan inside, lay on the bench next to Harry. She'd already read it at home, Summer having given her a copy at Mason's party, and Summer wanted to know what she thought, whether her best friend was keen to play an important part in *The Canal Boat Café*.

'Tell me about the compass,' Harry said.

'What do you think of my plan?' Summer stole a piece of cranberry slice out of the tin and bit into it, her eyes closing as the rich, tart fruit exploded on her tongue, merging with the butter of the crumbly pastry, crystals of sugar falling onto her shorts.

'I think it makes all kinds of sense and that you've thought of everything.' Harry sighed and looked at the floor, and Summer realized she was holding her breath.

'What's the sigh for?' Summer asked. 'Isn't Greg keen? Don't you think you'll have time when Tommy's at school? You're so close – and I'm not going anywhere. Willowbeck is my home now.'

Harry stared at Summer. 'It's a happy sigh,' she said. 'It's a relief.'

'What is? My business plan?'

'I'm going to do it,' Harry said. 'I always wanted to, from the moment it was a spark of an idea. And now, more than ever, it will give me purpose. Don't get me wrong, the money will be welcome too – Greg's not heard anything more about redundancy, but the work is patchy at best – but that's not the worst of it.' Summer thought she saw her friend's lip tremble, but she stayed quiet, letting her speak. 'It's feeling helpless. Looking after Tommy and doing the dinner and making our home nice? Somehow it seems like it's not

340

enough. I know . . .' She held her hand up. 'I know that of course they're the most crucial things, but I need to support Greg more, and this is how I can.'

Summer felt a tidal wave of relief that she could help her friend, that Harry wasn't turning down her offer. She felt the tension in her neck ease, felt happiness take up some of the space that was consumed by worries about Mason. 'You'll be brilliant,' Summer said. 'And it's going to be a feature of the café – I'm not going to put your creations next to mine, I'm going to sell *you* along with the cakes, so you get the recognition. *Harry Poole's perfect bakes*. I need to work on that.'

Harry laughed. 'You don't have to.'

'I do,' Summer said. 'People will have one taste, and your brilliance will spread like ripples, all along the fenland waterways. People will travel for days to eat your cakes. This,' she said, holding up her glass and waiting for Harry to do the same, 'is going to kick ass. What have you left the boys doing?'

Harry laughed, her long hair shimmering. 'Tommy is giving Greg an introduction to *Minecraft*. I'm worried I'll return to two pairs of square-eyes and monosyllabic answers.'

'You don't have to worry about that until later tomorrow,' Summer said. 'Harry, I'm so sorry I forgot you were coming.'

'You did,' Harry said, 'and that's not like you. And you have your mum's compass. So . . .' She crossed one leg over the other and turned fully towards Summer. 'What's going on?'

Summer bit her lip. It was a Monday evening, so the pub was noticeably quieter than it had been the day before, when she'd sat outside with Ross. The few couples sitting at the picnic tables were outnumbered by geese, and the breeze had an edge to it, as if it was annoyed by the sun's dominance. Summer thought it would get cold more quickly when dusk fell and wondered if there was a hint of thunderstorm in the air. The willow trees were plush and green, a parade of mallards weaving in and out of the obstacle course their trailing branches had made in the water.

'Summer?'

'Mason's gone,' she blurted. 'I found Mum's compass on board his boat, and I confronted him, and now he's gone.'

'*What?*' Harry leaned towards her, pressing her hand on Summer's bare knee. 'I think you need to back up a bit. That can't be the whole story.'

Summer told Harry everything, fuelling herself with delicious titbits from Harry's cake tin, infuriating her friend by asking what each one was, so she could write them down and start building them into her grand café plan.

'What's this? Has it got lavender in it?'

'It's a honey and lavender sponge. Summer! Stop changing the subject! How did Mason react when you mentioned Tania?'

Harry wouldn't let her leave out any details, and Summer had always been honest with her – about Ross, about Jenny, and about what had happened the day her mum had died. Nobody but Harry knew the whole story. 'It's happening again, isn't it?' Summer said, when she'd got to the end, to waking up to find *The Sandpiper* gone, and the carved wooden sun on the deck of her boat.

'What is?' Harry had lifted Latte onto her lap, and the dog was doing a bad impression of being asleep, while trying to edge closer to the cake tin. Summer moved it further away, and Latte's ear twitched.

'Me, messing up,' she said. 'Confronting people, creating

342

pointless arguments and never being able to make up for them.'

Harry fixed Summer with her stare. 'This is not the same. Firstly, Mason had your mum's compass, so you had to ask him about it. Maybe you could have waited to listen to the answer, but even so. Secondly, you are not responsible for your mum's death, I don't know how many times I have to tell you.'

'Yes, but I argued with her that afternoon,' Summer said, forcing the words out past the lump in her throat. 'I shouted at her for not coming clean about her and Dennis, for letting Jenny find out by herself rather than from them, for not ending the affair. I told her she was heartless, and selfish, and then I stormed off her boat.'

'Summer,' Harry said softly, 'I know all that, and I know you've been crucifying yourself with guilt ever since, but what happened wasn't your fault. And . . .' Harry paused, glancing beyond Summer to the quiet blue river before looking back, 'you were angry, your mum had told you she was going to break it off with Dennis. She'd told you she was going to do it and it hadn't happened, and then Jenny found out. Your anger was justified, and we all say things in the heat of the moment. You have been a victim of horrible, heartbreaking timing, but your mum knew that you loved her, despite what you said.'

'Strokes can be caused by stress – I read it. I caused her stroke.'

'No.' Harry shook her head. 'That is *not* true. You loved your mum; you were with her, on this boat, for years. She had your love and your company, and one argument isn't ever going to change that. You need to look past that last day.'

Summer tried to catch Harry's words and hold on to them. But they'd been here before and Summer hadn't ever been able to let Harry's reassurances sink below skin-deep. The guilt was always there, though recently Summer had thought she'd been getting past it, letting her own time running *The Canal Boat Café,* and the new life she was making for herself, override those feelings. Now, though, she had let her anger cause another huge rift with someone she cared about, and despite Harry being here, despite the fact they were going to work together, Summer felt like there was a hole that she wouldn't ever be able to fill. She tested it with her friend.

'But what about Mason?' she asked. 'I did it again; I flung accusations at him and then stormed off his boat. I didn't give him a chance to explain, even though he said he wanted to, and now it's too late.'

'Mason's not dead,' Harry said gently. 'And he'll turn his phone on eventually.'

'He's gone.' Summer shook her head. 'He realized I was too complicated a conquest and he's sailed off down the river like Claire said he would.'

'Hey!' Harry slapped Summer lightly on the arm and Latte squeaked and stood up, pretending to be affronted before sticking her nose into the cake tin.

'Oi, Latte. You're getting as bad as Archie.' Summer smiled as she lifted Latte's nose out of the tin, and then remembered that Archie, like Mason, was gone.

'You're not doing either of you justice there,' Harry said. 'You're lovely, you're not too complicated, and Mason does *not* want to sleep with you and move on. I've met him too, remember, and he's not like that, despite what happened with Tania.'

'I should have let him explain,' Summer said, cradling her

344

wine glass. She looked into the liquid, reflecting the golden haze of the late sun, and then downed it. 'I should have let him tell me about Tania and about the compass.'

'Yes,' Harry said, 'you should.'

'He's been so reluctant to open up to me. He was about to, and I flung it back in his face.'

'You were upset. It must have been a shock to find the compass on his boat.'

'I was irrational and hasty. You'd think I would have learnt my lesson by now.'

'Every situation is different. Don't beat yourself up because you don't have the perfect, measured reaction every time.'

Summer sighed and closed her eyes. The wind whispered around them, and Summer shuddered. 'What if he never turns his phone on again? What if I never find him?'

Harry shook her head, her mouth open, and for a horrifying moment Summer thought her best friend wouldn't have an answer. Then, 'Someone will spot him,' she said. 'Don't you have a network of spies on the water now anyway? Why don't you phone Claire?'

Summer didn't phone Claire immediately, but the realization that she could made her feel better. So many people had told her that the waterways were a tightknit community, and a beautiful boat like *The Sandpiper* would be hard to ignore, not to mention its equally striking owner or a badly behaved Border terrier. Summer shook her head and pinched another chip from the little metal bucket on the table.

They'd graduated to the pub when Summer had admitted that, due to forgetting about Harry's visit, she had nothing in for dinner. Now they had fat, juicy burgers and were sharing a bucket of chips. Latte lay peacefully at Summer's feet, and Summer wondered if she was quieter than usual, if she was missing Archie, or if that was just Summer projecting her own feelings on to her pet.

The wind was growing, whipping leaves and the feathers on ducks' backs into a frenzy, and Summer could see the surface of the water rippling with it, tiny waves chasing each other. She'd put a hoody on over her top, and Harry had her jacket on.

'Should we go inside?' Summer asked her friend. 'I'm not sure how long we've got before the sun gets blown away.'

'Is Latte allowed?' Harry asked.

'She is. Dennis and Jenny know how many dog walkers use the towpath and how much custom they'd lose if they were dog free.'

'Let's go in then. I was never the stoic British type.'

'I know that,' Summer said, laughing. 'You're as fond of a cushion and a fire as Latte is.'

'Or used to be,' Harry said, picking up her plate and the bottle of wine, while Summer grabbed the chips. 'Hasn't she found her adventurous side?'

'Yes,' Summer said, feeling another twinge at Archie's absence. Not only had she messed up her relationship with Mason, but she'd managed to deny her dog a lasting friendship as well. 'But when the fun's over she'll always seek out the comfiest spot. I'm sure she thinks the woodburner on the boat is solely for her enjoyment. I'll have to come back for the glasses.'

'Let me help.'

Summer turned to see Dennis standing next to the table, a tea towel flung around his shoulders. He looked like he'd been out in the sun, and his white shirt gleamed against his darker skin. 'Dennis,' she said, smiling, 'how are you?'

'Very well, Summer. How about you two? We'll get you inside in a jiffy.'

Harry picked a booth against the window, so they could still enjoy the sunshine, and Summer slid in opposite her. 'Thanks so much, Dennis,' she said, as he put their glasses in front of them. 'Has the pub been busy? How's Jenny?'

Dennis's face showed a moment of surprise, but he smoothed it back over with a smile. 'There's been no let up so far this summer, and it feels like we're only just getting started, what with the summer holidays to come. It could be our best year for a while. Nice to see you too, Harry.'

Harry smiled. 'Summer's stolen me away for a night aboard her boat. I just hope the rocking doesn't make me seasick in the night.'

'You can barely feel it,' Summer said, laughing. 'It's not like being on the high seas in a tiny rowing boat. It's perfectly safe and stable.'

Harry screwed her nose up. 'We'll see.'

'Brilliant pistachio cake, by the way,' Dennis said, patting his stomach.

'You had some?' Harry flicked a glance in Summer's direction.

'I was a latecomer to the party, but didn't want to miss Mason's birthday completely. I was lucky that there was a slice of your cake left.'

'He brought prosecco,' Summer told Harry. 'You'd better not tell Jenny how much you enjoyed Harry's cake, especially as she's going to be doing more baking for the café from now on.'

'You are?' Dennis asked.

Harry nodded.

347

'That's not going to make things easier between me and Jenny, is it?' Summer said.

Dennis sighed and gave her a rueful smile. 'I don't think things are ever going to be easy between you. You have to go about your business, Summer, and so does she. You can't worry about it – none of this is your doing. It's mine. Maddy's too, but . . . well, she's not here any more. I'm responsible, and I have to make it up to Jenny. Don't think badly of her, Summer. Think badly of me if you have to.'

'I want us all to get along,' Summer said, 'but I don't always make that easy.' Mason's face, anguished and defeated, flashed back into her mind, and she pushed her finger along the knots in the wood table. 'And I could never think badly of you,' she added. 'You rescued me. You and Mason.'

Dennis glanced towards the bar to check that everything was under control. 'I couldn't say no when Mason turned up,' he said. 'He was insistent. Apologetic, but determined. I'd never seen him like that, right on the edge of panic, but he . . . It must have brought back memories for him. He clearly cares a lot about you, Summer, and I think he was scared of history repeating itself. Of course, then, I didn't realize it, but when he told me, it all made sense.' Dennis shook his head, his gaze drawn to the view outside the window.

Summer gripped the stem of her wine glass, her knuckles going white. 'Memories?' she asked. Her voice sounded high and strangled, and she glanced at Harry, expecting a reprimand, but could see that her friend was equally intrigued. 'What memories?'

Dennis brought his gaze back to meet Summer's. 'Sorry?'

'My break-in,' she said. 'You said it brought back memories for Mason. What memories?'

Dennis frowned and rearranged the tea towel around his neck. 'You don't know? I thought you and he were——'

Summer shook her head quickly. 'We were friends. *Are* friends. I had hoped that . . .' She let her words trail away.

'What's happened, Summer? Is everything OK?'

She stared up at him. He was soft and warm and kind, and so straightforward. Her mind still couldn't wrap itself around him having an affair with anyone, let alone her mother. She could see instantly why someone would be attracted to him – she just couldn't imagine that he could ever be dishonest and underhand enough to go through with it.

'What did Mason tell you?' she asked.

'I'm not sure it's really my place,' he said, shaking his head. 'I mean, I don't know if he told me in confidence – it was on the way to seeing you at Tivesham and I think he felt like he needed to explain himself – why he was so desperate to get to you when he heard what had happened. It was almost like a confession and . . . it's very personal, Summer.' He worried at a scratch on his arm.

Summer's heart was thumping. This was the key – the key to everything that had happened. Was it right to hear it from someone other than Mason? She wasn't sure, but he'd gone, and she didn't know how she could get him back. Maybe Dennis had the answer.

'Please, Dennis,' she said, but it came out as a whisper.

'Mason's gone,' Harry said, her voice much louder.

'What?' Dennis looked out of the window again, in the direction of the river and the moorings, as if to confirm that *The Sandpiper* was no longer there. 'Why?'

'I had an argument with him,' Summer started, but Harry was taking charge.

'Summer cares about him,' she said, 'and he clearly cares about her. But they had a fight, and now he's gone and his phone's been permanently off, and anything you can tell us, Dennis, *anything* that would help us find him, or find out why he's gone, would make things so much easier. At the very least, we're worried about him, and it would help put Summer's – and my – mind at rest.'

Dennis sighed. 'I don't know . . . Why did you fight? Can you tell me that?'

'Dennis?' the voice cut through the general chatter of the pub. 'It's getting busy over here, can you come and help?'

Summer glanced up to see Jenny behind the bar. She looked ruffled, her hair falling around her shoulders, her eyes bright. Summer was struck by how pretty she was when she wasn't completely in control.

'Coming,' Dennis called, then turned back to the table. 'I can talk later, when it's quieter.'

'Mason had Mum's compass,' Summer rushed, not wanting him to walk away, desperate for him to tell them what he knew.

Dennis stared at Summer for a moment and then closed his eyes. 'Oh no,' he said. 'That's what you argued about?'

'What? What is it?' Summer was sitting up, almost ready to propel herself out of her chair and grab him if he tried to escape.

'Dennis?' Jenny called. 'Please, love.'

'Coming!'

'What do you know?' Summer pleaded. 'Please, Dennis.'

'Don't go anywhere,' Dennis said. 'I'll get someone to bring you another glass of wine, puddings, whatever you want. I promise I'll come back when it's quieter.'

'Why did Mason have Mum's compass?' Summer tried again.

350

Dennis glanced behind him, then back at the table. 'I gave it to him,' he said quietly. 'I gave Mason Maddy's compass. Now please, I have to go. Stay here, and I'll come and talk to you when things have eased off.'

He walked back to the bar and Summer watched him go, her mind racing, buzzing with questions, trying and failing to slot everything into place. She watched Dennis speak to a customer, start to pour a pint, his easy, relaxed demeanour ever so slightly strained. He kept glancing at their table, and Summer forced herself to drag her eyes back to Harry. Her best friend looked as shocked and intrigued as she was.

'What can we do?' Harry asked. 'Is there a fire alarm we can push? Something that will empty the pub and make him come over here more quickly?'

Summer managed a laugh. 'I don't think so,' she said. 'I think we just have to wait.'

Harry looked as pained at the thought as Summer felt. Summer got her mum's compass out of her pocket and put it on the table. It sat between them like an unexploded bomb.

'We'll just have to wait,' Summer said again.

Chapter 20

It was after closing time, and the wind was unpleasantly chilly, but Summer was sitting at a picnic table with Harry and Dennis. The fresh glass of wine that Dennis had brought them, on top of the others, and the intense orange glow of the outdoor heaters were making the edges of everything seem hazy, softer and less urgent. Summer stared at her boat, a portion of its blue and red paintwork standing out from the darkness under the towpath light, the rest in shadow, the river nothing but slivers of shimmer beyond it.

Latte was sitting next to Dennis on the bench, Harry was next to her, and the compass was on the table between them. She wasn't sure why she had got it out again, except that it was a symbol of everything, of how she'd argued with her mum, and then Mason. It was accusing, but it also reminded her that she could find things, she could resolve them. She had the power to fix her own mistakes.

'I'm sorry it's so late,' Dennis said, 'I didn't think it would stay busy this long on a Monday.' He still had the tea towel around his neck and was in just his shirtsleeves. 'Are you

sure you don't want to go back inside? I checked with ⏑
and she was OK with you being in the pub after closir.

Summer smiled and shook her head. Harry had manaş
to distract Summer while they'd waited for Dennis. They
shared an ice-cream sundae with butterscotch sauce and extra
nuts, and talked about Summer's plans for the café and Harry's
role in it. Summer wanted to do taster evenings and special
events. She wanted to open the café up to group bookings,
private parties where she could cruise down the river away
from Willowbeck to celebrate a birthday or an anniversary,
all with Harry's cooking at the heart. She had lots of plans
and Harry had discussed them all with her, taking her mind
off things for a couple of hours. Except that the compass had
sat on the table in front of them, reminding her.

When Dennis had finally been ready to talk, Summer had
felt so hot, so claustrophobic, that she'd asked if they could
sit outside in the fresh air. Now she felt slightly tipsy and
slightly cold, but those things didn't seem to matter against
the weight of what Dennis was about to tell them.

'Why did you give Mason my mum's compass?' Summer
asked, realizing that she couldn't cope with any small talk.

Dennis sighed. 'Because Maddy gave it to me – and it was
the thing that gave us away, in the end.' He ran his hand
over his short hair, from his neck to his brow. 'Jenny had
already figured it out, I'm sure, but it was finding Maddy's
compass in my jacket pocket that confirmed it. Why else
would I have a rose quartz compass? Who else could it have
come from? At the time, there was so much anger and hurt,
so much going on, and after . . . Well, after Maddy died, I
didn't know what to do. It reminded me of her and I didn't
want to get rid of it, so I hid it away. Jenny and I were just
getting back on track, then close to Christmas last year she

it again, among my things. She was looking for some-
g else, and she found it. It dragged everything up again,
l I knew I couldn't keep it.'

'Why Mason?' Summer whispered, thinking how hard it
must have been for Dennis, realizing that, in her own grief,
he was another person she'd completely disregarded. She
knew he'd loved her mum, and he'd had to cope with losing
her, as well as with the accusations and anger, the slow process
of trying to rebuild his marriage.

'I didn't know if you were ever coming back to Willowbeck,'
he said. 'Nobody had seen you since Maddy died, and Valerie
was struggling with her own grief. I also knew that the fact
your mum had given the compass to me might not sit well
with either you or Valerie. Mason pitched up here in
November, I think it was, and, as you know, he's instantly
likeable. We'd got to chatting before and once Jenny had
discovered the compass again I . . . I gave it to him. I asked
him to take some photos of the pub that I could send to a
local magazine for a promotional piece. I offered to pay him,
but he wouldn't hear of it, and so I gave him the compass
as payment. No story about where it came from, I just said
that I had to give him something, and that the compass
belonged on a narrowboat. He was taken aback, and probably
accepted it out of duty because he wouldn't take any money,
but I knew the compass would be in good hands, that it
would be close by. It was probably the wrong thing to do.'

Summer shook her head. 'You were hurting. It must have
been so hard, not being able to hold onto memories of Maddy,
having to struggle with losing her and with Jenny and . . .'
She swallowed. 'I'm glad you gave it to him. Shit!' She rested
her head in her hands. 'I accused him of *taking* it. I'd been
looking for it for so long.'

354

'I'm so sorry, Summer. If I'd thought about it for ev▨
moment . . .'

'It's not your fault. I should have given Mason time ▨
explain. I shouldn't have jumped to conclusions.' She wondered
if she'd be repeating that mantra for the rest of her life. She
glanced at her phone. The screen was blank. Her calls to
Mason throughout the day had remained unanswered, his
voicemail kicking in immediately. But she didn't want to talk
into empty air, and so she hadn't left him a message.

'It's good to know though, isn't it, that he had it for a
completely innocent reason?' Harry put her hand over Summer's.
'Confirming what you've believed about him all along.'

'That Mason is one of the nicest people I've met, and that
he's worth taking a chance on.'

Harry nodded. 'Exactly.'

Summer looked to Dennis for confirmation, knowing that
this bit wouldn't be so straightforward, and that he might
not even be prepared to tell her. 'What about his memories?'
Summer asked. 'Why was he worried history was repeating
itself?'

Dennis shook his head. 'Summer, I——'

'Please tell me,' she whispered. 'Please tell me something.
I'm worried I . . .' She thought back to how defeated he'd
looked after she'd asked him about Tania. 'I'm worried I've
really hurt him. He's always been there before. Not always
open, but always there to talk to, to spend time with, and
now he's just . . . gone.'

Dennis appraised Summer, and then Harry, and took a
sip of the whisky he'd brought outside with him. 'Mason lost
his wife,' he said.

Summer stared at him, wondering if she'd misheard. '*What?*'

'In a fire,' Dennis added. 'Their house caught fire when they

both inside. Mason got them out of an upstairs window,
Lisa was asthmatic. The smoke had done too much damage
d it was too late. She died on the way to hospital.'

The world seemed to expand and then contract around
Summer. As if there was only her in the world, and then the
sky was opening up around her, black and swirling and
endless. She pressed her hand against the table, steadying
herself.

'Oh my God,' she heard Harry say, and felt a hand against
her shoulder.

'Mason,' Summer whispered. 'Oh, Mason. Shit.' She put
her arms on the table and rested her head on them.

'He told me on the drive to Tivesham,' Dennis said. 'He
was so worried about you, and I think it brought everything
back to him: the fear, the devastation. It was five or six years
ago, and once Lisa . . . Well, she was gone, and the house
was destroyed, so he bought the boat. He was completely
lost, understandably. And of course it's something you never
fully get over, but . . . Well,' Dennis sighed, 'you'd hardly
know it, would you? He seems so well adjusted. So thoughtful
and kind, easy-going, as if he doesn't have a care in the world.'

'Mason,' Summer said again. She looked up at Dennis. 'He
had to bury his wife? He wasn't even thirty. She was . . .'
Summer swallowed, her eyes filling with tears.

She thought back to his shock at the sight of her boat
after the break-in and wondered if he'd had to go inside his
own ruined house, once the fire was out, once he had nothing
left. She thought of his stillness when she'd asked about the
photos he'd taken before he was a liveaboard. They must all
have been destroyed. She remembered him telling her he'd
had to work through things, and the way he'd appeared,
suddenly, on her boat the second morning she'd been back

in Willowbeck, responding to the fire alarm when she'd burnt the bacon and she'd thought he was just eager for a sandwich. 'Fuck,' she said, and closed her eyes.

'That's horrific,' Harry murmured, and Summer could hear the emotion in her friend's voice.

'It sounds like he doesn't really talk much about it,' Dennis said. 'I mean, if he's not even told you. I thought you were close.'

'We are – we were getting to be, but . . .' Summer shook her head. 'I can't believe it. I can't believe he's had to go through so much.' The anxiety she'd seen in him was nothing compared to the warmth, the care he'd shown her, helping when her boat leaked, cruising up to Foxburn to take her into the countryside, supporting her after the break-in despite, what she now knew, must have been unbearable memories. He'd been through the most traumatic event possible and, despite never having told her, he'd still given so much of himself to her.

'I need to get in touch with him,' she said. She felt it as an ache in her chest, an urgent, panicky feeling that made her sit on the very edge of the bench. She fumbled with her phone again, and Dennis put his hand over hers.

'If he's headed off, it's probably because he needs time. You said you fought? You brought up some personal things?'

Summer nodded.

'Right,' Dennis gave her a quick smile, 'well then, he's probably got a bit of stuff to sort through in his head. It might be that he'll come back when he's ready.'

'Or that he never wants to see me – or Willowbeck – ever again,' Summer said. She looked at Harry, whose big brown eyes were pools of emotion in the soft glow of the pub's lanterns.

'Didn't you tell me that the thing with Tania happened not long after he'd become a liveaboard?' she asked.

357

'That's what Claire said.'

'So maybe that explains his behaviour. Maybe he thought he was ready for a new relationship, but it was too soon.'

'Maybe,' Summer murmured. 'But I – I don't want to speculate. I want to find him and talk to him properly. No more jumping to conclusions.'

'I think that's a good idea, love,' Dennis said, giving her a warm, sympathetic smile. 'Mason's a good man, and if you were beginning to get close then he was probably going to tell you. You know, after the break-in, I saw how worried he was about you, how it brought back bad memories for him. That's why I was so keen that you came back to Willowbeck. You'd both been through a lot, and I thought that you could sort of help each other.'

'I remember,' Summer said. 'I was confused that you would want me back when it would only cause friction between Jenny and me. I had no idea.' She shook her head. 'I should have supported Mason more. I wish he'd felt able to tell me before I – I tried to force it out of him.'

'Things don't always go as planned, do they?' Dennis held her gaze, and Summer smiled at him, knowing that this was, in some way, a silent apology for everything that had happened before, with her mum. 'I think,' he continued, 'that Mason will come back to you. I don't think he's gone for good.'

'But if he's not answering his phone,' Harry said, 'if he wants some time away, then we should respect that. However, just because another liveaboard sees *The Sandpiper*, it doesn't mean that they have to disturb him. Surely just knowing where Mason is would be a comfort?'

Summer nodded slowly. 'You think it's time to call Claire?'

'I think it would help put your mind at rest.'

* * *

358

Summer called Claire the following morning, rubbing her temples to try and ease the headache that had appeared when she'd woken up.

'Summer Freeman, you bloody psychic!'

'What?' Summer frowned at Harry and handed her a coffee, the phone pressed to her ear. 'No, that's my neighbour, Val—'

'I was going to call you! We're coming to Willowbeck.'

Summer gawped. 'When?'

'This weekend. You know how I told you that Willowbeck was pretty but that I always thought it needed something else?'

'Ye-e-e-s.' Summer drew the word out, wondering what was coming.

'Well, that thing is my music festival! We're heading down this weekend, I want to talk to the owners of the pub about using their garden, and then if all goes well in a couple of weeks we'll have a humming, vibrant music festival.'

'A couple of *weeks?* Claire, how can you—'

'Because everyone's teed up. I've been banging on about having a festival this summer for yonks, and if Willowbeck's as perfect as I think it is, then all we'll need to do is get word out. And you know how quickly things spread up the river – it's like bloody wildfire.'

Summer winced. Claire's words reminded her of the reason she'd called in the first place, and then she wondered if she could ask about Mason without her friend thinking that her warning had come true, and that Mason had taken off because he'd gone as far as he wanted to with Summer.

'Will you be a part of it?' Claire asked.

'Yes, of course! I'd love to – and I took your advice,' she said, grinning at Harry. 'The café's going to be a lot more interesting from now on.'

'You went on a cooking course?'

'Nope, but I've roped in my best friend. We're going into business together.'

Once Summer had listened to Claire's whoops of delight they said goodbye and she hung up.

'You didn't ask her about *The Sandpiper*,' Harry said. 'I thought that was the whole point.'

Summer sat next to her on the sofa. 'It was, but Claire distracted me with the news that she and Jas, Ralph and Ryder and the others are all coming to Willowbeck to put on this summer festival, and then I realized if I asked Claire to look out for Mason, she'd know that he'd left, and she'd think that she was right. I can't tell Claire the truth about Mason's past – Dennis has confided in us, but we can't tell anyone else – so it's going to look like exactly what Claire was warning me against.'

Harry sipped her coffee and looked at Summer seriously over the edge of the cup. 'So what are you going to do?'

Summer shrugged, hoping that she looked more confident than she felt. 'I'm just going to have to wait for him to get in touch.'

That afternoon, after Harry had gone home with a promise to come back on Friday so they could start to plan what would be needed for the music festival, and making Summer swear she would let her know the moment she heard about, or from, Mason, Summer found that she couldn't focus. Harry had helped her in the café in the morning, and Summer had loved having her on board. It made everything about running the café easier and more fun, and it felt like they were the perfect double act. It had started Summer wondering if Harry baking cakes at home in her kitchen was as far as their business partnership would go, or if she could convince her friend to be an even bigger part of it.

Those thoughts, along with the revelation about Mason, and the fact that Claire and Ryder would soon be descending on sleepy little Willowbeck, meant that Summer got several drinks orders completely wrong, and found herself spreading chocolate icing on someone's scone instead of butter. Her customers were very good-natured, laughing off her failures, but Summer knew she needed to get a grip.

When the custom had died away, Summer made a large cup of builder's tea, cut a huge slice of coffee cake, and took them to *Celeste*. She had barely seen Norman since she'd been back in Willowbeck, and now that she was determined to stay, she wanted to try and grow some kind of relationship with her neighbour. She also thought Norman should be warned about the festival. Averting her eyes from the space where *The Sandpiper* should have been, Summer climbed on to the deck of *Celeste* and knocked on the door.

It took an age, but eventually it opened and Norman stood there, squinting up at Summer as if she was shining a torch into his face. 'Wharisit?' he asked.

'I brought you some tea.' She proffered the takeaway cup and the paper bag with the cake in it.

'Why?'

'Because I wanted to be friendly,' she said.

'No need for that,' Norman replied.

Summer counted to three inside her head. 'I know there isn't a *need*, but I wanted to. I'm back in Willowbeck for good now, and I think it would be nice if we got to know each other a bit better.'

'Suit yerself,' Norman said. He took the cup and paper bag, and nodded briefly at Summer. He backed into his doorway and Summer turned to go, but then realized he was coming back out onto the deck.

She stared at him.

'Puttin' the tea down,' he said, and angled his body back towards his door, as if explaining.

'Oh,' Summer murmured, 'right.'

'So you're stayin' then? Not chasing off after your fella?'

Summer blinked. 'S-sorry?'

'Mason,' Norman said. '*Sandpiper*. I heard him callin' t'you, t'other night. Bangin' yer door down.'

'Oh,' Summer said again. Something swooped, low and sickening, inside her stomach. 'Sorry.'

Norman shook his head. She could see flecks of pure white in his grey beard, the parts of his jumper that were worn thin. 'Ain't bothered, but sounded like 't'was sad for you. Decent man, Mason, even if his dog's a nuisance.'

Summer's laugh was slightly hysterical. She thought of Archie and how badly behaved he was, and how, though Norman stayed hidden inside his boat most of the time and was terminally unsociable even when he was fishing on his deck, even he knew that Mason was worth trusting. Was it only her that had been doubtful? Granted, she had more to lose if they started a relationship and things went wrong, but she'd still not had faith in him. She sagged her shoulders, wondering if she even deserved the chance to make things right between them.

'He's off after them cranes,' Norman said. 'Sure of it.'

'Cranes?'

'Seen 'em up at that reserve, ain't they? iPad told me.'

Summer resisted the smile. She thought Norman must be in his seventies, and wouldn't touch coffee because it was too modern, and here he was confessing that he had an iPad.

But her pulse increased, because he was also offering her an explanation for Mason's sudden disappearance. 'You think he's gone to the reserve because they've found cranes? You don't think that he . . . He . . .'

'Cranes,' Norman said again, nodding decisively. 'Mad about 'em, isn't he?'

Now the smile did creep onto her lips, and she fought the urge to reach out and hug him. She thought if she did he might be so surprised he'd fall over the edge of the boat. 'Thank you, Norman,' she said.

'Ta for the tea.' He turned in a small, shuffled circle and disappeared back inside *Celeste*.

Summer jumped down onto the towpath and raced back to *The Canal Boat Café*. She didn't know how true Norman's assertion was that Mason had gone after the cranes – the timing was a bit too perfect – but it had given her thoughts a lifeline, given her some breathing space if she imagined that he was out there being enthusiastic about the wildlife and not devastated because she'd forced him to drag up the past. She could rest easier, try and wait to hear from him, and look forward to Claire and the roving traders arriving.

She smacked a hand to her forehead as she realized she hadn't mentioned the festival to Norman. She would just have to go back tomorrow – as far as she was concerned he deserved tea and cake every day for the rest of his life. He'd given her a slice of the hope she was so desperate for.

Summer watched *The Wanderer's Rest* cruise into Willowbeck on Friday morning, followed by *Water Music* and *Doug's Antiques Barge* and all the other roving trader narrowboats, with a mix of excitement and trepidation. Only a few weeks ago she'd been part of their band and she'd had a lot of fun, but there were some bad memories too, and not just the break-in. Ryder would be there, ready to take over, and Claire would want to know what was happening with Mason. Summer suddenly felt protective of Willowbeck and Valerie, of Dennis, and Adam at the butcher's, and of Norman.

She'd taken him another tea and a cherry muffin, and told him about the festival. He'd looked at her with narrowed eyes and nodded, and then told her – though in not quite as many words – that there were *six* cranes, according to his iPad, and that meant Mason was bound to be busy for a while. Summer hadn't hugged him then, but she had reached out and squeezed his arm, feeling how thin it was through the threadbare jumper. She didn't want him to feel threatened by the newcomers.

Summer bit her lip and cleaned a table for the fourth time, and then Claire stepped on board her boat and all Summer's worries vanished.

'Summer, you beautiful creature.' Claire walked towards her, arms held out wide, filling up the café. Summer left her cloth and her antibacterial spray and hugged Claire back. 'You were never going to escape us for too long, did I mention that?'

Summer laughed. 'You didn't, but I always believed it. It feels a lot longer than a few weeks.'

'How are you? The café's looking tiptop, considering.' She fixed her gaze on Summer, asking an unvoiced question.

'Everything's going really well,' Summer said. 'It didn't take long at all to patch up the boat.'

'And how about your confidence? Is that patched up too?'

Summer nodded. 'I feel safe here in Willowbeck. And it's not that I didn't feel safe with you, or that I wouldn't consider roving again, but I need to be here for a while. I need to make this home first, so I always know I can come back when I need to.'

'That makes sense,' Claire said, folding her arms. They looked bronzed against the pale green of her dress, which looked far too floaty and feminine to steer a boat and work locks in, and then Summer noticed her orange Converse, and smiled.

'So this music festival's definitely going ahead, then?'

Claire nodded, her eyes lighting up. 'Sure. I just need to speak to the owners of the pub, but I can't see they'd turn down the opportunity for a shed-load of extra business, and then Ryder, Jas and I will get on the phones and it'll be all systems go.'

'Willowbeck won't know what's hit it,' Summer said.

'We're not going to wreck the joint,' Claire said. 'We're going to liven it up a bit.'

Summer gave her a warm smile. 'I know,' she said, 'just tell me what I can do to help. I can't wait.' And she meant it, too. In only a few moments, the presence of her bold, beautiful friend had made Summer feel that everything would be OK. There was no way Claire would allow the festival to harm Willowbeck or its occupants – she had one of the biggest hearts of anyone Summer knew. She didn't know how long she would get away with avoiding the subject of Mason, but she knew that the Willowbeck music festival was the perfect distraction, and would help to put *The Canal Boat Café* on the map.

Chapter 21

Willowbeck was transformed by the roving traders. Claire's boat set the scene, blasting out its usual array of musical genres throughout the day, though Summer thought that it was at a slightly lower volume than it had been in Foxburn or Tivesham, and the cluster of brightly painted narrowboats moored up in the visitor moorings and along the opposite towpath added vibrancy and colour that only served to enhance the small, riverside village.

Summer sat on a picnic table at the edge of the towpath, next to Valerie. It was early Saturday morning, and there was a layer of mist on the surface of the water, just waiting to be burnt off by the sun. It was too early for Claire's music to have started and there was a chill in the air, though Summer thought that, too, would soon disappear. Latte was chasing a leaf along the towpath and Harvey, Valerie's more adventurous silver tabby, sat watching her from the roof of *Moonshine,* Valerie's boat.

'I think it's lovely,' Valerie was saying. 'Claire and Jas and

Ryder all seem very nice, as do Ralph and Doug – such beautiful antiques on board his boat.'

'You've been?' Summer asked.

'Oh yes.' Valerie flicked her red hair over her shoulder. 'I've been on board most of the boats now.'

Summer stared at her for a moment, and then started laughing. 'You're a social butterfly, Valerie,' she said. 'How come I didn't realize before?'

'There haven't been lots of other liveaboards to get to know in Willowbeck before,' she said. 'But the music festival will bring them in, and I'm bound to get a good lot of interest in my readings. Have you got reinforcements for the café?'

Summer nodded. 'Harry came round yesterday and helped me plan it all out. She's going to help me on the Friday and Saturday, but she's got a wedding to go to on Sunday. I'll just have to manage, but it's only one day so I'm sure I'll be fine.' She sipped her spiced latte, trying to push aside the niggle that Harry had left her with the day before.

'You're rushed off your feet on a normal weekend aren't you?' Harry had asked her, when she'd told Summer about the wedding she and Greg and Tommy were going to. 'Can you imagine how much busier it'll be during the festival? You'll need some help on the Sunday.'

'I've done it before,' Summer had said, waving an airy hand in Harry's direction, hoping it would hide the fire of panic low down in her stomach, thinking that market day at Foxburn couldn't really be compared to a music festival.

Harry wasn't fooled. 'Summer, I really think you'll need an extra pair of hands. What about Charlie, the butcher's son? I'm sure that there'll be more demand for cappuccinos than raw sausages and mince. Why not ask him?'

Summer had nodded, but she didn't know Charlie very well,

didn't know if he had any experience beyond the butcher's shop, and the thought of working alongside someone she was unsure of in her precious café, on one of its busiest ever days, seemed even less appealing than working alone.

'And you'll be able to see the music in the evenings,' Valerie said, snapping her out of her reverie. 'It's very kind of Dennis and Jenny to let them use the grassland at the side of the pub.'

'I know. I was quite surprised – not at Dennis, he's a sweetheart – but Jenny.' Summer sighed. 'I think I may have been unkind to her.'

'Well,' Valerie said, bristling, 'she was unkind right back. You're in a difficult position with her and I think she's treated you very unfairly, although I do understand why it's not been easy for her to get past her anger. Maybe she isn't a monster, after all.'

'You're forgiving Jenny now? What *has* happened to you?'

Valerie gave a little chuckle, and Summer nudged her good-naturedly with her shoulder.

'And how are you otherwise, Summer? Have you heard from Mason?'

Summer pressed her lips together and shook her head. She'd tried calling a few more times, but it always went to voicemail, and Summer didn't trust herself to leave a composed message. 'Maybe he's really engrossed with the cranes,' Summer said. *For five whole days,* she added silently. She'd checked the nature reserve website after Norman's insistence that was where he'd gone and discovered that there *had* been crane sightings, which had reassured her slightly. But she wasn't a fool, she knew that what had happened between them on board *The Sandpiper* had made Mason change his mind about her, or at least take time to work out how he really felt.

'You know,' Valerie said, 'when someone has had something catastrophic happen to them, any further blow is harder to recover from. If a vase gets smashed and put back together, any subsequent break and recovery is slow and painstaking, because you can't ignore the earlier cracks.'

Summer looked at her friend, and swallowed. 'You know?' she whispered. 'Did Mason tell you?'

'No, Summer,' Valerie said, putting a hand on her knee, 'but I can tell. He's suffered a great loss in his life, and it's one that, as hard as he tries to push it away, will always affect him, no matter what else happens. He's a good, kind man, with a warm heart. He just needs a little more care and attention than he'd like to admit.'

Summer dropped her head, and then she had a thought. It was a crazy, wilful thought, but she said it before she could change her mind. 'Will you give me a reading, Valerie, and tell me what's in my future?'

'You don't want a reading from me, Summer.'

'Yes I do – I really do. Will you tell me?'

Valerie turned to her on the bench and Harvey sprang down onto the towpath and then up onto the picnic table in two leaps, his tail tickling Summer's nose. Summer lifted the cat into her lap, glancing at Latte to check the dog was otherwise engaged.

'I'm not going to give you a reading, Summer,' she said.

Summer's shoulders sagged. 'Why not?'

Valerie smiled at her, her eyes bright. 'Because you know what's in your heart, and you don't need me to tell you what you need to do.'

'But how can I do it – how can I do what I need to if he's not here, if he's gone?'

Valerie put a hand over Summer's and Harvey licked the

369

older woman's arm. 'Trust yourself, and trust that it will all work out.'

Summer looked at her, trying to read Valerie's meaning in her expression, and in the tone of her voice. She was smiling, which Summer thought had to be a good thing. Norman had told her about the cranes, Valerie was telling her to trust herself, and Dennis had said that he believed Mason would come back. She knew she was grasping at straws, trying to put the pieces together even though they were vague and insubstantial, but it was all that she had. And then Valerie said something that made Summer's mouth dry out for an entirely different reason.

'Have you spoken to Ross about it? Maybe he's heard from Mason.'

Summer replayed Valerie's words in her head before replying. 'Ross? Why would he have heard from him?'

'I got the impression they were good friends, from the things Ross says when he comes for his readings.'

Summer held onto Harvey, his soft ears tickling her chin. 'What kind of things?' she asked, the words coming out as a whisper.

'Oh, he just mentions him a fair bit. You introduced them, didn't you? Ross speaks very highly of him, and I have to agree, of course. It must be good to know that they get on, for if – when – Mason comes back.'

Summer blinked. This wasn't true. She knew it wasn't, because of what Ross had told her just before she'd gone to Mason's boat that evening, the doubts he'd stirred up in her about Mason's intentions. She knew because of Ross's hostility whenever he'd been in the same room as Mason, whenever she'd mentioned his name. She took a deep breath. 'Valerie, did you give Ross a reading saying that he would have to

370

look after someone. Someone who would end up getting hurt by a Lothario?'

Valerie turned slowly to face her, her brows knitted in confusion. 'No, I didn't say anything like that. Why on earth do you think that happened?'

Summer swallowed. 'Because Ross told me. He told me that, in his reading, you had warned him that he would need to be there for someone. He made it obvious that it was me; he said that I was going to be hurt by someone, and I tried not to believe him, but I let it cloud my thoughts about Mason, and then that night I discovered the compass on his boat . . .'

Valerie shook her head vigorously. 'No, you must have got it wrong. Ross wouldn't try and . . . no, he's Mason's friend. Maybe you misinterpreted what he was saying? Ross doesn't always explain himself very well, so—' She gasped. Harvey looked up at her, his green eyes wide, his purr loud.

'What?' Summer asked, a wave of nausea sweeping over her.

'Ross told me that you didn't believe in what I did, that you'd admitted to him that you thought I was a fraud. All those months ago.' Valerie pressed her fingers to her lips, her eyes bright with shock. 'He was so sweet, so apologetic, saying he hated telling me, but that he thought I needed to know when we were friends, neighbours. At first I was furious with you, but the more I thought about it, the less sense it made. I couldn't believe you would have said that, and thought I must just have misinterpreted his words. I didn't mention it to him again because I was sure it was my fault, that I must have got the wrong end of the stick. He's always so cheerful, so friendly.'

Summer stared at the blue water shimmering beyond the narrowboats as she tried to let the extent of Ross's manipulation sink in. 'I thought it was Jenny who'd told you that,

that she was telling lies because she wanted us to fall out, for me to feel unhappy enough to leave Willowbeck. And I did – I left! Ross got between us, and I think – I *know* now that he got between me and Mason.'

'Summer, I'm so sorry.'

'What for?' Her disbelief was slowly being overtaken by anger. 'You haven't done anything wrong.'

'I believed him,' Valerie said. 'I thought he was genuine, warm, sweet. I thought he wanted readings, that he was interested in what I did. I thought, when he asked about you and Mason, he just wanted to know how his friends were getting on.'

'Valerie,' Summer said, reaching over the silver tabby and putting a hand on her knee, 'I believed him too. I . . .' She thought back to the way he had comforted her, and then held her, after her mum's death. She closed her eyes, her jaw clenching. 'I have been taken in by him for a long time. Shit. He's never liked Mason, but he made you believe that he does, to find out more about him, to learn things that he can use as ammunition. Did you—' she started, then sighed, sure she already knew the answer. 'Did you tell Ross that Mick's nickname for Mason was Lothario? I had heard Mick call him that, and so when Ross used the same word, supposedly from your reading, the warning he'd got, part of me believed that it had been genuine, and that Mason really didn't care about me.'

Valerie stared at Summer's hand on her knee, and shook her head. 'He asked how you'd been. I told him about the leak on your boat, about Mick coming to help, that he and Mason knew each other because they'd worked on *The Sandpiper* together. I may have mentioned it, but . . . oh, no.'

'I should have known none of it was true,' Summer said, pressing her free hand against her forehead. 'If you'd really given Ross that reading, then you wouldn't be encouraging me to believe in Mason, to wait for him. You'd be as distrustful as Ross is about him. I've been so stupid.'

'No, Summer,' Valerie said. 'You've been manipulated. And that's not necessarily true. I don't always get names in my readings; I don't know all the details. I just get strong feelings, strong suggestions of what is happening or going to happen in a person's life. Ross was clever, using Mason's nickname, planting the seeds of doubt without being explicit. He's been learning how I work, learning the type of information I'm able to pass on. Oh Summer! What will you do?'

'I don't know,' Summer said truthfully. 'I'll have to confront him, but I – I think I need to focus on the festival first. I can't deal with it right now. But if Mason doesn't come back—'

'Trust yourself,' Valerie said vehemently, putting her own hand over Summer's and repeating her earlier words. 'Trust it will all work out. Don't let Ross come between the two of you.'

At that moment, Madonna's 'Holiday' burst out of the speakers on *Water Music,* and Summer knew it was time to start opening up. 'Thanks, Valerie,' she said, sighing. 'For listening. For helping me to see what's been going on.'

'I'm so sorry, Summer, for my part in this. But I am always here for you, remember that.'

Summer nodded and, collecting Latte on the way, and with a heavy mix of anger and regret churning in her head, went back to *The Canal Boat Café.* It was one thing telling Summer not to let Ross come between her and Mason, but what if it was already too late?

Her life, over the next few days, became a strange hybrid of her Willowbeck and roving-trader lifestyles. She spent the days working on board the café, which was noticeably busier since the arrival of the roving traders, selling bacon and sausage sandwiches, cakes and muffins, a variety of different traybakes that Harry had made in her country cottage kitchen, and a selection of flavoured macarons that they'd made together when Harry had come back for their festival planning session. Summer was ridiculously excited at the thought of having Harry's help for two whole days, and was already thinking about how best to ask her if she wanted a more permanent, varied role as a staple part of *The Canal Boat Café*.

In the evenings, after the café, the music shop, the sandwich boat and antique barge had all closed, Summer and Valerie would join the other roving traders on the grassland at the far side of the pub, away from the moorings. It was a large, unused patch of unkempt grass, partly hidden from the picnic tables and the towpath by the trees that bordered it. An outdoor stage was in the process of being erected, and Summer noticed that Ryder seemed to be in charge of it. He had probably sourced the equipment through one of his shady contacts, and every time she saw him he seemed to be ordering several sweaty men and women around from his relaxed position, cross-legged on the grass with a pint of cider in his hands.

Thursday evening was the night before the festival started and, as usual, Valerie and Summer went to meet the others. The stage looked ready, and the whole area had been adorned with fairy lights. They ran along the side of the pub, draped down on either side of the stage and even hung in the trees surrounding the area.

'Goodness me,' Valerie said, stopping on the edge of the grass. 'This looks incredible.'

374

Summer gasped, and then laughed. 'The roving traders do like their fairy lights. What a perfect setting.'

'Come on, ladies,' Claire called, 'stop gawping. Come and have a drink.' Claire poured wine into two glasses, and Summer noticed the trays of sandwiches and red velvet cupcakes in the middle of the cluster of people. Dennis and Jenny had agreed to them taking over the space on the understanding that, when they were using it, they would buy their food and drink from them. Summer had seen a large order of plastic pint glasses being hauled from a van into the back door of the pub, and knew that, like everyone else, the Greenways were excited about the extra custom and life the three-day event would bring.

Summer sat next to Jas and put her arms around Chester's shaggy neck. Latte bounded up and jumped on Summer's lap, desperate to be involved. Summer hugged the Bichon Frise and the Irish wolfhound at the same time, and Jas grinned at her from under his baseball cap.

'How's the blog going?' Summer asked. 'Still getting lots of followers?'

'Yup,' Jas nodded. 'Another few thousand since we were up at Tivesham. The summer months help because people dream about how great it would be to be on board a boat, cruising up and down with the sun shining on them, so you get lots of interested folk. It helps to remind them that the winters are very different.'

'Not that you want to put people off,' Claire said.

'No, no, of course not, but you need to be realistic. River life's not always easy.'

Summer nodded and sipped her wine. Though her time in Willowbeck and everything that she'd faced since she'd stepped back on board her mum's boat hadn't been plain

375

sailing, she wouldn't change it now. She wouldn't change what had happened, except for the one evening that was still haunting her thoughts.

'Are we going to have some stories?' Valerie asked. 'Summer's told me so much about them. She said that you were particularly good, Doug, that your Black Shuck story was really sinister.'

'It wasn't *that* scary,' Summer protested, trying to give off a confident air, remembering how terrified she'd been at Doug's words and hoping that wasn't the roving trader's lasting memory of her.

Doug sat up straight and rubbed his hands together, grinning at Valerie. 'Let me have a think,' he said. 'Give me ten minutes and I'll come up with something spectacular.'

'I can't wait.' Valerie's eyes met Doug's with a sparkle that Summer hadn't noticed before.

'The stage is set,' Ryder said, 'and all of us are merely players.' He sauntered over to the group and crouched down. He was wearing a loud, Hawaiian-style yellow and pink shirt and jeans so pale they were almost white. Summer thought she could see tassels on his shoes, but didn't want to look too closely for fear of being proved right. 'Looks pretty sweet, doesn't it?'

'That is an awful misquote,' Claire said, 'but it does look incredible. The bands will be so stoked. I've sorted out Herald at the last minute, and a good new indie band from Norwich called Swordfish with some pretty solid backing. I thought they could play Sunday night, close things down in spectacular fashion.'

'It sounds amazing,' Summer said. 'I'm just gutted I'll miss the early music while I'm working.'

'We'll make sure the volume's up,' Claire said. 'And with Harry along to help, you'll get breaks.'

'It depends how packed it is. From the conversations I've overheard in the café, it seems your stealth-marketing campaign has worked wonders.'

'We've got the river alight with it,' Ryder said, 'not to mention the fan-bases of the bands and artists. Willowbeck's not the biggest place, so I have no concerns about the atmosphere. It'll go off with a bang, and banging's what we're all about.' He gave Claire a sideways glance and she turned away, her cheeks reddening.

Summer covered her smile with her hand, and made a mental note to ask Claire what was going on with her and Ryder when they could talk in private.

'Shame about the empty berth though,' Ryder added, 'that's some custom, or help for the festival, that's going begging.'

'It's a residential mooring,' Valerie said, her voice stern, 'and Mason could return any day. He's only gone away for a few days for work. In fact, I bet he knows about the festival, and is planning on coming back over the weekend.'

Ryder raised his eyebrows, clearly unconvinced, but Summer was touched by Valerie's loyalty to Mason. She felt a tug on her T-shirt.

'Still no word?' Claire asked. Her voice was sympathetic, and Summer resisted the wall that was attempting to build itself up against the question.

'Nothing,' she said. 'Norman said he's gone after the cranes at the reserve, which I can believe, but I know that's not the whole picture.'

Claire squeezed Summer's shoulder. 'He'll come back,' she said.

Summer exhaled. 'You don't believe that.'

'I do. After what you've told me, about how he seemed prepared to talk to you about Tania, I do. He's a changed man, clearly – or you've made him see things differently.'

'You're kind, and I know you're trying to make me feel better, but I think I'm going to have to track him down if I want to try and explain. He's chosen to go off-grid, and I don't blame him.' Summer sipped her wine and then lay down, her head cushioned by the springy grass. She stared at the patches of blue sky through the pattern of leaves and branches above her. She'd told Claire that Mason had got close, about the compass, and about the night on his boat when she'd discovered it. She hadn't mentioned anything about his wife or the fire because that wasn't her story to tell, and Claire had seemed sympathetic, even though, without the tragedy in his past, it made Mason's disappearance seem irrational.

She blinked a couple of times, and when she opened her eyes, there was a face looking down at her, his features upside down, his smile appearing in her mind like a frown.

'Ross,' Claire said. 'Long time no see. I didn't realize you were joining us!'

'It sounded fun,' Ross said, 'I couldn't miss out now that Willowbeck is one of my favourite places.' He smiled at them, but it faltered slightly when neither Valerie nor Summer greeted him warmly.

Summer sat up. 'Hi,' she said. He was wearing a bright yellow T-shirt, his hair gelled into spikes, his knees poking out below black shorts.

'Summer, how are you? Ready for the festival?'

'Let's go and get a drink.' Her mind was racing. She hadn't prepared for this, hadn't worked through everything she needed to say to him yet. But he was here, and she couldn't pretend to be friendly now she knew what he was responsible for.

'There's plenty of wine here,' Claire said, holding up a bottle.

Summer shook her head and stood, beckoning for Ross to follow her. The picnic tables were busy, but Summer felt freer, more able to talk, away from the others. Inside the pub, blinking so her eyes could adjust to the gloom, she ordered a pint for Ross and a glass of lime and soda for herself. She took them back outside and sat opposite him.

Ross had his back to the river, a curious, amused smile on his face. Summer let her eyes follow the line of the boats: Purple *Moonshine,* closest to the bridge, *The Canal Boat Café* and then the gap where *The Sandpiper* had been, green and red *Celeste* and, finally, the cluster of roving trader boats in the visitor moorings and along the opposite towpath. The water was glittering and the breeze was warm, caressing Summer's arms. It was a perfect day.

'Summer, what did you want to talk to me about?' Ross puffed up his chest, as if he was preparing for good news. Summer wanted to feel sorry for him, for the desperate measures he'd taken to be in her life, but all she felt was anger.

'You lied to me about Mason,' she said.

It took a moment for Ross's grin to falter and for his chest to deflate. 'What? No, of course I didn't.'

'When you told me about Valerie's reading, I didn't want to believe it. You confused me, you made me doubt my own feelings, and now I know that none of it was true, that you made it all up.'

'I don't know what you mean.' Ross ran his fingers up the side of his glass.

'I spoke to Valerie. She told me that you and Mason were friends, that you chatted about him as if you got on, but I know that's not true. You've never liked him, and then, last time we met, you made out that Valerie had warned you to look out for me, to protect me from this Lothario character. It was obviously Mason.' She watched while Ross's lips tightened and his Adam's apple bobbed as he weighed up what to tell her. 'I wondered how Valerie could think you and Mason were friends; how Valerie could think Mason was a good person – if that reading had been real.'

'But she hinted at some of it, so—'

'No she didn't. She didn't say any of it. I asked her.'

Ross looked away, looked back. 'Summer—'

'Just tell me the truth! Admit that you made it all up, and then tell me why.'

'OK! No, none of it was real. Valerie's reading didn't say any of that.'

Summer sat back on the bench, feeling the wedge in her chest lessen a little at his confession. 'You made it all up to put me off Mason?'

Ross looked at her steadily. 'If you were sure about him, nothing I said could have changed your mind. I was only voicing your existing fears.'

Summer bit back her anger. 'You made me think he couldn't be trusted. You used Valerie – you made her think you were friends, but you were just using her to find out anything you could about Mason to turn me against him.'

'I like Valerie! That's not true.'

'Ross, come on. I've had enough of this. What about Lothario? I know you got that from Valerie.'

Ross folded his arms on the table. 'Summer, I care about you. It doesn't matter where I got the information from. Someone *did* call Mason a Lothario, didn't they? So maybe he is.'

'He's not.'

'How can you be so sure, Summer? Do you know him that well?'

Summer squeezed her hands into fists. 'No! No, I don't – I'm trying to, but people keep getting in the way! You've been keeping tabs on me: first trying to persuade me to sell the boat, then trying to convince me to come back to Willowbeck when I'd left. I *know* it was you who told Valerie that I thought she was a fraud. Not Jenny at all, but *you*. My friend. Someone I trusted, someone who has looked after me at my most vulnerable – and now I find out all of this! Ross, do you have any idea how much you've hurt me and Valerie?'

Ross stared at the table.

'How can I ever trust you again?'

'You stopped coming to my shop,' Ross said, his voice taking on a whining quality. 'I missed you, Summer, and I thought that if you gave up the boat, if you didn't have any friends here, then you'd come back to Cambridge.'

Summer's anger prickled like ice. 'So you tried to get me to sell the boat, tried to turn my friends against me, and when I left Willowbeck you came to track me down. And, not content with me moving back here, you tried to turn me against Mason?' She put her head in her hands. 'God, Ross. I can't believe I didn't see through you sooner. Did you really think I'd change my mind about you? I've told you so many times, I don't want to be anything more than friends.'

'But we're so good together,' Ross said. 'You have to believe that – you have to realize it. This Mason bloke doesn't care about you like I do.'

'How do you know that?' Summer shot back. 'You don't know *anything* about him. And you know very little about me if you think I'm just going to forgive everything you've done. The only thing that wasn't down to you was the break-in – someone else made me scared enough to want to come back here. I bet you wish you'd thought of that, too. But you planted the seeds, didn't you? Driving up to treat me to a takeaway, making a point of telling me how unsafe Tivesham was. I bet you were over the moon when your fears were realized.' She gave him a sharp, humourless smile, but froze when her words, played back to her, seemed like too much of a coincidence.

She looked closely at Ross, her heart pounding. He couldn't meet her gaze. 'Ross?' It came out as a whisper. 'You didn't, did you?'

'Of course not,' he said, chuckling and then taking a long swig of his pint.

Summer didn't believe him. Suddenly, she thought he was capable of going that far. He hadn't blinked at trying to turn everyone Summer cared for against her, so why wouldn't he take it a step further?

'Ross? Tell me the truth.'

'I am!' he shot back. 'I wouldn't do that to you, Summer. I care about you, I wouldn't try and hurt you like that.'

'So only by alienating me from my friends, making me doubt my own feelings? You'd hurt me in those ways, but not by breaking into my boat?'

Ross sighed. 'I was thinking of you, Summer. I looked after you, remember? I know what's good for you, *who's* good for you.'

'How can you say that?' She knew she was close to shouting, but she couldn't help it. 'How can you claim to know me so well, when you never listen to what I say? You never listen when I tell you I'm fine, or that I don't want to be more than friends. You turn up here and you manipulate everyone, and it's not going to work any more. I don't want to see you again.'

'Summer, please. I'll make it up to you.'

'I don't think you can,' she said, looking away. 'I just want you to go.'

'Please!' She felt his fingers touch hers and she pulled her hand away. 'I'll do anything, Summer. I'll apologize to Mason and Valerie, I'll pay for the damage to your boat, I'll—'

Summer snapped her head round to face him. 'Why would you pay for the damage if you weren't responsible for it?'

Ross shrugged, and hid his mouth behind his pint glass. 'I just want to help.'

'Did you do it?' she asked quietly. 'Did you break into my boat, to try and scare me into coming back to Willowbeck?'

'I would do anything for you, Summer, and I *knew* you weren't safe there. But you can't always see it.'

Summer felt splinters dig into her hands as she gripped the edge of the table. For a moment, she couldn't speak. 'I was *terrified*,' she said eventually. 'People went after you, the police were called, and there was so much damage.'

'I've said I'll pay you back. I know it was a bad idea, but I just thought if you came back to Willowbeck—'

'It's a criminal offence!' Summer shouted, and several people at the other tables turned in their direction. Summer leaned forward and lowered her voice, hissing at him. 'You have no idea how scared I was, how many other people were affected by your stupid actions.' She remembered crouching on the deck of her boat in the dark, Claire and her friends crowding round her, Jas chasing after him down the towpath. She could picture, perfectly, Mason's fear and shock when faced with her wrecked café, his reaction making complete sense now Dennis had told her what memories he'd been reliving. She stood suddenly, Latte yipping at her feet.

'I did care about you, Ross, and I will never forget what you did for me after Mum died. I would always have been your friend, but this, it – I can't take it in, and I don't – I don't know what to think. I want you to leave now.'

'Summer, please. If we just talk—' Ross stood as well, his face pale.

'I don't want to talk to you now. I can't.' She crouched and picked up Latte, turned in the direction of the stage and the roving traders, and then stopped. How could she explain it to them? That someone she had considered a friend had been manipulating her like that and had actually caused the break-in, the damage, and the fear that had at one point made Summer believe she could no longer stay on her boat. Ross had almost got his way. She wanted to tell Valerie that Ross had gone even further than they had thought, but she couldn't do it yet. She had to get her head round it first.

With the anger and shock making her feel restless and numb at the same time, Summer went back to her boat. She felt threatened by Ross. He thought what he'd done had been harmless, but to Summer it was sinister. He'd made Valerie question their friendship, he'd made her fear the open river, and he'd been trying to turn her against Mason. He hadn't managed that, but had his actions, his planted fears, worming their way into Summer's head, inadvertently caused Mason to turn against her?

Summer paced inside her cabin. Latte sat on the sofa, her little head moving side to side, following her owner's progress. It was a lovely evening; she could hear chatter and laughter filtering through the open window from the pub garden. Her phone beeped, but when she saw the name Ross she deleted the messages instantly. Harry got in touch to check timings for the following day, and Summer was reminded that the festival was starting tomorrow and she needed to prepare.

Grateful for the distraction, she went into the café, giving the tables and counter an extra polish, making sure the crockery and cutlery was clean and close at hand, checking on the cakes and cookies, the macarons and tarts waiting in the fridge. She poured fresh beans into the coffee machine and looked up at the blackboard behind the counter, wondering what to write. But she saw her message to Mason, running in red chalk along the top, and her resolve slipped.

It had been eleven days without any word from him. Not a single call or text, no message to let her know that he was OK – or even to tell her that he never wanted to see her again. Could he really be taking photos of cranes all this time? Summer was kidding herself if she thought that was what was occupying him. She could blame Ross – he certainly wasn't blameless in all this – but she couldn't really look further than herself.

She had asked Mason questions, and she hadn't waited to listen to the answers. She had forced him to drag up the past, and she hadn't been an outlet for him, hadn't trusted him enough to let him tell her. He'd been prepared to open up, to tell her about the biggest tragedy anyone could ever face – and she'd shut the door on him.

Summer went back to her cabin, but was unable to settle. She tried reading a book and then watching a film, but she couldn't concentrate. She even tried working on her present to Mason. The painting of the kingfisher was nearly finished, but the thought that she would never be able to give it to him lowered her spirits even more.

She changed into her summer pyjamas, climbed under

the bed covers, and stared at the ceiling for what felt like hours. Eventually, when cold air was slipping in through the window in her berth, and the pub garden was still and silent, Summer climbed out of bed. Latte was asleep at the foot of the bed and she moved quietly so she wouldn't wake her.

In only her shorts and vest top, Summer took her phone and went onto her bow deck, hoisting herself up onto the roof of her boat. Willowbeck was quiet, pockets of blackness interspersed with the soft, glowing lights on the towpath and a few of the visiting narrowboats. The cold air licked its way around her and, shivering, she lay down on the roof, jolting at how cold it was against her skin. She let her eyes adjust to the glittering star display above her. The moon was a thin, curved slice, the sky almost pitch black, and the stars popped out at her, alone and in clusters, so bright and vibrant that Summer felt she could reach up and touch one.

Her breath lodged in her throat, and goose bumps prickled on her arms and legs. She stared at the stars and let the emotions wash over her: her anger at Ross, her regret over Mason, and her longing to see him again. She thought back to the last time she had been lying on the roof of a boat, and how happy she'd been, and this, combined with the night-time wind and the celestial display, made Summer feel small, and lost. But she had to believe there was still hope.

She looked at her phone and, her pulse beating unhelpfully loudly in her ears, opened her messages. Mason's name hovered near the top, though it was a while since they had exchanged texts. Eleven days, Summer thought, and not one text.

Lying on the roof looking at the stars, she wrote, *but it's not the same without you. I miss you, and I'm so sorry. Xxx* She could have gone on and on, written out her apology in a long, heartfelt essay, but her fingers were trembling too much, and she didn't know if he was even at the other end of the phone. It would be easy for him to disappear to a different part of the country along the network of rivers and canals, replace his number and sever their ties completely. Summer didn't want to think that, but like Valerie said, he'd been traumatized. Maybe it was easier for him to start again, to put the pieces back together where nobody knew him – wasn't that what she'd tried to do when she cruised out of Willowbeck and ended up in Foxburn?

Summer stared at the sky, trying to pick out constellations, wondering which of the orbs far above her were planets and which ones were already gone, just the memory of a star, glinting its final, drawn-out goodbye.

At first she thought she'd imagined the beep. She'd been hearing it so often in her head, the hope of a message from him, that she thought it was just that. But she looked anyway – she couldn't not – and gasped when she saw the name on the screen. Mason.

She unlocked her phone and opened the message, squeezing her eyes closed and taking a deep breath before she allowed herself to read it.

Not the same place, the message said, *but the same stars. I miss you too. M xx*

Summer read the message over and over again, until her vision blurred and her toes turned to ice, and the stars slowly moved across the sky. She didn't know what to reply, didn't want to bombard him with questions, about where he was or when he was coming back or what he was thinking –

whether he hated her or forgave her, or if it really was the cranes that had taken him away.

Blinking the tears out of her eyes, she sent a reply: *I hope you sleep well. I've been doing a lot of hoping recently. PS,* she added, smiling through her tears: *The roof of my boat's filthy. Xx*

Chapter 22

The Willowbeck musical festival transformed the picture-perfect village into what felt to Summer like the centre of the world. Before she had a chance to open up, there were people milling about on the towpath, and narrow-boats mooring up along the opposite bank of the river, tying their ropes onto the posts positioned at regular intervals along the bank. It was the first day of July, and the weather was fitting, with lots of bare flesh on show even though the sun was a long way off being at its hottest. Summer was pleased, knowing that the weather would have a huge effect on the success of the festival, but she also had very little time, and a small wedge of panic that all her preparations – the baking and cleaning and stocking-up – wouldn't be nearly enough.

'I got the last space in the car park,' Harry said breathlessly as she came into the café carrying a tower of baking tins. 'This is mad. What time does the music kick off?'

As if on cue, James Bay's 'Craving' started blasting from *Water Music*.

'I think the first acts are on the stage at about eleven,' Summer said, 'but there's poetry and dance and all sorts before the bands start. I am so glad to see you, do you think we've done enough?'

Harry grinned. She was wearing tiny denim shorts and a bright-pink floaty top, her hair tied away from her face. 'Of course we have,' she said, and Summer couldn't detect a hint of uncertainty.

'You're right; we're as prepared as we can be. Let me help you with those,' she said, taking most of the tins from her friend, 'and get us both a shot of caffeine before we let the hordes in.'

'Caffeine would be good,' Harry said. 'You're a pretty shrewd businesswoman, you know that?'

'See if you still believe that at the end of the day.'

Summer looked out at the river. The opposite towpath was almost completely obscured by narrowboats, people sitting on their decks enjoying breakfast and soaking up the atmosphere. A gaggle of geese swam up the middle, their necks elongated, heads held high, as if they were the centre of attention. Summer switched on the coffee machine and got a fresh bottle of milk out of the fridge.

'Cheers,' she said, clinking her mug against Harry's when they were both full of frothy cappuccino. 'I've put an extra shot in each one. I think we're going to need it.' She soon discovered that she'd been too modest with the caffeine.

The people kept coming. The tables emptied and new customers took the chairs immediately, the café full of warm and cheerful chatter. A whisper of a breeze drifted through from the hatch where there was a queue that never seemed to diminish, however fast Harry and Summer kept serving. The dishwasher worked on overtime, and the contents of the cake tins and boxes on the kitchen counters and in the fridge were being bought and eaten at a rate that Summer had never seen before. All this against a backdrop of music, first from Claire's boat and then, as lunchtime approached, from the stage set up at the side of the Black Swan.

The river was thrumming with the boats cruising past and, whenever a space became available, mooring up to see what was happening in the usually quiet village. Summer wondered how the other residents were coping, though she thought Dennis and Jenny would be over the moon and just hoped they'd hired enough extra staff to cope with the influx of people, because all the picnic tables outside were crammed with festivalgoers. She hadn't seen Valerie, but thought that she probably had a full programme of readings, and she expected Norman was likely hibernating aboard *Celeste*, looking things up on his iPad.

Summer finally, reluctantly, closed the doors of the café at eight o'clock. The music had grown steadily in volume throughout the day and the current band, which Summer thought sounded like a cross between Of Monsters and Men and Placebo, were making the piles of cups reverberate on the café counter.

'That was a day and a half,' Harry said, when Summer brought them each a bottle of lemonade.

'I don't know what I would have done without you,' Summer admitted, pushing open the bow doors and flopping on to the deck seating.

'Lucky you didn't have to, then.' Harry sat down and slipped off her ballet pumps to rub the soles of her feet. 'I've got enough cakes and pastries back at the cottage to keep you going for the next two days. I'll bring them all tomorrow, and then of course I'll be able to help out, but if Sunday's anything like this, then you won't manage on your own. Have you decided what you'll do yet?'

Summer looked out over the water and narrowed her eyes. The light had taken on the pink haze of a hot, early evening, and she could feel the sweat at the base of her spine. She wiped hair from her face. 'Not exactly. I mean, I've thought about it, and about how hard it will be – and that was before today exploded around us – but I haven't come up with a solution.'

'Are you still open?' a young guy asked from the towpath. He had his arm draped around a girl, and she had daisies in her long, curly hair.

'Sorry, we're closed now. The pub's open though,' Summer said pointlessly, pointing to the hubbub. 'They do cakes as well – but we'll be open again tomorrow, early.'

'Cheers.' They turned and loped up the grass.

'You need someone else to serve,' Harry said. 'If I could get out of Sunday, I would, but it's one of Greg's closest friends and there's just no way.'

'I'd never ask you to miss a wedding to come and work your ass off for me all day,' Summer said.

'Is this perhaps . . .' Harry started.

'Perhaps what?'

'Something that Ross might be able to help you with? I'm sure he'd be happy to.'

'Yeah,' Summer said, her insides churning as she thought of everything she'd discovered and he'd – finally – admitted to. 'He would, but I wouldn't. Something happened yesterday that I haven't had the time to tell you about.'

Harry's mouth fell open. 'What? What's happened? Did you finally tell him to stay away?'

'I did,' Summer said, 'but from what I know now, it turns

392

out I should have listened to you in the first place and done it a long time ago.'

Summer told Harry everything that had happened, her incredulity at all that Ross had been doing to try and get his own way with Summer, and her surprise and relief when Mason had replied to her text, late the previous night.

'Summer, you have to report Ross to the police,' Harry said urgently. 'He can't be allowed to get away with it. Who knows what could have happened? You could have been seriously hurt.'

'I know, but . . .' Summer chewed her lip, not sure she could live with herself if she turned him into the police.

'But what? He broke into your boat. It was hostile – it was meant to frighten you. No way you can spin it round to helping, or supporting you, whatever he says.'

Summer stared at her shoes. 'I need more time to think. I don't want to see him again – I'm not *going* to see him again – but I don't know if I want to take it further. It would drag it back up, and I – I need more space after this,' she flung her arms wide, encompassing the festival, 'to decide what to do.'

'OK,' Harry said, rubbing her shoulder. 'I'm here for you whatever you choose. And it's good news, isn't it, about Mason? If you'd texted sooner, maybe he would have replied sooner. He could be as confused as you are, thinking you're still mad with *him.*'

'How could I be?' Summer asked, pressing her cool lemonade bottle against her forehead.

'How would he know you're not, if you left it so . . . so up in the air? The last time he saw you, you stormed off his boat and refused to open the door when he knocked.'

Summer sighed and rested her head on her arms on the

edge of the boat. 'All this could be cleared up if he just came back.'

'I'm sure he will,' Harry said, squeezing her arm. 'Especially now he's been in touch. Do you fancy going over to catch some of the band? I've got half an hour before I need to get back to Greg and Tommy, and it might take your mind off things.'

'Are they coming down tomorrow?'

'Yup. We might even get Tommy to help out in the café, if we're lucky.'

'What will we have to pay him in?'

'Ice cream should do it,' Harry said.

'That's good, because I've got quite a lot of that left.'

Saturday was even busier than Friday, with more people enjoying the festival as the weekend kicked in. Harry was good to her word and brought enough cakes to fill almost all of Summer's cabin. Greg and Tommy spent the morning exploring the other traders and watching the acts on the stage, and then Harry sent Greg off for a pint in the pub while Tommy cleared tables in the café, his cheery face and cheeky chat drawing admiration from the customers.

'How long have you been working here, young man?' asked a woman who Summer thought must have been in her fifties, but whose hair was enviably long and auburn, and dotted with tiny plaits. From where she was standing behind the counter, Summer could see one leg in flared jeans and a red wedge sandal.

Tommy glanced nervously at his mum, before turning back to the customer. 'This is my first day,' he said proudly. 'It's Summer's café, and we're helping because of the festival.'

'You're doing a great job,' the woman said. 'Any plans to open a café when you're older?'

Tommy shook his head. 'I'm going to be a professional fisherman. Dad's teaching me.'

Harry and Summer exchanged a grin, and Summer took over at the hatch while Harry ran to the kitchen to get a fresh batch of macarons – mocha and passion-fruit flavoured – out of the oven. Summer heard Tommy tell the woman how he wouldn't be able to be a fisherman in Willowbeck because there were definitely no fish in this river, and had to stifle her laughter.

Half an hour later she saw Tommy standing in front of one of the tables outside, talking to a family of three generations, two small children sitting on their parents' knees. He was gesturing wildly about something, miming running off down the towpath. The family were laughing, the granddad almost doubled over at the waist.

'Are you sure Tommy wants to be a fisherman and not a performer,' Summer said, pointing. 'He's a natural.'

Harry stared adoringly at her son. 'He's kept me and Greg going,' she said. 'He's been a bright light amongst all this gloom. Along with you and this café, of course,' she added, leaning out of the hatch and handing a bag of brownie bites to two teenage girls. 'Are you going to have a lunch break?'

Summer shook her head. 'It's too busy.'

Harry gave her a scornful look. 'You gave me half an hour,' she said. 'Go and ask Tommy to get to the final act of whatever he's performing on your way out, and I'll be fine.'

'I'll take ten minutes.'

'If I see you back here before two, then I'll push you in the river. Go!' Harry flapped her hands in a shooing gesture, and Summer gave her friend a grateful smile and hung her apron over the corner of the blackboard.

Summer could barely move on the towpath, but she made

it through the crowds to the picnic tables and wove through those to the stage area, where an acoustic singer was sitting on a stool and playing a large, ochre guitar, his voice carrying easily over the attentive crowd. Summer stood with her arms folded, watching him, enjoying a few moments of doing nothing but drinking in the atmosphere.

'He's good, isn't he?' said a male voice at her ear.

Summer turned, her eyes narrowing in recognition at the man who greeted her. He was a bit older than she was, with green eyes and fair hair. 'Yes,' she said, trying to place him, 'he really is.'

'Taking a break?' the man asked, nodding his head in the direction of the river.

Summer glanced behind her. 'Just half an hour,' she said. He was a customer, that was it, though she couldn't remember serving him.

The man looked in the direction of the stage, then turned his green eyes back to Summer. 'And did Mason come back?' he asked softly.

It hit her then. The businessman who'd asked for the same order Mason always had, espresso and bacon sandwich, the day she'd woken up to find *The Sandpiper* gone. Today he was suitless, looking much more relaxed in a loose-fitting white shirt and navy shorts.

'Not yet,' she said, her happy mood dipping.

'But he will,' the man said, angling his beer bottle in her direction. 'And you think it too, or you wouldn't have said yet.'

'I'm hopeful,' she said, trying to believe her own words.

'Who couldn't be hopeful on a day like this?' He smiled at Summer, and it was such a genuine, warm smile that Summer felt instantly reassured. She opened her mouth to thank him, but the singer on the stage finished his song and spoke to his audience.

'We're coming to the end of my set,' he said, 'and I hope you've enjoyed it.' The crowd whooped and cheered and Summer joined in. 'Now, for my last song I'm going to need some help. I hope you've all whetted your whistles with beer from the Black Swan, because you're all going to sing along. You up for it?' He held his guitar up by the neck, his arm stretched towards the blue sky.

Summer could stay for this song, and then go back to the café. 'Yes!' she called, joining in with everyone else. She turned to grin at the green-eyed man, and he held out his beer to her. Summer took a quick swig and thanked him, and they sang along together, both deciding that volume was more important than accuracy, sharing a few minutes of fun before Summer went back to work, the cheerful chorus playing in her head for the rest of the afternoon.

Summer again closed at eight o'clock, knowing she needed to save stock – and some energy – for the next day, when she would be working entirely on her own. She toyed with the idea of asking Dennis if he could spare a staff member, and then decided she would play it by ear, only calling on help if things got desperate. She went with Harry, Greg, Tommy and Valerie to watch Herald's set, dancing along to the songs with Tommy and Claire, despite her sore feet.

'This,' she said, breathlessly, raising her arms up to the star-filled sky and the fairy lights, the thrum of electric guitar and the crowd all around her, 'is incredible. You're so clever, Claire, I would never have imagined Willowbeck could host a festival.'

'You need to let your imagination run wild,' Claire said, 'and believe anything is possible.' She gave Summer a wide, slightly sweaty grin, and Summer bounced forward and hugged her.

'I'm going to do just that,' she said, 'starting with tomorrow. I believe I can run the café single-handedly on the last day of the music festival.'

'Or you could ask Norman to help,' said Harry, joining them.

'That might be stretching it a bit far,' Summer admitted, and they all laughed.

'We've all agreed to close up at six tomorrow,' Claire said, 'so we can enjoy the last evening of the festival and Swordfish. It's going to be a cracking night; we'll have done pretty good business and I think we could all do with an evening of festival fun by then.'

'If I'm still alive,' Summer said.

'Hey,' Claire said, 'you're going to be brilliant, remember?'

'I can help,' Tommy said.

'No, we're going to Steve and Sophie's wedding.' Harry smoothed down her son's hair.

Tommy screwed his face up. 'But I have to wear a suit,' he said. 'If I'm in the café I can just wear shorts and T-shirt, *and* eat ice cream.'

'Weddings are fun,' Summer said, 'and I'm sure there'll be other guests your age.'

'I want to come back here tomorrow,' Tommy said, his petulance a telltale sign of tiredness.

'You can come back whenever you want – *after* tomorrow,' Summer confirmed.

'But now,' Harry said, 'bed. We've got a long day ahead of us.'

'It's a shame you'll miss the last night.' Claire hugged Harry and Greg, and gave Tommy a shoulder squeeze.

'I've had a blast,' Harry said. 'Who thought working in a café could be so much fun? I could teach my previous employer a thing or two.'

'I'm glad you think that,' Summer said, 'and thank you so much – for everything. I'll be in touch after the weekend.' She would wait until things had calmed down to speak to Harry about working in the café with her.

'Good luck tomorrow, and don't forget about Norman if you get really stuck.'

Summer laughed, and Claire looped her arm through hers as Harry and her family wove their way through the crowd.

'Bed for me too, I think,' Summer said.

'Let me know if you really struggle tomorrow,' Claire said. 'I'm sure we can drag some help up from somewhere. What about Ryder?'

Summer winced. 'I think I'd rather take my chances with Norman.'

For the last day of the festival, Summer wore a lilac dress that skimmed her knees. It was comfortable but pretty, and went with the red and blue gingham apron she put on whenever she was working. Latte sat on a chair in the café, watching the boats pass by while Summer made herself a coffee and arranged her cakes under the domes on the counter. Even with the craziness of the previous two days, she had enough varied stock to keep the customers happy, and with her cut-off time set at six o'clock, Summer was confident that she wouldn't run out.

At first she found it easy. She was methodical and organized, splitting her time between the queue forming at the hatch, and the people sitting at the tables. She cleared the used crockery quickly, set the dishwasher going as soon as it was half-full, and was proud that nobody was having to wait too long. But as the stage started up and lunchtime drew near, the crowds seemed to swell. The river was busy with passing narrowboats and the sun was even warmer than it had been the previous day. Summer got stuck for longer than usual at the hatch when a woman in her forties with bright pink lipstick and pearl earrings read out a long order written down on a piece of paper, and when she turned back to the café there were several displeased faces looking back at her.

'I'm so sorry about that,' she said, approaching a young couple at one of the tables, the woman with a toddler on her lap. 'It's so busy today.'

'Your café's beautiful,' the woman said, flicking back her short blonde hair, 'no wonder it's packed. And you're doing a brilliant job.'

'Thank you, that means a lot. What can I get you?'

When an older couple came in, Summer felt a flash of recognition. 'Are you regulars?' she asked, wiping down the table and stacking the previous occupants' used cups and plates onto a tray as they sat down.

'No,' the woman said, 'but we have been aboard – though it didn't look anything like this.'

Summer frowned.

'You gave us a cup of tea on a bitterly cold day,' the man added. 'You were on the roof of the boat, I'm not sure you were even open.'

Summer gasped as realization dawned, remembering the day she'd cruised away from Willowbeck, wondering whether she should try and make the café work or if she would be better off selling it.

'I have to say,' the woman said, in the face of Summer's stunned silence, 'it looks amazing now. You must be so pleased you decided to stay.'

Summer nodded, snapping herself out of her reverie. 'I am, and it's so lovely to see you! I can't believe you came back.'

'When we heard about the Willowbeck festival, we couldn't miss it. And look how incredible it is – I've found some old vinyl that I used to have as a boy.' The man held up a carrier bag. 'It's such a good idea.'

'I know Claire, the organizer, and she's worked miracles in such a small amount of time.' Summer grinned down at them, wishing she could chat all day, her mind whirring at how much had happened since the first time she'd met the friendly couple, on a freezing day back in February.

'Excuse me,' someone called, and Summer looked up to see the queue at the hatch snaking up the towpath, as far as the eye could see.

'Crap,' she murmured. 'I have to get on,' she said to them, 'but I'll be back with your order in a second.'

Summer realized the few minutes she'd spent talking had pushed her off track. She worked as fast as she could, but the queues and orders and questioning expressions seemed endless. Summer told herself she wouldn't panic, and she kept her head down, frothing and pouring and plating up, serving and clearing, smiling and trying to breathe. She heard people exclaim at something on the water, the sound of another boat chugging slowly past, hoping to squeeze in along the towpath, but then she was back at the hatch, handing out paper bags full of ginger cookies.

She made three espressos for a group of young men who looked like they were having a shot of caffeine before moving seamlessly onto beer, and gratefully accepted a bag of bacon from Adam, who had appeared at the counter.

'Thought you could do with this,' he said, handing it over. 'We'll sort out the money later.'

'Thanks, Adam,' she said, 'you might just have saved my life.'

'See you later, at the festival?'

'I'm counting down to six o'clock,' she said quietly, not wanting the customers to know she was wishing her time, and them, away.

She turned back to the hatch, handed over four Magnums, and then heard someone putting crockery down on the counter, probably clearing an empty table themselves so they could sit down.

'Just a sec,' she said, turning back to the counter, and her breath left her in one swift exhale.

Summer couldn't do anything but stare. Mason was standing on the other side of the counter, looking at her. His skin was darker, the freckles across his cheeks more pronounced, and his hair was longer, the curls as dishevelled as ever. He was wearing a royal blue, V-necked T-shirt and his camera was around his neck, the silver glinting in the sunlight.

Summer felt a flood of emotion, of desire and relief and elation, so that it was suddenly hard to swallow and she felt giddy. His dark eyes found hers, and though his lips weren't smiling, the warmth in his gaze set fireworks off inside her.

'Hi,' she said, her cheeks bunching into a smile.

'Hey,' Mason said. 'You look like you could do with some help.'

She thought she might have nodded, but she was transfixed, unable to look away from him. He had a tiny, white petal stuck in his hair, and she imagined it drifting lazily through the summer breeze to land there, while he was at the helm of *The Sandpiper*, cruising on his way back to Willowbeck.

Mason glanced behind him, then gave her a nervous smile.

'Summer? The queue . . .' He pointed outside, and Summer forced herself to look at the row of people waiting at the hatch.

'Help would be amazing, thank you.'

'Right.' Mason nodded decisively, and started clearing up tables.

Summer blinked. Her heart was thudding so loudly that she couldn't hear anything else. She wiped her hands down her apron and smiled at the young boy who was peering in at the hatch, wondering if she looked slightly hysterical.

'What can I get you?' she asked him, and concentrated hard on the answer, wishing she could turn round and look at Mason again. She could hear him chatting with people, could hear Latte's adoring barks and wondered where Archie was, whether *The Sandpiper* was back in its rightful place or if an opportunistic festivalgoer had snuck into his residential mooring. But she knew that she needed to concentrate on serving the queue, which would be both easier and harder now that Mason was on board.

They worked together, Summer serving at the hatch and making hot drinks, Mason plating up scones and muffins, macarons and miniature praline and coffee tarts, clearing tables, loading and unloading the dishwasher. There was no time for chat and Summer was glad, because she needed to speak to him properly, once everyone had gone and the café was closed. But their eyes kept meeting across the tables and though their smiles were hesitant, Summer found that Mason's gaze was as penetrating as ever, his dark eyes latching onto hers and holding her captive.

With him there, Summer felt invincible. Lunch passed, people came and went, and Summer kept serving and chatting, her confidence sky-high with Mason at her side. He must have forgiven her, she thought as she served two cream teas, or he wouldn't have come back. He wouldn't be here, helping her, if he didn't think there was anything to talk about.

She thought she would be counting the seconds, willing the clock hands to find six o'clock, but it came around so quickly, with a quick blast from *Water Music*, followed by an announcement through a loudspeaker that Summer didn't realize Claire had.

'The roving trader boats are now closed,' she called, 'but the Black Swan is serving food and drinks all evening and we're delighted to announce that, at seven-thirty, acclaimed band Swordfish will be making their way to the stage. Thank you so much for coming to the inaugural Willowbeck music festival. We hope you've had a good time – we've all had a blast.' The horn sounded again and a round of applause and cheers went up from the people on the boats, the towpath and the pub garden.

Summer waved goodbye to the last of the customers and walked to the bow deck, closing and locking the door while Mason shut the hatch. Latte jumped up onto a table and barked at Mason, her tail wagging madly.

Summer turned and leaned against the door, butterflies dancing in her stomach. Mason rested his elbows on the counter, and Summer was drawn to his tanned arms and strong hands as he picked up the carved wooden sun.

'You got another one,' he said, holding it close to his face and turning it over.

'I did,' she said, walking slowly towards him. 'The day you left. The day after I – I stormed off your boat.' She forced herself to hold his gaze, and saw a flicker of pain cloud his features, before disappearing. 'I'm so sorry, Mason. I'm sorry for what I said, and I'm sorry I didn't listen to you.'

Mason put the sun back down, and Summer saw his shoulders rise and then fall. 'Where can we go to talk? It's a beautiful evening.'

Summer nodded. 'Come with me,' she said. 'And get Archie on the way.'

They crossed Elizabeth Proudfoot's bridge, against a tide of people making their way towards the stage. Latte and Archie were on leads at their feet, trotting along happily in each other's company. Summer and Mason walked side by side, Summer's heart thudding in double-time as they turned left at the end of the bridge, to where the river was quieter and the towpath was surrounded by greenery. As they walked further away from the festival, from the people and the music, Summer's heart began to settle.

There was a bench ahead of them, just a few wooden slats on top of metal legs, the wood warped and disfigured by time and the damp atmosphere, and Summer stopped in front of it. She brushed a few leaves off and sat down. Mason sat next to her, his body angled slightly towards her, his bare knee, below grey cargo shorts, touching hers. It was cooler beneath their leaf canopy, the light tinged bright green, the sounds of the festival muted.

'Mason——'

'Summer, I——'

Summer laughed nervously and shook her head. 'You go first.'

'Sure?'

She nodded, realizing that just hearing his voice made something settle inside her, easing her tension. She looked at him as he narrowed his eyes slightly, and chewed down on his bottom lip. She waited, holding her breath.

'I'm sorry I left,' he said, 'the day after you found the compass. It was partly for work, but it – I needed to get away, to have some time by myself, to think.'

'I'm sorry too,' she said.

'What for?' he asked. 'For being angry that I had something that belonged to your mum?'

'For asking about Tania and not waiting to hear your answer, and for leaving the way I did.'

Mason dropped his head and nodded. 'I thought I'd blown it, that you'd made your mind up and I'd lost my chance. I tried to follow you, to call you, but when I couldn't get through I thought that was it.'

Summer closed her eyes. 'I was mad, shocked – I think, about the compass. It took me a while to calm down and then, when I had, you'd gone. But of course I wanted to talk to you – I planned it all out that night, that in the morning I would come bearing an olive branch, but when I woke up you were gone. I tried calling . . .'

'I know,' he said quietly. 'But by then I didn't know if I could speak to you. What I would say to you.' He shook his head. 'Summer, there's something I need to tell you, about why I ended up on *The Sandpiper* in the first place, what led me here.'

Summer inhaled. 'I know,' she whispered.

Mason looked at her, his lips parted in surprise. 'What? How do you know?'

'Because I saw Dennis. I explained that you'd gone and mentioned the compass and he said – Mason, it wasn't his fault; I *begged* him to tell me. He said you probably needed some time to think after everything you'd been through, assuming I already knew. He told me about the compass, how he'd given it to you as payment for some photos. I'm so sorry I accused you of taking it.'

'He told you about Lisa?'

Summer nodded. 'He didn't want to, but I knew there was more to it than just a messy ending with Tania, and so I made him tell me. He said you told him on the drive up to Tivesham, after my break-in?' She risked putting her hand on his knee. He didn't seem to notice, but turned towards the river, rubbing his jaw.

Latte and Archie were snuffling in the undergrowth, their tails wagging, and Summer thought how simple it must be to be a dog, and have an uncomplicated friendship like theirs.

'I'm sorry,' Summer said again, 'I should have waited to hear it from you. I'm so, so sorry, Mason, I can't imagine what it feels like to lose someone you love like that.'

'The worst thing was, I thought I'd saved her.' His voice was calm, but Summer could hear the roughness at the edge of his words. 'I thought, after the panic and fear, after getting away from the flames, the awful heat and the smoke, that we were OK. We got out of the bedroom window, onto the kitchen roof. Lisa was in and out of consciousness by then and I had to carry her – drag her – but I thought we'd made it.'

Summer squeezed his knee. Tears stung her eyes, forcing their way out to her cheeks.

'But then we were on the grass and I could hear the sirens, but she wasn't breathing. I tried to resuscitate her, and then the paramedics took over and I . . . Part of it is so clear in my mind, and part of it's a blur. I spent months going over and over it, trying to make the pictures clear, wondering what I could have done differently.'

407

'You did all you could,' Summer said. 'I'm sure of that. I know you would have done everything in your power to save her. It was a tragic accident.'

He turned towards her, the pain of reliving it etched on his face. Summer took his hand, blinking away her tears.

'It's hard to talk about,' Mason said, 'even now. I can't get over the fact that I survived and she didn't. I'm not sure I ever will. But I should have told you sooner.'

'You don't owe me anything,' Summer whispered.

'Not even the truth?'

'You would have told me, if I'd let you that evening. That perfect evening that I ruined when I flew off the handle.'

'I had no idea the compass was your mum's.'

'I know that now,' Summer said, 'but I shouldn't have jumped to conclusions. I was so relieved to see it, but at the same time it raised a whole load of questions and I couldn't think straight. With that, and what Claire had told me about Tania, I was confused.'

'I should have been honest with you that night in Foxburn, when Claire appeared.' Mason sighed. 'It wasn't long after I'd bought *The Sandpiper.* I'd started to rebuild my life and I was trying, so hard, to move forward. I thought Tania could be part of that, but it was far too soon. I know I treated her badly, but I never meant to. I hadn't even begun to deal with losing Lisa, and I was finding it hard enough to look after myself, let alone care about anyone else, so I just left. I thought it would be better for both of us. I knew Claire would have been fiercely loyal to her friend, so when I saw her in Foxburn, with you, I panicked. I didn't want you thinking badly of me.'

Summer squeezed his hand. 'Thank you for telling me,' she whispered. It was as she'd imagined, as Harry had suggested once they'd found out about Lisa, and the tragedy Mason had faced. He had never meant to hurt Tania; he had been trying to grasp hold of normality before he was ready. Summer swallowed. 'I think, now,' she said, 'I need to be honest with you.'

Mason sat up, suddenly wary. 'OK,' he said, 'about what?'

Summer sighed. 'About Mum. About why I feel so guilty, why I've struggled to cope with everything, and why I was reluctant to come back to Willowbeck in the first place.'

Summer told Mason about the accusations she'd thrown at her mum on the day of her stroke, about how irresponsible she was, how heartless and selfish, how those were her last words to her. She was comforted by Mason's hand in hers, the way he tightened his grip but didn't interrupt her. She told him about finding comfort with Ross, about how that had been a mistake and what it had led to. She took a deep breath and told him how Ross had been manipulating her ever since.

'Mason,' she said, 'he was the one who broke onto my boat.'

'*What?*' Mason let go of her hand. 'Are you sure? He admitted it?'

'He did. He said he realizes now it was a bad idea, but . . .'

Mason shook his head, his jaw clenching. 'I was jealous of him when I thought you were together. I didn't like him, but I didn't realize he could be dangerous. Anything could have happened – you could have confronted him, gone into the water to try and escape – *anything.*'

'I know,' Summer said. 'But it didn't. I'm OK, the boat is – *everything* is.'

'Are you going to tell the police?'

'I don't know. I – I know how wrong it was, but I don't

want to even think about him at the moment, let alone have to face seeing him again. For now, I just want to concentrate on this, on us.'

Mason looked at her, his eyes hard with anger, his chest rising and falling.

Summer took his hand in both of hers. 'I'm fine, Mason. We don't have to worry about Ross any more. You're back in Willowbeck and that's what I care about the most.'

'So you forgive me?'

'For what? What is there to forgive?'

'For Tania, for disappearing like that?'

'You needed time,' Summer said. 'And I forced you to do that – to confront your feelings, and your fears, again. I should be asking you to forgive me, but I'm not sure I deserve it.'

Mason's tired, tanned face suddenly broke into a grin, the kind that made Summer feel dizzy with desire. 'You deserve forgiveness,' he said. 'In fact, I think you deserve a lot of things. And this is definitely one of them.' He leaned in towards her, cupped her face in his hand, and kissed her.

Summer closed her eyes, moved closer to him on the bench, and kissed him back.

Mason's skin was warm, he smelled of coffee and icing sugar, and he was back in Willowbeck, kissing her, his hand leaving her face and his arms circling her and pulling her against him. It was the resolution she'd been hoping for, and now that it was happening and she was in his arms, Summer realized she could finally let go of her hopes, because they were no longer figments, floating through her mind. Her hopes had become reality, and she thought, as she kissed Mason, felt his strong arms around her and the tickle of his hair against her cheek, that the reality was every bit as good as she'd imagined.

410

Chapter 23

Summer and Mason walked slowly back towards the bridge, their fingers entwined, and then stopped on it for a moment before making their way towards the festival. Summer could have spent the whole evening on the bench with Mason, getting a bottle of wine and some of the leftover cake, and returning and hiding with him under the tree canopy until dark, but Claire had worked so hard – she couldn't abandon her on her last night. The sound of the band, Summer assumed Swordfish's support act, was filling the air. Their music was loud and vibrant, and as she stared up into the blue sky, she wasn't sure she could imagine a more perfect end to the festival.

The river, sparkling and resplendent with narrowboats, was below them, the garden of the Black Swan was full of people drinking and lazing in the sunshine, and she could hear the shouts, the crowd singing along in front of the stage. For the last night Dennis and Jenny had agreed to let Ralph set up a food stand outside, to help cope with demand, and so while the sandwich boat was closed, the smells of grilling meat drifted up into the air. Summer looked down into the water and thought of Elizabeth, whose ghost was supposed to haunt the bridge, and how she would have found happiness if she hadn't listened to the rumours that her father had killed Jack, her lover. She leaned into Mason, and he kissed her forehead.

'OK?' he asked.

'Better than OK,' Summer said. 'I meant to ask, did you find the cranes?'

'I did – three pairs of them. The owners of the reserve are ecstatic and I've got lots of work ahead of me, documenting their arrival. How did you hear about it?' He gave her a curious look.

'Norman,' Summer said, laughing. 'He overheard you knocking on my door that night. The next day I took him some cake and he said you were off chasing cranes, but you'd be back. He was trying to reassure me. He's really lovely when he's prepared to talk to you.'

'How did Norman know about the cranes?'

'His iPad. I guess he looked at the reserve website.'

'Wonders will never cease,' Mason said. 'Should we take Archie and Latte back? I'm not sure two errant dogs would go down well in that crowd and I don't want to risk them getting trampled.'

'Sure, but I want to remind you that only one of our dogs is badly behaved.'

'Oh, give it time,' Mason said. 'I'm sure Latte will come round to Archie's way of thinking.'

'Well, I'd put money on Archie mellowing, now that we're—' She stopped, finding Mason's eyes with her own, unsure what to say.

'Together?' Mason asked. 'Is that what you were going to say?'

Summer nodded, feeling the unhelpful flap of butterflies in her stomach.

'Why didn't you say it?'

'I wasn't sure if I should.'

'Be sure, Summer,' he said, kissing her. 'I am.'

They left Latte and Archie on board Summer's boat, with the windows open and bowls of dog food and water, and then made their way up the side of the Black Swan and into the crowd, just as the support act finished. Holding tightly onto Mason's hand, Summer wove through the throngs of people, looking for Claire or Ryder or Jas, and eventually found Ralph's food stand at the back of the area, a queue snaking into the trees.

'Summer!' Claire called, 'there you are! We thought you'd got lost.'

Summer went to meet her friend, pulling Mason with her.

Claire and Mason eyed each other for a moment, and then Mason held his hand out. 'Oh come here,' Claire said, pulling Mason towards her and giving him a tight squeeze.

'Claire, hi,' Mason said, struggling for breath.

'Good to see you've morphed into a proper liveaboard,' she said, after she'd let him go.

'What do you mean? I've been on my boat for years.'

'I mean this,' Claire said, pulling his T-shirt. 'You've lost that neatness you had back then. You're looking properly scruffy.'

Mason looked affronted. 'I'm not scruffy.'

'When was the last time you had a haircut?'

Mason opened his mouth, and then turned to Summer in exasperation.

Summer laughed. 'I like him just like this, all tousled and dishevelled.' She pulled at one of his curls, and it sprang back into place.

'Oh yeah?' Claire raised an eyebrow. 'Well, I'm very happy for you. And glad you made it back in time for the grand finale.'

'This is pretty amazing,' Mason admitted, glancing around him. 'I can barely believe we're still in Willowbeck.'

Jas appeared with Ryder, both carrying trays of beer in plastic pint glasses. They handed them out and Summer introduced Mason to everyone. She wasn't quite ready to say *please meet my boyfriend,* but she couldn't stop looking at him, so thought it was probably obvious anyway. She chatted to Jas, who told her how much traffic the blog had been receiving, and how Chester was becoming the star of the festival, everyone wanting to have their photo taken with the sedate Irish wolfhound.

Summer listened to him as she watched Claire and Mason talking, their heads close together, trying to hear each other against the sound of the crowd, anticipating the appearance of Swordfish. She saw Claire gasp and press her hands to her mouth, and then give Mason another of her bear hugs, and thought that he must be telling her about Lisa, perhaps trying to explain why things had fallen apart with Tania the way they had.

She wasn't sure if it would get any easier for Mason, but she could at least be confident that she could be there for him now, whenever he wanted her to be, whether he wanted to talk about it or not. She turned away, leaving them to their conversation, and saw Valerie striding towards her, beautiful in a long, scarlet dress. Doug was with her, and both of them were smiling.

'Good lord, Summer, I never knew this many people could fit in Willowbeck. I've had nonstop readings all weekend, and I've grown my regular client list by about a third. I'm going to have to train Harvey up to be my protégé at this rate.' She embraced Summer in a Frankincense-infused hug, and Summer hugged her back. 'Doug was saying that this area's a treasure-trove for antiques. He's arranged visits over the next few weeks to see several pieces in situ.'

'Not to mention that I've sold a lot of my stock,' Doug added. 'The boat's looking pretty barren, so hopefully these visits will be successful. I'm not sure anyone's had a bad time at this festival. Claire's done us all proud.'

'You all had a hand in it,' Summer said, 'but I think there's one person who may not have relished it as much as everyone else.' She pointed towards the river. 'Poor old Norman.'

'Wha'about me?'

Summer gawped as Norman appeared alongside Doug, his threadbare green jumper in place, but his beard significantly neater than the last time she'd seen him. His cheeks were pink, as if he'd spent the whole festival sitting in the sun.

'N-norman,' she said. 'Wow, I didn't—'

'Think I liked music?' He shook his head. 'Big fan o' Swordfish, I am,' he said. 'Got their album on me iPad.'

Summer laughed incredulously, and hugged him. 'It's lovely to see you.'

'I' been enjoyin' it all. On me boat. You been stuck in that café the whole time.'

'That's true,' Summer said, still unable to believe it. 'Come and get a drink.'

She tried to introduce Norman to Claire, Jas and Ryder, but they'd already met, and Summer was left shaking her head, wondering how she'd managed to misjudge her neighbour so much. Mason came and put his arms around her waist and Valerie gave an unmodified squeal of delight.

415

'Mason, you're back and you're – you're—'

'Head over heels about Summer?' he asked. 'Guilty as charged. And I did see the cranes,' he said, turning to Norman. 'They're beautiful – very impressive, great to photograph. You should come with me next time.'

'I'd like that,' Norman said, and then to Summer, 'Told you he was off seeing t' cranes, tha' it'd all come good.'

'You were right,' Summer said. 'Thank you, Norman.'

'Keep bringin' t' cake and bacon butties, we'll be fine.' He nodded conspiratorially at her, and Summer laughed and pressed her head into Mason's shoulder.

'Ooh look,' Claire said, 'here they come.'

The laughter and chatting fell to a hush as the lights around them dimmed, so only the spotlight and Ryder's fairy lights lit up the space, and then three young men and a woman, all in their twenties and dressed in carefully deconstructed jeans and T-shirts, the woman with a shock of bright pink hair, appeared on the stage. The crowd erupted, even Norman raising his hands in the air as the guitars played their first chord and they launched into their best-known song. Summer had heard of them, though she didn't know their music very well, but she was soon caught up in their upbeat songs, jumping along with Mason at her side, stealing kisses and embracing between each track.

Summer couldn't remember when she'd felt happier, more alive or more confident. She stole a glance at Mason, who was intent on the stage, and saw the whites of his eyes in the low lighting, the shape of his jaw, his neck and the suggestion of dark hair appearing at the neckline of his T-shirt. She gave an involuntary shudder, reached up and kissed his cheek. Mason turned to her and wrapped his arms around her, pulling her against him. They couldn't speak while the music was so loud, and so instead they kissed, as the stars began to emerge, glimmering through the trees above them, and the air cooled to a delicious, whispering breeze. As people danced and sang around them, Mason and Summer were locked into their kiss, a perfect moment that held only the two of them in its grasp. Summer thought that she'd be content to stay there forever.

When the band played their last track, and the crowd cheered and whooped and clapped with exhausted, sweaty limbs, it was close to eleven o'clock. Swordfish bowed and thanked everyone for coming, and Summer turned to Claire.

'Wow,' she said. 'That was brilliant.'

'I know,' Claire said, her eyes bright. 'They're a sure thing, Swordfish, and they didn't disappoint tonight.'

'I can't believe it's over. I mean, it might be nice to have a couple of slower days in the café, but it's been so much fun. How will Willowbeck cope with going back to being quiet and picturesque?'

'You want it to be like this all the time? I think everyone needs a break. But it's certainly proved itself as a good venue.'

'So you'll be coming back?'

'Try and keep me away,' Claire said. 'But I guess you're staying for good.' She nodded her head in Mason's direction. He had his arms folded, his hair pushed back from his forehead, and was chatting to Valerie. Summer's heart gave a little jolt.

'Yes,' she said. 'Willowbeck is my home. It doesn't mean I won't ever want to go cruising again, but maybe we'll come together next time.'

'I'm so happy for you, Summer,' Claire said. 'Mason told me what had led him to this lifestyle in the first place, and

– God, I had no idea. He wants to get in touch with Tania, to explain that he wasn't ready, that he was grieving and handled things badly. I've not seen her for a while, but I'll put the feelers out, see if she's prepared to listen. She should be, and it's in the past now. I'm prepared to say I was wrong.'

'That's pretty astounding,' Summer said, grinning. 'But you weren't wrong, not really. You just didn't have the whole story, and I should have been confident enough to make up my own mind. But now I have, and . . .'

'And now you get to tug those curls as often as you want, you lucky thing.'

They laughed and settled onto the grass as the crowd drifted away, back to cars and boats and houses. Ralph put some more meat on the grill, Ryder went into the Black Swan to get more drinks before last orders, and the others joined Claire and Summer.

There was a general sense of exhaustion and contentment as they chatted quietly, and then Swordfish came to say goodbye to Claire, and headed off with their manager and cases full of their instruments.

'Dismantling starts tomorrow,' Ryder said, leaning back on the grass. 'I wish we could leave it up permanently. We could tell our stories on the stage, under the lights.'

'I'm not sure what Dennis and Jenny would think of that,' Valerie said. Summer noticed that she was sitting close to Doug, and felt a swell of happiness.

Their talking and laughter continued into the night, after the temperature had dropped and the darkness above them was broken only by the map of stars, competing with the soft glow of the fairy lights.

'Time for me to turn in,' Valerie said, standing and stretching her arms up to the sky. 'How can it feel so cold suddenly? I may need to put the woodburner on before I get into bed.'

'Don't say that,' Summer said. She'd been trying to ignore the goose bumps on her arms for the last half an hour, reluctant for the night to end.

Doug, Ralph, Norman and Jas all agreed that they were knackered. They said their goodnights and made their way down the hill towards their boats, leaving Claire, Ryder, Summer and Mason.

'I was pretty sceptical about Willowbeck when Claire suggested coming here,' Ryder said, 'but as usual she's been just the right amount of confident and bossy, and look what it's resulted in.'

'The best mini music festival that Fenland has ever seen,' Claire said.

'I think you're being too modest. I think word will stretch beyond Fenland, and you're going to have to think bigger for the next one.' Mason held up his plastic cup in a toast to Claire.

They'd moved on to spirits, and Summer was slowly getting used to the burn of the whisky as it slid down her throat. She felt happily hazy, and knew that the days ahead would not only be full of sunshine and her café and the possibility of Harry becoming a more permanent fixture, but that they would also be full of Mason, of getting to know him and lazy kisses, of Archie and Latte and long, languid evenings close to the water. She closed her eyes in contentment.

'I think it might be bedtime,' Claire said.

Summer opened her eyes. 'No, I'm fine, I was just thinking.'

'And we can all guess what you were thinking about!' Claire raised her eyebrows.

Summer blushed and looked at Mason. He pushed a strand of hair back from her face. 'It is late,' he said.

'Ooh, whose boat?' Claire asked. 'How will you decide? Kidding, kidding.' She held up her hands in submission as Summer pretended to be annoyed.

Summer collected their glasses and put them in the bin outside the pub. There was a light on inside and she wondered if Jenny and Dennis were still awake, clearing up after what must have been one of the pub's busiest-ever days.

The four of them made their way down to the boats, then Claire and Ryder said goodnight and strolled along the towpath towards the visitor moorings. Summer and Mason stopped outside *The Sandpiper* and he put his arms around her. They were in darkness save for the glow of the towpath lights and Summer could smell smoke lingering in the air, left over from Ralph's barbecue. It was much cooler, the breeze caressing her face, and she felt giddy with exhaustion and happiness.

'This has been a good day,' Mason said. 'One of the best. Except I can't feel sad that it's over, because now I know there are so many more good days to come.'

'Not all of them will have Swordfish in, though.'

'But they will all – or most of them, at least – have you in.'

'Ain't that the truth,' Summer murmured, reaching up to kiss him.

Mason put his hands in her hair and Summer felt her whole body respond to his touch.

'You could come to mine,' she said, breaking away, 'though it might be a struggle to convince Latte that she won't be allowed to sleep on the bed tonight.'

Mason smiled down at her. 'I think that—' He stopped, his breath catching in his throat, and then looked up, past her. She felt him tense.

420

'What is it?' she whispered. 'Mason?'

'Can you smell that?' His voice was sharp. 'Burning?'

Summer shook her head. 'It's just the barbecue,' she said, but her words trailed away, because she realized that the smell had got stronger, not weaker, and now she could hear the unmistakable crackle of flames. It reminded her of the nights with Claire and Ryder, telling stories in the woods around an open fire.

Mason moved past her and down the towpath, in the direction of the bridge. After a few steps he broke into a run, and Summer noticed, under the glow of the towpath light, the smoke. It was coming from *Moonshine*, Valerie's boat.

Summer was gripped by fear, but Mason was running towards the boat. 'Call nine-nine-nine!' he shouted. 'Fire brigade and ambulance!'

'*Mason*,' Summer called, 'don't . . .' But she didn't know what to say. Valerie was on board that boat, and while she didn't want Mason to face any danger, she needed Valerie to be safe.

Somehow she made her feet work. She followed Mason along the towpath, pulling her phone out of her pocket at the same time and calling the emergency services. The smell and the thickness of the smoke got stronger as she approached, but she couldn't see any flames.

'Valerie!' Mason was shouting and banging on the door of the stern deck. 'Valerie!'

There was no response and Mason wiped a hand over his face then took a deep breath and barged his shoulder into the door, once, twice, three times. Summer was telling the dispatcher where to send the fire brigade. She stepped closer to *Moonshine*, but Mason held his hand up.

'Don't,' he said. 'Stay there, Summer.' He was breathless,

his voice ragged, but he put his shoulder into the door again, and this time it sprang back, coming off one of its hinges. Black smoke poured out into the air, and Mason started coughing.

'You can't—' Summer began, but Mason put his arm up over his face as the acrid black smoke billowed around him and disappeared inside the boat.

'Mason!' Summer called. 'Valerie!' She stood on the towpath, wondering what to do, feeling numb and helpless and panicked. The smoke continued to pour out of the door and now she could see the orange of flames licking at the window at the bow end of the boat. A silver tabby appeared, bounding out of the open doors, its paws black with soot. Summer scooped it into her arms.

'Harvey,' she said, noting the cat's thinner face. 'Oh God, Harvey.' She hugged him to her, and then gasped as Mason appeared, pulling Valerie out. Her nightdress was smudged with black and they were both coughing. Summer put Harvey down and ran forward, taking Valerie's other arm and helping to carry her onto the grass. She was half-awake, dazed, everything sooty and smelling of smoke.

'Valerie,' Summer said, as they lowered her onto the grass. 'Are you OK? Valerie?'

She murmured something that Summer couldn't make out, and Mason crouched next to her.

He tried to speak, but the words wouldn't come through the coughing. Summer reached out to him, squeezing his arm, and realized that he was shaking.

'They're on their way,' she said, 'the fire brigade and the ambulance. Are you all right, Mason?'

He nodded, still coughing, and wiped his streaming eyes.

Summer felt a tug on her dress, and looked down at Valerie.

422

'M-Mike,' she managed, through wheezy, laboured breaths.

Summer went cold. 'Valerie, was he—'

'Mike,' she said again, and then closed her eyes.

'Who's Mike?' Mason managed.

'Her other cat,' Summer said, 'but Mason, you can't—'

He pushed himself to standing and ran back towards *Moonshine*, and Summer scrambled up, skidding on the grass, racing after him and calling his name. She looked back to see Dennis and Jenny rushing out of the pub door, dressing gowns on, and thought she could hear the sound of sirens in the distance.

'*Mason!*' she called. 'You can't! Please, Mason!' but he was gone, back inside the boat, the black smoke pouring into the sky in huge, dark plumes, the orange lick of flames eating its way down the boat. Summer stepped onto the deck and put her hand over her face. Even here, the smoke was acrid. Her heart was hammering in her chest, the tears streaming down her face a mixture of smoke and panic. '*Mason!*' she called again. 'Please, Mason!'

'He's not gone back on there, has he?' Dennis was at her side.

'He's gone back for Mike,' she managed, 'one of Valerie's cats.' She took a step towards the door and Dennis pulled her back onto the towpath and away from the burning boat. At first Summer struggled to escape his grasp, but Dennis held on tightly, saying words that Summer couldn't take in. He led her over to a bench and sat her down, and Summer stared at *Moonshine* through her streaming eyes, thinking as every second passed that it was too late, he'd been on there too long. She kept repeating his name, over and over again, until the sirens got louder and blared out their approach, and people began to emerge from other boats, Claire and Ryder and Norman.

423

Summer stared at *Moonshine,* willing Mason to appear, not daring to think about the other possibility.

And then, behind the noise of the sirens, and the confident words of the paramedics as they approached Valerie, and Claire shouting her name and asking her what had happened, she heard coughing. She stood, shrugging off Dennis's hand, and rushed towards *Moonshine,* but was overtaken by four firemen who approached the boat ahead of her. She kept her eyes trained on the stern doors and billowing smoke, trying not to look at the flames curling along Valerie's boat, creeping closer and closer to where she'd seen Mason go in, and then there was a glimmer of movement at the stern and suddenly Mason was there, staggering, coughing, his face smudged and sweating – and he had Mike in his arms.

Summer raced forwards, but this time one of the firemen held her back while the others took hold of Mason and lifted Mike gently out of his arms. They led him to the grass and lowered him carefully down, and a paramedic crouched next to him.

Summer tried to pull herself out of the fireman's grasp. She could feel Claire squeezing her arm, but she couldn't look away from Mason.

'Is he OK?' she asked nobody in particular. 'Please, can I go and see him?'

Mason was coughing relentlessly, his whole body shaking, and the paramedic was kneeling beside him, calmly taking an oxygen mask out of her pack and placing it over his mouth and nose.

'Give them a moment,' the fireman said. 'He's awake, that's the main thing.'

Summer thought of Lisa, who had been semi-conscious

when Mason had got her out of the house, and felt another swell of panic, so overwhelming that she felt dizzy.

Jenny was crouched next to Valerie, stroking her hair while the paramedic made his checks. Summer's friend was shaking her head slowly, her mouth also obscured by a mask, her red hair fanned out around her on the grass. Jas was sitting on one of the picnic benches, holding both silver tabbies. Mike was purring and snuggling into Jas's arms, alert despite his ordeal and the smoke he must have inhaled.

The fireman let go of Summer's arm and patted her on the shoulder, and Summer raced forwards, falling onto the grass next to Mason. She couldn't restrain the sobs and looked at the paramedic, unsure what she was asking, but needing reassurance.

'He won't be able to speak for a while,' she was told in a soothing voice. 'He seems unscathed, but we'll need to take him to the hospital to check him over, and monitor his lung function for a while to see if the smoke has done any lasting damage.'

Summer swallowed. 'He's going to be OK?'

'Let's get him to hospital,' the paramedic said cautiously, 'and let the doctor look at him first.' But she gave Summer a reassuring smile.

Summer looked at Mason, who was sitting up but only just, his body slumped forwards, his chest heaving. She reached out, and gently pushed his hair back from his brow. Mason raised his head. Despite the ash and the sweat on his face, the tears streaming down his cheeks and the oxygen mask, his dark eyes held on to hers, and Summer felt a flood of relief.

She put her arm around him and he leant against her, his hand finding hers. He wrapped his fingers around hers and squeezed, and though there was chaos around them, the paramedics, and the firemen and -women calling to each other as they began to douse Valerie's boat with water, Summer could only focus on Mason, on the fact that he was still here, that she hadn't lost him, and that he had done something so brave that she could barely take it in.

Summer held on to Mason and wondered if she would ever be able to let go.

Chapter 24

Summer found herself in the back of the Greenways' Land Rover, her hand being squeezed by Jenny. The paramedic had said that Mason would need to be monitored for several hours, have his blood gases checked, and have a thorough examination to make sure he'd suffered no burns or other injuries. Valerie, too, would need to stay in hospital until they were confident she was on the road to recovery. Jenny squeezed her hand again, her grip strong, and Summer forced herself to look at the woman and try to smile.

'They'll both be fine,' Jenny said, her voice confident. 'Valerie was conscious, there were no signs of burns that I could see, and the ambulance got here quickly.'

'That man of yours is a hero,' Dennis called from the driver's seat. 'An absolute, bloody hero. Especially considering what he went through before.'

'I know,' Summer said, but she wasn't sure she'd said it loudly enough for anyone else to hear. She didn't know why Jenny had sat in the back with her, instead of in the passenger seat alongside Dennis, but she thought it might be for comfort. Summer tried to feel comforted – Mason was all right, she had hugged him and he had responded – but her head was hammering. She couldn't help thinking about the last time, driving to the hospital in her little Polo after Valerie had called her, her angry words at Mum flinging around in her head like a caged bird trying to escape, and then stepping into the corridor and seeing Valerie standing there, conveying, with wide, disbelieving eyes, the worst possible outcome.

Panic swelled in her chest at the thought that this time would be the same. She'd get there to discover something horrendous had happened in the ambulance, that Valerie's heart had given out, or that Mason had suddenly stopped breathing. She wished that there had been two ambulances so she could have gone with one of them, kept them in her sight the whole time, held on to them. She was worried what would happen in her absence.

'Jas is calling the emergency vet,' Jenny said. 'He'll get Mike checked out, but he seemed quite lively, didn't he?'

Summer nodded. 'Animals have good instincts,' she said. 'Maybe he was hiding somewhere the smoke couldn't get to him. We can ask Mason when he's recovered. And Jas is looking after Latte and Archie and Harvey.' Summer longed to hold on to her soft, wriggling dog, so alive and innocent and loyal. She wished she could see Archie too – they had both been on Summer's boat for most of the evening, and Summer hadn't had a chance to go to them and comfort them after the fire had broken out. She hoped Jas was doing that for her.

Dennis swung the Land Rover into the hospital's car park, and they got out. Summer shivered in the night air, and Jenny got a coat from the boot of the car and put it over her shoulders. Summer walked with them to the Accident and Emergency doors, blinking at the harsh white lights, the solid, square lines of the reception area and the long corridors branching off it. It was so different to Willowbeck, with its overhanging trees and kingfishers and birdsong, where the pub was the biggest building and nature was still fully in charge.

Dennis found the reception desk and Summer stood alongside him, wondering how someone could seem so perky and awake in the depths of the night. She knew that she had to take control of herself, that she couldn't allow the panic to overwhelm her.

'We're here to see Valerie Brogan and Mason Causey,' she said, before Dennis had a chance to speak. 'They were being brought in by ambulance after a fire at Willowbeck.'

'OK,' the woman said, turning to her computer. Her nametag read *Samira,* and she had large, smiling eyes. 'Ah yes,' she said, scanning the screen, 'they've just arrived. The doctor will look at them shortly, so if you want to take a seat . . .?' She indicated the waiting room, which was about half-full, with morose, stunned or ill-looking people sitting on the red-cushioned chairs.

Summer sat with her back to the wall, and Jenny and Dennis sat opposite her, the silence lasting for only a few moments before Dennis asked if they wanted a drink. Summer said she'd love a cup of tea, and watched him disappear down one of the long corridors.

Dennis and Jenny had both managed to fling on clothes instead of their dressing gowns before driving Summer to the hospital, and Jenny was wearing jeans and a hoody, her hair loose and her face make-up free. Summer cleared her throat.

'Thank you,' she said, 'for bringing me here. I'm not sure I would have been up to driving myself.'

'Of course not,' Jenny said, her eyes flitting between Summer and the hard linoleum. 'Very happy to. It's a terrible thing.'

'Yes,' Summer said, 'but at least they're both going to be fine.' She tried not to let it sound like a question.

'They are, thanks to Mason. Dennis told me what had happened to him, to his wife, and I can't imagine how he could have rushed onto that boat so readily, to face another fire, to get Valerie out and then go back for Mike.'

'Perhaps that's why he did,' Summer said quietly. 'He tried to save Lisa and, though he did everything he could, she still died. Maybe he felt he needed to, that he wasn't going to let it happen again. Surely it's what everyone would *want* to do, but I don't know if I'd be brave enough to face the flames, that thick black smoke.' Summer shuddered and rubbed her eyes. Her fingers came away black with soot. 'In fact, I know I wasn't. I didn't follow Mason on board.'

'I don't think I could have done it either,' Jenny said. 'But you phoned the fire brigade. And having both of you on that boat as well as Valerie, in such a small space, might have created too much confusion. You did what you could, Summer, but how awful for such a wonderful few days to end like this.'

'You've enjoyed the festival?' Summer asked, trying to lighten the mood.

'We've never been busier,' Jenny said, giving her a faint smile. 'I love Willowbeck and how sleepy it can be, but to have so many people, so much life here for a while – I loved it.'

'I think Claire will want to make it a regular thing, if everyone's willing to do it again.'

'And you coped – in your café?' Jenny's voice was tentative, but Summer met her gaze head on.

'I did, I had help from friends.' She thought of the moment she had turned to see Mason standing at the counter, back to rescue her in her hour of need like a knight in shining armour. Well, she thought, he'd done enough rescuing for the time being, and once they got out of there, she was going to put all her effort into looking after him.

'I'm glad,' Jenny said, 'to see your café doing so well.' She couldn't quite meet Summer's eye, and Summer realized how hard it must be for her to say it.

'Thank you,' Summer said. 'And the chips and gravy you do at the pub are the best I've ever had. I love Willowbeck, and I want to stay.'

'I know,' Jenny nodded, 'and I'm sorry if I made that . . . hard, at the beginning.'

'You did,' Summer said. 'It was hard enough anyway, after . . . And I just wanted a fresh start, to see if I could do it. I know my mum did an awful thing,' she continued, 'and I'm sorry for that, for what she did to you and to Dennis. But she was still my mum, and I will never stop loving her.'

'You shouldn't,' Jenny said. 'And my attacks on you were petty. God,' she shook her head, and indicated the waiting room, 'there are more important things, really, aren't there?'

'There are.' Summer nodded. 'And in order to help you deal with it all, you need lots and lots of cake. Red velvet cake and cupcakes, and cream cakes and macarons. I think we can work alongside each other. We don't have to be competition.'

Jenny sighed and looked at the floor, her dark hair falling towards it like the willow trees over the river. When she looked up, she was smiling. 'Your macarons are delicious.'

Summer's mouth fell open. 'H-how . . .?'

'I got one of our waitresses to go and buy a bag from you when the festival was on. I thought you'd be too busy to recognize her.'

'I was! I mean, I didn't. You liked them?'

'I loved them,' Jenny admitted.

Summer felt a swell of pride. 'I made those,' she said. 'Me. Not Harry.'

'You're a great baker.' Jenny sat up and glanced sideways. Summer followed her gaze and saw Dennis walking back towards them, holding three takeaway cups between his fingers, his movements slow and careful.

Summer turned back to Jenny and held her hand out. 'Truce?' she asked.

Jenny paused for a moment, then stood and sat in the seat next to Summer's and, ignoring Summer's hand, gave her a soft, soap-scented hug instead. 'Truce,' she said quietly.

Summer, smiling into Jenny's shoulder, felt fresh tears threaten and gave a large sniff.

'Here you go,' Dennis said, grinning as he waited for the hug to end, and then handing out the drinks. 'I'm not sure this can actually be called tea, especially to those who work in the catering industry, but I think we should give them the benefit of the doubt.'

Jenny took the lid off hers and made a pained face, as if she'd been served a cup of river water. She sniffed it and took a tentative sip. 'No, Dennis,' she said, giving him a rueful smile, 'we really shouldn't give them the benefit of the doubt. This is nothing short of hideous.'

The three of them kept up a stream of chatter while they waited. Summer told Dennis and Jenny about her time in

432

Foxburn and then Tivesham, meeting Claire and her friends, and the plans she had for the café. Jenny told Summer about her own cakes, and invited her to come and have a look at her beautifully kitted-out kitchen.

'It's a lovely place to work,' she said, 'but sometimes nothing beats a hand whisk, or just using your fingers. But don't tell Dennis I said that.'

'I like the food processor,' Dennis said, indignant. 'I use it to make soups.'

'There you go, then,' Jenny said, 'we're all happy.'

They both refused to give Summer their gravy recipe, saying it was a family secret, and Summer was grateful that they were taking her mind off the fact that there was still no news from the doctor.

Eventually, when Dennis, ever hopeful, had bought them all a coffee and then a hot chocolate, Jenny accepting that the hot chocolate could, at a push, be considered passable, a pair of double doors further up the corridor thwacked open, and a tall, fair-haired doctor emerged, with Mason at his side.

Summer jumped up from her chair and raced towards them, but the doctor held his hand out in front of him.

'Steady,' he said.

Mason met Summer's gaze and gave her a weary smile. He was still covered in soot, still in his ruined blue T-shirt and grey cargo shorts, and he looked exhausted, but he was here, standing in front of her, and Summer knew the rest could be fixed – it was her turn to look after him. She took a deep breath, calming her nerves, pushing away the swell of emotion.

'How are you?' she asked. 'Are you OK?'

Mason opened his mouth to speak, and a cough came out instead. He turned away and put his hand over his mouth.

'He's all right,' the doctor said, 'but the cough will last for a few weeks and he'll need a lot of rest. There's no lasting damage though, so he's very lucky.'

Summer nodded, not sure she trusted herself to speak, and reached her hand out to Mason. He took it and treated her to a smile that, while small, reached his eyes and made Summer's heart skip. 'Thank you,' she said to the doctor. 'And what about my friend, Valerie?'

'She's doing well. We're going to keep her in for the day, do a few more tests and continue to give her oxygen. All being well, she should be ready to go home tomorrow.'

Summer dropped her head and sighed.

'Brilliant news,' Dennis said, putting his hand on her shoulder. Summer hadn't realized Dennis and Jenny were there, she had been so focused on Mason.

'Can I hug him?' Summer asked the doctor.

'Yes please.' Mason's voice was raspy, but just hearing him was enough. She flung her arms around him, almost knocking him backwards, and felt his arms go around her. He smelled strongly of smoke, but the feel of him, being able to be close to him when only a few hours earlier she thought she might lose him, was overwhelming. She pressed her head into his shoulder, and only let go when Dennis gently pulled her arm and said they should be going home.

They walked out into bright sunshine, the day having arrived while they'd been in the timeless, white waiting room, and Summer climbed in the back of the Land Rover next to Mason. Within moments his head was back on the headrest and he was dozing, his breaths wheezy. Summer watched him sleep all the way back to Willowbeck.

The small riverside village was a hive of activity when they got back, with lots of people on the towpath and at the picnic tables, despite neither the café nor the pub being open. Claire spotted them first and hurried towards them, gently embracing Mason.

'Mason! God, are you OK?'

'I'll be fine,' he managed, smiling and rubbing his eyes.

'What's going on?' Summer asked.

Claire glanced behind her and sighed. 'Mick's here, and there's an investigation team too. *Moonshine* isn't salvageable, Mick says. He's got his towboat, and he's going to take her back to the yard once they're done trying to find out what happened.'

They walked closer to the river, and Summer felt Mason tense beside her as they saw *Moonshine*, the bow of the boat entirely blackened, the stern retaining some of the purple paintwork, though it was blotchy and burnt-through in places.

'Sorry about *The Canal Boat Café*, too,' Claire said.

Summer saw that the bow of her boat had been affected by fire damage, though from where she stood it looked structurally intact.

'What will Valerie do?' Summer asked, the superficial damage to her boat low down on her list of concerns.

'The insurance should get her a brand-new boat,' Dennis said, 'providing the investigation's straightforward; in the meantime, she can stay at the pub. We don't want her uprooted from Willowbeck while she's waiting. Do you know what happened?'

Summer shook her head. 'I remember her saying she was going to light her woodburner, so maybe that's where it started. That's just a guess, though. How are the cats?'

'They're OK.' Claire nodded. 'Jas had the emergency vet check them over and Mike's surprisingly well, considering how long he was on there. Though, of course, he wouldn't even be here if it weren't for you.' Claire looked at Mason and everyone fell quiet, reminded again of what Mason had risked to save Valerie and then her pet.

He waved her away. 'I just—' He coughed harshly and shook his head. 'Where's Archie?'

'Oh, Jas's boat is hosting the Willowbeck home for stray cats and dogs at the moment. Let me go and get him.'

Jas emerged with Archie and Latte, and Summer was almost reduced to tears again when the Border terrier flung himself at Mason, barking madly. Mason crouched on the grass and hugged his dog, while Summer picked up Latte and squeezed her close.

'I'm sorry I left you,' she said into the dog's silky ears. 'I didn't mean to. Are you OK?' Latte licked her cheek and Summer laughed. 'Good,' she said. 'And you'll be able to spend much more time with Archie from now on, though if you start misbehaving then we'll have to have a serious talk. The four of us,' she added, glancing down at Mason and Archie, and feeling a swell of something that felt dangerously like love.

Even though she was exhausted, Summer took Latte and Archie for a long walk over the fields, while Mason went to get some rest on board *The Sandpiper*. He hadn't said much, and Summer thought that, even if he hadn't been coughing relentlessly, he would still have been quiet. She couldn't imagine the strength it must have taken for him to face the fire on Valerie's boat after going through one at his own home, and losing his wife to it. It must have brought so much back to him, and Summer thought that over the coming months he would struggle with his memories, and with the shock of what had happened. But she was prepared for that, and she was ready to do anything for him.

The sun baked down on them, and Summer, carrying a bottle of water and a metal dog bowl with her, and stopping to hydrate Archie and Latte as they went, stayed under the shade of the trees where possible. It was cool and quiet in the woods, and Summer slowed her steps, enjoying the peacefulness. The dogs were energetic in spite of the heat, having been cooped up on board the boats for too many hours, and as they reached a clear, grassy glade, Summer let them off the leads and lay on the plush, springy grass, staring at the endless blue above her.

Six months ago, even the name Willowbeck had sent a shudder of dread through her, and now she couldn't imagine being anywhere else. She had begun to make peace with Jenny, she had taken steps towards accepting her mum's death, and facing her guilt. She had found a man she believed she could be truly, gleefully happy with, and she was the proud owner of a vibrant, beautiful café. OK, so at the moment the paintwork was less than perfect, but she knew exactly what she could do to change that, and she was relishing the thought of it. Valerie would return soon, first at the pub and then in a new boat, back in her place as Summer's neighbour. It hadn't always been easy, and Summer had made many mistakes along the way, but, she realized, it had all been worth it.

She strolled slowly back across the fields, the dogs on leads at her feet, and stopped on Elizabeth Proudfoot's bridge. Willowbeck shimmered in the afternoon sunshine. Valerie's boat was gone, and the bow of hers was blackened, but *The Sandpiper* and *Celeste* were in their rightful places, people were beginning to fill up the picnic tables in front of the pub, oblivious to the drama that had unfolded the previous night, and the visitor moorings were still full of roving traders.

Summer knew they would be moving on soon, but she was confident that, following on from the success of Claire's festival, they would be back. She heard a high, sharp keening behind her, and turned just in time to see a kingfisher, flying low and fast over the water in search of a new fishing spot. Suddenly, the urge to see Mason was overwhelming, and she picked up her pace.

She tapped gently on the door of *The Sandpiper* and then pushed it open, stepping inside. Archie and Latte, released from their leads, skittered forward, back on familiar ground.

'Ssshh,' Summer hissed as Archie yelped, but the door to Mason's berth opened and he emerged, wearing only a pair of scruffy jeans. Summer stared at him, knowing she was smiling idiotically, but unable to help it. His hair was haywire – he'd probably slept on it wet after showering to remove the grime and soot – and he was blinking tiredness out of his eyes, but he looked a lot better than he had a couple of hours ago, less pale and less smudged.

'How are you feeling?' she asked.

'Better,' he said, and then tried to clear his throat. 'Not brilliant, but better.'

He sat on the sofa and Summer joined him, handing him a glass of water. He put his arm around her and pulled her close, into his bare chest. Summer breathed in his citrusy, vanilla scent, and his warmth, and the faintest trace of smoke that she knew would take a while to leave.

'I missed you,' she said.

'You were only gone a couple of hours.'

She could tell it was an effort for him to speak, and she rubbed his chest, wondering if it was sore. 'I've realized that

I will always miss you when I'm not with you. You're very missable.'

'Thank you,' he said, 'so are you. Except I was asleep, so actually I didn't—' He broke off and coughed, and Summer winced. Archie put his paw up on Mason's knee and looked at him quizzically.

'He knows you're not well.' Summer stroked Archie's ears.

'I'm fine,' Mason said.

'I nearly lost you.' She sat up and looked him in the eye.

Mason's face was passive, but she could see his Adam's apple bobbing. 'No, you didn't. I would never have risked . . . that.'

'Fires are unpredictable,' Summer said softly. She didn't want to argue, or tell him off, she just wanted him to know how much he mattered. 'No more rescuing, for the time being. I'll tell everyone to be extra specially careful so you don't need to.'

'I'd appreciate it,' Mason said.

'Or maybe, if we just stay here for the next few days, then you won't be tempted even if someone *does* need rescuing, because you won't know about it.' She ran her hand through his curls, and kissed him softly on the lips.

'Now that,' Mason said, his voice rasping, 'sounds like an excellent idea.'

'I'm full of good ideas.' Summer kissed him again.

'Why do you think I was attracted to you in the first place?'

'My incredible bacon sandwiches,' Summer said.

Mason leaned back and looked at her, his dark eyes fixing on to hers and his face suddenly transformed by one of the grins that made Summer glad she was sitting down. 'Fair point,' he said, 'but you're pretty special too.'

* * *

439

When Summer made it back to her boat later that day, leaving Mason to sleep, she found another wooden sculpture on her bow deck. It was clean, while the wooden slats and the paintwork surrounding it were blackened and sticky with soot. She picked it up, frowning. It was a flag, crafted with a slight ripple in it, as if it was blowing in a breeze. There were stripes and stars, and even though it didn't have the required fifty, Summer could tell it was the American flag. This one, she decided, was the most baffling of all.

She went inside the café, which felt hollow and empty after the rammed, bustling days of the festival. She walked up to the counter and laid her flag alongside the others, looking at them each in turn. She had no connections to America, no reason to be given a flag, and its appearance confirmed that Mason hadn't been leaving them for her, unless he'd made it while he was away on the reserve. Besides, wouldn't he have told her by now if he were responsible?

Her phone buzzed and she pulled it out of her pocket, smiling when she saw that it was a text from Mason. *Miss you already,* he'd written. She replied quickly: *Go to sleep.* Xx She looked down at her home screen, and noticed the date at the top. The fourth of July. Independence Day. Her mouth falling open, she stared at the flag, and then went back to each of the others in turn.

She'd received the heart the second day she'd returned to Willowbeck, in the middle of February. She'd made heart-shaped cookies because it had been Valentine's Day. Then there was the frog, which she'd received a couple of weeks later, on the twenty-ninth of February. Leap day.

'Oh my God,' she murmured. The daffodil – St David's Day, the rabbit for Easter, and the Jester's hat, which she'd thought was a dig at her, someone telling her she was a joke, was on April Fool's Day. She picked up the sun and turned it round in her hands, wondering if it was just because it was summer, or whether it, too, had a special meaning. She tried to remember the exact day she'd received it – it was the day after she'd argued with Mason.

She didn't hear Claire come up behind her.

'Oh God, look how many Norman originals you've got.'

'What?' Summer spun to face her. '*Norman?*'

'Those gorgeous little sculptures. He's given us all one as a leaving gift. An LP for me, a sandwich for Ralph, a little dresser for Doug. Jas has got a computer, and Ryder's is a little stage. The detail is incredible, and Doug got quite worked up about them. They're new, not antiques, but he says the quality is amazing. Better not show him your collection, or he'll swipe them.'

'*Norman* made these?'

'Hello, earth to Summer? I know you haven't had any sleep, but did you not hear what I just said?'

'But he . . . he's been leaving them for me, anonymously, on my deck. I had no idea. Look.' She went through the different models, explaining them.

'Summer solstice,' Claire said when Summer got to the sun. 'Got to be.'

'Oh, of course! But why did he leave them for me?'

'To cheer you up? To give you something to look forward to? You were pretty down when you first came back to Willowbeck, weren't you? Maybe it was just a little mystery to keep you interested. Gifts cheer everyone up, don't they?'

Summer leant on the counter, examining the rabbit. 'Norman was looking out for me. I thought he was mad at me for coming back when I'd abandoned Valerie for so long, but he wanted me to stay. He was encouraging me in his

441

own way. And these are . . . I'll have to tell Mason. We'd been trying to work the mystery out together.'

'I bet you'll be doing lots of things together from now on, won't you?'

Summer smiled down at the counter.

'Yes,' she said, 'yes, I think we will.'

Chapter 25

Summer stared at her boat. It was her boat, her café, and it was about to have its grand reopening. Mason came and stood beside her, wrapping his arm around her waist in a gesture that now seemed so natural to both of them, but still sent a happy shiver through Summer's whole body.

'You've done an incredible job,' he said, bending low to whisper into her ear. 'It's the most beautiful boat in Willowbeck.'

'More beautiful than *The Sandpiper*?' Summer asked, laughing.

'Yes,' Mason said decisively. 'Definitely.'

The landscape of Willowbeck looked slightly different to how it had done six weeks ago, with *Moonshine* moored next to *The Canal Boat Café*. *Celeste* and *The Sandpiper* were still in place, but *Moonshine* was gone, replaced by a deep purple boat with gold trim, called *Cosmic*. The investigation had ruled that the fire had started because a spark had left Valerie's woodburner and fallen on a curtain, a terrible, but innocent, accident.

Summer had, very briefly, entertained the thought that Ross had been behind it – a last, vindictive act because Summer had finally told him she didn't want him in her life. But, she'd reasoned, everything he'd done he thought he'd been doing to help her, however misguided his actions had been. She hadn't reported him to the police, unable to be the cause of any more pain or suffering, but instead had written him a long letter, telling him that they could never be friends again, and asking him to stay away from Willowbeck. It had hurt, but she knew she had to leave it behind her, those horrible few months after her mother's death, and the memory of the break-in. While Harry and Mason had, at first, been adamant that she should go to the police, once she'd explained her reasoning they had understood why she didn't want to go through with it.

Valerie, too, had been forgiving, also choosing to focus on the future, rather than the past. Out of hospital and in one of Dennis and Jenny's spare bedrooms, she had found *Cosmic* searching on websites of boats for sale, and said she had to have it – the name was perfect. It's fuchsia paintwork, however, was not.

'I can't have that, Summer! It'll clash with my hair. What should I do?'

Summer knew exactly what Valerie needed to do, and that was let her paint her boat.

Summer had spent most of July and August at the boatyard with Mick, working first on Valerie's new boat and then the repaint of her own, finishing her kingfisher painting for Mason in the few quiet moments in between. Mick was great fun to work alongside, their days were filled with laughter, and he showed her how to prime and sand and paint the boats, giving her full rein on the design and details once the base colours were in place. Summer was concerned that she was losing custom, but, with Harry's help, she'd worked on a plan and geared it towards a big relaunch at the beginning of September.

Jas had agreed to spread word on his blog, and Adam, Carole from the gift shop, and even Jenny, were handing out flyers, explaining that the café was closed for refurbishment and would have a grand, Indian Summer reopening.

While she worked, and on the days that Mason wasn't at the reserve, he brought them both sandwiches and cake, and the odd home-made espresso from his cafetiere on board *The Sandpiper*. Summer loved the work, creating beautiful designs on the boats, but she relished these moments, when Mason would come and interrupt her, sit outside with her for half an hour, Archie and Latte scrapping playfully at their feet. It seemed he missed her as much as she did him, and in the evenings, with her boat in the boatyard, Summer stayed on *The Sandpiper*, sharing Mason's bed and finding out about him slowly and deliciously, in a way that was as far from an instant download as possible.

His cough had taken several weeks to go completely, and Valerie had stayed in bed at the Black Swan for nearly a month before she felt strong enough to get up and move about properly. Mason's physical recovery had been quick, but she knew that the emotional scars would take longer to heal. He talked to Summer about it, the fear he'd felt battling against the determination that he wasn't going to let anybody else die in the way that Lisa had. Sometimes he would disappear in the evenings, taking Latte and Archie along the towpath or across the fields, always returning to Summer with a hug and a kiss, his skin warm and his hair smelling of late summer. She knew it would take time, but also that they had all the time in the world.

'I asked Mick,' Summer said as she looked at her boat, with its new, improved paint job and its new name.

'Asked him what?' Mason murmured into her ear.

'Why he calls you Lothario.'

'I didn't know that he did until you told me.'

'Well, it's because they all agree, at the boatyard, all those big burly men, that you're a lady-killer. He didn't go as far as to say that he fancies you, but his admiration was pretty clear. You set people's hearts fluttering, and I can vouch for that.'

'Well, that's a relief. It'd be a sad state of affairs if I couldn't make my girlfriend weak at the knees.'

'It's all right,' she said, patting his hand, 'you definitely do that.'

'Summeeeerrrrrr!' called a voice from behind them, and they turned to see Tommy racing along the towpath towards them, Greg and Harry hand in hand behind him.

Summer embraced her friend, and gratefully accepted the cake tin that came in between them. 'A little something for the grand opening,' she said. 'Just to sit alongside your wonderful offerings.'

Summer narrowed her eyes. 'I think wonderful is taking it a bit too far.'

'Well, I don't,' Harry said, 'and nobody else will either.'

People had begun to arrive, clustering towards the towpath, eager to see what the grand ceremony involved. Summer and Harry went on board the boat and opened up the hatch, Summer starting up the coffee machine. She looked at the display of wooden objects on the counter in front of her – cakes and narrowboats, kingfishers and herons – all for sale for what Summer thought was a modest price.

She had gone to Norman after the revelation about his

carvings, and thanked him for keeping her spirits up. He had been as gruff as ever, hardly daring to admit it, let alone accept the compliments she thrust at him. Over the weeks she had convinced him that his carvings were special, and that anyone would be delighted to own one. Selling them in her café wasn't about making any money for Norman – he almost flat out refused to accept any – but about spreading the joy they had given her, and giving her guests mementos of their visit to Willowbeck and *The Canal Boat Café*.

'All set?' Harry asked.

'All set.' Summer nodded. 'Thank you so much for coming on board with this,' she said, and Harry rolled her eyes. 'Sorry, sorry, no pun intended.'

'Your café is a million times more fun to work in than my old place,' Harry said. 'Working with my best friend, in an idyllic river setting, is a dream job. And it's helping us to get back on our feet. Greg is as grateful as I am, though I'm not sure his pride will let him admit it to you.'

'Well, neither of you can be as grateful as I am,' Summer said. 'This café is going to fly with you baking *and* working here. We are the perfect team.'

'I hope it doesn't fly. I think sail would be more appropriate.'

Summer tutted. 'Narrowboats don't sail, they cruise. You've got a lot to learn.'

'Well, as hard as this might be to believe,' Harry said, 'I'm looking forward to every minute. Do you have the bottle?'

Summer grinned and went into the kitchen, getting the bottle of champagne that Mason had bought out of the fridge. She carried it through the café and out to the towpath, where the crowd had gathered. There was Greg and Tommy, Dennis and Jenny, Adam from the butcher's and Valerie and Norman. She could see a few of her regular customers, Barry

447

and even the green-eyed businessman who she'd sung with at the festival. She was almost tempted to run over and point Mason out to him, telling him that they had both been right to believe he'd return. Mason was there with Archie and Latte, both of whom were looking up at the roof of *The Sandpiper,* where Harvey and Mike were sitting next to each other, sunning themselves in the late summer glow.

Since the fire, Mike had gained a new lease of life, and no longer stayed inside. Summer thought that was probably to do with the fact that for a few weeks they had been forced to stay in the noisy, busy pub rather than on a narrowboat, but she didn't want to burst Valerie's bubble of enthusiasm. Mason, it seemed, had not only rescued the cat, but had also shown him what he was missing.

'Right,' Summer said, standing and facing the crowd, clutching the bottle of champagne. 'Thank you so much for coming today, to the grand reopening of *The Canal Boat Café*, and the renaming ceremony of my boat. As lots of you will know, a few weeks ago Valerie's boat *Moonshine* suffered a devastating fire. Her own boat couldn't be saved, and the damage to the café was superficial, but enough to warrant a repaint. As you can see, Valerie's new boat, *Cosmic,* is even more beautiful than *Moonshine* was, and if you want to talk to her about psychic readings or astrology, then please do.' She gestured towards Valerie, who gave a quick wave.

Summer took a deep breath, and continued. 'When it came to repriming and painting *The Canal Boat Café*, I discovered that, beneath the existing paint job, this boat had another, real name. That name,' she said, glancing at everyone staring back at her, 'was *Summer Breeze*.' She heard a familiar snicker from Mason's direction, and saw Valerie bite back her laugh. 'It seemed a bit ridiculous – and a bit arrogant – to have a boat that was named after me, and it also suggested that I might be slightly flatulent. So, anyway, it had to go – but it gave me an idea about what I could call my boat, my beautiful café.

'I thought it would be straightforward, but apparently, changing the name of a boat is very unlucky, and that's the last thing I wanted. Mick, the boatbuilder . . .' she searched for him in the crowd, and he gave a quick cheer, 'taught me the steps I needed to perform a thorough and disaster-free renaming ceremony, and I started by finding, and then obliterating anywhere the name *Summer Breeze* appeared. Since I hadn't noticed it anywhere outside or inside the boat, the search had to be thorough.

'Now that's been done, and the boat has been repainted, we can get rid of the old name.' She unfolded a piece of paper, held up a metal tag with the name *Summer Breeze* written on it, and stepped onto the bow deck of the boat.

'So,' she said, feeling her cheeks redden, 'here goes. Oh mighty and great ruler of the seas and oceans, to whom all ships and we who venture upon your vast domain are required to pay homage, implore you in your graciousness to expunge for all time from your recollection, the name *Summer Breeze*, and submit this ingot bearing her name to be corrupted and forever be purged from the sea.' She glanced around her, at the barely straight faces, Tommy grinning and Adam's shoulders shaking gently.

She had wondered aloud to Valerie whether this was really a ceremony for narrowboats, that surely it must only apply to sea-going boats, but Valerie had said that all rivers were connected to the sea in some way and was, like Mick, adamant that it needed to be done. She had also wondered if her mum had known about the original name, and had simply had it painted over with *The Canal Boat Café* when she bought the boat, rather than expunging it completely, because of the connection to her daughter. Maddy had only introduced the boat to Summer once it was finished and in the water, showing it off proudly as her new home, her new life, after her divorce from Summer's dad.

Trying to push away her embarrassment, Summer threw the tag in the water, then poured half the bottle of champagne in after it. 'In grateful acknowledgement of your munificence and dispensation,' she said, watching the fizzy liquid get swallowed up by river water, 'we offer these libations to your majesty.'

'Now,' she said, turning back to the befuddled and amused faces, 'that's done, which means we can get on with the naming ceremony. Here.' She jumped down onto the towpath, her heart pounding, and stood next to Mason and the large piece of paper that was covering the boat's new name. It was still painted red and blue, but Summer had used an attractive gingham design for the trim work, and added paintings of different types of cakes, and mugs of tea and coffee along the length of the boat.

Mason reached to the floor behind him, and handed Summer another bottle of champagne. 'You need a new one for the renaming ceremony,' he said. 'You can't use the rest of the first bottle.'

'You're as superstitious as the rest of them,' Summer said, laughing and accepting it gratefully. She turned to the crowd, held up the new bottle of champagne, and read out the second part of the speech.

'Oh mighty and great ruler of the seas and oceans, to whom all ships and we who venture upon your vast domain are required to pay homage, implore you in your

450

graciousness to take unto your records and recollection, this worthy vessel . . .' She glanced at Mason, who gave her an encouraging smile, and then gripped the corner of the paper and carefully pulled it away. 'This worthy vessel, hereafter and for all time known as *Madeleine.*'

She looked at her handiwork: *Madeleine* written in a fluent, flowing script in dark blue against the faded blue background, the words *The Canal Boat Café* painted below it in red. There were cheers of appreciation and a couple of gasps from the crowd. Summer looked up and caught Jenny's gaze, and the older woman gave her a nod and a small, understanding smile. Summer's return grin was pure relief.

'In appreciation of your munificence, dispensation, and in honour of your greatness, we offer these libations to your majesty and your court.' Summer sacrificed most of the bottle of champagne to the river, and turned back to the crowd. 'To celebrate the new name of the café, we have fresh madeleine's for everyone, full of jam and cream. Please stay for a while, have a tea or a coffee, and sample some of our cakes. I've got wooden carvings made by the wonderful Norman for sale inside, and if you fancy something bigger or stronger, then the Black Swan pub is also open. If you want to discuss any bookings – we do private parties, which involve a trip along the river – then please talk to Harry or me. Thank you for coming to share this special day with us, and I hope you'll have many return visits on board *Madeleine.*'

As the crowds began to disperse, some heading inside the café where Harry was waiting, others drifting towards the Black Swan and the picnic benches, Mason pulled Summer aside. 'That,' he said, kissing her on the nose, 'was beautifully done. It's a beautiful tribute to your mum.'

'It seems like a bit of a faff,' Summer admitted. 'Not the

new name, but the ceremony. And it's a waste of a lot of perfectly good champagne.'

'I don't think the river gods would see it that way,' he said. 'Besides, I've got another bottle waiting in my fridge for when today is over – and it's just for the two of us. Those deities have had their fill.'

'Mason Causey,' Summer said, looking up at him and letting herself get lost, for a moment, in his gaze, 'you are the perfect boyfriend, you know that?'

'I know,' he said, kissing her again. 'But the longer you stand here gazing at me, the longer Harry has to run the café by herself.'

'Good point,' Summer said. 'What are you going to do?' she asked as she turned back towards the café.

'I'm going to come and order an espresso and a bacon sandwich,' he said, grinning. 'What other choice is there?'

Summer changed out of her grand reopening dress and put on jeans and a grey hoody. She ran round to *The Sandpiper* and Mason welcomed her onto his boat and into his arms, giving her a long, lingering kiss.

'You smell of cake,' he said.

'It's a special new perfume,' she said. 'I thought I'd go the extra mile for the café.'

'You always go the extra mile. Was it a successful day?'

'Yes,' Summer said, smiling. 'The best.' She sighed, delighting in the feel of weary limbs from a day on her feet, clearing and serving, chatting and laughing with her customers. 'The new cakes went down well, we had no real disasters apart from a squirrel trying to climb in the window and Latte going barmy trying to chase it, and I've had lots of messages of support on the Twitter and Facebook pages. *Madeleine* is officially launched.'

'And it'll have nothing but good luck,' Mason said, 'because you appeased the river gods.'

'I did,' Summer said, triumphantly. 'And I've come to collect my reward.'

Mason slowly tugged at Summer's hair, pushing it behind her ear, and bent down to kiss her neck. 'Don't you want the champagne first?'

Summer wriggled and laughed. 'Mason!'

'Come on, then.' He grinned at her and got two glasses out of a cupboard, and the bottle of champagne from the fridge. Summer noticed it was better quality than the others, the outside of the bottle glistening with condensation.

They stepped out into the cool evening air and Mason hoisted her up onto the roof of *The Sandpiper* before passing her the bottle and glasses. He lifted Archie and Latte up and then climbed up himself, sitting close to Summer as he popped the cork and poured champagne into the glasses.

It was just after seven, and the sun had begun its slow, beautiful descent, with the endless turquoise of dusk above them, the brightest stars the first to show themselves. Lights from the boats in the visitor moorings, and the large windows of the pub, glowed golden in the approaching gloom. Summer could hear the flutter of wings as ducks took flight, and Valerie calling Mike and Harvey in for their dinner. Willowbeck was slowly shutting itself up for the night, doors closing, birds going to roost, the surface of the water settling into a dark, inky nothing.

Summer gave a shiver of delight and moved closer to Mason, putting her arm around his waist and clinking her glass to his.

'To Willowbeck, and all the magic that it has to offer,' she said quietly, not daring to break the stillness of the evening.

'To Summer Freeman,' Mason added, 'and to *Madeleine*. To *The Sandpiper,* to flourishing wildlife and endless cake-lovers, and to our future on the river. Together.'

'To us,' Summer said, and they both drank. It was as perfect, as cool and refreshing as she'd anticipated.

'I have to go to the reserve tomorrow,' Mason said. 'I'd love to stay in the café all day drinking coffee and sampling your new cakes, but they want me to take photos of a new area they've just cleared.'

'There's no sign of your work there running out?'

'Not a glimmer. And when it does,' he said, 'well, there's lots more work I can do in the area. Work that means I can stay here, in Willowbeck.'

'I know we can go where we choose,' Summer said, 'and that there are other beautiful villages and stretches of river and canal, but Willowbeck feels like home, and I don't want to leave.'

'You won't have to,' Mason said. 'I love Willowbeck, and I love you, and I'm not going anywhere.'

'Ah,' Summer said, 'but do you love me *as much* as you love Willowbeck?' She turned to him, picking out his features in the gathering dusk.

'Surely you know the answer to that?'

Summer took his face in her hands, kissed him firmly on the lips and then said, 'I do. Willowbeck is very lucky to have you.'

As night fell and the stars came peeping out, winking down at them, Summer and Mason lay on the roof, looking up. She felt Mason sigh, his chest rising and falling, his fingers tracing patterns on her waist.

'Penny for your thoughts,' Summer said quietly.

'I was just thinking,' Mason said, 'how happy I am.' She

could hear the gravel in his voice, like a trace of the smoke inhalation left over from the fire, but she knew him well enough now to know that it was the telltale sign of emotion. She stayed silent, letting him speak. 'Even before I moved to the river, even after everything that's happened, I don't think I've ever felt as content, or as hopeful as I do now – hopeful for the future. That's all down to you, Summer. Do you remember that first day, when Archie stole your bacon and you were angry with Valerie for talking about Maddy watching over you, and you gave me Jenny's poisoned cake?'

Summer laughed. 'How could I forget? I was pretty awful, wasn't I?'

'You were trapped, like a caged bird. Somewhere you didn't want to be. I could see past that.'

'Well, I thought you were scruffy and disorganized,' Summer said.

'You did?' She felt Mason sit up slightly, the challenge in his voice.

'And completely adorable,' Summer finished. 'I wanted to run my hands through your hair, even though I was angry.'

'This hair,' Mason said, shaking his head, 'it gets to everyone. It's like my super power.'

'*Such* a Lothario,' Summer said. They fell into an easy silence, and Summer narrowed her eyes, trying to pick out the constellations amongst the glittering clusters far above them. She still couldn't remember any of their names, and thought she would have to get a book, or an app. Latte lay down with her chin on Summer's ankle.

'Mason?' she said.

'Yes?'

'Do you think Mum is really looking down on us, like Valerie said?'

'If she is, she's congratulating you on your choice of boyfriend.'

'I'm being serious.'

'I know,' Mason said, kissing her forehead. 'Sorry.' She heard him sigh. 'I think she'll always be with you, in your heart and your memories, and in the things she taught you – how to run the café, how to be strong in the face of adversity, how to forgive. She'll always be a part of your life, but looking down on you? I'm not sure. I don't believe in ghosts, but please don't tell Valerie I said that.'

'Don't worry,' Summer said, 'your secret's safe with me.'

When the sun fell behind the horizon, and the temperature fell with it, they decided to take the rest of the bottle inside, to Mason's cosy cabin. As he helped Summer down off the roof, she glanced in the direction of Willowbeck bridge. The light was gone now, the glow of the towpath lights not reaching as far as the brick structure, but for just a second, Summer thought she saw someone standing there, a woman, a glimmer of blonde hair in a ponytail. She blinked and the image was gone, there was nobody on the bridge and she was standing on the deck of *The Sandpiper*, in Mason's arms.

'OK?' Mason asked, giving her a puzzled smile.

'Yes,' Summer said. 'I thought I saw something, that's all. But there's nothing there, it's just my eyes playing tricks. Let's go inside, it's getting cold.'

As she followed Mason inside, she hovered at the door, looking again at the curve of the bridge. She wondered how much truth there was in Valerie's beliefs, whether her mum was still there at her side, unseen, and if Elizabeth Proudfoot and the gardener, Jack, had found each other in the end.

She thought if it was going to happen anywhere, then it was likely to be in Willowbeck. Who could fail to want to stay, and fall in love, in Willowbeck? Summer had. She'd decided to stay, and she'd fallen in love with the place and with the scruffy, delicious nature buff who was pouring out the rest of the champagne and whistling tunelessly to himself, while Archie and Latte skittered at his feet, tripping him up, hoping for a morsel of something tasty from the fridge.

Summer stared out at the bridge for a few more seconds, found herself giving a quick, ridiculous wave into the darkness, and then closed the door on the night and went to wrap her arms around Mason. It was here, with him, as much as in Willowbeck, that Summer truly felt at home.

The End

Archie's Adventure

Mason Causey had lost his dog. He stood on the black and white checkerboard floor in the galley of his narrowboat, *The Sandpiper*, and turned in a slow circle, absentmindedly running his hand through his dark curls. He couldn't have been distracted for that long – and besides, where could Archie realistically go? It was a narrowboat. He checked in his berth and his small bathroom, but there was no sign of the Border terrier, and he wasn't in his usual place, lying full length along the sofa, turning lazily onto his back whenever Mason passed, demanding to have his tummy tickled. Except, he now realized that the sofa was completely covered in his photography paraphernalia; lenses and cases, his tripod. He hadn't even left a place for Archie to snooze in comfort.

Mason sighed. Archie had clearly decided to play a game of hide and seek, disgruntled that his owner had been concentrating on reviewing the photos he'd taken at the nature reserve that morning rather than on his dog. Mason went through his boat, checking under the bed and sofa – though there wasn't room to hide a mouse, let alone a scruffy terrier – even looking in the washing machine. Feeling a sudden knot of anxiety, remembering how he'd been struggling to get his muddy boots off in the doorway when he got back, Mason went to the bow doors and stood in front of them. He pushed the door gently and it swung backward, away from him. Not on the latch.

'Shit,' he murmured. Pulling his boots quickly back on and untangling himself from Archie's lead, which had decided to attach itself to him as if making a point, Mason picked up his keys and locked the door behind him.

It was a beautiful, fresh autumn day, the kind that made you feel like a criminal for spending any time inside. Maybe Archie had a point. 'Archie!' Mason called, hopping down from the deck and onto the towpath. 'Archie, come!' He cupped his hands around his mouth, hoping the sound would carry, that his dog would hear him and come racing back. Fat chance, Mason thought, heading in the direction of *Madeleine*, The Canal Boat Café, and Summer. Summer, he knew, would have the answer – after she'd stopped laughing at him.

Willowbeck was resplendent in its autumn coat. The river was indigo, deep and cool and rippling, and the leaves of the willow trees lining its edge had begun to turn a golden colour, like the setting sun. The breeze was cool, but not unpleasant, and the sky was a heady, cloudless blue.

As Mason approached *Madeleine*, a figure, in shadow up until that moment, appeared at the hatch and, despite his predicament, Mason felt the smile reach his lips.

'Do you want a bacon sarnie for lunch?' Summer asked,

459

reaching out her arms as he approached and pulling him forward for a kiss. Mason banged his head on the top of the hatch, but he barely felt it because being with Summer, kissing her, made everything else fade into the background. Almost everything. He couldn't get distracted – he had to find Archie.

Summer leant back and rubbed his curls, her eyes dancing. 'Are you OK?' she asked, and a laugh slipped out. 'Sorry.'

'My head's fine,' he said. 'It's Archie.'

Summer's expression clouded. 'What's wrong? What's happened?'

'He's gone,' Mason admitted. 'I was working on my photos from this morning, and when I looked round, he wasn't anywhere. I, uhm, I think I might have forgotten to latch the door, so . . .'

'He won't have gone far,' Summer said quickly. 'You know Archie, always chasing the next adventure, but he knows how good he's got it with you. He'll come back.'

'I can't just sit at home and wait for him,' Mason said, 'I need to look for him.'

'OK, then take Latte. He'll probably seek her out like a homing pigeon.'

'Sure,' Mason said, his shoulders dropping. 'Thank you. And can you—'

'I'll keep an eye out.' Summer smiled. 'If he turns up he'll just bark on the doorstep. Keep your phone on.' She disappeared for a moment and then returned with a squirming Bichon Frise in her arms, attached to a bright red lead. She handed Latte over, and Mason let the little dog lick his cheek before putting her on the ground.

'You always know what to do,' Mason said, leaning towards her again, careful to keep his head away from the edge of the hatch. He gave Summer a long, lingering kiss, feeling the

460

familiar twinge of excitement and contentment, pressing his hand against her cheek and wiping away a smudge of flour. 'I'll let you know when I find him.'

'Come back for an espresso and a sandwich when you do. I want to hear about your morning at the reserve.'

'Can't wait.' He waited until she'd turned back into the café, to the customers who adored her almost as much as he did. Glancing quickly at *The Sandpiper* to check Archie hadn't returned with his tail between his legs, Mason walked purposefully up the towpath, Latte trotting along at his side.

'Right, Latte,' he said, 'let's think. Where's Archie gone? Where would he take off to on a beautiful day like this – the fields? The woods?'

Latte angled her head up, and gave a little bark. Mason stared down at her, wishing – and not for the first time – that he understood dogs. Maybe if he did, Archie wouldn't outplay him quite so often. But this was the first time he had completely disappeared, and Mason felt a twinge of panic, along with a prickle of sweat on his palms. Knowing he had to be decisive, he walked further along the towpath, towards *Cosmic*, the purple and gold boat where Valerie lived.

He knocked on the door, and a moment later it opened to reveal the fortune teller, her long red hair uncharacteristically smooth around her shoulders. Harvey, one of her silver tabbies, snaked out of the door and Latte started barking. 'Shhhh, Latte,' Mason said, pulling against the lead as the little dog tried to reach Harvey, who had jumped up onto the deck seating, just out of reach.

'Mason,' Valerie said, beaming at him. 'What can I do for you and Latte?'

'Have you seen Archie?' he asked, slipping straight past any small talk. 'He's managed to escape from my boat.'

Valerie narrowed her eyes. 'How long ago?'

'I don't know, maybe an hour?' Mason shrugged, realizing how hopeless he sounded. 'I was working, and I didn't notice that I'd left the door open.'

'Oh, Mason.' Valerie sighed good-naturedly, reaching out to squeeze his shoulder. 'That dog of yours . . . I haven't seen him since you were out walking with him yesterday evening, but I'll keep an eye out – as I'm sure will Harvey and Mike.'

Latte made one more, concerted attempt to launch herself at Harvey, and Mason scooped the little dog into his arms, trying to control her warm, wriggling body. 'Thank you Valerie,' he said.

'And make sure you don't lose Summer's dog as well. One at a time.'

Mason gawped, but Valerie gave him a mischievous smile and waved him away. Mason turned back to the towpath, wondering what to do next. Neither Summer nor Valerie seemed surprised, or remotely worried, that Archie was missing, which he had to take as a good sign. The next stop, he thought, was the Black Swan.

There was a smattering of people sitting at the picnic tables outside, not yet ready to give up on summer and al fresco drinking, and Mason asked each of them if they'd seen a Border terrier running around. There were looks of concern and shaken heads, but nobody had seen his dog. Looking under the tables as he went just to make sure, Mason approached the large wooden doors and stepped inside.

He blinked, taking a moment to let his eyes get accustomed to the gloom, and saw Dennis standing behind the bar.

'Mason! Bit early for you, isn't it? Unless you're here for some lunch?' On cue, Mason's stomach rumbled, and he thought of the bacon sandwich waiting for him back on

462

Summer's boat, once all was well and Archie was at his side.

'Have you seen Archie?' Mason asked, and went through the story again, watching Dennis's expression turn to genuine concern.

'Sorry,' he said. 'Not seen him today. And as clever as he is – which he must be to outfox you – I'm not sure he can open those big, heavy doors.'

'Thanks, Dennis,' Mason said, trying not to feel despondent. Maybe this was it. Maybe after several near misses, of Archie acting up and pushing him to the limits, he really was gone this time. Mason hadn't paid enough attention, he'd always been fairly relaxed about his dog's behaviour – as long as it didn't harm or upset anyone else – but maybe he should have seen this coming.

Blinking as he stepped back into the autumn sunshine, Mason let his eyes linger over the beautiful, riverside tapestry of Willowbeck: the colourful narrowboats moored up, ducks gliding serenely along the water, geese pecking at the grass and waddling amongst the picnic tables. The visitor moorings were empty, and Mason tried to remember if they had been when he'd got back from the reserve. A sudden, horrific thought that Archie had been stolen flashed through his mind. He crouched down and stroked Latte, rubbing her fur all over, comforted and saddened in equal measure by her presence. He *had* to find Archie. After Summer, he was the one thing Mason couldn't live without.

Norman was his next call, the old man shaking his head slowly when Mason explained his predicament. Mason felt immediately chastised, even before Norman had spoken.

'Wa'rra you doin' leavin' t'door open? Mind you, dog's a Houdini anyway. Surprised yer've kept hold o'im this long, t'be fair.'

463

'You've not seen him?'

'Not since 'e knocked me fishin' rod over day before yesterday.' Norman nudged his head behind him, as if to indicate the past.

'I am so sorry about that,' Mason said, 'truly.'

'No 'arm done.' Norman had a glimmer of amusement in his eyes. 'You find 'im,' he added. 'Th'place won't be t'same wi'out him, even if he is a mischief.'

'Thank you,' Mason said, his voice rough around the edges. He stepped back onto the towpath and stood, hands on hips, waiting for inspiration to strike. Latte lay down on his feet, snuffling gently, and Mason wiped a hand over his face. If only he had checked the latch on the door. If only he hadn't been so absorbed in his photos. He'd taken some really good ones of a group of long-tailed tits up in a high tree, their fat little dusky pink bodies clustered together, their long tails flicking and wagging behind them, almost like tiny, fluffy dogs.

'Archie,' he called. 'Come on, Archie!' Latte took up the mantle, barking her soft, high bark, and Mason felt a tug of love at her loyalty. Only a couple of weeks before, Mason had showed Summer photos of the birds, and told her how they were sometimes referred to as 'bumbarrels', because their nest was barrel-shaped and they went in and out of it through a hole in the bottom. Summer had laughed so hard she'd had tears in her eyes, and almost fallen off Mason's desk chair and onto the floor of *The Sandpiper*.

'Mason!' He looked up at the familiar, beautiful voice, and saw Summer waving to him out of the hatch of *Madeleine*. 'Any luck?' she called.

'No, not yet!' He gave a shrug, hoping that he seemed nonchalant, that Summer wouldn't see how anxious he was.